THE UNFORTUNATE
Miss FORTUNES

Jennifer Crusie

Eileen Dreyer

Anne Stuart

St. Martin's Paperbacks

THE UNFORTUNATE MISS FORTUNES

Copyright © 2007 by Jennifer Crusie Smith, Eileen Dreyer, and Anne Stuart.

Excerpt from *Agnes and the Hitman* © copyright 2007 by Argh Ink and Robert J. Mayer.

ISBN: 0-312-94098-X
EAN: 978-0-312-94098-0

Printed in the United States of America

St. Martin's Paperbacks edition / July 2007

St. Martin's Paperbacks are published by St. Martin's Press, 175 Fifth Avenue, New York, NY 10010.

10 9 8 7 6 5 4 3 2 1

For the real
Queens of the Universe . . .

Kate Christlieb
Kate Ohlrogge
and Mollie Smith

We would like to thank . . .

Charlie Verral for hosting our brainstorming and combination sessions and not turfing us out when we lost his key, the readers of the Well-Behaved-At-All-Times blog for following our progress and making encouraging sounds, Heidi Cullinan and Sally Floody for being our take-no-prisoners beta readers, Meg Ruley, Andrea Cirillo, and Jane Dystel for midwiving our sisters, and Jennifer Enderlin for taking a chance on them and then sticking with us while we wrote and rewrote and rewrote, and especially Jenny, Eileen, and Krissie for not killing each other no matter how sorely tempted.

CHAPTER ONE

Mare Fortune bounded down the stairs of the family home in her ragged blue running shorts just as the wind caught the front door and blew it open, sending coppery dust swirling in. She batted the dust away and looked out, but instead of Mrs. Elder's beat-up front porch across the street, she saw golden sunshine beaming down on a red tiled roof and a fat laughing baby toddling in a dusty road while a tough dark-haired guy chased after it, laughing, too. She sucked in her breath and thought, *Crash,* and reached out into the sunlight for him, but he vanished, him and the baby and the red tiled roof and the sunshine, and it was just boring old Duckpond Street under cloudy skies in Salem's Fork, West Virginia, with Mrs. Elder's peeling porch across the way, no coppery dust at all.

"Oh," Mare said, feeling bereft and then feeling stupid for feeling bereft. *He left you, he's gone, it's been five years, you're over it.* She turned to close the heavy door, just as her oldest sister Dee took down their mother's jewelry chest from the mantel in the living room and, beyond her, their middle sister Lizzie bent over her metallurgy book at the battered dining room table, everything normal, nothing to worry about.

"Big storm coming in." Mare yanked down on her tank top, shoving Crash and the whole vision thing out of her mind. "Big old Beltane storm." Her tiger-striped cat, Pywackt, padded down the narrow stairs with dignity, and she made kissing sounds at him, which he ignored. "Lightning on the mountain just for us, Py, baby."

"Didn't we throw those away?" Dee said, cradling the brass-bound jewelry box in her slender arms as she frowned at Mare's tattered shorts.

"You tried," Mare said.

Dee nodded, looking distracted. "Come on," she said and turned toward the dining room, her gray wool suit perfectly fitted to her tiny waist. Mare stuck her tongue out at Dee's auburn chignon and followed her into the dining room where ethereal Lizzie sat hunched over her book in her purple silk kimono, her blond curls tangled and blue eyes wide, dripping muffin butter onto her notebook as she ate.

Dee put the jewelry box on the table and said, "Mind the butter, Lizzie," and Lizzie turned another page, oblivious to Dee, the butter, and the wind whistling outside the open garden windows.

Mare plopped herself down at the table and looked at the muffins. "They're all apple bran, Lizzie. That's boring. I like blueberry and lemon poppy seed and—"

Lizzie moved her hand over the muffin basket, still not looking up from her book, and tendrils of violet smoke trailed from her fingertips and across the apple bran.

"Thank you." Mare craned her neck to look into the basket and then went for a newly transformed blueberry, but Dee moved the basket out of her reach.

"First we vote." Dee straightened the jewelry box.

Lizzie looked up from her book. "Now?"

Crap, Mare thought, and looked longingly at the muffins. Lizzie had baked them so they were bound to be munchable.

"Yes, now." Dee sat down at the head of the table. "If Mare's going to college, she has to register now. Which means we have to decide if we move so she can go to a school we can afford. And which piece of Mother's jewelry we sell to finance it. And I have to be at the bank in an hour, so we have to do it now."

"*Not* now." Mare stared at the blueberry muffin just out of her reach—*come here, damn it*—so that a couple of dust motes lazing in the air sparked blue. "Not now, not ever." She lifted her chin, feeling the weight of the muffin in her mind, and it rose slowly until it hovered at eye level.

"*Mare,*" Dee said. "*Not in front of the window.*"

Mare grinned and crooked her finger, and the muffin floated toward her, sparking blue once or twice, like a misfiring muffler.

"Oh, dear." Lizzie waved her hands a little, as if to warn Mare off, tendrils of violet smoking from her fingertips, and her butter knife turned into a rabbit.

Py sat up and took an interest.

"Easy there, Lizzie," Mare said, staring cross-eyed at her muffin, now floating in front of her nose. "You know Py and bunnies."

Dee flushed. "Put down the muffin, please, Mare. You know how important this vote is."

"It's important to you," Mare said, concentrating on keeping her muffin afloat. "It's not important to me. As mistress of all I survey, I feel that college is, how can I put this? *Unnecessary.*" She scowled at Dee—why were they having this conversation again? She was twenty-three, if she didn't want to go to college, she wasn't going to go—and her annoyance broke her concentration and the muffin dropped and broke, and Mare said, *"Damn."* She focused on another one, lemon poppyseed this time, making it rise from the muffin basket while Lizzie's butter-knife rabbit began to forage for crumbs on her notebook page.

At the end of the table, Py began to forage for the rabbit.

"You are not mistress of all you survey," Dee said, exasperated, "you're—"

"Queen of the Universe," Mare said.

"—assistant manager of a Value Video!!"

Mare pulled the muffin toward her with her eyes. "That's temporary. It's only a matter of time until I'm queen of the company."

"I don't think Value Video!! has queens," Dee said.

"I know, they have presidents. But when I get to the top, that's gonna change."

"Well, to become queen of Value Video!! you have to go to college." Dee opened the jewelry box. "It was always Mother's dream that we'd all go, and it's your turn. It's past time for your turn. So we vote."

"I don't want to," Mare said. "Lizzie doesn't want to vote, either, do you, Lizzie?"

Lizzie looked up. "What?"

"It's time to vote," Dee said gently.

"All right," Lizzie said, her focus drifting again.

"Lizzie!" Mare shrieked, betrayed.

Lizzie jerked back, startled, and Mare saw her fright and said, "Lizzie, it's okay, *it's okay,*" but it was too late. Lizzie was waving her hands, fingers trembling, as she warded off Mare's anger, purple tendrils of apology wafting over the table.

"Oh, hell," Mare said as lavender smoke rose around them.

Lizzie let the purple cloud engulf her. It was so quiet in there. Two more bunnies had popped up, depleting the knife count on the table and drawing Py closer. She blinked rapidly as the cloud grew thicker; it felt as if coppery dust had gotten into her eyes. For a moment she'd drifted away from her contentious sisters and their tiny living room in Salem's Fork, and she was floating, distant, in a castle in Spain, lying on her back, and someone was leaning over her, and it was . . .

"Lizzie, honey, take a breath," Dee said, as the smoke cleared.

"I'm sorry," Lizzie said to Mare, pulling herself together. "I wasn't paying attention."

"It's okay." Mare floated a muffin over to her, dispersing more smoke with blue sparks. "Dee's trying to get us to vote and I don't want to because I don't want to move again."

Lizzie picked the muffin out of the air and sighed the rest of the purple away. Violet smoke, drifting around a castle in Spain, moody and romantic. *Stop it.* "I'm not sure I want to, either."

"We're *voting*," Dee said sharply.

She startled the bunny and made it quiver, and Lizzie picked it up and petted it, trying not to quiver herself. They were fighting again. She hated the days when they voted. Three more bunnies had popped up on the table during the argument, and Lizzie wondered whether she could take them and sneak back into her room while Mare and Dee glared at each other.

"Then I vote we don't vote," Mare said. "It's my future, and I'll take care of it when it gets here."

"And just how is refusing to plan for your future going to protect you from Xan the next time she finds us?" Dee said, goaded.

"What makes you think we need protection from her?" Mare said. "She's our aunt. And she hasn't come after us in years. I'm not even sure she's the demon you make her out to be." Dee began to protest and Mare overrode her. "And anyway, I don't see the connection between going to college and escaping Xan. I don't see your college degree getting you much protection or anything else except stuck in that damn bank. At least I get to watch movies."

"I wouldn't be stuck in that damn bank if you'd grow up and take care of yourself—" Dee stopped.

Oh, Dee. "I'm sorry," Lizzie said into the silence, trying to fight the sick feeling inside her. "Dee, I'm sorry about the bunnies and I'm sorry about the bank. I'll get us money, I'm almost there, I've almost got it, I'll get us the money and you can quit and paint full-time, I swear—"

"No, Lizzie, it's all right." Dee patted Lizzie's hand. She reached out to Mare and Mare pulled back. "Mare, I didn't mean it, I'm fine at the bank. We're fine. I just want you to have a future."

"I have a future." Mare focused on the muffin crumbs and they piled onto each other in lumpy parodies of muffins, little Frankencakes, misshapen and wrong.

That's not how you make a muffin, Lizzie thought. Mare didn't know how to make things. Making things took time and patience and thought and understanding.

Mare shook her head and let the muffins fall apart again. "You don't need to work at the bank for me, Dee. I don't want college."

"You haven't even tried it," Dee protested.

Mare met her eyes. "College can't teach what I need to know, Dee. I need to know how to use my power, we all do, we're cramped here in this little house, hiding our powers from everybody, and they're rotting inside us. The only one who can show us how is Xan."

"No," Dee said. "You don't know her. You were too young when we ran, you don't remember. She killed Mom and Dad, Mare. She could—"

"She didn't kill anybody." Mare flipped her hand as if she could flip the idea away. "They died of stupidity, just like the coroner said. You really have to get over that, Dee."

Dee clenched her hands. "Trust me. She's dangerous. Isn't she, Lizzie?"

"Yes," Lizzie said. *I can't stand this,* she thought, picking up her book again.

"At least Xan doesn't hide who she is," Mare said. "At least Xan doesn't tie her own hands and hide from the world."

Dee straightened. "We are not going to Xan, and that's final. Now it's time to vote." She turned their mother's jewelry box so they could see inside. "I vote yes. We use one of Mother's necklaces to send Mare to college."

"Not the amethyst," Lizzie said from behind her book, and blinked as she felt that coppery dust in her eyes again. She could feel the satin sheets against her naked skin, the weight of the purple stone between her breasts, his breath warm and . . . She shook her head. *Not the amethyst.*

"Not any of them," Mare said. "I vote no."

"Lizzie?" Dee said to the cover of the metallurgy book.

Lizzie lowered the book. "You really don't want to go to school?" she asked Mare.

Mare rolled her eyes in exasperation. *"No!"*

Lizzie looked at Dee. "I'm sorry. I don't think we should force . . ." Dee scowled at her, her eyes stormy, and Lizzie sucked in her breath. "I abstain."

Dee drew a deep, angry breath, and green fog began to rise, swirling around her.

"Oh," Lizzie said faintly. "Oh, no . . ."

Well, *that tears it,* Dee thought, coughing green fog. It wasn't bad enough that her head was about to explode, now the rest of her was, too. Her skin burned. Her heart pounded like a jackhammer. Her body was in the throes of cataclysmic change, and there wasn't a damn thing she could do about it.

Couldn't she just cry when she got upset like other women? Maybe throw a tantrum? Hell, even spinning muffins would be better. No, she had to be theatrical. But *God,* didn't the two of them understand? Did they *want* to end up stuck here for the rest of their lives?

She didn't. She wanted what she'd seen when that copper dust had blown through the door and into her eyes: a high, white studio in Montmartre and paint on a canvas, and a model she seemed to know. A breathtaking man who smiled as if he'd waited just for her . . .

"Oh, *Mare*," Lizzie said.

"I am *not* taking responsibility for this," Mare said.

Dee could feel her cells metamorphosing, twinkling into new patterns like the transporter beam in *Star Trek.* Her throat tightened, her vision sharpened, the colors faded. Damn it, this was the worst time for this to happen. It was tough enough to get Mare to take her seriously. It was even harder when she was—

Poof!

"An owl!" Lizzie said, as she waved away the green fog. "Oh, dear. Are you a screech owl?"

"I'm a pissed-off big sister owl," Dee said, but it came out in screeches and chirps only her sisters could understand. She wasn't sitting at the table anymore, she was on top of it, clad in cinnamon feathers and perched on a set of talons, frantically scrabbling for purchase in the nest of her collapsed clothing.

"You sound like a screech owl." Mare stood up and shoved her chair under the table. "Not that you don't most of the time anyway." She looked down at Dee, perplexed, as if she were ready to continue the fight but wasn't sure how. "Listen, I think I'll just go ahead and do my morning run now. You have a nice, uh, flight."

She did *not* always screech.

"You're not going anywhere until I return to form," Dee screeched.

Mare bent down, so that they were eye to eye, which made Dee blink. "You look very Disney, all ruffled up like that. You should have a perky little musical number with the other forest creatures coming right up. Call me if the urge to sing sweeps over you."

"Go on and run like the dog you are," Dee said. "But I'll be here when you—"

The doorbell rang.

For a second, they froze, looking at each other.

"I'll get the bunnies," Lizzie said.

"I'll check the window," Dee said.

"I'll get your clothes," Mare said and scooped up the nest out from under her.

Lizzie shoved the bunnies into the kitchen. Mare tossed Dee's clothes into her room. Dee focused on the view out the front window, which revealed nothing more than the jungle of flowers that was their front yard and the picket fence that contained it.

"One person at the door," she said. "No official vehicles at the gate."

Lizzie sat back down and tried to look calm. Dee tried to look as normal as an owl could under the circumstances. They all nodded to each other, and Mare opened the door.

"Good morning," a baritone voice said. "You must be Moira Mariposa Fortune."

"What's it to you?" Mare snapped, but Dee's beak dropped open. That man. The one she'd just seen posing for her in Montmartre, there in the swirling dust: she swore it was him. Tall, lithe, and dark, his sable hair just a little too long, his leather jacket a little too worn, and his battered jeans a little too tight. In short, as wicked as sin. Especially when he smiled. When he smiled he was Dennis Quaid in Daniel Day-Lewis's body. And in her fantasy he'd been smiling at *her.*

"Well, if I'm right," he said with a big smile at Mare, "it means I can stop tramping across this town like a door-to-door salesman."

"Then move on, Willie Loman," Mare said and tried to shut the door.

The guy stuck his foot in her way. "If you'll just listen . . ."

Dee'd listen, all right. She'd nestle against his neck and trill in his ear. She might be the oldest virgin in

North America, but she wasn't a dead virgin. And she could swear she knew what every inch of him looked like without those clothes.

"Good heavens," Lizzie whispered from behind her. "You're preening."

Good heavens, she was. Fluffing her feathers and twitching her tail and tucking her head, as if the guy standing in the door was a big barn owl.

"Did you know you have a screech owl on your table?" he asked Mare.

"No," Mare said. "I hadn't noticed."

"Close the door, Mare," Dee begged.

It came out as a descending carillon of chirps. The guy on the other side of the door lifted amazed eyebrows at her. "And I think she likes me."

Leave it to her to turn into an owl in front of an ornithologist. Who else would recognize the mating call of the Eastern screech owl?

"You think wrong," Mare said to him, trying to close the door. "And good-bye."

"Good," Dee said, panting. "Get him out of here."

It wasn't often a man got under her skin like this. She didn't allow it; it was too dangerous. She'd tried a few times, letting herself believe that the arousal from hormones would affect her differently than the agitation of anger or fear. She'd been wrong. She'd ended up sending two guys into therapy and another to an ashram in India. She could still hear him screaming as he ran into the night, her bra dangling from his hand after she'd shifted right there in the back seat of his Jeep. And not into anything as cute as an owl. No, she'd shifted into his mother. Just like she had with the other two guys. And she hadn't even liked their mothers.

She'd been celibate ever since, and assured herself she was happy that way. She didn't have a choice, after all. But for some reason, this man suddenly made her feel like a nun peering out the convent gate, longing for what she could never have.

Thank God he was leaving.

He kept his foot in the door. "Wait," he said. "Please. I'm looking for Moira Mariposa, Elizabeth Alicia, and Deirdre Dolores Fortune. I'm researching a book."

"Our name's O'Brien." Mare stopped trying to kick his foot away. "A book?"

He nodded. "About Phil and Fiona Fortune. That's your real name, isn't it? You just took O'Brien as an alias when you moved here."

Dee shut her eyes, suddenly sick. Oh, hell. Didn't it just figure? She couldn't even have a decent fantasy without it blowing up in her face.

"No, our name really is O'Brien," Mare said. "And we don't know anybody named Fortune. Would we lie to you?"

"Since I got your alias from your parents' old commune members, I'd say that's a yes," he said, perfectly calm for all the disaster he was unleashing. "I was hoping to at least talk to your oldest sister, Deirdre."

"She doesn't want to talk to you," Dee chirped. "Get rid of him."

Her heart was slamming against her tiny chest. Her head threatened to explode again. It wasn't fair. They'd run so far, hidden so well. And here was the man of her dreams—well, her dust—blithely threatening to do a great big Geraldo on them.

"Thanks," Mare said, "but no thanks. Now if you'd move your foot so I could close this door—"

He just kept smiling. "That's what I was told you'd say."

"Really?" Mare asked. "And here I thought I was being delightfully unpredictable. Go away."

"Find out who told him who we are," Dee begged.

"How about we start over?" he asked, putting out a hand. "I'm Danny James. Like I said, I'm researching a book—"

He never had the chance to finish. Mare stomped on his toes, and when he winced and jerked his foot back, she slammed the door. Then she turned and looked at her sisters. "Well, this is another fine mess the 'rents have gotten us into."

Dee was frantic. That was disaster standing on their front porch. How could Mare just dismiss it like an inconvenient Mormon on a mission? "We have to find out what's going on," she said. Flapping her wings, she swooped over to perch on the living room windowsill.

"I don't have to find out," Mare said. "I don't care. I got rid of him. He's gone."

"I don't have time," Lizzie said, picking up her book. "I have work to do. I'm really close to a break-through."

"Well, I have time." Dee stared out the front window where she could see Danny James pause out by the curb. "What if *she* sent him?"

"Who?" Mare asked.

Dee glared. "Xan."

Mare shook her head. "She's your nightmare in the closet. Let it go, Dee."

"Open the door." Dee ruffled her feathers, preparing to fly. "I'm going after him. Somebody has to keep an eye on him. I can do it without being caught."

"You don't think he'll find an owl on his ass suspicious?" Mare asked.

"He'll never see me."

"How about when you change back to human form in the middle of the sidewalk and you're naked?" Mare stopped and looked thoughtful. "Actually, men usually don't ask questions about naked women, so you might get away with that one."

Dee ruffled her feathers again. "I have clothes stashed all over this town. Nobody's going to see me naked. And anyway, we have to know. I can at least see where he goes before I have to be at the bank."

"Couldn't he just be what he says?" Lizzie asked. "A book researcher?"

Dee inched her way to the edge of the table. "Mother and Dad have been dead for twelve years. Why would anybody do a book now? And exactly who gave him our alias? We can't just assume Xan isn't behind this. The last time she came after us, we almost didn't get away in time. Open the door."

Lizzie and Mare looked at each other.

"Maybe we should vote on it," Mare said. "Just because Dee is over twenty-eight, that doesn't mean she gets to choose her own life—"

"MARE!" Dee screeched, and Lizzie slipped around her and opened the front door.

Dee shoved off the dining room table and launched herself past them, out into the morning sky.

Xantippe Fortune put aside her silver spell bowl, the coppery dust of the True Desire spell gleaming in the bottom, and then wiped her see glass clean while the short, dark-haired woman next to her looked defiant but nervous. Very nervous.

Good, Xan thought and settled into the silver brocade

wing chair, the folds of her red gown falling smoothly over her wrists.

It was hell finding competent help for a supernatural power heist in the twenty-first century, especially in a place as small and clueless as Salem's Fork.

"All I did was sneeze," Maxine said, smoothing down her polyester peasant blouse.

Fashion always tells, Xan thought. "You sneezed on a magic glass, Maxine. Twice. The first one blew the front door wide open, which made the sisters close it instead of leaving it open to the screen door, which made it impossible to hear what was happening in the front of the house. The second sneeze almost made them close the garden windows, and if they had, I would have lost the dining room conversation. Because you were never taught to use a handkerchief, they think a hurricane is coming. Plus it's *unsanitary.* You just bought a diner, woman. I shudder to think what happens in your kitchen."

"I'm going to call it Maxine's," Maxine said in a dreamy voice.

"No, you are not," Xan said. "You are going to do nothing to call attention to yourself or to the fact that you have suddenly acquired enough money to buy a diner. Our arrangement was that I would give you the money to buy the diner in exchange for your *clandestine* services for the next three days, but you must not call attention to yourself. That's where the 'clandestine' part comes in, Maxine. Until Monday, the Greasy Fork stays the Greasy Fork. Do you understand?"

"There are gonna be *big changes,*" Maxine said, looking off into the distance at her magnificent future.

"Maxine!" Xan snapped, and Maxine jerked to attention. "What are you going to do for the next three days?"

"I'm gonna watch the Fortune sisters and not make any big changes because I'm clandestine," Maxine said.

"And?"

"And I'm gonna keep an eye on the three men who come for them."

"And?"

"And I'm gonna tell you everything."

Xan settled back into her wing chair again. "Good, Maxine."

"And then I'm gonna sell martinis at the Greasy Fork."

"Maxine!"

"But not until Monday," Maxine said hurriedly.

When hunting season comes, Xan thought. *I'm going to turn you into a rabbit.* "Good, Maxine. You may go."

Maxine looked around the room. "How do I—"

Xan waved her hand and Maxine vanished, only to reappear in the see glass, looking dizzy and slightly nauseated behind the Greasy Fork's Dumpster.

I know how you feel, Xan thought. *The whole town makes me feel that way.*

Then she turned her attention back to the Fortune house, her heart beating a little faster now that her plan was in motion. She'd cast one spell and brought the sisters' True Loves to Salem's Fork, then cast another and the sisters had seen their True Desires. Now Danny James had met Dee and Dee was on her way after him. Lizzie was about to turn around and meet somebody amazing. And Mare—

"Xantippe?"

Xan sat bolt upright as Maxine stood before her. "How the *hell* did you get back here?"

Maxine blinked. "The portal by the Dumpster was still open."

Xan closed her eyes. If someone breathes in the

natural psychic energy of a supernatural center like Salem's Fork her entire life, Xan told herself, even if she's a dolt like Maxine, she'll pick up some basic skills. "Yes?"

"Danny James just checked into the Lighthorse Harry Lee Bed and Breakfast Inn."

Xan nodded. "Thank you."

Maxine nodded back. "About the martinis, I—"

"Maxine, do you have any idea how powerful I am?"

"No, Xantippe."

Xan waved her hand and Maxine became a mouse, frozen in terror on the floor, the only part of her left that resembled Maxine her tiny horrified beady black eyes. Xan waited a beat and then waved her hand and Maxine stood before her again, shaking so hard, her head bobbed.

"Never forget, Maxine," Xan said gently, "that I turned you back by choice. The next time, I may leave you turned. And you might not be a mouse."

Maxine sucked in a terrified breath.

"But of course, I won't," Xan said. "I need you, Maxine. You're *my friend*." She smiled into Maxine's eyes, radiating hypnotic goodwill, and after a moment, Maxine relaxed.

"Good one," Maxine said, still a little rocky.

"Go watch the girls." Xan waved her hand and Maxine disappeared, only to reappear in the see glass, next to the Dumpster again, stumbling as she landed. "Next time, it's *in* the Dumpster, Maxine," Xan said to the glass, closed the portal, and sat back, catching sight of the sisters in another angle of the see glass: Dee flying away in the shape of an owl, and Lizzie and Mare in the doorway, talking.

Xan leaned closer to the glass and whispered, "It'll be a fair trade, darlings, those spells were true," and

Lizzie looked up, startled, and said something to Mare, who looked stolid as ever, shaking her head and then pounding off down the pavement like the draft horse her nickname said she was.

They didn't know it, but they were lucky to have Xan looking out for them, taking care of them, making them the deal of their lifetimes. It wasn't going to hurt, it truly wasn't, and they'd be better off in the end. She wouldn't miscalculate, nothing would go wrong this time, and if it did, it would hardly be her fault. No, they were very lucky.

Especially Lizzie, Xan thought, feeling a pang of jealousy as Lizzie turned to go inside.

Especially Lizzie . . .

CHAPTER TWO

If this had been any other morning, Dee would have been delighted to be flying off from the house. Her favorite times had been spent as a bird. She loved flight: the sudden lift, the ruffle of air through her feathers, the illusion of freedom. She adored the patterns and colors the earth revealed from this indifferent height. But mostly, she liked being alone, responsible for nothing, failing no one, just focused on the scene around her and how it would translate onto the canvas that waited her back in her studio.

Not today. Today, she had to waste her precious time trailing Danny James.

He was trouble, she just knew it. And not just because he exuded enough pheromones to melt a girl into a coma. Dee couldn't believe that neither Mare nor Lizzie had reacted to him. She still felt as if she'd been gigged like a frog.

He was trouble because he knew who they were. Because he wanted to know more. Because, damn it, she couldn't be sure he hadn't come from Xan.

Ah, there he was. On a motorcycle, of course, hot

enough to make Mare notice as he rolled past. But then, who wouldn't notice Danny James? Heck, every woman he passed turned for a second look. Some a third. Of course, it wasn't often that strangers made the turn into the blind valley that cradled Salem's Fork. Maybe it was just curiosity.

Uh-huh. And maybe the next time Dee tried to have sex she'd stay her own shape.

She watched closely, hoping against hope he'd betray himself quickly so she could waste a bit of time skimming the warm air currents before heading into work. He didn't oblige. He rode straight through Salem's Fork toward the river. He didn't stop to talk to anyone or pass incriminating notes. He did seem compelled to wave and smile to every person he passed. And everyone seemed equally compelled to smile and wave back.

Oh, he was real trouble.

He made her suddenly yearn for things she couldn't have, him and that happy smile and that damned motorcycle of his. He probably felt as if he were flying down there on his bike. She bet he felt free.

"Mrs. Washington!" he called as he pulled the bike to a stop in the driveway of Lighthorse Harry Lee, a lurid pink and chartreuse Queen Anne monstrosity that sat a block from the town square. "I was hoping I could ask a favor from you."

He'd caught little Verna Washington at her biweekly hedge pruning. She was in overalls and a floppy straw hat, a living lawn ornament. Like every other female in this benighted town, she smiled, almost impaling herself on her pruning shears when she tried to pat down her tightly permed gray hair. "Why, of course, honey," she caroled. "Didn't you see the girls, then?"

"I did. Thank you."

And here Dee had thought Verna was a friend. Dee alighted in the willow that grew at the northwest corner of the house to see Danny lope up the sidewalk, another of those bright smiles crinkling his eyes.

"Would you mind if I checked into my room a bit early?" he asked Verna. "Since I have to wait to interview my subjects, I was hoping I could catch a shower and make some calls."

"Don't be silly," Verna trilled, sounding just like Dee in her mating-owl mode. "You go right on up. I had Mel take your bag up to 3B. It's the Lighthorse Suite, Mr. James. We call it that because Lighthorse Harry Lee himself came through town on his way to the Revolution and left behind a boot. See the planter on the porch? It's an exact replica."

Verna pointed to the boot, now sporting pink begonias, but Dee was fixated on her good luck. The Lighthorse Suite was situated no more than ten feet from where she sat. She felt like a good smile herself. The window was open. Could be a good chance to see what secrets Danny James might reveal.

Danny was trying to go inside, but Verna was still talking.

"You sure you don't want to give me just a little hint about what the girls' story is?" Verna asked, snagging Dee's attention. "I know it can't be bad. They're such good girls. Why, they can't even seem to shoo all those bunnies out of their yard, and them with that big garden and all. Soft hearts, you know. But you were saying . . ."

Don't blow our cover, Dee silently begged. *Not yet.*

Stupid to worry. Their cover was already blown. There wasn't a person in town who wouldn't find a reason to ask just what that handsome stranger had been doing at the O'Brien house at eight in the morning.

"Oh, it's no mystery," Danny James assured the little woman. "I'm just researching some history for a book, and I was hoping they might be able to help me."

Verna patted him on the arm as if he were a gentleman caller. "Well, how fascinating. Maybe you'd like a cup of tea while you tell me all about it."

And, of course, he smiled and offered her his arm. "What a lovely offer, Mrs. Washington."

Excellent. Verna would keep him talking for hours, while Dee searched his room. She quickly scanned her target. Verna had decorated the inn in Early Ruffle, all lace and chintz and vacant-eyed china dolls ranged on high shelves. Danny James was going to look like a panther at a tea party tucked under Verna's pink sheets. His luggage sat by the door, just waiting to be searched: a backpack and a wheeled softsider, both unopened; a briefcase that sat tantalizingly open on the wedding ring quilt.

Making sure the coast was clear, Dee lifted off and slipped smoothly in through the open window.

She must not have been as smooth as she'd thought. She hardly made it into the room before there was a loud slam behind her. She turned to see that the window had fallen closed.

Oh, dear God. She was stuck. She plopped down on the quilt right next to the briefcase and tried not to panic. The door was open into the hall, but she sincerely doubted that an owl could flap right down the stairs without being noticed. Maybe she should hide in the closet until Danny James got too warm and opened the window again—hopefully before she turned back into a naked human. Of course, if she was a human, she could get the window open . . .

There was a big time planner on the desk. Dee tilted her head. Hmmm. Not a very modern man, with no

PDA. No, he had a book with everything she needed to know about him, right there for God and the world to see. She looked toward the open door again and then the closed window. She did her best to tamp down the instinct to batter herself against the glass to get out. She had to stay calm.

She decided she could stay calmer if she distracted herself with her mission. She had turned pages before as a bird. Maybe she'd have enough time to turn these and see what she could find out. Flapping as quietly as she could, she flew over and settled on the desk.

The address book was open to the *D*s. She scanned it to see only two names that meant anything: Dellwood Press and Mark Delaney. Tidy. Dellwood Press was the publisher who put out the wildly popular Mark Delaney books.

Was that who he worked for? If it was, he had a great job. Delaney was a legend. Best-selling, award-winning, as notorious for his obsessive reclusivity as his immense talent. Easy to be reclusive if you have this many addresses, Dee thought in passing. New York, L.A., London. Detroit. *Detroit?* Not her idea of a world-famous hideaway. The question was, what was a genre writer who penned alternative historical novels doing researching Phil and Fiona Fortune?

Dee hopped closer. Balancing on one claw, she reached over to try and flip pages. She needed the *X* page. Maybe the *O*. She needed to know if Xan had sent him. *D* . . . *E* . . . damn, this was hard. If she'd been human, she'd be sweating. Hop, pull, hop, flap . . .

She was concentrating so hard that she missed the sound of approaching footsteps. Suddenly the top stair creaked. Dee spun so fast, she almost fell over.

"Remember," Velma's voice trumpeted up from the

front hallway, "the window's a little loose and can close sometimes. If it does, just prop it with that big old dictionary on the desk."

"Thank you, Mrs. Washington," Danny James answered from right outside the door. "I'll be fine."

Dee had to hide. The minute Danny James turned from calling down to Verna, he'd see her. She didn't even think about it, just swooped straight up to the top of the chifforobe, her tiny heart stumbling. She tucked herself in among the garden of silk flowers Verna had crammed onto the cherrywood top. Maybe if she sat very still she'd look like décor—if the dust up there didn't make her sneeze. Besides, she needed to see what Danny James was going to do. He was already closing the door before it occurred to her that if she changed back, she might have a better time of it under the bed.

At first the situation looked promising. Once he was in the room Danny James walked straight to the window and yanked the sash open. A fresh breeze wafted in along with the sound of desultory traffic. Verna could be heard chattering with Mrs. Phipps from next door. Grabbing the huge dictionary from the desk, Danny James wedged it in the window to keep it propped open.

She could get out now, Dee thought, shifting from foot to foot. If he'd just turn his back, close his eyes, and ignore the sound of wings. Instead, he stood right in front of the window. Stretching his arms overhead, he slowly arched his back until Dee could hear little popping noises. "Oh, yeah," he muttered, stretching sideways. "I've been wanting to do that for about five hundred miles."

Dee knew she should scrunch down so he wouldn't notice her up there, especially with his eyes facing the ceiling. But she was terrified into immobility, an owl statue surrounded by silk flower bouquets.

Facing out the window again, Danny pulled out a cell phone and punched buttons. "Hi," he said. "It's Danny. No luck so far, but I guess I expected that. I'll call when I get something."

And?

And he'd evidently finished with phone calls. Tossing the phone onto the bed, he shucked his jacket. Not just a leather jacket. An old, battered bomber jacket with the 390th Fighter Wing insignia. The Fighting Boars. The plain white T-shirt underneath betrayed every muscle in his chest and torso, and highlighted rock-solid shoulders.

Now, leave, she thought desperately. *Give me a little space to get out the window.* She sat as still as stone, terrified he'd see her. Holding her breath so she didn't sneeze. Praying he'd take his shower.

She'd obviously prayed for the wrong thing. He was going to take his shower, all right. It was just that he was going to strip right here in the room. Sinking onto the iron bed, he pulled off his old battered cowboy boots, and Dee realized he had great biceps.

No. No time for biceps. Don't look.

She looked. She loved biceps.

She really should go. *Please turn around. Let me out.*

He pulled off his shirt.

Dee gaped, frozen to the spot. It was like watching a theater curtain rise, only this one exposed the most incredible torso she'd ever seen: taut pecs and cut abs and a dusting of mahogany hair that curled at his throat and trailed right down to his waistband and beyond, and oh, God, he even wore a silver medal, the chain glinting against his tan skin.

Hadn't she seen that this morning? When he smiled at her in that brief, tantalizing flash of fantasy in the dust? Dreaming about painting was one thing. But dreaming about painting *him* . . .

She had to close her eyes. She had to turn around. He had no idea what disaster he was courting just by shucking his shirt. He reached up to pull the silver chain over his head and dropped it on the nightstand, and Dee almost groaned out loud.

Was he humming or was she? She couldn't tell. She just knew she should move. She should fly away, right now, no matter the cost. The danger certainly couldn't be greater than what would happen if she shifted right on top of his chifforobe. Because the way her body was reacting to him, even her owl body, she just wasn't sure it wouldn't happen.

Concentrate on something else. He was out to get her parents. Not enough. Something else. Xan. He could be from Xan. She had to . . .

She forgot what she had to. He was unsnapping his jeans. She held her breath, terrified that if she so much as gasped, she'd start chirping like a car alarm. Her tiny heart was thundering. Her feathers had suddenly grown too heavy and hot for her skin. Warnings shrilled in her head.

Any other time, she'd already be seeing green fog. But she'd never become this aroused when she was already shifted. She had no idea what would happen. Would she change again? Would she change back into herself? Maybe she'd simply explode. She could just imagine owl feathers showering down from that chifforobe like fireworks.

Well, it couldn't be any worse than what usually happened. She could just imagine what Danny James's reaction would be when his mother appeared crouched on the top of his chifforobe wearing nothing more than a blush.

As for her, she might as well just kill herself and be done with it.

It didn't seem to matter. Even at the real risk to life, limb, and both their psyches, she simply couldn't look away. She couldn't think of anything but how breathtaking he was, how he made her want things she'd never allowed herself to want. Her very cells were glowing hot, a core meltdown that presaged disaster of monumental proportions. Her energy was coagulating, gathering to change, and she was trapped in a room with the man who'd come to investigate her.

Please . . .

She was terrified she was already sparkling. The green fog clogged up inside of her, stealing her breath. And still he didn't leave. Instead he pulled a file from his briefcase. She saw him bend over it and just closed her eyes.

"I wonder what you look like now," he said suddenly. "And what you're going to end up telling me about those bloodsucking charlatans you call parents."

Dee's eyes snapped open to see him looking at an old magazine article of her in her Darling Dee-Dee dress. It saved her. His words sent a chill straight through to her talons.

Danny James tapped the picture. "Ready or not, Deirdre Dolores Fortune, here I come."

Then he sauntered on into the bathroom, never once noticing that he had an owl on his furniture. Dee shot him a scathing look. Then she wasted a moment yearning for that file. It was too late, though. She had to leave. Dee barely made it out the window and next door to Pete Semple's toolshed before the green fog enveloped her.

Lizzie stood in the open doorway, staring out in the bright morning sun as her sister disappeared into the sky in search of her prey. Dee made a lovely owl, she thought absently, all brown feathers and piercing eyes.

"Should I follow her?" Mare said, sounding exasperated. "You know, in case she ends up naked in a tree someplace, and I have to kick that Danny guy's ass? After which she'll bitch at me because I'm not going to college?"

Lizzie shook her head. "I'm not taking sides on that. You know she works hard at that bank for us and—"

"Right." Mare went down the porch steps. "Gotta run before I go to work. If I see our sister naked, I'll beat up anybody who's looking at her, no matter what she says."

The wind blew like a whisper, and Lizzie looked up. "Did you hear that?"

"Hear what?" Mare frowned at the breeze. "I didn't hear anything. Back in an hour. Thanks for the muffins."

She pushed off, hitting a full run before she was through the front gate, and Lizzie breathed a silent sigh of relief as her youngest sister disappeared down the road. Time to herself, a quiet house, and no more fights. She could even finish her cup of tea before she retreated to her workshop. She was about to close the door when she felt a shiver run down her spine.

It wasn't a particularly unpleasant shiver. Not a sense of danger, or impending doom. But something was definitely off, and she turned back to the kitchen slowly, and then had to stifle her instinctive scream.

He was leaning against the kitchen counter, and for a moment she couldn't see him clearly. He was a mass of changing colors—swirls of vivid brightness dancing, and then everything settled down, like a camera coming into focus, and it was only a man standing there, a tall man in a dark suit and blond hair, watching her.

The back door to the house was still closed and locked with a chair full of unread newspapers in front of it, and Lizzie had been standing in the only other door, watching her sisters take off. That door was still open behind her back, and she ought to run for it, fast. She was a chicken and she knew it, but the one thing stronger than her fear of confrontation was her curiosity.

"How did you get in here?" Dumb. She should have asked him who he was.

"Doesn't your sister know better than to turn into an owl in the middle of the day? Owls are nocturnal—if someone notices, there are bound to be questions, even in this town. Especially in this town." His voice was deep, mesmerizing, and just slightly annoyed.

She stared at him. He hadn't been there when Dee shifted, and even if he'd seen it he wouldn't have believed it. "What do you mean, especially in this town?"

One of the bunnies hopped across his foot, and he leaned down and picked it up, a soft, tiny creature in his elegant hands. She watched, mesmerized, as he stroked it, the long fingers caressing the fur lightly before he set it down on the table, where it lay in silver splendor, a fork once more.

"Who the hell are you?" she said, finally asking the right question.

He moved into the light, and she could see him quite clearly. Elegant, with long golden hair, dark eyes, impeccably dressed, with a silver stud in one ear. A little on the thin side—he was too well dressed for Mare, and Dee didn't like blonds. He was probably in his early thirties, though there was something almost ageless about him.

"Either your worst nightmare or your salvation," he said. "It's up to you."

She didn't like men in suits, she didn't like men who just showed up in her kitchen, no matter how gorgeous they were, and she definitely didn't like his lack of answers. "I'm getting out of here," she said, turning to make a run for it.

The door in the hall slammed shut, followed by the very audible click of the lock.

"I don't think so," the stranger said. "You've been causing too much trouble, and I intend to put a stop to it. There's nothing worse than amateurs messing with the laws of mutability. The repercussions can screw things up on a global level, and it can't be ignored any longer."

"Amateurs?" Lizzie echoed, seizing on the one tangible insult.

"Well, you could hardly consider yourselves in any way adept. Your sister Deirdre transforms herself without any control; sooner or later she's going to do it with a full audience and then where will you be? And your younger sister's attempts at psychokinesis are pathetic, though so far not intrinsically dangerous. You, on the other hand, are likely to blow up this house and the entire neighborhood if you don't cease your brainless experiments."

"Who the hell are you?" she said again, trying for a tone as cold and deadly as his. It wobbled a bit, but it was a fair approximation.

"Elric."

"Elric? That's a ridiculous name."

He closed his eyes in exasperation, and for a moment she could look at him without him seeing her. He really was quite astonishing, even if he still seemed to shimmer a bit about the edges. She didn't like men in suits, but it was still the best-looking suit she'd ever seen. Or maybe the best-looking man . . .

He opened his eyes. "You've never heard of me."

She shook her head. She could dive out the window, she supposed. If she'd only had Dee's ability she'd be something entirely different at this point—with luck she'd have turned herself into a man-eating tiger and disposed of him.

There had to be something she could do. Like turn the floor into Jell-O, but then she'd be trapped, as well. And she'd be just as likely to turn the worn wooden flooring into a sea of rats.

"Sit down." Elric picked up another bunny as it hopped across the floor.

She didn't move, staring at his hands as he stroked the furry creature. Elegant, dangerous hands.

"I want you to go away," she said.

"I'm sure you do." He set another fork on the table, then began to scoop up the other three that lay scattered on the floor. "But you'll sit anyway. We need to talk."

"If you don't leave I'll call the police."

"You're not calling anyone. You don't want people knowing your secrets any more than I do."

He had a point.

"Then I'll turn *you* into a rabbit."

Oh, my God, it was the wrong thing to say. He

laughed, and it was like a rainbow of color flashing through the room. A woman could be fool enough to fall in love with a laugh like that.

And then he put his hands on her, and she was lost. It was nothing more than the touch of his strong fingers on her shoulders, pushing her down into the kitchen chair, the same long fingers that had been so gentle with the baby rabbits, but it felt as if those shimmering colors shot through her body, and she sat down, hard, staring up at him.

He looked startled himself, as if he'd felt those strange colors, too. But then, of course he would— they emanated from him. He reached for a chair, then changed his mind, choosing one farther away from her, and sat. "Don't look so nervous, Elizabeth Alicia," he said, his voice gentle on the Spanish pronunciation of her middle name. "I'm simply here to stop you. You're messing with things you don't understand, and those things could explode in your face. Literally. Apart from the fact that you're drawing unwanted attention, you could wind up dead. Alchemy is a tricky business, and you don't seem to have the first clue on how to go about it."

"Lizzie," she corrected him. "And how do you know my name? Know so much about us?"

"Everyone knows about the three of you, everyone with our kind of power. I've come to stop you before you do something irreversible."

She was halfway to the door before she remembered it was locked, and any man who could turn her bunnies back into forks had to be capable of stopping her escape with little more than a blink. She felt completely foolish in turning around, but she didn't have much choice. He was waiting for her.

"I'm not going to hurt you, Lizzie. But you're too dangerous to be left on your own. You need to make peace with your family. Someone your age should be in much greater control of her gift. You need guidance, teaching, things you gave up when your sister took you and disappeared. It's a wonder you haven't been caught—your half-assed attempts at alchemy upset the tenor of the cosmos."

"The tenor of the cosmos can take care of itself," Lizzie said. "We're not going anywhere near our family or anyone else. We do fine by ourselves, thank you very much, and we don't need anyone interfering."

"You screw up by yourselves. Haven't you practiced your craft, learned its possibilities?"

"No. We don't want to do anything that could bring us unwanted attention, either from the people in town or People Like You."

"You can't just ignore your powers. They misfire if you don't work at them."

"We don't want them."

He raised an eyebrow. "All right. Then give them up. I can make arrangements."

"Not yet."

She was really beginning to annoy him. "Whatever the problem is, I can fix it."

"You can't fix everything," Lizzie said gloomily. "God knows I've tried."

"Maybe *you* can't fix everything, Elizabeth Alicia," he said, "but you don't even know me. Your sisters' mistakes are only minor inconveniences—they might draw unfortunate attention but they don't disturb the flow. You, on the other hand, are messing up big time, and I have no intention of leaving until you agree to stop what you're doing."

"Then prepare to be here for a while," she said. "I'm on a mission, and I don't give up easily. Once it's accomplished I don't intend to do magic ever again. Until that point there's nothing you can do to stop me."

"You'd be surprised. Why are you planning to give up your powers?"

"They've never brought me anything but trouble. I want to be normal."

He let his eyes drift over her a brief, pregnant moment. This was a good thing—it was what he wanted. So why was he reluctant? "And just what is that noble mission?" he said. "I can't for the life of me figure it out. Every time you get upset, things change shape, and your workshop is a nuclear meltdown waiting to happen."

"My workshop is locked!"

"Locks don't have any effect on me," he said in a mild voice. "Tell me what you're trying to do, and maybe I can help."

She looked straight into those dark, mesmerizing eyes.

"I'm trying to turn straw into gold."

Change straw into gold? You're kidding," Elric said to Lizzie in a flat voice, though he knew she wasn't. *Oh, Christ,* he thought, staring at her. He couldn't quite believe how someone so angelic looking could be causing this much trouble. Her guileless blue eyes didn't begin to hint at the intelligence behind them, and with her tousled blond curls and slender body she looked like an impish teenager, not the woman he knew her to be. And what was it with her shoes? She was wearing Road Runner high-tops—how could he be attracted to a woman wearing Road Runner high-tops? Because he was.

"We need money," Lizzie said. "That's all Dee can think about, and if she didn't have to worry about it, she'd stop trying to force Mare to go to college, and Mare would stop arguing, and if we needed to pick up and leave we could . . ." Her voice trailed off, as if she'd realized she'd said too much.

"And that's what you think you need to do as soon as you can warn your sisters," he supplied for her. "But I'm not going to let that happen. You don't need money, you need to stop what you're doing."

"I need you to go away and leave us alone," she said, her voice stronger. She shifted, and he was afraid she was going to try to run for it. He could stop her, of course, without moving. But he was still shaken from their earlier contact, and he couldn't figure out what had happened. Maybe all that random psychic energy that she and her sisters couldn't control had managed to get between them and set off sparks. Maybe.

"Too bad. Whatever made you think straw was a good base for gold?"

"It's traditional in alchemy," she said stiffly.

"It's traditional in fairy tales. Rumpelstiltskin, spinning straw into gold. In alchemy you turn base metals into gold. Like lead."

She blushed. He liked his women sleek and sophisticated, dark-haired and whippet-thin. So what was he doing, fascinated by a pretty little girl who blushed? Besides, he was here for a reason, and getting distracted wasn't part of his plans.

"It doesn't work," she said. "I've tried lead, copper, iron, Teflon. None of it works, so I went back to straw."

"And what happens with straw?"

"It catches on fire."

He shook his head. "There are laws that govern this sort of thing, and you seem to have no notion what they are. No wonder you're on the edge of disaster."

"We're doing just fine," she said, shoving her blond curls away from her face, trying to look fierce and failing. "We don't want you here. I can figure things out on my own, and I don't need your help. I'm not the total idiot you think I am."

He was silent a moment. What would happen if he touched her again? Would there be sparks? Or nothing but this mild irritation combined with a surprising rush of attraction? He'd find out before this was over, just out of curiosity. He wasn't going to do anything about the attraction; he didn't want to get mixed up with the Fortune spawn if he could help it. But there was something about her that drew him, made him want to . . .

"I don't think you're a total idiot," he said, banishing his errant thoughts. "You've just been living in a vacuum, away from people who could help you."

"The people who helped us when our parents died? I don't think so. We can take care of ourselves."

At that moment a baby rabbit hopped across her feet. She leaned down to pick it up, stroking it. She was something like those bunnies, pretty and soft and seemingly helpless. But she wasn't, even if she herself wasn't convinced of it.

"Stop thinking so hard," he said.

She glanced up at him. Blue eyes, clear and wide and wary. "What do you mean?"

"You're trying to change him back, and you're trying too hard. You have to let go, make it instinctive. Think about something else."

"Like what?"

"Think about how much I annoy you, put the rabbit on the table, and tell me I'm an asshole."

"You're an asshole," she said promptly, setting the rabbit down. A silver fork lay there for a moment, and she stared at it in disbelief, and then a moment later it turned into a lemon.

He shook his head. "You have to stop thinking about things. And one of the first rules of mutability is that you don't cross elements. Animal turns into animal, mineral to mineral, and so on. You can't turn a fork into a living animal or even a plant."

"I just did," she said smugly. "And I could turn straw into gold."

"That's because you didn't know what you were doing and you were trying too hard. If you cross elements you disrupt everything, and it affects whatever you're working on, not to mention those around you. Turn it back into a fork."

"You're an asshole," she said promptly, trying it again, but of course the lemon just sat there.

"It's not an incantation. Think of something besides transmutation."

"That's hard to do when I'm thinking how much I'd like to turn you into a toad," she said. The lemon flattened out to a spoon. A yellow spoon, but it was a step in the right direction.

"I wouldn't try it if I were you," he said. "You forget who I am."

"I don't know who you are," she said, cranky. He suspected she didn't get cranky very often—she didn't seem to know how to carry it off. "Apart from Elric the Magnificent or something like that. I'm guessing you're some kind of cheesy charlatan like my father."

"Really?" She was making him cranky, as well, which was unusual. He'd expected this to be far simpler; he'd show up, stop Lizzie from screwing up the universe, send them all back to Xantippe, and get on with his life. But Elizabeth Alicia Fortune was getting under his skin, and it was enough incentive to make him drop his protective coloring. Just for a moment he was no longer a somewhat staid-looking man in a dark suit—he was a blaze of color and light that could blind the unwary, and then a second later he was ordinary again. Or as ordinary as he could carry off.

She blinked. That was it: she simply blinked at his temporary transformation, and then dismissed it. "I live with a shapeshifter, remember?" she said. "I'm not impressed."

"That's because you're naïve. I didn't change shape. I simply changed your perceptions."

"Now that I don't believe. You can't alter the way I think," she said fiercely. She looked at him a little closer, and there was sudden doubt in her eyes. "Can you?"

"Maybe there's hope for you yet," he said. "No, neither I nor anyone else can make you think things that aren't already inside you, not unless you're particularly empty-headed. But I can alter the way people perceive me. People see what I want them to see. Or not see me at all if I so choose."

"You can become invisible?"

"You aren't listening. I don't become invisible—people just don't see me."

"Can I do that?" she asked, fascinated.

"God, I hope not," he said. "You're trouble enough as it is."

She looked oddly pleased at the notion. "So what do you want from me? From us? How do I make you disappear?"

"You need to stop these dangerous experiments and return to your family."

"Not on your life."

It was nothing more than he expected. "Then—" The sound of the doorbell cut through his words. "Get rid of him," he said.

"How do you know it's a him? Do you have X-ray vision?"

"It's a him. If you were still enough you'd be able to sense the same thing. And I don't like him. Get rid of him."

"It's probably just a poor UPS man," Lizzie said, rising. "I ordered some supplies for my workshop a few days ago."

"I hate to think what kinds of things he's bringing," Elric said with a shudder. "We'll just ignore him and maybe he'll go away."

The doorbell had given way to a peremptory pounding on the door, and Elric knew he was no deliveryman in brown shorts. And he didn't like that at all.

"I'm answering the door," Lizzie said. "You can turn me into a pillar of salt if you want, but I'm going."

It wasn't worth arguing about. He followed her, of course, though she wasn't aware of him, and he waited behind her left shoulder, out of sight, as she unlocked the front door and opened it. He'd considered keeping it locked, but the man on the other side wasn't going to give up, and the noise he was making annoyed Elric. The sooner Lizzie faced him, the sooner he'd go away and Elric could get on with his mission.

He moved out of the way as she opened the door, shielding himself from the intruder. The man standing in the doorway was negligible; Elric was sorely tempted to flick his hand in his direction and make him disappear, but he suspected Lizzie wouldn't like that.

"What took you so long, Lizzie?" the man demanded. "Sometimes I think you'd lose your head if it wasn't attached. I tried calling you but your telephones aren't working."

"They're not?" she said, glancing over her shoulder toward the kitchen, looking straight through him, not realizing he was directly behind her.

"I need an answer about the date. You said you were going to tell your sisters about us. July twelfth works best for me—it's a slow time at work and I can afford to take a couple of days off for a honeymoon without it affecting my career. If your sisters put up a battle, then the next best time is mid-August, but I don't see what it has to do with them. They don't like me anyway."

And who could blame them? Elric thought. He hadn't paid any attention to the diamond on Lizzie's left hand. No wonder; it was so small it would take a magnifying glass to see it.

He took another long look at the man who'd interrupted them. Why in the world would Lizzie choose someone like this as a mate? He was handsome enough, Elric supposed, in a toothy, all-American way, but he was quite possibly the most ordinary man Elric had ever seen. He'd always believed everyone had some touch of magic, some hidden gift, no matter how small. For the first time he was beginning to doubt that.

Marriage to a man like this would strip Lizzie's powers from her and leave her as ordinary as he was. He really ought to encourage her to marry this idiot and abandon her abilities. Safer for everyone.

"Charles, I really can't talk about this now," she said. "I'm working on something—"

"Those silly experiments? Honestly, Lizzie, you need to grow out of that—it's time for you to settle down," he said with exasperated, condescending affection. "The sooner we get married the sooner you can put all that silly stuff behind you."

No, Elric really didn't like Charles, and the fact that he was temporarily engaged to the woman in front of him surely had nothing to do with it.

"I don't want to argue, Charles. I haven't had a chance to talk to my sisters—something came up this morning—but I promise as soon as they come home I'll tell them about our engagement and see if the date works for them. And it's not that they don't like you— they don't know you. I'm just worried they'll think it too soon—we've only been seeing each other for a few weeks."

"I'm a man who makes up his mind," he said, smug. "I took one look at you and knew you'd make the perfect wife."

"Fine. In the meantime I need to—"

"Is someone here?" Charles demanded, suddenly suspicious.

"No," she said quickly. "I'm just trying to get some work done."

But Charles had already shoved past her, and Elric moved out of the way so Charles wouldn't run into him. Someone like Charles would never see him, but even Elric couldn't make his corporeal form disappear.

Lizzie went racing after Charles into the kitchen, then came to a halt, doubt and confusion on her face. She glanced behind her, looking directly at Elric without seeing him, but for a moment her gaze narrowed, and he wondered if it was possible for her to look past the veil he'd put up. No, she was too young, too untried, and he was too good. But that moment of uncertainty in her blue eyes had been unnerving.

She turned back, and he could see her shoulders relax. "No one's here, Charles. Don't you need to be at work?"

"If we're alone in the house maybe we could go into your bedroom . . ."

Lizzie's aversion was so strong it cut through his own illogical fury. "I don't think so," she said, taking his arm and pulling him toward the door.

"And you certainly don't want me watching," he whispered in her ear. She jumped, banging her elbow against the doorframe.

Charles was already at the door, dutifully enough. "What did you say?"

"Nothing," she said, rubbing her elbow. "I just said you ought to get to work."

"I thought you whispered something."

"Why would I do that?"

Charles, totally without imagination, shrugged. "You sure you're alone?"

"Do you want to check my bedroom?"

"Not a good idea," Elric whispered.

"There it is again!" Charles said. "That whispering sound."

"It's the wind," she said. "There's a storm coming. You need to get back to work."

"I need to get back to work," Charles said. He leaned forward and kissed her, a closed-mouth, possessive kiss on Lizzie's soft mouth, and Elric decided he hated him. Intensely.

"You'll call me tomorrow," Lizzie said in the same dulcet tone.

"I'll call you tomorrow," Charles said, again as if he'd just thought of it himself. Miss Lizzie had more skills than Elric had realized. What else was she hiding?

He waited until the door was closed behind Charles, waited until he heard the sound of his car drive away, and then he dropped the veil, and Lizzie jumped.

"You do that again," she said, "and I'll . . . make you wish you'd never come here."

It was too late for that. He looked at Lizzie's badly kissed mouth, and wondered just how much trouble he was in.

Mare pounded the streets of Salem's Fork in her blue running shorts, trying to obliterate the morning from her memory. Her argument with Dee was easy to evict, she'd been ignoring Dee's arguments for years, but that coppery, dusty, sunny dream stayed with her, which was ridiculous. She did not miss Christopher Duncan in the slightest. Crash. What kind of a man had a nickname like that? Especially a guy who rode a motorcycle; there was a vote of confidence for you.

She turned up the path to the top of the mountain and the circle of stones the locals called "the Big Rocks" with "the Great Big Rock" in the center. That was a mistake; she and Crash had made love up there at least a thousand times, maybe more, although they'd only been together for two years, so maybe not, but it had been wonderful. The thought of him made her dizzy now, so when she ran back down the mountain she was in a lousy mood. Stopping at the Greasy Fork diner for a doughnut and orange juice, and having Pauline the waitress point out that eating a doughnut wasn't good for her, did not improve her morning. Running past Mother's Tattoos and seeing Mother wave at her gave her the warm wash of peace Mother always did, so that was something, but getting home and hearing Lizzie talking to herself in her workroom and not getting a chance to apologize to her for being snippy at breakfast was awful. *What is it with the universe this morning?* Mare thought. First with the dust and the daydream and now with the general thwarting. She shook her head and went to shower and then changed into the white overalls she'd painted with the Anti-Pesto logo from *The Curse of the Were-Rabbit,* put on her black-rimmed, pink-lensed, heart-shaped sunglasses, and then walked the quarter mile to the red plastic wonders of Value Video!!, where things were going to go her way. Or else.

"Hello, Mare!" Dreama, their little blond counter clerk, sang out as Mare stormed in. "Ooooooh, the coveralls look good! Nice job on the Anti-Pesto logo!"

"Thank you." Mare slammed her bag on the counter. "The universe is behaving badly, so I will be making adjustments." Then she smiled at Dreama. "You, however, are always good. How's my favorite apprentice?"

"I'm fine, thank you, Mare," Dreama said, straightening her baby-blue sweater, her ponytail bobbing.

"Not fine," Mare said.

Dreama winced. "I'm *glorious,* thank you, Mare."

"Damn straight." Mare patted her shoulder. "So, what's new at Value Video!!?"

Dreama leaned forward. "There's this gorgeous guy in the office with William."

Mare thought, *Crash,* and then mentally slapped herself. She had no idea where Crash Duncan was, but she was positive he wasn't in the manager's office in the Salem's Fork Value Video!!

Dreama jerked her head at the door that said MAN-AGER in gold stick-on letters, her round face wide-eyed. "He's a vice president from headquarters."

Mare tilted her head and thought about it. Crash had been gone for a while. There was an off chance he could have made it big and come back as a Value Video!! VP. It didn't seem like him, but still . . .

Dreama leaned still closer, her pouty lips parted in wonder. "I think they heard about William trying to off himself."

"William was not trying to off himself." Mare frowned at the door, aware of the new threat. "What does the head office want with William? He didn't try to hang himself in front of the customers." Of course, if the VP was Crash, it wasn't a problem. She could take care of Crash.

"The VP looks just like Jude Law." Dreama sighed, obviously dazzled.

"Oh," Mare said, fighting her disappointment. Crash didn't look like Jude Law. Crash looked like a really good-looking biker. Of course, there had never been any chance the VP was Crash. That had been dumb—

"I swear to God," Dreama said, "I thought it really was Jude. And you want to know what's funny? His name is Jude. Look."

Dreama shoved a business card at her and Mare took it. Under the Value Video!! logo it said, JUDE GREEN, VICE PRESIDENT SALES.

"He's really *gorgeous*," Dreama said. "Oh-my-God gorgeous. And he just came back from the Italian office—"

"Value Video!! has an Italian office?" Mare said, stunned.

"So he says 'ciao' a lot and it's so *cool*," Dreama said. "And did I say he's *gorgeous*?"

"Gorgeous men do not faze us, Dreama," Mare said, giving the card back, reality making her cranky again. "They are merely flesh and blood, arranged in a pleasing manner. They too shall pass, while we remain immutable and eternal. And, of course, unfazable. That's why we rule the universe."

"Yes, Mare," Dreama said.

Mare gave the situation some thought. Okay, Crash hadn't come back, but if she played everything right and William didn't do a reprise with the rope in front of the VP, she might get a raise out of this. She looked around the store, trying to see it from a vice president's point of view. Aside from the mess of returns on the counter, the place looked pretty good, several customers already there, mostly kids but they were being quiet, nothing to get a VP upset. Mare frowned as the fact of the kids being there registered. "What are all these kids doing in here? What are *you* doing in here? Get back to school. That's all we need is the head office busting us for illegal use of high school help."

"Teacher conference day," Dreama said. "I'm legal. Mare, he is so *hot*."

"We're unfazable, Dreama." Mare went behind the counter to clean up the mess on the desktop. She stacked the DVDs and then started sorting the receipts before the VP could get a look at the chaos and harass William into looking for more rope.

"I bet his suit is Armani," Dreama said. "I bet he's *rich*."

"Is there anything I need to know?" Mare said, comparing two receipts. "You know, *about the store*?"

"One of the beanbag chairs sprung a leak. I tried to fix it with duct tape, but I think it's dead. He has *green eyes*, Mare. He's like—"

Dreama hoisted herself up on the counter and smacked into the stack of DVDs, and Mare, her hands full of receipts, caught them with her mind, blipping down them mentally to hold each one separately, trying to dampen any little blue sparks so Dreama didn't see. She shot a glance at Dreama, who was still talking, all Jude Green all the time.

Okay, then, Mare thought and let go of the DVDs. She looked at the stack with pride: she was getting *good*. It had taken years of practice, but now with concentration, she could stack DVDs with her mind almost as well as with her hands.

God, she had the suckiest power in the family.

Mare realized that Dreama had stopped talking and was smiling past her, swinging her legs against the counter and biting her lower lip. Mare turned around.

Ah, yes, the VP. Smooth gleaming blond hair. Glistening deep green eyes. A broad curving smile. All aimed at her, dressed in a very expensive charcoal-gray suit and very ugly green tie, topped off with a silver tie tack that gleamed almost as brightly as his teeth.

Gimme a raise, Pretty Boy.

"Miss O'Brien?" the vision said. "Ciao! I'm Jude Green, vice president in charge of sales for Value Video!!" He took in her coveralls and faltered a little, evidently expecting more tailoring and less Anti-Pesto from his assistant managers.

Ciao? "Nice to meet you, Jude." Mare shook his hand. It was a little damp, but not completely off-putting. "So, you're from Italy?"

He nodded. "Originally from France, but then we migrated to Italy. Just over the border."

"Oh, you're *French*," Dreama said, practically swooning.

He looked at Mare's overalls again, shook his head, and then soldiered on. "I'd like to talk to you."

"I'll just go check that beanbag chair." Dreama boosted herself off the counter, grinning like an idiot.

Mare smiled at the VP, but before he could say anything, Brandon Upshot, the O'Briens' paper boy, came up to the counter with a girl who looked familiar, which wasn't unusual. Everybody looked familiar in Salem's Fork. What didn't look familiar was Brandon looking nervous. Brandon could hit the front porch with the daily paper dead center, eyes closed, while riding his bike no hands, just like magic. Brandon had nerves of steel.

Brandon looked like he was going to throw up.

First girlfriend, Mare thought and told the VP, "With you in a minute." She smiled at Brandon. *I'm Queen of the Universe and I've got your back, babe. Calm down.*

"We'd like to reserve the love seat for the nine o'clock show," the girl said, a giggle in her voice, and Brandon blushed.

"Let me check." Mare pulled out the clipboard that listed the seating available. "For the nine o'clock, the big couch is gone and the two La-Z-Boys, and all the beanbag chairs, but amazingly yes, the love seat is available and is now yours for the nine o'clock showing of *The Curse of the Were-Rabbit*. Excellent choice, Brandon."

The girl looked at him with new respect. People knew Brandon. Brandon was somebody.

Brandon got calmer.

The VP moved closer.

Watch and see how the pros do customer service in Salem's Fork, Ciao-hound. Mare smiled at the girl. "Do I know you?"

"I'm Katie Rose," the girl said. "My mom works at the bank with your sister."

"Oh, sure, Linda Rose, right?" When Katie nodded, Mare said, "Good to see you again, Katie." She handed the clipboard to Brandon. "Write your name and Katie's and your phone number right there." She pointed at the blank space for the love seat sign-up.

Brandon took the pencil with nervous fingers, and Mare saw it start to roll out of his loose grasp. She froze it long enough for him to get a grip on it and begin the serious business of writing his name and Katie's together on the same line, then she glanced at Katie. She was smiling at Brandon, adoration in her eyes.

I used to smile at Crash like that, Mare thought, and then evicted Crash from her mind to glance back at Jude Green. He was watching her, not the customers. So much for his interest in public relations. "So you're a vice president," she said to him, folding her arms and leaning back against the counter. "What brings you to Salem's Fork?"

Jude moved a little closer. "We understand you had a disturbing event this week."

"Disturbing?" Mare said, thinking, *Oh, hell, William.* "I don't recall anything disturbing. There's never anything disturbing here. We don't do disturbing. Everything's under control." *My control. Gimme a raise and go away.*

A sulky boy came up to the counter and shoved Brandon aside to drop *Girls Gone Wild Cleveland* in front of her. "Great flick," the boy said to Mare. He nudged the tall kid who'd followed him to the counter. "It's got naked chicks in it. Topless."

He looked back at Mare as if to say, *How about that, baby?* and she picked up the DVD to sign it out, repressing the urge to smack him upside the head with it since Jude Green was standing right there. The VP was stifling her flair. Another good reason to become queen of Value Video!!: stomp out all that flair-stifling.

"Cool. Naked chicks," the other kid said. Mare squinted at him. He looked to be a junior in high school. One of the Bannisters. They all had those noses that turned up at the end like elf shoes.

Mare ran the rental automatically while she tried to figure out Jude Green's angle—why would he care about William and the rope?—and kept an eye on the sulky kid.

"You're coming back here to see a *puppet movie*?" he said to Brandon. "*Chick flick*. Guess *she* picks out the movies, huh?"

Brandon flushed, Katie stepped closer to him, and Mare gritted her teeth.

Jude Green was still watching. Not a good time to take steps with a customer.

"Whipped," the sulky boy said to Brandon.

On the other hand, Mare thought, *this* is *my universe.*

"*You,*" she said to the sulky boy, handing him his credit card receipt. "*Sign that.* And you," she said, turning to the younger boy. "What's your name?"

"Algy Bannister," the tall kid said, looking wary.

"Algy." Mare leaned forward. "Before you now are two possibilities, two paths you may take. One is represented by your buddy here"—she jerked her thumb at the sulky boy—"the guy with the boobs-and-butts movie. The other is represented by Brandon, the one coming back to see Wallace and Gromit solve *The Curse of the Were-Rabbit*. You understand the choice that lies before you, grasshopper, a choice that could determine your future happiness and satisfaction?"

"Hell, yes," Algy said, and reached for *Girls Gone Wild*.

Mare slammed her hand down on it, making Jude jump. "One thing to consider. This guy you're with . . ." She looked at the sulky boy's Value Video!! membership card. "Shawn. Shawn is going home with you tonight to watch this video, right?"

"Right," Algy said, confused.

"But Brandon is going to be sitting on a love seat tonight with his arm around Katie."

Algy looked over at Katie, now linking her hand through Brandon's arm protectively.

"The thing about chick flicks," Mare said to Algy, "is that chicks like them." She picked up *Girls Gone Wild* and handed it to Shawn. "Here's your dick flick. Enjoy."

"Funny," Shawn said, handing back the signed receipt.

Algy said, "Yeah, funny," but he watched Katie smile at Brandon.

"Choose wisely," Mare said. "Do not listen to the words of others who have chosen a lesser path, but follow your bliss."

Shawn snorted but he looked confused.

Algy thought about it. "*Girls Gone Wild*," he said defiantly, and high-fived with Shawn.

Mare shook her head sadly as they left, probably taking her raise with them. "Next thing you know, it'll be human sacrifice, dogs and cats living together."

"Pardon?" Jude said.

"*Ghostbusters*," Mare said, and took the clipboard from Brandon and Katie, smiling at them as they left.

"So everything's under control," Jude said with a definite undercurrent of censure in his voice.

"Yes," Mare said. "Algy gets to choose. It's that whole free will thing."

"That doesn't sound like control to me."

Mare frowned at him. "Do not confuse control with tyranny, Jude. That mistake has screwed up entire continents. Imagine what it could do to a video store." She cocked her head at him. "So, why are you here?"

"Your manager tried to hang himself," Jude said.

"Not really." Mare went back to tidying up the counter, radiating unconcern as hard as possible. "Besides, it's all taken care of now, William is just fine, and everything is under control."

"Could you tell me what happened, please?"

Mare sighed and leaned back against the counter. "Well, I'm in charge of the weekend events and tonight we're showing *Curse of the Were-Rabbit* and tomorrow night *Corpse Bride,* and then Sunday we're doing a triple feature of the *Were-Rabbit, Corpse Bride,* and *Howl's Moving Castle,* so when I was making the posters earlier this week, I wanted to call it 'Scare the Shit Out of Your Kids Weekend,' but William said I couldn't advertise anything with 'shit' in it. So I changed it to 'Scare the Stuffing Out of Your Kids Weekend' and did this display with dolls with the stuffing coming out of them, but William said that was too gruesome. So then I put up a sign that said, 'Scare Your Kids Silly Weekend' with photos of kids crossing their eyes and sticking their tongues out at the camera, and William went in the back room and tried to hang himself, and I found him and cut him down. And we've got almost a hundred people signed up to come for the three days combined and that's not counting the drop-ins so I'm thinking it's going to be another huge success for the Salem's Fork Value Video!!" She beamed at him.

Jude did not beam back. "As I understand it, he talked to you before he hung himself."

"Well, yes, but that wasn't because of me," Mare said, thinking, *Jesus wept, what is this, Pin It on Mare Weekend?* "He'd brought the rope from home."

"And . . ." Jude consulted his clipboard. "He left a note that said, 'Blame it on Netflix.' "

"Who told you about the note?"

"Uh," Jude said, his eyes sliding over to where Dreama was restocking the games, looking like an efficient Catholic School Girl, which was probably a vice-presidential fantasy.

Dreama looked up and saw him looking at her and blushed.

Traitor, Mare thought and turned back to Jude, smiling. "Look, it wasn't that big a deal. The rope would have broken anyway. It was really more like twine. I think it was a cry for help. Netflix really does depress the hell out of him. And anyway, it's over. It's fine. Moving on now—"

"So you've been acting as manager all week." Jude turned back to survey the store. "Putting up all these displays—"

"No, no, William's been quieter but he's been managing the place. I always do the promotion stuff. We're right back to normal."

"Normal being Algy getting his lesson in free will."

"And Brandon and Katie getting their love seat to watch Wallace and Gromit," Mare pointed out. "Everybody's happy. There are no problems here. We are back to normal. Not that we ever left normal. We are normal twenty-four/seven." She smiled, determinedly cheerful.

"I wouldn't call these displays normal. Unorthodox, maybe."

"You say that like it's a bad thing." Mare smiled at him harder. "Here's the problem, Jude. The people

who do the Value Video!! displays have souls made of
plywood. They are pressed and cut to measure, Jude,
they have no flair. I have flair."

Jude looked around. "Yes, Miss O'Brien, I would
have to agree you have flair. The furniture alone—"

"Isn't it great?" Mare put as much bounce in her
voice as possible. "It's amazing the things people leave
out in the street. A little paint and it's better than new."

"I see," Jude said. "And then there's the display of
'Movies That Are Much Worse Than They Sound' over
there. It's almost empty."

"We can't keep it filled, Jude," Mare said. "People
just have to see for themselves. We've had to order
more copies of *Bell, Book, and Candle* and *Bewitched*."

"And the 'Cry Till You Puke' display?"

Mare leaned closer, trying to look confidential and
trusting. "You know, weepers are not my thing. But if
you're into them, you really want to go the whole way.
Beaches, *Terms of Endearment*, *Shadowlands* . . . Actually, *Shadowlands* is a damn good movie. Anyway,
you want to be pointed to the ones that are going to
get you there. It's like emotional porn, you know? It
isn't really the story that matters, it's getting that release."

"I see," Jude said, looking more interested.

"Because that's really what we're selling here,"
Mare said. "Emotional catharsis, vicarious release.
You want to experience the hell of war without getting
killed? We have 'Movies Your Recruiter Doesn't Want
You to See.' You want to know what it's like to fall in
love without having to get a background check on the
person you're dating? We got 'Bad Dates Gone Good.'
You want to know—"

"Right," Jude said. "That's all very interesting."

"I've been doing this for a while, Jude. Our sales

are up. William was really happy about that. I think that's why he used such thin rope. He knew there were good times ahead." She leaned back against the counter. "I can't believe the central office sent you down here because William had one bad day."

"They didn't."

Jude opened his mouth to go on and Mare braced herself for whatever was coming next, but then the door opened again and Algy came in, looking furtive.

"Back with you in a minute," Mare said to Jude, and turned to face Algy. "Have you reconsidered your choice, grasshopper?"

"Why do you keep calling me that?" Algy said.

Mare sighed. "What do you want?"

Algy leaned over the counter, looking around to make sure he wasn't overheard. "What kind of movies do chicks like?"

"Luckily for you, I have a list." Mare reached under the counter for her accordion file of recommendations and flipped through it until she found one that was headed "Movies Girls Like." She pulled it out and handed it to him. "Of course it depends on the girl. But I have it broken down into the most common stereo-types."

Algy squinted at the list. "Yeah. This is good."

"And I'm pretty sure that if you reserve it now, the love seat is still open for the six-thirty show. If you know a girl, I mean."

"I know a girl," Algy said, looking first outraged, then thoughtful. "Yeah. Put me down for that."

Mare handed him the clipboard. "Put yourself down."

Algy filled out the clipboard and handed it back. He'd left the space for the other name blank. Probably a good idea until he'd found somebody to say yes.

"You have chosen wisely," Mare intoned, and when

Algy frowned at her, she said, "That's from *Indiana Jones and the Last Crusade*."

Algy looked confused again. So did Jude.

"Don't worry about it," Mare said. "Just remember: no *Girls Gone Wild*. Ever."

"Right." Algy folded up his list and stuffed it in his pocket. "Thanks." He leaned closer. "Don't tell Shawn."

"Wouldn't dream of it." Mare stashed her recommendations folder under the counter again as the door closed behind Algy. Then she turned back to Jude.

"That's amazing," he said. "You are unstoppable."

"I know."

"Dreama said you were Queen of the Universe, but I thought she was joking."

"She wasn't. So why are you here exactly?"

He flashed his smile at her, and she saw how attractive he was, now that he wasn't criticizing the place. "The head office sent me down because your sales have consistently been the highest in the area even though you have a relatively small customer base." He stepped closer. "I'm assuming that's because of you."

"And William," Mare said. "So we're doing good. That's great. Thanks for stopping by to tell us. Anything else?" *Like a raise?*

"Oh, yes." He flashed his movie-star smile again. "I was sent to find out why the store was thriving and I think I have." He held out his hand. "Congratulations, Miss O'Brien. You are now the new manager of Salem's Value Video!! Your salary will, of course, double."

He went on but his words faded as the dusty Tuscan sunlight swirled into the store in a cloud of coppery dust and that damn baby laughed again and Mare felt the whole place swing around her, and she said, "No."

Jude stopped. "No?"

Mare swallowed. "No." She put her hand out to the counter, her whole world unsteady, thinking, *Tell him yes, you idiot, it's a raise,* but she knew she didn't want it, clear as that sunshine. "No, thank you, no, I don't want to be manager."

Jude blinked slowly, his eyelids moving like shutters. "Was it the part where I said you'd have to behave normally, no funny stuff?"

"No," Mare said, surprised. "I missed that part. What happened to William?"

"We feel William will be happier in another line of work."

"No." Mare took a deep breath, surer every time she said it. "No, no, no." She took a step back and bumped her butt into the counter, knocking off a pencil and letting it roll to the floor. "We need William here. He's the voice of reason. He does math. We need William as manager. I refuse to be manager. Go back in that office and tell William he still has a job."

Jude picked up the pencil and handed it to her. "Miss O'Brien . . . may I call you Mare?"

Mare repressed an exasperated sigh. "Sure, Jude."

"Mare, I realize that some women have a fear of success—"

"I'm not afraid of success. I embrace success. Success and I are practically twin souls. I just don't want to manage a video store. Where's the fun in that?" As soon as she said it, she knew it was true.

"Well, *this.*" Jude gestured to the promotional displays.

"Yes, but if I'm manager I have to have somebody else do that while I do the ordering and the books and all the dull gray dead stuff. No. No, no, no. Go tell William he's manager again. I'll wait here." Mare folded her arms and stared at him. "Go on."

"Well . . ." Jude leaned against the counter, closer to her, smelling faintly of good, expensive cologne. He had a really large Adam's apple, but on the other hand, his suit was very good. You couldn't have everything. "There is another possibility."

"William is still the manager."

"Yes, fine, William's the manager," Jude said. "But I'm really intrigued by your displays. I think other stores in the chain could benefit from your imagination. Would you be open to working in the promotions department at the head office in New York City?"

"You're kidding." Mare frowned. "The promotions are designed in New York? You'd think they'd be more creative there. Greatest city in the world and their idea of a hot promotion is Two for One Tuesdays? Jeez."

"That's why they need you," Jude said. "I can arrange for you to work outside the department, be your own boss. I get the feeling you don't respond well to authority."

"Authority has never responded well to me." Mare stared off into space for a moment, considering this new possibility. "New York. Huh. That could be good. The Statue of Liberty. I've always considered her a kindred spirit. Maybe . . ." The dusty Tuscan sun tried to swirl in again, but she kicked its ass out of her frontal lobe. She had a real life to live here. And pay for.

"Uh, well, that's good," Jude said, clearly lost. He polished his tie tack with his finger for a moment and then he cleared his throat. "It's Friday, so it's going to take me a while to pursue this, I'll have to make some calls, but can I say that you would be interested in relocating to New York?"

Mare almost said yes, and then remembered Dee

and Lizzie. Would they like New York? Art museums for Dee, the New York Library for Lizzie, lots of anonymity, a good place to hide from Xan. It could work. "I'll have to ask my sisters."

"For permission? Surely you're old enough to make this decision on your own."

"To see if they want to move," Mare said. "We stick together." *We have to. We have strange and unusual powers, Jude. Lizzie could change you into a toad before you could polish your Rolex.* "But I'm interested, yes. Go ahead and make your calls. And tell William he's still the manager."

"Yes, Mare," Jude said and went back to the office.

Mare turned and crooked her finger at Dreama.

"What?" Dreama said as she got closer.

"So you told Jude about William and the rope," Mare said.

Dreama flushed again. She put her hands behind her back and stuck her chin out, trying for innocence and missing by a mile. "He was asking me things and I just told him. It slipped out. He's so gorgeous, Mare, don't you just want to tell him everything?"

"No," Mare said. "And neither do you. You almost got William fired."

"Yes, but then you could be manager," Dreama said.

"So you had a *long* talk with Jude," Mare said severely.

Dreama leaned closer. "You'd be a much better manager, Mare. You really would. William *hates* being manager."

"So would I. Listen to me." Mare fixed her with a steely gaze. "Do *not* tell Jude anything else. Ever. We are us and they are them. Got it?"

Dreama looked annoyed. "Then how are you ever going to get a promotion? You said you were gonna be queen of Value Video!! Well, you're gonna need a promotion for—"

"I changed my mind," Mare said, equally annoyed because she didn't know that the hell she was doing, either. "Queens of the Universe do not get into ruts, Dreama. They stay fluid and unpredictable—"

The door chime rang and Mare turned to smile and then sucked in her breath, like a punch to the stomach. He stood there, tall and dark and blue-eyed as ever, the dusty Tuscan sunlight behind him, and Mare thought he was a hallucination and almost had words with her frontal lobe until Dreama said, "Oh, my," and then she put up her hand to ward him off and knocked over the stack of DVDs, scattering them all over her nice, tidy desktop.

"Hello, Mare," he said and shoved his hands in his pockets, looking pretty much exactly the way he'd looked five years before when she'd been so in love with him that the world had tilted sideways every time she'd looked at him. "Uh, I'm back." He waited a minute while she stood breathless, speechless, and then he said, "You gonna say anything?"

"Hello, Crash," Mare said, hating it that her voice cracked, and then she went toward him and all that sunlight, which wasn't easy because the world was tilting again.

X an put the shallow silver bowl in front of the see glass, now a mirror on her silver-paneled wall. As she reached to take down a gilded box from the shelf beside it, the angle of light changed and she caught her own reflection. The light of day wasn't kind to a woman at midlife, she thought.

She looked closer. Even with magic and plastic surgery, the skin lost elasticity. Last night Vincent had leaned close to her, his tux immaculate in the low light of the restaurant, his white hair perfectly styled, and said, "We should always dine by candlelight," and she'd been fairly sure there'd been a snicker in his voice.

But then, Vincent was such a bastard. A gorgeous one if you liked graying distinguished men who could have headed the cast of an eighties television show, and adequately talented in bed if you liked choreography and a man who kept looking in the mirror admiring his own technique, but his charm was wearing thin. Thank God she was almost done with him. She was going to take a great deal of pleasure in casting Vincent aside, especially in front of everyone in their social circle, all those smirkers who'd watched last night while he'd flirted with a very young brown-haired witch named Jennifer, whose weight seemed to be entirely concentrated in her bust and her behind, which was evidently where she kept her brains if she thought Vincent was a catch. Xan had smiled, outwardly amused but inwardly seething that the moron would humiliate her in her own circle. It shouldn't matter what any of them thought, she was the most powerful of all of them, they were just her court . . .

She had been the most powerful of all of them.

Age, she thought. *Age brings wisdom. Who the hell wants wisdom?*

Youth and power. That was—

Somebody sneezed behind her and she jerked back. "Sweet hell, Maxine, how did you get in here again?"

"The portal—"

"I closed the portal."

"Well, there was a little crack of light and I kind of—"

I'm going to have you killed and stuffed. "What do you want, Maxine?"

"Oh. Right. Well, it's coming up on Friday night. Martinis would really sell—"

"Maxine, you will do *nothing* to call attention to yourself or the diner until *Monday*." Xan put down the gilt box and began to wave her hand.

"No!" Maxine said, waving both of hers. "Wait! I have news! There's a new video store guy named Jude. He's your guy for Mare, right?"

"Yes?" Xan said, stopping in mid-wave.

"Well, he's *really* cute," Maxine said. "Looks just like Jude Law. But the one everybody is talking about is the writer guy on the motorcycle. Ohmigod. Dee won the hottie lottery with that one."

"Thank you," Xan said icily.

"Haven't seen the third one. Lizzie's."

Elric. He made Vincent look like a roadie for a boy band. "He's there."

"Oh. Okay." Maxine hesitated.

Xan sighed. "What is it, Maxine?"

"Well, I really don't know what's good stuff to tell you and what isn't. It would help if I knew what these guys were doing in town."

Xan thought about turning Maxine into a rabbit now, but she needed her. "All right."

Maxine came closer, glancing at the silver bowl and the liquid simmering there, probably avid to ask what it was but wisely keeping her mouth shut. *Even Maxine has a learning curve.*

Xan smiled at her. "I am concerned about my nieces, so I have cast a spell to bring them their True Loves."

Maxine's mouth dropped open. "You can do that?" Xan looked at her, and Maxine nodded like a bobble-head doll. "Of *course* you can do that, you can do anything, but I mean, geez, do you know what kind of money you could make doing that for real? I mean, people would pay *hundreds of dollars* for that kind of stuff."

"Right, Maxine," Xan said. "Hundreds of dollars. May I go on?"

"Oh, yeah," Maxine said. "This is good stuff."

"I'm afraid that just bringing the men into Salem's Fork won't be enough. The girls are very stubborn. So I have to keep an eye on the way their romances are going." *I have to make sure that Dee knows Danny hates magic so that she'll give her power up to me. I have to make sure that Elric takes Lizzie's power from her because she's too dangerous and gives it to me. And I have to make sure that Mare discards her magic for earthly power so that I can take it for myself.* "You know how easily young girls can throw away good men through inexperience."

"I know." Maxine's face crumpled. "My Boyd. If I could do it all over again—"

"I'm sure," Xan said. "So we're keeping an eye on Dee and Danny, Lizzie and Elric, and Mare and Jude."

"Lizzie and who?"

"Elric," Xan said. "He's probably not going to be outside much. Tall, blond, beautiful, you'll know him if you see him."

"Wow," Maxine said. "You sure are good to your nieces."

"Yes," Xan said. "I sure am."

She turned back to the see glass where Danny was heading for the bank; inside Dee was bent over her desk. Lizzie was at the kitchen sink, doing dishes; Xan sighed for a woman so lacking in passion that she'd do dishes alone in a house with Elric. And Mare was heading for the diner, probably meeting Jude there for lunch; who could resist a movie-star-handsome boss who'd just offered her the promotion of her dreams?

She opened the gilt box and sprinkled the contents into her right hand until the red spicy powder made a mound there. Then she waved her left hand over the bowl, drawing up a spiral of vapor, then another, then another, until she had the three coiling together, a silver arabesque above the bowl in front of the see glass.

"Wow," Maxine said.

"Quiet," Xan said. A little refresher course in "Xan Is Magic, Don't Disobey Her" wouldn't hurt Maxine. "This is an impulse spell, Maxine. It's very delicate. Don't move."

"Right," Maxine said, leaning closer to see.

Xan thought about explaining "don't move" in detail, but since an impulse spell was one of the sturdiest spells in existence, she decided to let Maxine go.

Xan held her right hand in the middle of the vapor arabesque and waited. In the see glass, Danny walked into the bank and began to talk to Dee. Xan looked closer at the house and saw Elric standing behind Lizzie in the kitchen window. And much harder to see, Mare was sitting in the diner with someone, leaning forward—

Xan gently blew the red powder through the arabesque and into the see glass, and the peppery vapor spiraled into the see glass, down into Salem's Fork, into a bank, a kitchen, a diner—

"Wow," Maxine said, her eyes wide.

"It's lunchtime, Maxine," Xan said. "Go sling hash."

"But," Maxine said, and Xan waved her hand and then there was silence.

In the see glass, Maxine reappeared in the Dumpster, staggering among the green plastic bags.

Xan closed the portal and stuck a psychic brick behind it.

Find a crack in that, Maxine, she thought and then poured herself a glass of wine.

As she sat back with her wine, the see glass gave her back her reflection. "Only by candlelight," Vincent had said. And the bastard was older than she was.

But if she had the girls' powers, she'd also have the girls' psychic energy, all that juice flowing through her veins. She closed her eyes and imagined the swell of youth again. The loss of power probably wouldn't hurt the girls if she took it carefully; they'd probably age like normal humans, they'd fit right in and have the ordinary lives they craved, but she . . .

She'd be young again.

And then she could put that bastard Vincent in the Dumpster with Maxine.

She shifted again to watch Maxine in the see glass, outside the Dumpster now, patting down her uniform. Hell, maybe she wouldn't wait. The memory came back to her of Vincent and that little witch Jennifer last night, she of the big brown eyes and big brown hair and very small power, laughing in a corner while the rest of the party watched Xan avidly. If Vincent was going to chase trash, Xan could at least put him in the vicinity of it.

The thought of impeccable, immaculate, tuxedo-clad Vincent in a diner Dumpster in Salem's Fork, Virginia, cheered Xan so much, she smiled.

And then she looked closer at the glass . . .

CHAPTER THREE

Dee yanked her skirt into a more comfortable position and prayed for the day to pass. This was the fifth time in three hours she'd had to stand, wriggle, and then sit back down, just to get some relief. She had a headache from the sudden cellular disruption. She was still jumpy from the close call she'd had that morning. And she was dressed in heavy wool and starched cotton.

The good news was that she'd been able to reach Pete Semple's toolshed and change without attracting any attention except from Pete's dachshund Eddie, who was used to seeing Dee walk naked out of green fog. The better news was that Pete hadn't found her clothes and tossed them before she needed them.

The bad news was that the suit she'd stashed with Pete was the heaviest one she owned, meant for winter. Since the day had grown unseasonably warm and muggy, she itched like a mange victim and smelled vaguely like damp motor oil. Worse than that, though, it seemed she'd forgotten to pack underwear. Which was why she kept readjusting her clothes. The wool skirt was bad. The stiff cotton blouse was pure torture.

"Anything else, there, Dee?" a gravelly voice asked in her ear.

She jotted down the information she'd just received from Salem's Fork's only police detective and fiddled with her Bluetooth. "No, Larry. I think a clean police record is all a girl could ask for. Thanks. I really appreciate the help."

"Not at all. The chief gave me a heads-up on this guy when he heard he was at your house this morning. I know we didn't find nothin', but you be careful."

"Thanks, Larry. You give my best to Eleanor."

She hung up, checking off another item on her list. She wasn't going to be caught unprepared again. By the time she got off work, she was going to know everything there was to know about Danny James. Then she was going to make a preemptive strike and surprise him before he surprised her. He could use a little unsettling. Actually, he could use a mallet to the head. *Ready or not, here I come*, indeed.

Of course it didn't go the way she planned. God forbid she should ever once be prepared for the disasters in her life. She'd just added her notes from Larry to the ones she'd shoved in her desk drawer when a shadow fell across her desk.

"No, Mike," she said, expecting to see the latest junior VP standing there asking for a sexual harassment suit. "I won't suck your toes and make you a happy man."

She looked up and froze.

Danny James was standing there right in front of her desk, his hair damp enough to curl, his physique a thing to make grown women weep. Oh, she hadn't realized it before. His eyes were blue. Not just blue. Cobalt-teal blue. Drop-your-business-suit-and-take-a-sailboat-to-paradise blue. Breathtakingly bright and shrewd as sin. Dee was mesmerized.

"Ca . . ." Embarrassed at the squeak that came out of her throat, she tried again, perfectly aware that her cheeks were flaming. "Can I help you?"

She tried so hard to ignore the pure shaft of heat that ripped through her. Sharp heat, sizzling like hot oil in a frying pan. She wondered if Mr. James could possibly have felt it, too. His smile sagged, and his eyes had suddenly grown very dark.

"If sucking toes is part of this bank's service," he said, "I'm surprised you don't have a line all the way around the block."

Dee flushed like a hormonal teen. Lovely. Multiple humiliations in a single day. "Please excuse me. Now, can I help you?"

His smile reappeared. "They said I should see you to open an account." He held out his hand. "You are Deirdre O'Brien?"

Dumbly, Dee took it. He didn't shake, though. He just held on. Dee just stared.

This had to stop. She'd never reacted to anyone like this in her life. And to make matters worse, he was conjuring up that damn fantasy again. Just a flash, the way it had appeared in that swirl of dust. His skin had been tanned, she would swear it, with just a sheen of sweat across his back, so that it gleamed in the light of the high sun. And his smile. Oh, his smile.

It couldn't have been his smile. She had to stop this. *Ready or not . . .*

She pulled her hand back and cleared her throat. It was better than cursing.

"May I sit?" he asked.

He was in a blue open-neck oxford shirt now, the sleeves rolled to his elbows, his jeans newer, but no less obscene. Dee ran her tongue over suddenly dry lips.

"Uh, of course." She gave a limp little wave to the chair across from her. "What kind of account do you want, Mr. . . . ?"

"James," he said, settling into the chair. "Danny James. Didn't your sister say I'd be by?"

"Oh." She sucked in a breath, trying to look calm. "That."

"Yes." His smile expanded, all teeth and delight. "That. I'd like very much to take you to dinner tonight."

She did not smile back. "I thought you were opening an account."

"Well, I can do that, too. I just didn't want to miss you again. I'd really like to talk to you."

Dee made it a point to open the drawer that held her paperwork. "And I really don't want to talk to you. Exactly what kind of account would you like, Mr. James? We have several excellent ones to choose from."

"Don't all those bobby pins hurt your head?"

Dee caught herself before she instinctively reached up to check her chignon. It was her work hair. Clean and tidy and out of the way. Her hair was long and curly and bright red, the banner of an Irish witch, Aunt Xan had always told her. So it was always a battle of wills for control. And yes, the pins did hurt her head. It took a lot to subdue all that unruliness.

"Oddly enough, Mr. James, that doesn't answer my question. What kind of account did you say?"

How could that grin get brighter? He leaned back in his chair as if he were in his living room. "You pick one for me. I'm sure you know better than I."

Dee sighed, her headache suddenly worse. "I really

do have work to do, Mr. James. If you aren't here on bank business, I'd have to ask you to excuse me."

He pulled a checkbook from his breast pocket. "But I am. I told you. I'd like to open an account. With . . . will fifty thousand do?"

Dee almost choked on her tongue. "Fifty . . . yes."

Her hands actually trembled as she separated out the papers for the interest-bearing checking account—with overdraft protection—and passed them over. "And you'd like to transfer that from your bank in Chicago?"

He smiled, an eyebrow lifted. "You do research, too, do you?"

"It's why God invented Google." She pulled out a Third Virginia Bank pen and laid it on top of the forms. "From what I've learned you are a book researcher, which must pay better than I thought, if you have fifty thousand dollars to throw around. You work for the author Mark Delaney, which is impressive, as he actually does make quite a bit of money and has quite a few literary awards for a horror writer."

"Alternative history. Please. And just to set the record straight, you were right to think that researchers don't make much money. The money's Mark's."

Dee shrugged. "You have no wants or warrants, you rent your apartment, and you have current licenses for a motorcycle and a Jeep. I'm still waiting on your credit report. All told, though, pretty boring."

He grinned up from where he was signing his check with a flourish. "Actually, not boring at all. I get to go places other people don't and talk to people I'd never get to meet and learn things I've always wanted to know. Since Mr. Delaney doesn't like to mingle, I get to do it for him. I even get to meet lovely people like you and your sisters. It may not be romantic, but I'm having fun."

She bet he was. If the reactions she'd seen in town were any indication, he could get a rock to talk to him. And he'd probably enjoy it. For a few moments, she allowed herself to actively envy him. She was stuck here in *Office Space* central until the day both Lizzie and Mare were safe and independent, and she could learn to control her unfortunate tendency to morph. Researching alternative histories suddenly sounded exciting as hell.

As if to remind herself again of where she belonged, she tapped the form in front of him. "I can't imagine why you would want to open a new checking account for the short time you'll be here, Mr. James, but this should probably be adequate for you."

He ripped the check off and handed it over. "Who said I was going to be here a short time, Ms. O'Brien?"

She tried to stare him down. "I did. I'm afraid there's simply nothing here for you."

"You don't know what I need, though."

This time she glared. "Whatever it is, I don't have it."

Oh, crap. Had she really said that? She flushed again, a mottled red that was sincerely unattractive on a redhead, while he made a slow perusal of her, tucked away beneath her boring gray suit and bobby pins.

"Oh, I wouldn't say that, Miss O'Brien. Are you sure I can't talk you into dinner?"

She did her best to reclaim her dignity. "I'm sure, Mr. James."

"What about a drink? Surely a drink won't overset the delicate balance of of the universe."

A drink. With Danny James. Who was he kidding?

"Mr. James," she said, ready to deal him the setdown of his life, when something tickled her nose and she shivered hard, once. "I'd love to have a drink."

Dee wasn't sure who was more surprised. She did know who was more appalled.

This day was going from bad to worse, Lizzie thought unhappily, staring up at the now visible Elric. Charles's appearance had been even less welcome than the stranger's—she'd already been rethinking her precipitous decision to marry him, and seeing him with Elric's dark, unreadable eyes made her choice seem even more absurd.

"That's my fiancé," she said, unnecessarily.

"Not for long," Elric said, turning and heading back into the kitchen, obviously expecting her to follow. She glanced at the door longingly for a moment, and as if on cue the lock clicked. "He's not your type."

"I'm not going to discuss my love life with you," she said stiffly. She began scooping up the silverware from the table, including the yellow spoon, and dumped it all in the sink.

"What are you doing?"

"Washing dishes," she said without turning around. Maybe if she just ignored him he'd go away. "We have a deal, my sisters and I. I take care of the household, they bring in the money."

"You don't strike me as the Susie Homemaker type."

"I'm not. I like to cook—that way I can mix things together and make something without it exploding or catching fire. Traditional jobs are a bit of a . . . challenge for me. Things change form when I don't expect it, and I have a hard time explaining."

He came up behind her—she didn't have to turn to feel him, she didn't have to have any special gifts. He was everywhere. "The dishes can wait. I want you to tell me why you're marrying that weak-minded bully."

"He's not—"

"You've got him wrapped around your finger. I was impressed—that kind of mind magic is very advanced, and doesn't usually go along with transmutationary gifts. Though maybe that's why you can control him when everything else in your life is out of your control."

She turned at that one, glaring at him. Or tried to, but every time she looked at him he seemed to shift a little, those streams of color distracting her. "You're a psychiatrist as well as a charlatan?" she demanded. "Go analyze someone else."

He was unfazed by her insult. "Did I touch a nerve, Elizabeth Alicia? You don't need a man telling you you're a useless idiot."

"That's what you've been doing ever since you materialized in my kitchen," she snapped, turning back to the dishes.

There was silence for a moment, and she wondered if she'd finally managed to puncture that calm certainty.

"You have a point," he conceded finally. "But in my case I think you're too smart and too gifted to be making stupid mistakes and endangering yourself and those around you. Your boyfriend seems to think you're useless. What in the world made you think you should marry him?"

"I told you, I want a normal life, one without magic."

"I think I can safely assure you that a life with your future husband will be completely devoid of any sort of magic." His voice was dry.

She dumped the silver and yellow flatware into the drainer and turned to look at him. Again, that odd little pinging feeling inside—as if her hormones had short-circuited.

Her hormones had nothing to do with the stranger who'd shown up in her kitchen, she reminded herself sternly. In fact, her hormones were barely operating at a normal level, despite the strange, erotic dreams that had been tormenting her the last few nights. All those had managed to do was ensure she had a lousy night's sleep, and right now she'd had about as much of the mysterious Elric as she could handle.

"You want to leave," she said, her voice soothing. "You want to forget you ever found us."

His hoot of laughter might have been insulting if she'd had even the faintest hope it would work. "I told you, that only works on the weak-minded, and those whose minds are clouded by lust. Haven't you ever wondered why it didn't work when you tried it with your sisters? And don't tell me you haven't tried—I won't believe you."

"I've tried. You're right, it only works with men. And clearly not all men," she added. "Lucky for you your mind isn't clouded by lust for me."

"Lucky for me," he said, his still dark eyes watching her. "Why did you choose Charles? The weak-minded part, I imagine. You wouldn't have any trouble finding men whose minds are clouded by lust, but you must have wanted someone who was easily controllable. And you seem like such a sweet girl."

"Charles is none of your business," she said. "Who

I choose to marry and what I do with my life is none of your business."

"You're a fool. You deserve better, and instead you choose a backwater town and an idiot boyfriend and sooner or later you're going to end up blowing up this house and your sisters with it until someone puts a stop to it."

She turned her back on him, shaking. More anger, and she hated it. Though the odd thing was, she was getting angry in return, when she usually just hid in her room. "Leave me alone." She picked up the dishpan to dump the soapy water out. "Get the hell out of here and leave me alone."

"I'm not going anywhere," he said.

Lizzie gave up and began to the tip the dishpan, and then something tickled her nose, and she shivered hard twice.

"Then *I am,*" she said and whirled around, flinging the soapy water directly at him.

And then she ran.

The Greasy Fork was crowded by the time Mare got her lunch break at noon, but Crash had snagged them a booth, as always. She threaded her way through the crowd, keeping her heart-shaped sunglasses on to hide her eyes so they wouldn't give anything away, like maybe that she was glad to see him and might still be hopelessly in love with him except that she wasn't that much of a loser, hell, she was Queen of the Universe, he could kiss her foot. Or something else.

He saw her and stood up, looking tall and broad and solid as ever, and really, really good, and she remembered how it had felt to have his arms around her. *Doesn't matter.* She was going to be cool, she didn't care—

"Thanks for meeting me," he said, and his voice sounded so deep and good, just *hearing* him felt so good, she closed her eyes to savor it.

"I had to." Mare slid into the booth. "I couldn't talk to you at the store. We have a vice president there."

"Yeah, I saw him." Crash sat down across from her and that felt right, being back in a booth at the Fork with him, and Mare thought, *No, this is how you got hurt before, he won't stay . . .*

"So it's *been a while*," she said.

"Right." Crash picked up his empty coffee cup and tilted it, and Mare thought, *Coffee, that's new, he didn't drink coffee five years ago.*

"Well, welcome back." She picked up the menu and flipped it open, holding it in front of her so she couldn't see him, especially because she thought there might be tears in her eyes, tears of rage, damn it, but he wouldn't get that; if they slipped down her cheeks from under her sunglasses he'd think she was crying for him.

"You don't need to look, you have that menu memorized," he said.

Mare sniffed and thought, *Yeah, remind me again of how my life never changes.* "There might be something new on here."

He hooked a finger over the edge of the menu and pulled it down to look at her, exasperated. "There's never anything new in this one-horse town."

Mare snapped the menu down. "Something new happened once. *The horse left.* Why did you leave me without a word, *you bastard*?"

He scowled at her. "Hey, I called three times the next day and got the usual runaround from Dee. I came to see you but I couldn't come in, like always, and you wouldn't talk to me."

Mare blinked. "Talk to you? I had *three pins in my arm.* I was *doped to the gills on Percocet,* for crying out loud. *Of course* I wanted to talk to you when I was *lucid again.* I was *in love with you.*"

"Well, you didn't call *me,*" Crash said, looking around the diner as Mare's voice rose. He leaned forward as he lowered his voice. "I figured since I'd almost killed you, and you never called me back, you were done with me."

"And you didn't stick around to ask?" Mare said, madder than ever. "You just *left the next day?*"

Crash sighed. "Mare, I didn't see much future for us. At the best of times, your sister hated me, and you never let me get too close. After the accident . . ." He looked down into his coffee cup. "I didn't think dumping you on my bike in the middle of the road and breaking your arm was going to make things any better. So yeah, when you wouldn't see me, I left."

"Oh, well, so *fine,*" Mare said. "You want to end the relationship, you say—"

"No." He met her eyes. "I didn't want to end anything, I just wanted . . . out. Out of Salem's Fork, I'd wanted out of here for a long time. But I couldn't leave you. And then I called and you wouldn't talk to me, and things were lousy with my dad, and he kept telling me I almost killed you and didn't deserve you—"

"Well, your dad's a jerk, we all knew that," Mare said. "But—"

"—and Dee felt the same way and Dee's not a jerk—"

"Dee's overprotective," Mare said, starting to see

the past more clearly. "But you still should have *talked to me,* damn it. You didn't even *talk to me.*"

"I tried," he said, and tilted his empty coffee cup again, and Mare sat back, knowing he had tried, and that he was right about her keeping him away before that, too, keeping secrets like *I'm a witch,* because that kind of thing was hard to explain and could get Dee and Lizzie burned at the stake or whatever they did to witches in the twenty-first century, probably studied in Area 51 or something, and then Pauline stopped to fill his cup for him, peering at him over her glasses.

"So you're back, are you?" she said. "Where you been?"

Mare looked up. "Pauline, we're having a conversation here."

"Yeah, everybody heard you." Pauline raised her penciled-in eyebrows. "Just like old times, you whipping him into shape again. You can take your sunglasses off. The sun went down in here after breakfast." She nodded at Crash again. "So where you been?"

"Italy," Crash said.

Italy. Mare looked away, at the jukebox selector on the tabletop, biting her lip. *Italy.* She began to flip through the cards. She'd stayed in Salem's Fork and kept her secrets and cried for months, and he'd gone to Italy. Where there was probably dust and sunshine.

"No shit." Pauline balanced her arm on her hip, holding the coffeepot dangerously near Crash's ear as she absorbed that.

Crash slid two quarters across the table to Mare— *just like old times*—and she swallowed hard. It didn't matter that he hadn't taken her to Italy, she didn't speak Italian anyway. Of course, neither did he back then. He probably did now. Italy. She blinked back tears. Hell, she'd have gone to Outer Mongolia if he'd asked.

No she wouldn't have. Dee and Lizzie would have gotten burned at the stake without her. She was the only one who knew how to use the shotgun. *Lizzie can make muffins,* Mare thought, *but I can lock and load.*

"Good food in Italy?" Pauline was saying.

"Yeah," Crash said, and Mare could tell from his voice that he was watching her, so she put the quarters in and punched some buttons at random.

"Italy," Pauline said, as Kim Richey began to sing. "Damn."

So I didn't punch the buttons at random, Mare thought as Kim sang about buying a new red dress to keep her spirits up because her boyfriend was gone. *Damn subconscious.*

"So in Italy—" Pauline began.

"You should go tell someone about that, Pauline," Mare said from behind her sunglasses. "That's hot news. Don't want it to cool off."

Pauline nodded. "Back in a minute," she said and headed for the kitchen.

Crash didn't look exasperated anymore, just tired. "Mare, there wasn't any reason to stay if you didn't want me around, if you wouldn't talk to me. And I knew why you wouldn't. I swear, I didn't see that trash barrel roll into the street. I was watching the road, I don't know where the hell it came from. I have replayed it over and over in my head, and I swear—"

Mare blinked at him. "That's okay, that could have happened to anybody, I'm not mad about that." She shook her head. "That's not it at all."

"I wouldn't have taken any chances with you behind me." He met her eyes, straight on. "You were everything to me."

Kim sang, "You'll never know how much I love you," and Mare sat back. "Well, I'm nothing to you now, so it doesn't matter, does it?"

He leaned forward, and Pauline came back to take their order.

"Maxine says welcome back, and she saw this movie about Tuscany and wants to know if that's where you are."

Mare scowled at her. "Since when do you ask questions for Maxine? You've had Maxine completely terrorized for years and now you're her lackey?"

Pauline grimaced. "It's supposed to be this big secret, but Maxine bought the diner two days ago."

Mare's annoyance vanished. "Oh, bad luck, Pauline."

"No shit," Pauline said. "You're not going to believe this one: starting tonight, we're serving martinis."

"No." Mare leaned closer. "How the hell did she get a liquor license that fast?"

Pauline leaned in, too. "You got me. I'd say she was giving blow jobs, but I don't think Ferris Tuttle over at the license bureau has a dick."

"Good point," Mare said.

"Do you mind?" Crash said to both of them.

"So is that where you are?" Pauline said to him. "Where Maxine said? Tuscany?"

"Yes," Crash said.

Pauline turned around and yelled, "That's where he is, Maxine."

Over behind the counter, little dark-haired, rumpled Maxine gave him a thumbs-up, and Crash gave her a nod and turned back to Mare, looking as if he were thinking, *This is why I left.*

"So," Pauline said. "What'll it be?"

Crash said, "Two hamburgers, one medium well, one medium rare, pickles on both, cheese on the medium well, fries, two Cokes, one diet, with water chasers. Wait fifteen minutes then bring a chocolate milkshake. Large."

"*Hungry*, are you?" Mare smiled at Pauline. "I'll have—"

"I just ordered for you," Crash said, looking impatient. "That's what we always got. Can we finish our conversation now?"

"Well, I've *changed*," Mare said. "You leave a woman alone for five years, *she's gonna change*." She smiled at Pauline again. "I'd like ketchup on the medium rare burger and a lemon slice in the Diet Coke *and* in the water, please. And make the shake a strawberry."

"I like chocolate," Crash said.

"Then get your own," Mare said, and he ordered a chocolate shake.

"Not much of a change," Pauline said to Mare.

"*Thank you*," Mare said, and Pauline topped up Crash's coffee cup and left.

Crash picked up the sugar dispenser. "She's right. Adding lemon doesn't change the basic order. I still know you. And you are something to me, damn it. You're—"

"You do not know me," Mare said, staring at Crash's coffee cup.

"You ran five miles this morning and waved to Mother at the tattoo parlor," Crash said, getting ready to pour sugar into his coffee but keeping his eyes on her. "Then you came here and had orange juice and a doughnut for breakfast. Why are you making this so hard? Why do there have to be so many secrets and so many rules and why does everything have to be so damn hard?"

"I have no idea what you're talking about." Mare stared at the coffee cup until it sparked blue, and then she slid it over two inches as Crash glared at her and poured sugar onto the table where the cup had been.

"And I know you. I'll bet you five bucks that you're wearing blue lace under that god-awful coverall. You always wore blue lace under anything butch." He grinned at her then, for the first time since he'd come back, and she lost her breath because she'd forgotten how his smile lit up his whole face.

"I am not wearing blue lace," Mare lied, and tried to think of anything besides how good it felt to have him smiling across the table from her again. Like how easy it was to move things like muffins and coffee cups and how hard it was to move little things like sugar grains. She stared at the sugar and began to separate out grains, biting her lip as she concentrated.

"I can see the lace." Crash put the sugar dispenser back. "Right there at the top of your zipper." He picked up his spoon, looked down for his cup and saw the pile of sugar instead, and said, "What the hell?" as Mare looked down to see her zipper had slipped enough for a flash of blue lace to show at the top.

It looked pretty good so she left it.

"You peeked so that's cheating," she said. "No bet. There are many new things about me."

Crash shook his head, cleaning up sugar as he spoke. "Nobody knows you like I do, Mare. I know you, the real you, the part that doesn't change. There's nobody else in the world like you. And I know because I've looked."

"Knew me, maybe," Mare said. "But not anymore. There's a lot new about me, like . . ." Her voice trailed off as she realized there wasn't anything new if you didn't count being able to move sugar granules. "I have a new tattoo," she lied, and watched with satisfaction as his eyebrows went up.

"Where?" he said, grinning, and the light in his eyes made her want to grin back at him. "Give me a map and a flashlight. I'll find it."

Kim sang on in the background and Mare thought, *Do not get sucked into him again, he left you,* and said, "You'll never know. So why did you come back?"

"For you," he said, and she went very still. "I miss you, Mare. I've been everywhere and seen everything, but there's nothing and nobody like you."

Mare took her hands off the table and put them in her lap. "Oh." *Concentrate on the sugar.* She tried to make the sugar swirl, thinking of each separate grain. It gave her a hell of a headache but that beat heartache any day. *I love you so much. I never stopped loving you. I never will stop loving you.*

"I didn't have anything when I was here." He pushed his coffee cup away to lean across the table to her. "I was just Crash the Loser who almost killed you on my bike on your prom night. But things are different now. I've got my own business in Italy. I was roaming around over there and I met this guy, he's as nuts about bikes as I am, and Mare, the Italians, they really know motorcycles, they're an art form over there, and this guy, Leo, he loves the old ones and he's been restoring them and he showed me how." Mare nodded and Crash went on. "I've been working on this bike for you. It's back in Italy, all done, ready to go. Here." He got out his wallet and took out a photograph and handed it to her.

The bike was a thing of beauty, a moped on steroids, sleek and black with a baby blue tank and seat and piping.

"It's a Kreidler Florett," Crash said. "Built in 1964, 49cc, but it moves like you wouldn't believe. Lightweight but fast, just like you. Took me a long time to find all the parts but it's cherry now . . ." His voice trailed off.

"It's beautiful," she said, trying to keep her voice flat.

"The Florett is considered the best 50 cc bike ever made," he said, pulling back, clearing his throat. "It's a real collector's bike."

"I like the blue," Mare said.

"It's your color," he said.

"And the logo thingy, that's cool."

"That's the Florett logo."

Mare nodded. "The seat looks like leather."

"It is."

"Baby blue leather."

"Yep."

Mare nodded again. The bike was perfect. She handed the picture back to him, glad she had her sunglasses on. Her eyes were probably glowing.

Crash put the picture back in his wallet. "The thing is, I have a business there. I just bought a house. And it's beautiful there, you'd love it. I can just see you riding that bike through the hills, and the Italians, they'd love you. I can take care of you now, Mare." He swallowed and then took a deep breath. "I think we should try it again. I'll do better this time. Come back with me." He looked into her eyes, the blue depths of his aching with honesty. "We belong together. Come to Italy with me, Mare."

Yes, she thought, but she sat back and tried to be cool. "Just like that. Five years go by, you don't call, you don't write, and just like that it's 'Come to Italy with me.'" *God, yes.*

"I know." He ducked his head a little. "I was going to try to take it slow, but we never did that." He looked at her, solid as ever. "We were always going ninety miles an hour, Mare."

"Yeah, that's how we hit the trash can," Mare said, trying not to think, *Italy. With Crash.* She stared at the sugar dispenser, watching the granules inside start to stir. *Italy.* Where the sky was as blue as his eyes and he'd built a perfect bike just for her.

"I know you need time to think about it," he said. "I have time. I don't have to leave until Monday—"

"Monday?" The sugar dispenser rocked as Mare sat up, and she slapped her hand over it so Crash wouldn't notice. "You think I can decide to just run off to another country with you in a weekend?" She leaned forward, trying to make him understand. "I have a job here, I just got offered a great promotion, I'm on my way to the top, Crash. And by the way, have you *met* my sisters?"

"You're twenty-three," he said. "You can leave your sisters. I want to show you Italy. I can take care of you, Mare."

"You can't." She took her hand off the sugar dispenser where the sugar granules were heaving on their own now, peppered with little blue sparks, probably because her heart was beating like crazy because she was leaning so close to him, kissing distance, and the excitement had to go somewhere. *I can move that sugar with my mind. How are you going to deal with that?*

"I can," he said, leaning closer to her, too. "I love you, Mare."

She pulled back at that, and he leaned to follow her, into the space where she'd been, and then his nose twitched and he shivered hard, three times.

"Crash?" she said, alarmed.

"Marry me," he said.

Mare was the runner in the family, but Lizzie knew how to make tracks when she needed to, and the last thing she wanted was for a gorgeous, pissed-off, soaking wet wizard to catch up with her. She couldn't believe she'd lost her temper enough to actually throw the water at him, and for half a moment she'd been paralyzed, half expecting him to dissolve into the floor like the Wicked Witch of the West. He'd just blinked at her as the soapy water landed, and she'd disappeared, racing out the front door before he could try any of his fancy tricks.

The sky was cloudy with the approaching storm, and the wind was growing stronger as she made her way up the cliffs outside of town.

She saw the huge oak first with nothing beneath it—no wet wizards lying in wait for her—and then she went into the stone circle, slightly out of breath, and started to climb up onto the great lump of boulder affectionately known as the Great Big Rock. Some ancient glacier had dragged it down, but now it was smooth and rounded by thousands of years of weather, and she reached the top of it easily enough, hunkering down, trying to catch her breath.

Something was definitely wrong, and Dee must have been right to call for the vote this morning. She'd been a fool to abstain.

She shoved her tangled hair out of her face, lifting

her head to look down at the peaceful little town beneath her. No sign of any mysteriously colorful wizard searching for her—maybe his powers were like electricity and he'd shorted out. Maybe he'd given up . . .

"I'm sorry."

She almost fell off the boulder, but he reached out his hand to catch her. Touching him was even worse, but she managed to regain her balance on the rock without it, turning to look at him, fighting the impulse to run once more.

"You're not wet," she said.

He shook his head. He didn't look the least bit ruffled—however he'd managed to follow her, it clearly hadn't been at the same dead run. "I could see what you were going to do. It was easy enough to put up a barrier. I'm afraid your floor's a mess."

She sighed. "My fault," she said. "It needed washing anyway. Why did you follow me?"

"We haven't finished. I'm sorry I insulted your choice of life partners. Clearly there's no accounting for tastes."

"Clearly," she said. She'd underestimated him. Her parents could never have appeared as he had, crossing time and space with seemingly no effort. They'd been better at flashy tricks to delight their television audience, not real power. She was dealing with something more complicated than she'd even known existed, and she had to be careful not to lose her temper again. Which shouldn't be hard—she never lost her temper. Except for today. With this man.

"I really don't want you here," she said in what she hoped was a reasonable voice. "How can I make you just go away and leave us alone? Go back to where you came from, wherever that is."

"Toledo."

"Toledo?" she echoed. "As in Ohio?" Somehow he didn't strike her as the Midwestern type.

"As in Spain."

She digested the information, ignoring the little pang of envy. She'd always wanted to go to Spain. "Listen, we have a comfortable life here, and we're not bothering anyone. Can't you just forget you ever found us?"

He looked at her for a long moment. She would have thought being outside would have muted him, made him less formidable when she wasn't trapped in a room with him. She was wrong. Even at the top of a mountain he was a disturbingly powerful presence. One she needed to get rid of, fast.

He didn't look like he was going to be easily swayed. "You want me to disappear from your life, forget you ever existed?"

"Yes."

"Fine. Then you do what I tell you and we'll have a bargain."

She didn't like making bargains with the devil, and Elric whoever-he-was was downright satanic. But she wasn't sure she had much choice. "And what are you going to tell me to do?" she asked, wary.

"Isn't it obvious? I'm going to show you how to turn straw into gold."

She stared at him. "I thought we weren't supposed to cross elemental boundaries. I thought you were going to *stop* me."

Elric shrugged, a sight beautiful to behold. "I have a feeling you're going to anyway, so I might as well accept the fact and make certain you're prepared for the ramifications."

"And what might those be?"

"It won't stay gold. But if you're lucky it'll stay that way long enough for you to cash it in and get out of here. Assuming that's what you want to do. Somehow I can't see the children of Phil and Fiona Fortune living in suburbia. They were a little more upscale."

"I'm not my parents," she said stiffly. "I have no intention of ripping people off, and I'm not interested in fame. I need to make money fairly."

"And you think using magic spells is a fair way to make money? That's one thing that never tends to work—if it did, the twenty richest people in the world would be ones with our kind of gifts. Personal gain is frowned upon, and it never works out well. Look what happened to your parents."

In fact, she didn't know what happened to her parents, only that they'd died. Dee didn't like her asking questions, and something had kept her from looking into it. She barely remembered those years in the limelight—she'd hated the attention from the media, the indifference of her parents. Their quest for fame and fortune had killed them—she knew that much. And she had no interest in following in their footsteps.

Her motives, however, were pure. She needed the money for her sisters, but she wasn't about to waste time with explanations. She wasn't about to tell him anything more than he needed to know. He knew too much already. "Is there anything I can use to turn into gold that will stay that way?"

"Some base metals. If you go about it the right way, and your intentions are pure. I'm just not sure I can teach you that much in the next three days."

"Three days?" she said faintly. "You're planning to stay in the area that long?" She was horrified, though she wasn't sure if it was because he was staying too long or leaving too soon.

"No," he said. "I'm planning to stay in your house that long."

"Not if my sisters have anything to say about it. Dee doesn't allow sleepovers."

"If Charles is any example, I can see why not. However, she isn't going to know. I have no intention of letting her see me."

"Dee sees far too much," Lizzie said, glum.

"This isn't a case of a teenage girl trying to break curfew," Elric said. "Trust me."

That's not going to happen anytime soon, she thought. "There isn't an extra bedroom. There's no place for you to sleep."

"Your bedroom will do."

"I only have one bed."

"We'll take turns."

She stared at him, frustration bubbling up. She would have told him what he could take turns doing, but it wouldn't have any effect and would only upset her stomach.

"I don't like you," she said in a sulky voice.

Again that demoralizing smile. "Of course you do. That's part of the problem." Before she could open her mouth to protest he went on, "Why don't we go back to the house and you can show me what you've been working on, show me what you've learned so far? We can take it from there."

Back to the house that suddenly seemed way too small with him in it? She didn't really have any choice. "Give me a minute," she said. "I'm not quite ready to hike back."

"No need," he said, and took her right hand in his before she could stop him.

Colors everywhere, with the wind streaming through her hair, pulling it free of the pins she'd stuck into it to hold it in place. The smell of lilacs, a sea of pinky-white dogwoods like a carpet beneath her, and she was back in their kitchen, ready to throw up.

He was no longer holding her hand, a small mercy, and she couldn't read anything in his dark, mesmerizing eyes. "You'll get used to it," he said. "If you keep having problems, a little Dramamine will do wonders."

"What . . ." Her voice came out in a choked gasp. "What did you just do?"

"I didn't think we had time for a leisurely stroll through Salem's Fork, and your fiancé might start asking questions if you were seen with me. I just got us here a little quicker."

"Don't do that again," she said. "Or at least give me a little warning."

"Agreed," he said. "Are you ready to start?"

Her workshop was a closed-in sun porch, and the only entrance was through her bedroom. She wasn't sure which would feel more intimate: taking him through her bedroom or letting him into her work-space, a place no one else had ever intruded on before. But clearly she had no choice. There was no other way to get rid of him.

"You leave me no choice," she said.

"You look like Joan of Arc facing the stake," he said. "Trust me, this will hurt me more than it will hurt you."

She'd heard that before, and it was usually followed by something awful. The last thing in the world she was going to do was trust the shimmering stranger who had invaded her life.

She would take what she needed from him, learn what she could, and then get him out of her life, along with the gift that felt more like a curse.

"And once you teach me, you promise you'll go?"

"I'll be gone in three days. By the Feast of Beltane."

And all she could do was hold on to that hope, as she led him into her bedroom.

Sugar shot straight up out of the pouring spout of the shaker, and Crash ducked back, saying, "What the hell?"

Mare slapped her hand over the top of the shaker again. "Earthquake. Did you just ask me to marry you?"

"No kidding?" Pauline said, and Mare looked up to see her standing there with their Cokes. "He proposed?"

"Thank you," Crash said, taking the Cokes from her. "We're good here."

Pauline stood there for a minute, her face avid, and then when they both looked at her pointedly, she rolled her eyes and left.

"You *proposed*?" Mare said when she was gone.

"Yeah." Crash sounded surprised himself as he passed over her Diet Coke. "I did."

"You didn't mean to do that, did you?" Mare said, relieved and disappointed. "It's okay."

"No, I did. I mean, yes, I want to marry you." He shook his head as if to clear it, and then thought about it for a minute. "Yes, I do. Yes, Moira Mariposa O'Brien, I want to marry you—"

Yes, Mare thought.

"—yes, I want to have kids with you—"

A fat laughing baby toddling down a sunny dusty road . . .

No, Mare thought. How would he feel if his baby turned out to be a freak like her?

"—yes, I want to . . . what's wrong?"

Temper tantrums with blue sparks and teddy bears flying across the nursery? Purple smoke rolling in and bunnies leaping from the bassinets? A puff of green fog and your firstborn is a frequent flyer?

"Okay, not kids, not right away," he said. "In a couple of years. Five years. Ten years. We don't have to have kids." He looked confused, as if he were in over his head.

She knew how he felt.

"Stop," Mare said. "It's just . . . things are complicated. I just got offered a promotion at work. And call me feminist, but I think working at my own career instead of following yours around might be a good idea for me." *Except yours is in Italy and I bet I could do something amazing in Italy, too. Better than rent videos anyway. And I know I could do amazing things with you. Just lunch with you makes me breathless.*

"I didn't mean you'd just follow me around," Crash said. "I don't know what I meant. We'd work it out." He looked at the sugar shaker again. "I'm doing this all wrong. What the hell just happened here?"

"And we really don't know each other," Mare said. "Five years have changed both of us. A weekend isn't enough for us to know, not after five years. And you *left* me. How do I know you won't do that again?" *I can't even tell you the big secret of my life. How can I marry you?*

Crash shook his head. "Look, I waited to come back until I had something to give you, until I was ready to say, 'Come back with me.' I'm ready, I'll stick, I swear I will, Mare. I'm not going to pretend that all I did was work. There were other . . ." He frowned, as if he knew he was screwing up again. "Look, no matter what I was doing, who I was with, I couldn't forget you. I had to come back to get you."

Mare sat back, exasperated. "Why do I feel like I'm being ordered at the pickup window at the Big Fast Food Restaurant of Love? You got a weekend so you're driving through. As long as you're here, you'll take the Combo Mare. Supersize it, to go."

"That's not fair," Crash said. "Look, you want me to go away, just tell me to go."

He met her eyes straight on and she thought, *Don't leave me,* and put her head in her hands.

"Mare?"

Italy and the dusty sun and the bike and Crash and maybe that baby, and she loved him, she'd never stopped loving him, if she just wasn't one of the gifted Fortune Sisters, the Head Bouncer at Witch Central . . .

"Don't go," she said.

"Does it have to be this hard?" Crash said. "Does it always have to be secrets and misery? Can't it just be 'I love you, too,' and a trip to goddamn Italy?"

"No." She drew a deep breath. "This is going to take some thinking."

"Thinking." He nodded. "Sure, why not? Thinking. Some women answer proposals with just 'yes' and a kiss, but you need to think about it."

"Hey," Mare said. "It's been *five years.*"

Crash sat back. "You got a time frame on that thinking?"

"I don't get off until ten-thirty," Mare said. "I'll probably need longer than that. Tomorrow."

"Okay. Tomorrow."

"Is that when you're doing it?" Pauline said.

Mare glared up at her. "Excuse me?"

Pauline put their food on the table. "Is that when you're getting married? Did you say yes? Maxine is back in the kitchen and she's dying to know."

"You *know*," Mare began dangerously, and then realized the diner had grown quiet.

"And a few others, too," Pauline said. "You know how word gets around here."

"Oh, hell," Crash said. "I had to come back, I couldn't just stay in Italy."

Mare stood up and looked at everyone in the diner looking back at them. "So here's the story, and let's get it right when we repeat it, people. Christopher Duncan, whom we all know and love as Crash, is back in town after establishing a successful business in Italy. He has come back to discuss the possibility of my joining him there to live happily ever after as his wife in the dappled sunshine where we will have many blissful days and passionate nights. I'm trying to decide if I want that, or if it would be better for me to stay here in Salem's Fork and rent videos to all of you. I'm thinking about it. It's not an easy decision. There are ramifications. I am cogitating. In the meantime, your food is getting cold. Eat up, Fork People. Cold food is bad for the digestion."

She sat down again and looked at Crash, ignoring the sugar granules in the shaker, which were now pulsing gently, happily, like a good strong heartbeat.

"You're insane," Crash said, "but I love you."

"Eat your lunch," Mare said, and ignored the sugar.

Elric shouldn't have been surprised by Lizzie's neat bedroom—pale pink wallpaper, white-painted furniture, gingham curtains, and a bedspread that looked as if it belonged on the twin bed of a thirteen-year-old, not the slightly more generous double bed. The only anomaly was the pairs of shoes lining the white baseboards—there had to be at least fifty pairs, of every possible shape and style. He glanced at Lizzie's feet for the first time, and a slow smile spread across his face. The Road Runner high-tops had disappeared—at some point her shoes had become tropical espadrilles with fake fruit dripping off the straps. Lizzie Fortune had a hidden wild streak, at least when it came to shoes.

She was already looking defensive. "If you're thinking I've been extravagant you're wrong. I didn't buy all these shoes. I haven't worn half of them."

"I don't care how you got the shoes, Lizzie. I will admit it interests me that you have so many. You don't strike me as the Imelda Marcos type."

She shrugged. "I like shoes."

"Apparently. I'm assuming these appear whenever you try to transmute something?"

She looked guilty. *Adorably so,* he thought, not happy about it. This was far too slippery a slope for him.

"I'm not quite sure why they appear or where they come from. It's usually when I'm . . ." She stopped, suddenly embarrassed, and he took pity on her.

He knew perfectly well what would call forth the odd appearance of extraneous footwear—shoes had a strong connection to sexuality, and the shoes must manifest when she was sexually distracted, or excited. Maybe he'd underestimated Charles's abilities, though he hated that possibility. Or maybe, just maybe, he was having as strong an effect on her as she was having on him.

And that made things even more dangerous.

"Don't worry about it," he said, just as happy to

change the subject. He went over to the white-painted dresser and pulled open a drawer, ignoring her screech of protest. Her underwear was all neatly sorted and folded—white cotton bras and cotton underpants decorated with bears and butterflies and lambs. She had the underwear of a thirteen-year-old, as well, he thought. He glanced back at her. But the shoes of a courtesan.

She pushed past him and slammed the drawer shut, carefully managing not to touch him. "There's nothing in there that's of any interest to you," she said sternly.

He said nothing. He was much more curious about her underwear than he cared to admit, and keeping her distracted and unsettled was part of his master plan, but she was nervous enough around him as it was. He needed to lull her into dropping her guard if he was going to accomplish what he'd set out to do. And he had little experience with failure.

"So show me your workshop," he said, turning his back on the enticing shoes. It wasn't possible that she'd manifested them out of nothing—alchemists had to start with something, even dust. Except that the rental home of the Misses Fortune seemed antiseptically clean.

The workshop itself was messier than he'd expected—maybe she'd conjured her shoes out of any of the strange artifacts littering the old sun porch. The room was dark—sunlight filtered through the bamboo shades with a sullen glint, and the long workbench was scarred with spilled chemicals and gouged by who knew what. A bale of straw sat on the floor, half decimated, with bits of straw everywhere, as if a giant mouse had gotten into it. Either that, or the Scarecrow had met with the flying monkeys.

"Eleven fire extinguishers?" he murmured. "You need them all?"

"I was expecting another from the UPS man. I go through them fairly quickly," she said, a defensive note in her voice. "It used to be just small fires, but now they come with explosions, so I figure I'd better be prepared."

She didn't realize that her penchant for setting fires was also a sign of potential power. When he'd first set eyes on her he'd assumed the power surges coming from this little town in Virginia had been a fluke—no one that innocent-looking could be causing such chaos. He was rapidly learning otherwise.

"So what do you use for focusing your power? Some kind of array?"

"What?"

"Do you make a circle of some element like salt, do you draw a circle, do you . . . ?"

"I don't do circles."

He stared at her. "What do you use, then?"

"I don't use anything. I just concentrate, and things change. Not the way I want them to, but I've gotten some great shoes out of it."

Ah, she was getting feistier. He'd terrified her when he first showed up, and he should have pushed his advantage. Now she was getting sassy, and she was going to be a hell of a lot harder to intimidate into doing what he wanted.

"No talisman? No philosopher's stone?"

"Life is not a Harry Potter novel."

"You and I both know it's not as far removed as people might think," he said beneath his breath. "Okay, that's lesson number one. You need something to feed your power through. Concentrating as hard as you can on something doesn't work. It's like trying too hard for an orgasm—the harder you work, the more elusive it becomes. You have to let go."

She blushed. "I'm afraid you must be more of an expert at difficult orgasms. Are you talking about you or the women you sleep with?"

"Actually, it's pretty much a no-brainer for men. And with no false modesty I have to say that I'm very good in bed. Years of experience does wonders." He tilted his head. "I'm thinking more of young women with little experience who sleep with the wrong men."

A crackle of energy, and a pair of narrow stiletto heels appeared on the scarred workbench. Hot-pink fuck-me shoes. *Very interesting,* he thought.

She grabbed the shoes and threw them under the workbench. "I really don't want to be discussing sex with you," she said in a strained voice.

I know you don't, he thought. *But why?* He took a step toward her, trying to forget about the very sexy shoes. "We need to find you a talisman . . ." he began, automatically reaching for her hand.

The spark between them made him jump, and she let out a pained little scream. It wasn't a sexual spark, not the disturbing current that he'd felt before when he'd put his hand on her shoulder and when he'd taken her hand to bring her back home—it was static electricity magnified a hundred times, and it hurt.

"What was that?" she demanded in a shaky voice.

He'd touched her ring. It was no wonder he hadn't noticed—anything that tiny was easily overlooked. "It's that pitiful engagement ring," he said. "Your body's rejecting it."

"Give me a break," she said. "And it's not pitiful. Charles and I agreed it made more sense to put money into something that benefited both of us in the long run. This is merely a symbol."

"If that's a symbol of your great love, then you're in deep shit," Elric said. He stared at the nasty little thing in fascination. He wasn't going to touch it again, not as long as it was on her finger.

"I don't want to discuss this with you," she said stiffly.

"Fine. We won't discuss sex and we won't discuss your fiancé, though if you're that uptight about things it's no wonder you've been screwing up in the workshop. People like us need to be comfortable in our bodies, not nervous and twitchy. It throws everything off."

He'd expected her to argue again, but she looked momentarily distracted. "That would explain Dee's problem," she said, half to herself.

"What is Dee's problem?"

"None of your business."

Elric bit back his irritation. He was going to have to immobilize Deirdre as well, plus the youngest, and he was going to have to do it without anyone realizing it. He didn't have enough information; he only knew their gifts were backfiring. Now he was beginning to wonder if he'd made a grave mistake in coming here.

He dismissed it a moment later. The disturbances emanating from this area had been felt worldwide, and he'd known, with that instinctive sureness that had been with him most of his life, that this was where he was supposed to be.

"Take off the ring," he said.

"The hell I will."

He blinked. She was looking very defiant, even though her voice had wobbled slightly, and he wondered if another pair of shoes were about to appear. Maybe they'd be combat boots.

He tried another tack. "The ring is interfering with the flow of energy through your body," he said patiently. "You said the fires and explosions were getting worse. Starting when?"

She glanced down at the tiny chip on her hand. "Around the time we got engaged," she said reluctantly.

"I rest my case. The ring disrupts things when you try to channel your gift. Your body is fighting it—I'll leave it up to you to draw whatever conclusions you want."

"Someone must have . . . hexed it or something," she said.

"Take it off and I'll tell you."

She pulled at it, and it came off easily enough—a little too easily for a ring that wasn't loose. She held it out to him, but he shook his head. "Put it on the bench."

"Chicken," she said, but she sounded relieved as she set it down.

He picked it up, half expecting another crack of painful electricity, but it was nothing more than a plain, cheap ring, devoid of power. "It's just a ring," he said. "Harmless. Except if the wrong person wears it."

She started to reach for it, but a sizzle of blue electricity danced between them, and she jerked her hand back. "You're doing that," she said in a sulky voice.

"Believe what you want. But you're not wearing it until I leave. We aren't going to get anywhere if we practically get electrocuted every time I touch you."

"I don't see why you need to touch me," she protested.

He closed his eyes in momentary exasperation. "Didn't you have any training at all? I can help you channel your energy—you don't have to start getting paranoid."

"That's right, your mind isn't clouded by lust. If it was I'd be able to make you do what I want."

He wasn't about to argue with it. His mind wasn't clouded with lust—he'd been able to compartmentalize it very neatly. Yes, there was a strong, deep attraction that made no sense, and it was entirely inconvenient and, as far as he could tell, completely one-sided. So he'd banished it with the ruthless efficiency he'd perfected, never to think about it again until he was far enough away from her that it wouldn't be a danger.

He put the ring back down on the workbench. "You can have it when I leave. In the meantime, I'll show you what I mean."

He had no idea why he did it, when he'd just been thinking how dangerous she was. Maybe he hadn't banished that errant strain of lust as efficiently as he thought. He reached out to put his hand on her shoulder, as he had before, but for some reason it slid up the side of her neck, cupping her face, and there was no snap of static power between them. Instead it was a pulse, strong and powerful, flowing between them, awash with color and the heartbeat of the universe. And without thinking he moved his head down to kiss her.

Danny James opened the door to the Greasy Fork and ushered Dee in. Dee couldn't think of any-place more platonic to have her one drink with Danny than the Greasy Fork, the epitome of the small-town diner with its scarred Formica and Coke-and-hamburger menu. Plus no alcohol. She'd be safe there.

She led him through the bustling early-dinner crowd over to her favorite booth by the front window where she could see the town square, the river, and the cliffs beyond that were her favorite haunt. The sun was low, throwing a golden wash over the red brick buildings and limning the trees. Dee sighed. What the hell had she been thinking? She needed to be outside in that perfect light. Not here. Not with Danny James, for God's sake.

She'd laid in a few brushstrokes of burnt sienna along the lines of his throat, where the warm sun had left shadows.

Dee shook her head, feeling oddly bereft. Damn fantasy.

"Nice place," Danny said behind her with a suspiciously dry voice.

"Did I tell you the drink choices here are Coke, Coke, and coffee?" she asked as she tossed her briefcase onto the seat and slid in.

Danny looked around. "Yeah. I can see that."

"No, no," the waitress said as she bustled over. "It's your lucky day. We got a liquor license. I know how much you like a good martini, Dee. How 'bout it?"

"Wonderful," Dee said faintly. "Thanks, Maxine."

Without taking her eyes off Danny, Maxine dug into her pocket, where she usually kept her order pad. "And you, sir?"

"I'll just have a longneck," Danny said with another one of those killer smiles as he settled across from her.

Every person within a four-booth radius turned their way. Maxine headed off to get their drinks, making it a point to wait until she was out of Danny's line of sight before vigorously fanning herself for Dee's benefit. *Yeah,* Dee thought. *He's all that and more.* She just wished she knew what that more was.

He looked like a yuppie exec on casual day, his oxford shirt open and rolled up to his elbows, his hair just that much disordered, his shoes tasseled. He smelled like the male animal. Dee recognized the scent from her times as a fox. Musk and power and salt. The clean hint of soap, and something that was particularly Danny James. Something deadly she couldn't quite identify. Probably the uncut scent of pheromones. And she was sitting across from him in hundred-weight wool and a pool of sweat. Very attractive.

She was feeling flushed again. Just who'd thought this would be a good idea? Across from her, Danny pulled a tape recorder from his jacket pocket and set it on the booth.

"Oh, I don't think so," Dee said, stone-faced.

He gave a wry shrug and put it away. "You can only say no."

"I could beat you into insensibility with your own equipment."

She could change into a wolverine and chew his face off. But it was too nice a face.

"Oh, you don't want to do that," he said without looking up. "I have such a nice face."

Dee went very still. Just which bit of vitriol had he been responding to? And if he was letting her know that he'd heard her thoughts, why wasn't he flashing her an "I know what you are" smile?

She surreptitiously took another sniff. Again, she caught the man scent, the soap. And . . . ah, hell. She should have known. That mystery scent hadn't just been pheromones. It held the tang of ozone before a storm. The crackle of electricity. Whatever else this guy was or wasn't, he was one of them. He smelled like psychic power.

Dee fought to keep from sweating like a suspect. What did it mean? Why was he really here? And damn it, how could just smelling the power on him make her so darned itchy? No, that was the wool against her ass, which she suddenly couldn't seem to hold still, as if rubbing it against Naugahyde would relieve her distress.

Danny James replaced the tape recorder with a notebook and a Third Virginia Bank pen. "You don't like talking about your parents?"

She looked around for that martini, suddenly grateful the Greasy Fork had sold out. "What are you researching?"

Smooth, Dee. Very smooth.

He didn't seem in the least disconcerted. "A book for Mark Delaney."

She scowled. "Yes, I got that part. What could my parents have to do with alternative history?" Except the alternative history she used to imagine for herself. Clair and Cliff Huxtable as her parents and a house in the suburbs where the silverware stayed silverware and stress caused nothing more than headaches.

"Mark wants to do a nonfiction work on psychics," he said. "Since your parents were the most famous ones, he thought we should start there. I'm sure you know that they were sometimes referred to as—"

"The Jim and Tammy Faye of psychics. Yes, Mr. James, I know all the pejoratives." Like "charlatan." She wondered when that one would come up. "And keep it down, please. I'm happier if no one in Salem's Fork thinks I know anybody famous."

"I was sure you'd rather I got my information from the source, which would be you."

"Not really," Dee said, seeing Maxine set a full martini glass on a tray and salivating. "There's plenty of video on them. I doubt I could add anything."

"I've seen the video," he said. "No offense, but it all struck me as a cross between Ed Sullivan and Elmer Gantry."

"With just a soupçon of the Partridge Family. They did know how to put on a show."

"I'm sure that accounts for some of it," he said. "Their rise to fame was pretty meteoric. From neighborhood psychics to international stars in a matter of three years."

Dee tried to see where Maxine was with that martini. "The neighborhood they worked was West Hollywood," she said. "They numbered quite a few producers and agents among their clients."

It had been Xan who'd spotted the opportunity. The producers had never known it wasn't their idea.

Danny James consulted something in his notebook. "Well, it certainly was a winning formula. Especially when they added you girls to the show. You were naturals for the bright lights, all ruffled and sweet and singing those cute songs. You did a hell of an 'I'm a Little Teapot.' "

Dee scowled. "If you're trying to butter me up, Mr. James, that probably isn't the way you want to do it."

His eyebrows headed north. "You didn't find it as charming as the rest of us."

Being blinded by those hot, hard lights? Hundreds of hands on her; people bending so close she could smell fetid breath, smiling and smiling and lying? And her parents always standing apart on the other side of the stage like benevolent deities while she waited for just one word of praise? What more could a girl want?

"I guess I must lack that showbiz gene."

"Yeah, I can see that," he said. "You couldn't be more buttoned down if you were a nun."

Dee went rigid. "Well, thank God you've come along and shown me the error of my ways, Mr. James. Now you have the length of one martini to talk."

Right on cue, Maxine stopped at their table, drinks

in hand. "Thatta girl," she said with a sharp nod as she set the longneck down. "Even if he does have a point, a gentleman has no business being rude when he's courting."

Mortified, Dee shut her eyes and held out her hand. "Can I order my second martini now?"

Maxine laughed and settled Dee's first martini right into it. "You bet." Balancing her tray against her hip, she turned to Danny James. "So, it was like love at first sight, huh? You just met, right?"

That got Dee's eyes open fast. What the hell? Maxine was spacey, but even for her that was a bizarre question. On the other hand, it might be a better line of inquiry than the real one. Especially since the other waitresses were standing back by the kitchen door waiting for Maxine's report on the new man in town.

"No," Danny said, picking up his longneck. "We met in college. I haven't seen Dee since junior year, isn't it?"

Dee almost couldn't get her mouth closed enough to form consonants. "Um, yeah."

Was he really covering for her? Hell, he was here to expose them. Wasn't he?

"Really?" Maxine said, sounding confused. "College?"

"Loyola," he said.

"Butler," Dee said at the same time, and damn near winced.

"For senior year," he retorted easily. "She left before I could ask her to the fraternity formal, and I never got over it. So I'm using this research project as an excuse to see her again."

Dee felt as confused as Maxine. Did Danny really mean to protect her? Maybe she could at least listen to what he had to say.

"Well, that's just *great*," Maxine said, still sounding bewildered. "So you're like in love and everything?"

Dee damn near spilled her martini. "We're in *what*?"

Danny gave her a conspiratorial look. "Give us time, Maxine."

"Give me another martini, Maxine," Dee said, in a tone that said, *Get out of here, Maxine,* and Maxine, evidently realizing her tip was in jeopardy, made tracks back to where the rest of the waitresses waited.

Dee faced Danny James. "Why did you do that? You could have outed me like Rock Hudson."

He lifted an eyebrow. "You're not escaped felons. I figure you have your own reasons for protecting yourselves. And while I'd dearly love to know why, that's not why I'm here. Okay?"

She found she could breathe again. At least for now. "Thank you."

He picked up his longneck. "No thanks necessary. Maxine was right, though. I wasn't being a gentleman. I'm sorry. It just seems such a long way from that 'Delightful Dee-Dee' on the show who always sang in her pretty pink dresses."

So that quickly he was back on the hunt. Dee went after her martini. "I'll have you know crinoline itches like a bitch."

So did wool, but he didn't need to know that.

"What else itched?"

Dee stared. He'd just done it again. "What?"

He leaned closer to her and kept his voice down. "You and your sisters disappeared twenty-four hours after your parents' death, and haven't been heard from since. What have you been hiding from?"

"Nosy researchers."

"I thought you might like to tell your side of the story. Did you really go to Butler University?"

"If we wanted to tell our story, we probably would have done it anytime during the last twelve years." She reached for her purse, trying to force an end to this nonsense. "There is no story."

He didn't move. "It's not just that you've never even gone back to your parents' commune—who would all like to hear from you, by the way. You're living in seclusion half a continent away under an assumed name. Why?"

She stopped again and faced him with a semblance of calm, even as her pulse skittered around like a pea in a hot skillet. "Who wants to live in a commune of psychics? Everybody knows your business."

"And now nobody does."

"And oddly enough, they don't seem to mind."

"What about your sisters?"

"They don't mind, either."

"Even the name change?"

She was getting frustrated. "You don't like O'Brien? It was my grandmother's name."

He jotted something down, although Dee couldn't figure out what it could have been. She hadn't said anything yet.

"Your parents," he said, his posture still comfortable. "They were both gifted?"

He looked so objective. Too bad Dee had already heard his opinion on the matter.

"You really want to know?"

He looked up, surprised. "Of course. If anybody knew, it would be you."

"And you'll believe me."

He offered a wry grin. "You seem a trustworthy sort."

She wanted to shake her head. This was going to be such a waste of time. "Yes. They believed they were gifted."

"And you?"

"Me what?"

"Are you gifted?"

"Why, yes, thank you. I can knit and tap-dance a little, and I'm a whiz with a block of ice and a chain saw."

"What about . . . ?" He let his hands drift through the air, the universal sign language for "woo-woo."

"Looking for somebody to entertain at parties?"

"Looking for the truth about your parents."

"No you're not." She shoved her drink away and sat back. "You're trying to prove they were frauds. I mean, they must have been, mustn't they? After all, they were convicted of it. They were convicted because they are fairly credulous and believed the wrong financial advisors." And Xan, who had known better. "I'm not going to help you vilify them further."

"And what makes you think I'm going to do that?"

Dee gave him the benefit of sincerely considering her answer. "You don't believe it's real, do you?" she asked.

He never hesitated. He didn't even smile. "No," he said. "I don't."

Dee almost laughed. She should have known. He was a psychophobe with a pile of psychic magazines in his bedroom. "Not ghosties nor ghoulies nor even things that go bump in the night?"

"Swamp gas and overheated imaginations."

Lord, was she tempted to show him. It would be so easy. All she had to do was reach across the table, grab him by the ears, and kiss him. Really lip-lock in on him so that she sucked on his tongue like a Popsicle and he suddenly looked up to see his mother sitting in front of him. Wouldn't he be surprised?

"Would you mind talking about the show?" he asked. "I mean, nobody was closer than you three."

Dee reached for her martini again. It would be such a good moment to shift. It didn't have to be his mother. Just something startling and very mobile. "We weren't involved at all," she said. "Just trotted out on special occasions. Other than that, we had nannies."

And Xan. Always there, whispering in her ear, dripping uncertainty like acid. Especially, inevitably, around her twelfth birthday, the day her world changed.

"Why don't you just tell me about the book?" she asked. "Why is Mr. Delaney so interested in psychics all of a sudden?"

Danny James eased back in his seat. "Not all of a sudden, really. It's a subject he's been fascinated by for a while. Especially . . . shall we say, 'professional psychics.' "

"Ah." Dee took a sip of gin. "I recognize that tone of voice. The 'all psychics are frauds or delusional' tone. Cops and fundamentalists are particularly fond of it."

"Well, were they? Frauds, I mean."

"You obviously think so. Who am I to argue?"

He should have looked piqued. He laughed. "Oh, I do love a challenge. I don't suppose you'd like dinner after all, would you?"

Of course she'd like dinner. Who was he kidding? But she couldn't risk it on so many levels.

Then he reached across the table. "Please," he said. "I don't bite. I promise."

He did even worse than that. He touched her. Laid his hand over hers and squeezed. Lightning burst behind Dee's eyes. A shock of heat shot up her arm and scorched her. That dusty image blossomed again, paint and sunlight and Danny James. Worse, this time it brought with it the sound of laughter. The sense of joy.

Dee gasped, stunned to silence. She looked up to see that Danny had lost color. His pupils were suddenly the size of dimes. Oh, God. He could see it, too. He could hear it.

Dee yanked her hand away, fully intending to turn him down. To climb regally to her feet and walk purposefully out the door.

She took in a breath, all set to shake her head. "Actually," she said instead, "I'd love to."

Lizzie stared up at Elric, into his dark, fathomless eyes, and she knew he was going to kiss her. She wanted him to. She was fascinated by his mouth, by his cool voice, by his eyes and the long elegant hands. She was fascinated by him, and half terrified.

She still wanted him to kiss her. She could feel the power pulsing between them, threading through her body so that she could feel him everywhere, and the sensation was so terrifyingly wonderful that she wanted to feel his mouth as well, everywhere, and see what kind of colors it brought.

But then he dropped his hand, stepping back, away from her, and the connection was broken, and she felt suddenly drained. Thankfully unkissed. Damnably unkissed.

"You're very susceptible," he said, and if she didn't know how powerful he was she might have thought there was a shaken note in his cool voice.

"Susceptible to what?" She took a step back herself, for safety's sake. A thousand miles between them would make things even better, but so far he'd been immovable.

"To me."

The sting to her pride was enough to override her fears. "Yes, I'm absolutely quivering with desire for you," she said. "We're long-lost soul mates, and I can't live without you." The problem with sarcasm, she thought, the moment the words were out of her mouth, was that you had to have practice. She was so seldom sarcastic that her haughty little speech sounded far too much like she meant it.

It would have helped if he'd said something, anything. But he just looked at her for a long, measuring moment, before changing the subject. "We need to find you a talisman."

"What for? To keep me safe from you?" she shot back.

"We're not going to talk about that right now," he said. "Maybe later. Right now we have work to do."

Talk about what? she thought with just a trace of desperation, but for once she kept her mouth shut. The longer she was around him the more dangerous he became, though she wasn't quite sure why.

"What kind of talisman?" She went back to the original subject. "What do I need it for?"

"To focus your energy. Do you have any old jewelry, maybe something that belonged to your mother?"

There was no way she could lie to him.

"We have some jewelry," she said reluctantly. "But it's not mine. We've been using it to support ourselves—every now and then we sell off a piece and it keeps us going."

"Where is it?" He moved past her, and in the crowded workshop it was a difficult thing to do without touching her, but he managed.

"I told you, it's not—"

He left the workshop, moving through her room

without even glancing around him. She didn't blame him—the sweet, neat confines of her small bedroom didn't hold anything arcane or mysterious.

She rushed after him, about to argue some more, to find him standing at the table by the open window, looking down at the brass-bound trunk Dee had left there. He glanced up at her. "I presume this used to belong to your feckless mother. Come here and choose something."

"I shouldn't . . ."

"Don't be tiresome, Lizzie. This is all very simple—either you learn to use your gifts or you keep exploding things and courting dangerous attention from people you'd rather avoid. Open the box."

Dangerous attention from people she'd rather avoid. Did he mean Xan? If so, he couldn't have come up with a better argument. She opened the box, looking down at the tangle of brilliant, gaudy jewelry.

"You know which one is yours, Lizzie," he said in a more gentle voice. "Just trust yourself."

She really didn't like a man who was right all the time, she thought, picking up the one piece that had always fascinated her.

It was the Borgia pendant, a huge rich amethyst, set in silver and looped on a silver chain, the violet catching the light from the setting sun through the window. It felt alive in her hand, and her fears, the ones she thought she'd banished, came rushing back. She put it down on the table, backing away from it. "I don't want it."

She was too rattled to realize he'd moved, scooping up the pendant, or she would have tried to get away, but he simply put one hand on her shoulder, stilling her, and placed the pendant around her neck. She could feel the weight settle between her breasts, and it vibrated against her heart, warming it, like a fire glowing inside her.

And then he kissed her.

It was the last thing she expected—the touch of his mouth against hers—and he pulled back, looking as startled as she felt. She stood frozen.

"Ah, shit," he said, and catching her face in his hands, he kissed her again.

It was like nothing she'd ever felt before, and she reached for him, holding on, afraid she might fall. A swirl of color, greens and blues and lavenders, all dancing around in her head as he kissed her, with slow, deliberate thoroughness. Charles preferred closed-mouth kisses—

But Elric didn't. He stroked the sides of her face until she opened her mouth for him, and he used his tongue, kissing her with a slow, deliberate care that left her shaking, cold and hot. She had no choice, no thought but to kiss him back, sliding her arms around his neck, pressing her body up against his, the living amethyst between the two of them, between their hearts, and it glowed, burned, sang, as she closed her eyes and let herself sink into the breathless wonder of the kiss.

She didn't know what would have happened next if the ferret hadn't scampered across her foot. She jumped away from him, banging her head against his jaw, and looked around her in dismay. Two ferrets, six mice which should have been white but were instead varying shades of purple, and Pywackt, staring at her in haughty disdain, a deep lavender himself, before he started after the mice.

"You've got to stop doing that," Elric said. "There are already too many rodents in this world."

Lizzie ignored him, scooping up the mice before Py could get them. A moment later she was holding flowers in her hands, the same roses that had been residing in the now empty vase, and she realized she hadn't transformed the silver this time. She stuffed the flowers back into the vase, but by this time the ferrets were a pair of leather shoes once more, though Py seemed determined to prove otherwise.

"That's a step in the right direction," Elric said in a cool voice. "At least you didn't cross elemental boundaries this time."

"I did that?"

"You did. I, however, was the one who turned them back. I think that's the first thing I need to teach you. How to undo the messes you make."

She would have argued with him, but she had something more important on her mind. "Why did you kiss me?"

He shrugged. "I don't know. Maybe you just needed kissing."

"Don't do it again," she said.

Except that he really did have the most melting smile. "I can't promise that. But not unless you want me to."

"Then I'm safe," she said firmly.

"I wouldn't count on it," he murmured.

It made her stomach jump in anticipation. "Are you going to teach me or not?" she demanded, half shocked at her cranky tone of voice. Elric the Magnificent was enough to try the patience of a saint, and she was feeling less and less saintlike.

"I'm going to teach you," he agreed. "Everything I know."

Lizzie wasn't even going to consider why that

sounded so deliciously frightening. All she knew was
that she didn't want to change things, even if she could.

W*hat*?" Xan said, glaring down at the see glass
on the table. "The *hell* you'll teach her everything you know!"

A loud sneeze made her jerk up so fast she almost
knocked the glass off the table. "How did you get up
here this time?"

"Well, it wasn't easy," Maxine said, looking perturbed. "Somebody had put a *brick* in the portal, some
big ol' shiny invisible thing, and—"

"What do you want, Maxine?"

"Boy, you look good."

Maxine's eyes were frankly admiring, and Xan was
in a place where a little frank admiration was welcome, so she relaxed.

"Thank you. Now what do you want?"

"Is that dress silver? Like real silver?"

"Yes. What do you want?"

"You goin' out tonight? Like to a party?"

"A gala at the Kennedy Center with a small party of
friends afterward." With Vincent for the last time.
Knowing Elric was near was speeding up the inevitable.
Every man paled beside Elric, but Vincent became invisible. And after tonight, all his power taken, he'd be dis-
pensible, too. Used up. Discarded.

Xan began to feel almost cheerful.

Maxine sneezed again.

"Maxine, can't you take something for that?"

"Allergies," Maxine said. "I've always had 'em, not the regular kind, the doc can't figure out what I'm allergic to, but it's worse in here."

Magic, Xan realized. *I picked the only person in Salem's Fork who's allergic to magic.* She sighed. "Did you have something to tell me, Maxine?"

"Yes. Did you know that Danny knew Dee in college?"

"No, he did not."

"Well, he said he did," Maxine said, as if it were irrefutable.

"He lied to you, Maxine."

"Really?"

"Men do that. Was there anything else?"

"Well, he's not in love with her. I asked, and he said to give him time."

Xan sat back. "You asked. He just got into town this morning, and you asked if he loved her."

Maxine nodded. "I thought—"

"Don't think, Maxine. It's not good for you." Xan took a deep breath. "Now that you're here, I have a job for you."

"Okay," Maxine said. "You want me to slip him a love potion? I bet you make a great love po—"

"Maxine, he's her True Love. He doesn't need a love potion. He's destined to love her. They all are. I cast the spell to find their real loves. It's fate. It'll happen. Leave them alone."

"Right." Maxine nodded. "Got it. Still, a love potion. Couldn't hurt."

"Maxine."

"Don't mess with fate. Right."

"Someone else is messing with fate," Xan said grimly, looking down at the Fortune house. "After I expressly told him not to." *You were supposed to take her powers, not teach her to use them, Elric, you double-crosser.*

"Whoa," Maxine said.

"The bastard never does anything I want him to," Xan said, thinking of all the things she'd have liked Elric to do.

"Oh," Maxine said knowingly. "A woman scorned."

"I beg your pardon," Xan said.

"What a dummy," Maxine said, shaking her head. "You'd have thought he'd have gone for it. I mean, you're no spring chicken, but you've definitely got it going on."

"Maxine, do you *want* to die a slow, agonizing death?"

"No."

Xan waited for a moment, but Maxine seemed to have gotten the point. "Lizzie is at home wearing an amethyst pendant. Get it from her and bring it to me."

"Amethyst . . . ?"

"Purple stone pendant. Get it."

"Okay." Maxine saluted. "Uh, Xantippe?"

"No, you cannot give Danny and Dee a love potion."

"What about Mare?"

"Jude already loves Mare. Go."

"What about Crash?"

Xan stared into the see glass, trying to find Elric. "Who?"

"Mare's old boyfriend. He's a mechanic who's living in Italy and he came back to town and proposed to her at the Greasy Fork at lunchtime."

Xan turned her head slowly to look at Maxine, standing there in her diner uniform with MAXINE embroidered over her left pocket. She looked a little more full-breasted than usual and a lot more uneasy. "At lunchtime?"

"In front of God and everybody. Mare stood up and announced it."

"And you waited until now to tell me because . . . ?"

"It was *lunchtime*," Maxine said, outraged. "We were *busy*. And then I forgot. But then Dee and Danny came in for drinks and dinner and I remembered and . . ." She faltered. "You want me to do anything about Mare?"

"No," Xan said. "Stay away from Mare. Stay away from Dee and Danny. Your job is to get the amethyst pendant away from Lizzie and stop by the video store and tell Jude—"

"The one who looks like Jude Law?"

"Yes, tell Jude to get to work on Mare, that he's got competition. I'll take care of Crunch."

"Crash."

"Whatever. Get that pendant and warn Jude." Maxine turned to go and Xan got a look at her chest in profile. "Maxine, what the hell are you wearing?"

"Push-up bra," Maxine said, adjusting her breasts. "I'm making all the night waitresses wear them. We'll get more customers."

"It's a diner, Maxine, not the Salem's Fork Hooters."

"I bet the tips go up." Maxine checked her watch. "My break's over. Gotta go."

She disappeared into the portal without so much as a "See ya," let alone a genuflect, and Xan thought about smiting her through the see glass and decided that being Maxine was probably punishment enough.

She looked back at the glass, worried now. Dee and Danny were still in the diner; she could see their heads bent close together over the table. They'd be fine, they were half in love now and would fall completely by Sunday.

The glow from the workroom window told her that

Lizzie and Elric were there. She ignored a stab of jealousy to focus on the problem: Elric had no business teaching Lizzie to use her magic, but if Maxine got the amethyst it would slow down her learning curve so badly he might get frustrated and just take Lizzie's power from her. And then take Lizzie, keeping her safe and powerless in Toledo. Xan felt a real twinge at that; being kept in Toledo by Elric would be dark and erotic and mesmerizing, and her hand slipped on the glass just thinking about it; maybe when she was young again—she closed her eyes at the thought, young again—maybe when she had the girls' powers, Elric would look at her differently, but no, he was meant to be with Lizzie and there were other men, although none like Elric. But then, accidents could happen. And Lizzie might not make it through.

Of course she was going to do her best to see that the girls survived the loss of their powers. She was their aunt, after all—she only wanted the best for them. But Lizzie was already more frail than the other two . . .

No. Youth is enough. Youth and power. Who needs Elric?

And then there was Mare. Xan could see her through the hideous neon that filled the plate-glass windows of Value Video!!, Jude gazing at her adoringly. He really was attractive, Mare surely would prefer him over some mechanic named Crash. Loud, oblivious Mare, who never stopping clumping around shouting long enough to notice what was going on around her. She was going to be the easiest, if she'd just ignore the mechanic and take the vice president, who had to be far superior . . .

She looked down at the diner. Maxine was heading for Dee and Danny again.

It was damn difficult getting good help for a supernatural power snatch these days. The awe just wasn't there. She glanced at the time and realized that Vincent would be there soon. It was damn difficult getting good supernatural lovers, too. It might almost be easier being human.

Don't be ridiculous, she told herself, and double-locked the portal.

CHAPTER FOUR

Dee picked at her mandarin chicken salad and wondered what the hell she'd been thinking. Dinner with Danny James, the most sensual man she'd ever met? The very man who was threatening her with her past?

Who was she kidding? She'd been thinking that it was yet another Friday night in an endless series of Friday nights she'd sat home alone while Mare and Lizzie were off having normal social lives. But this one time, she had a chance to throw over the traces just a little. Just enough.

And she'd enjoyed this last hour. They'd talked about inconsequentials: Danny's travels, small-town life in Salem's Fork, popular culture, sports. And Danny had stayed so far away from his true purpose here that Dee had almost been able to think he'd asked her to dinner just because he wanted to spend time with her.

He finished wiping his hands with the red and white checked napkin and set it down. "Well, that was good," he said, leaning back in his seat. "I can't remember when I had such a good dinner. Tough to find good burgers in France."

Dee looked up from the scattered lettuce on her plate. "I'd love to find out someday."

He shook his head. "I'm still surprised that you haven't traveled. I mean, you have to admit there was some high living with your parents."

Dee just shook her head. She really should have left while she had the chance. "We didn't travel."

"Can I ask you why?"

Dinner, it seemed, was officially over. The chicken salad threatened a surprise return.

"You mean you don't want to talk about travel?"

His grin was bright. "Sure. When we see each other again for fun instead of business."

Those images were back, and this time there was no question. He was starring in them. His bare back, his smile, the wash of golden light on his skin, and her at her easel. She sucked in a breath, trying her best to ease her heart rate a little. "Again with the lame come-ons. Don't you have anything better?"

The gleam in his eyes was as amused as it was delighted. "You'll just have to hang around and find out, won't you?"

Picking up his second longneck, he took a deep swig, never looking away. And that bead of perspiration just had to slide right down his Adam's apple. He made her want to laugh. He made her restless and unsure and hungry.

"Do you think your sisters would mind talking to me?"

"Yes." The answer was instinctive. *She'd* mind. How could he possibly appreciate her sisters on such short association? It had taken the people of Salem's Fork a solid year to look past Mare's outfits and Lizzie's shyness to discover the real beauty beneath. And this was the first town where they'd actually felt as if they belonged. Dee didn't want them hurt again.

But, oh, hell, it wasn't her call to make. It hadn't been for a long while. She shifted her shoulders a bit, trying to work out the stiffness. She shook her head. "They were pretty young when my parents died. I'm not sure they'd have much to say. But it's their decision."

Come to think of it, it might be worth the price of admission to see what Mare could do to this guy. He might work for a world-famous author, but she'd bet he'd never dealt with the Queen of the Universe.

Just that thought soothed her enough to relax again and finish her drink.

"What do you think they'd say about your parents' deaths?" he asked. "I know you're aware of the suggestion that their deaths were suspicious, coming on the eve of their incarceration."

She should have expected this. It was definitely the wrong time to run out of martini. "The coroner ruled that they died of hypothermia. They'd been participating in a spiritual cleansing in the ocean, and stayed in the water too long."

"You don't think it was suspicious?"

Yes. *Yes.*

"Of course not. My parents were rather notorious for their lack of common sense. They went swimming alone in a cold ocean and lost track of time. I'm just surprised they made it all the way home before they collapsed."

In the middle of the foyer. She'd found them there, lying on the floor with Xan bent over them, smiling. *Smiling.*

"And you disappeared after they died because?"

Because my aunt had just murdered my parents and

was turning her sights on us. It had all been there in that smile. Only no one else had seen it.

"It was decided that it would be healthier for us to be out of that environment."

He considered her a moment, which ratcheted up her nerves. "And you don't think they might have stayed in the water accidentally on purpose?"

Dee was having trouble breathing again. But then, she always did when she thought of her bright, frivolous, unworldly parents. "No. They might not have been the most mature adults on earth, but they wouldn't have left us on purpose. My mother was upset enough that they had to leave us to go to prison."

She'd made Dee promise to take care of her sisters. And she'd given her the jewelry box.

"And have you been here all this time?" he asked.

"Places like it."

"Your family took you in?"

"Yes."

It didn't seem to occur to him that she might be lying through her teeth. Before he could continue, Maxine returned.

"Here you are, honey," she announced, handing the bill to Danny. Sometime during dinner she'd applied a fresh coat of black eyeliner and, evidently, her Wonderbra. She was bending way over now, as if she couldn't quite see over her breasts, which was a distinct possibility. "I hope everything was to your liking."

Danny reached around to pull out his wallet. "I haven't had a hamburger this good since BillyBurgers closed back home."

"Then I'm glad Dee brought you here." Maxine gave him a little smack on the arm. Maxine smacked everybody. "So, you in love with her yet?"

His smile damn near sent Maxine toppling over. "I

even offered to have her babies. She was sensible enough to say no."

Maxine laughed and gave him another open-handed smack and then turned to Dee. "Dee, you tell Mare that Italy is no place for a good American girl like her."

Dee found herself blinking a bit stupidly. "I'm sorry. What?"

Maxine perked up, "You didn't know? Crash is back, honey. He asked Mare to marry him and go off to Italy, if you please. She said she'd think about it, but you know that's no good . . ."

Dee tuned her out. Crash? *Crash?* Dee had to get herself over to the Value Video!! and find out what the hell was going on.

"Oh," she said, interrupting some diatribe Maxine was giving on some wonderful guy named Jude. "Yeah. That."

"The betting's at two to five she'll say yes," Pauline informed her on the way by.

Dee shook her head. Crash. "Well, put me in for a tenner."

"For or against?"

Italy. Dee grabbed her briefcase. "Either way. You should never think you can predict what Mare's going to do." Pauline laughed and Dee slid across the seat. "Uh, I have to . . ."

Danny James was already on his feet, sliding his wallet into his back pocket. "Come walking with me," he said, taking her by the hand. "You know you want to."

Dee damn near pulled him over on his head. Of all the things to whisper to her.

You know you want to, Deirdre, Xan had whispered. *You want to be like me. But you can't without my help. Without me, you'll create disaster.*

Dee's stomach dropped. Hell, she was nauseous. "No, thank you. I need to talk to my sister."

But he was already dragging her to her feet. She barely hung on to her briefcase as she was summarily yanked from the booth, with not one patron of the Fork coming to her aid. No, *they* were smiling, as if they were extras in *Love Story*, or something. Before she could so much as protest, she was out the door onto the sidewalk.

"Now," Danny said, making it a point to fill his lungs with air. "Isn't this better?"

"No," she said, even though it was a lie. "It's just windier."

He tapped her on the nose. "Live a little."

Dee struggled to keep her skirt pulled low and her dudgeon high. How did he do it? She wanted to go with him. She wanted to run down the sidewalk hand in hand like a kid and whoop at the moon. And if anybody knew better, it was Deirdre Dolores Fortune.

"Mr. James . . ."

"Danny." He took her hand and turned her toward the river. "If you want, we'll walk over to ask your sister why she'd ever want to get married and move to Italy with somebody who sounds like he can't drive. But on the way, there are still some questions I have."

"Lucky me."

"It's painless, I promise," he said with that sly grin of his. "What's up there?" he suddenly asked, pointing toward the orange-tinted trees that crowned the bluffs across the river.

Dee followed his gaze. "Salem's Mountain."

"Can you see the sunset from up there?"

"What's left of it." The clocks had just turned the week before, and it was still a surprise to see the sun up at seven.

"Let's go see."

Dee just blinked at him. "Now?"

He laughed and Dee wanted to smile right back. "It would be pointless to do it later. C'mon."

Her heart was stuttering again. Temptation whispered in her ear. Mare could wait. The rest of the world would continue to spin on its axis if she took just a little time and watched the sunset with a handsome man. Before she had a chance to really think about it, she let him pull on her hand, and she followed him down the street.

They only made it as far as the corner when Dee dragged Danny to a stop. She'd just spotted his mode of transportation.

"That's a motorcycle," she accused.

He straightened, insulted. "This is not just a motorcycle. This is a 1956 500 cc Triumph TR6."

It sat sleek and low and menacing against the curb. And, damn it, bloodred. Xan red.

"I'm sure it must be very proud. But I'm not going anywhere on it. My sister was almost killed on one of those things."

"Ah," he said. "Now I know where that guy's name came from. And why you aren't interested in letting your sister travel to Italy with him. But no one has ever called me 'crash.'" He leaned close again. "Come on. You know you want to."

This time the words almost made her groan. He was right. She did want to. He was rubbing his thumb over the palm of her hand and setting up showers of heat all through her. "It's . . . oh, I can't do this in a dress."

And no underwear.

"Of course you can," he said. "You probably don't want to do it with your hair held hostage, though."

And before she could so much as protest, he managed to pluck out the one bobby pin that anchored every other bobby pin in her hair so that it all came tumbling down, pins flying everywhere.

"How *dare* you?" she demanded, grabbing her hair in an effort to corral it.

It was too late, of course. Her hair exploded into curls.

"Perfect," Danny crowed. "This would happen sooner or later on a motorcycle anyway. Come on."

She wanted to. She wanted to climb aboard that bloodred disaster machine and wrap her arms around his chest as he kicked the thing into action. She wanted to feel the engine in her chest. She wanted to feel the vibration of the bike in places that were dangerous, places she spent most of her time keeping under strict control. Places that would be pressed snug against his jeans. She wanted to just take off and find out where she went when she got there. And that scared her more than anything.

"Why are you doing this?" she demanded.

Danny's smile grew even larger. "Pure impulse."

She shook her head. "Pure impulse is what gets people into trouble."

"Pure impulse is what gets inventions invented and great thoughts thought."

"And young girls pregnant."

Danny stepped closer, crowding her against the bike, and laid his hands on her shoulders. "Haven't you ever given in to impulse, Deirdre Dolores?"

Dee found herself grinning against her will. "As seldom as possible, Danny James."

"Well, that's where we differ. I do nothing that's not spawned by a walloping dose of whimsy. And my whimsy right now is telling me I need to get up that mountain. With you."

He was so beautiful, so alive, a shock to her senses. He was magic and freedom, and she was suddenly drunk with him. And she didn't even know what his secret was. Because he had at least one. She could smell it on him, just like that power he refused to believe he had.

He lifted a finger to trace her lower lip. "You really are beautiful," he said, his eyes hooded and compelling. "I wasn't lying about that. But especially with your hair down. You should wear it down more often."

She couldn't move, couldn't think. Couldn't so much as get a breath past the sudden fire in her chest.

"Now," he said, fingering one of her curls like a silk ribbon, "I say we find out what my girl can do."

Dee took a breath of him and lost what sense she had. "Which one?"

He dropped a kiss on her nose. "The one I named after another special lady." He still had hold of her hair, and was using it to draw her closer. "But not, I think, as special as you . . ."

Dee wanted to ask. She thought she did, anyway. But when she looked up into his eyes she lost herself. Blue was the hottest fire, wasn't it? She simply couldn't look away from him, from his hot blue eyes. The gathering dusk settled in his hair and sharpened the lines of his face. The scent of power drifted off him, setting up a resonance in her, like a tuning fork. And he was stroking her face, his work-roughened fingers trailing sparks. What did a researcher do to get hands like this? What could those hands do to her?

"Xantippe said you looked like her," he murmured, bending closer. "She was wrong. You're so much more beautiful."

Dee lurched back. "*Who* said I looked like her?"

He blinked, bemused. "What?"

But Dee's eyes were already closed in despair. "You named your motorcycle after my aunt, didn't you?"

By nine o'clock that night, Mare was depressed as all hell. Algy had not shown up for the six-thirty showing, thereby shaking Dreama's faith in her as Queen of the Universe; William was reaching new depths in moroseness, looking so depressed that she had to keep an eye on him at all times; and Jude repeatedly told her that the New York job was hers for the taking as long as she shaped up and gave up anything that wasn't "normal," looking at her as if he expected her to do something in return, like fall into his arms or something. On the positive side, she'd made a noon appointment at Mother's Tattoos the next day to get the tattoo she'd lied about to Crash so she'd have a new one to show him if he talked her into taking off her clothes before he went back to Italy. But the only really cheerful thing that happened all night was that Pauline from the Greasy Fork stopped in to rent *My Dinner with Andre* and told her that Lizzie's incredibly dull boyfriend, Charles Conway, had left for Alaska that afternoon. "Why?" Mare said. "Who cares?" Pauline answered. Since Mare was pretty sure the answer would be "Not Lizzie," she said, "Good point," and went back to work.

"So that man who was here earlier," Jude said from

behind her. "You're not supposed to entertain friends during working hours. Was he your boyfriend?"

"Yes . . . he vas . . . my boyfriendt!" Mare said.

Jude looked confused.

"Young Frankenstein," Mare said. "Cloris Leachman. It's a classic."

Jude still looked confused.

"He's not my boyfriend," Mare said.

Jude looked relieved.

"Mare!" somebody whispered loudly, and Mare jerked to her feet and saw Dee over by the door, motioning for her.

"Customer needs me," Mare said to Jude. "Back in a minute."

She went over to Dee and pulled her behind the game shelf. "Make it quick, that blond guy in the bad green tie is a VP from the head office, and he's stalking me. Hey, what would you think about moving to Tuscany? Lizzie would like Tuscany and so would I—"

"Can we talk about it later?" Dee said, looking upset.

"Sure," Mare said. "Or I just got offered a promotion if we move to New York . . ." Her voice faded as she saw that Dee's hair was loose, a riot of coppery curls, not like Dee at all. "What the hell have you been doing?"

"Nothing," Dee pushed her hair back and then stopped, as if she'd just realized what she must look like. "Do you have a rubber band?"

"Nope, but I can fix it, although it's a shame, it looks great like this." Mare tilted her head to concentrate as she began to pull the strands together at the top of Dee's head, little blue sparks among the copper. It was like the sugar grains; the key was to think of the hairs individually and then to align them so that—

"Stop it," Dee said, trying to shove her hair back into place, "it's *Xan.*"

Mare stopped and Dee's curls dropped back to her shoulders. "You saw Xan?"

"No. Danny did. Xan sent him." Dee's voice was miserable. "He hasn't said so, but it's a fact."

"Oh, hell," Mare said, feeling lousy for her. "Damn, I'm sorry, Dee."

"I think she's close by," Dee said. "I can feel it."

Close by, Mare thought, and her pulse kicked up a beat. Xan who really was Queen of the Universe and who could teach them how to control their powers and then . . . "Listen, she could set us free." *And I could go to Italy.* "She—"

"*No.*" Dee grabbed Mare's arm. "She's *dangerous,* Mare. She has *real power,* and she wants *us.* She's *unstoppable, so we can't let her start.*"

"But she's—"

"And now I can't find Lizzie." Dee sounded truly upset. "I left Danny as soon as I learned the truth and ran home to find her, but she wasn't there. I'm going back out to find him and ask him where Xan is. If I can't find out, we'll have to run again. We'll vote on it, but I just don't think we have a choice. We'll have to go."

Oh, *hell.* Forget ever seeing Italy or even New York, Dee was going to bury them in another nothing little town again.

Unless something stopped her.

What would make Dee stop running?

Danny James.

Mare surveyed her sister. "We can't vote until we know more about what's going on. So I'm thinking, with your hair down like that, if you unbuttoned a couple of buttons on your blouse, Danny would probably tell you anything you wanted to know." She tried to unbutton Dee's top button with her mind, but the material just puckered as the button pulled on it.

Dee slapped her hand over the button, her green eyes clouded with worry. "Stop it, this is serious. Xan's tried to find us before, but this time feels different. I can feel it like that storm coming in. Can't you?"

"Yes," Mare said. "You wouldn't believe what's already come in for me. Crash is back in town."

"I heard. You don't think he—" Dee's face changed and she said, "Shhhh."

Mare turned and saw that Jude had come closer and was watching them, not even pretending to be doing something else. "That's the vice president." She stopped, struck by a thought. "You know, the VP turned up about the same time Danny did. You don't suppose Xan sent him, too, do you?"

Jude cleared his throat.

Mare turned back to Dee. "Never mind. Xan's a lot of things, but she's not lame. Listen, I gotta go. The bottom line is, you have to seduce Danny to find out what's going on. If he's from Xan, he's used to magic, so the whole mom-in-bed thing won't faze him. And if it turns out that he's just a pawn, he'll leave and recover. Eventually."

"It's not that easy," Dee said, her voice bleak. "Just keep your eyes open for Lizzie and *stay away from Xan*. You want an education, go to college, not to Xan."

She headed for the exit, as sure as ever that she was right, so just as she opened the door, Mare messed up her hair, ruffling her curls in all directions, and Dee snapped around, looked enraged and really, really beautiful.

Go look like that at Danny, Mare thought, but she called, "Must have been the wind. Big storm brewing out there." Then she turned to see Jude right behind her, watching everything. "Yes, Jude?"

"Was that your sister?" he said as Mare heard the door slam behind her.

"Yes, it was." Mare started to head for the counter and then stopped. "What makes you think that was my sister?"

"You're a lot alike," he said, meeting her eyes.

No we're not, Mare thought. *We look nothing alike. So how did you know?*

Maybe Xan was that lame.

Up on the big flat screen, Victor Quartermaine fired at a little gray bunny that went hurtling backward toward a white light. *I know how you feel,* Mare thought, and then the bunny ended up in the BunVac 6000 floating in rabbity ecstasy, not dead after all.

"I love the BunVac," she said.

"What?" Jude said.

"The BunVac 6000," she said, nodding at the screen. "You're vice president of a video company and you don't know the BunVac?"

"Oh, that." Jude polished his silver tie tack with his finger, almost a nervous twitch by now. "I don't watch children's movies."

"Uh-huh," Mare said, and turned back to the screen to watch Victor put a bunny on his head.

"Have you thought about my New York offer, Mare?" Jude said. "It would give you tremendous power. With your abilities you could go right to the top. Vice president in no time. President even."

"Queen," Mare said, her eyes on the bunny.

"The sky's the limit. No, not even that, no limit. Limitless power. You'd like that. Of course, you'd have to stop doing strange things . . ."

"I'm thinking about all my offers, Jude," Mare said.

The problem was, the offer she needed most, the one that might set her free, that one she hadn't gotten yet.

Maybe I need to talk to Xan, she thought, and turned speculative eyes on Jude.

Dee was still futzing with her hair and waving off blue sparks as she stalked out of the video store. Every strand of her hair still shivered in outrage from Mare's trick.

Seduce him. Easy for Mare to say. She had the courage to try something like that. Dee had spent so much effort trying *not* to have sex, she swore she'd forgotten how. She—

"Need this yet?"

Dee jumped a foot. There, leaning against a lightpost, was Danny himself. Smiling, rumpled, and holding out her briefcase like a Christmas present.

Dee wondered if he knew how good he looked in that Marlon Brando pose or whether he just couldn't stand up straight for long. It didn't matter. Her brief dalliance with the illusion of mutual attraction was over. Fantasies survived only in the dust.

"Are you stalking me?" she demanded, snatching the briefcase and hugging it to herself.

Danny looked around at the fairly deserted streets. "I must be. Here you are. Here am I. Waiting for an explanation for why you disappeared like *The Runaway Bride.*"

Giving her hair one last agitated yank, Dee sighed. "Please. If you like me, don't quote movies."

He didn't like her. He was using her, just like the

other men Xan had sent to smoke her out. Xan dealt in men the way a Crip sold crack.

"You ran off so fast, I wasn't sure what happened," he said, looking concerned. "Is there anything I can do?"

He stepped closer. Dee stepped back. The street by the store had emptied, and the wind had kicked up, catching a flyer for the Elks' chicken dinner and plastering it against the Civic Pride trash container on the corner. At the horizon, a gathering of clouds showed purple. Portents of the storm to come.

"You can explain about my Aunt Xan."

He offered a chagrined grin. "She said you'd be upset."

"And she'd be right." Dee shoved her hair off her forehead. "I'm not fond of liars. I'm even less fond of people who play games."

He held up his hands, the image of innocence. "No more games. No lies. I shouldn't have done it in the first place, but this was important to Mr. Delaney. And . . ." He shrugged, looking faintly ashamed. "I didn't know you then."

"Well, you know me now," she said. "So you can begin to make amends. And that begins with how you really found us."

"Will you tell me more about your parents?"

Dee couldn't help staring at him, presumptuous prick. "You're just going to have to stick around and find out, aren't you?"

She really hated this. How could she know what to do? Her instincts were to run. Well, first to beat the crap out of him with her briefcase and *then* run. But if she ran, she'd never know just what his relationship was to Xan. What Xan really wanted.

If only she hadn't seen him in the dust. If only Mare hadn't put that suggestion in her head.

"Would you like to go back to the Fork?" he asked. "I think they like me there."

Dee snorted. "They'd have your babies there. But no, I'd rather have some privacy."

"My room?"

"Privacy, Mr. James." She looked around the uninspiring streets for inspiration. "I walk up the stairs at the Lighthorse with you, and by morning every woman in town is going to be camped in my front garden wanting details."

"Your place."

She didn't even bother to answer. Danny James was not coming anywhere near her house.

"It's a nice night," Danny said, looking back toward the river. "You want to try the mountain?"

Dee looked that way herself. The late light bathed the cliffs in gold, and the moon hung half seen amid the trees. Maybe that wasn't a bad idea. She did feel as if she had power up atop those cliffs.

Danny waited patiently for her, his hands still stuffed in his pockets, his hair rippling in the gusting breezes, that silver chain glinting just once against his neck. Dee still didn't have on any underwear. She'd still be forced to snuggle up to him all the way up the mountain . . .

Slapping the briefcase against Danny's chest, she stalked over to the bike. "Fine. But it had better be everything I've ever dreamed of."

She caught Danny's delighted smile out of the corner of her eye and decided to ignore it. Within five minutes, she was glad she did. And not because she wanted to see the cliffs. Danny had taken the route along the old Cobblestone Road, something Dee had never done on a bike. Maybe it was the no-underwear business. Maybe it was because Dee was already about as on edge as she could be. Suddenly the bike was acting like a big, bloodred vibrator. Good God. Did Mare know about this? Considering all the time Mare had spent on a bike with Crash, Dee'd bet it was a certainty. Maybe if things worked out, Dee'd spring for a bike herself. And find another town with lots of cobblestones.

They left the cobbles somewhere between delight and disaster, and made it the rest of the way up Salem's Mountain without incident. If Dee hadn't known any better, she would have sworn Danny had been up here before. He didn't just instinctively ride right to her favorite spot. When he climbed off the bike, he walked straight into the stone circle by the edge of the cliff.

Dee loved to stand dead center in the circle by the standing stone, where she swore she could gather power through her fingertips. Danny James stopped in the same exact place. Dead center.

Digging his hands back into his jeans pockets, he looked around him. "This place should be reserved for pagan rituals, ya know?"

Dee should have known. "Really? Why do you say that?"

He shrugged, looking a little uncomfortable. "Oh, I don't know. I can see witches dancing here, I guess. Right at the edge of the world, with the full moon rising over this big rock."

She found she could actually smile. "Did you know you're standing in a stone circle?"

He literally jumped back. "Here?"

She walked in through the southernmost portal and lifted her face to the sky, just like always. "Legend has it that about three hundred years ago witches used to dance here during the full moon."

He stared at her. "You're lying."

"Nope. Lots of magic here. You must have felt it."

That made him look spooked. "Not at all. I'm a researcher. I imagined it. I'm always doing things like that."

Or he heard the old voices, just as she did. When she wasn't crouched in the grass nibbling clover, that is. She spent a lot of time on this mountain in fur.

"It's time to talk," she said.

He refused to face her. If she'd tried to pull the scam he had, she wouldn't have faced her, either. Still, she couldn't believe how sad she was. Just more proof that she had no business fantasizing, she guessed.

Danny deliberately walked outside the circle and eased down against the big oak that shaded it. "Come into my office," he said, arms on bent knees.

Dee was sure she should say no. She needed to protect herself from this man, after all.

No she didn't. Xan was coming for them. By tomorrow night, she'd be gone from Salem's Fork. How much could Danny James hurt her in twenty-four hours? More than he had, anyway. So she eased herself down to the ground, close enough to him to feel the heat from his body in the cool evening air.

"I'm glad you left your hair down," Danny said, as Dee stretched out her legs and tugged her skirt over her knees. "With your hair down, I can imagine you dancing up here with the old girls. Come to think of it, that might be fun. Full moon's coming in a day or two. Why don't we come back up and dance?"

Beltane, ancient holiday of fertility. Just the idea sent a waterfall of shivers through her. If there was anybody she wished she could have danced for on the night of Beltane, it would have been Danny James. Especially considering what traditionally came next. Literally.

"My Aunt Xan," she said out to the deepening cobalt of dusk. "How did you find her?"

But Danny just shook his head, slipping his arm around her shoulder. "Not yet," he demurred, resting his head atop hers. "Let's just enjoy the night for a bit first, huh?"

Damn him. He fit so comfortably. He sounded so reasonable. She had no business trusting him, especially considering the fact that just his touch was setting off more electricity than Mare in the throes of her power. But it was so beautiful up here. So spiritual in a way no modern church leader would comprehend. There was power and grace and bone-deep joy here, where the witches had danced. It had always been her spot. Now, she'd never think of it again without feeling Danny James's cheek resting against her hair.

"Actually," he said after a few minutes of companionable silence, "Xantippe found me."

Dee closed her eyes, stricken. Then Xan *had* sent him. Could there be any way on earth to separate them in her mind now?

He lifted his head. His arm stayed where it was. "I had . . . um, just gotten the assignment," he said, "and had spent time doing the primary research. I contacted your parents' organization, and a few of their old employees. Who wouldn't talk, thank you very much. Whatever else your parents did, they inspired loyalty."

"I know. And Xan?"

"Said that she'd heard about me from one of them. Wanted me to get the story right, and thought the best place to start would be with you three."

"You never met her?"

"I'd planned on going to Santa Fe from here. That's where she is."

It still sounded plausible. "And she told you how to find us."

He shrugged. "She said you'd probably go by Murphy, O'Brien, or Ortiz, and that it should be easy to find a Deirdre, Elizabeth, and Moira in the same place." She thought he smiled. "It wasn't, but I managed."

"Have you talked to her since you found us?"

"Just to tell her I had. She asked me to call her after I talk to you."

"Where?"

"Her cell phone. In Santa Fe."

But Xan wasn't in Santa Fe. Dee didn't know how she knew that, but she did. Xan had used Danny as a stalking horse. And just like twice before, she was now coming for them.

"And exactly why would you name your bike after her, Danny? Bikes are very personal. They're . . . they're . . ."

"Sexual substitutes?" He fingered the loose curls by her temple. "I guess it was the sound of her voice. Throaty and sexy, like a bike engine. Just a whisper, so you had to really listen closely, ya know?"

Dee pulled away from his fingers, but she didn't get up. "Yeah. I know."

She wondered just what it was Xan had whispered. There was no way she wouldn't have known how sexy Danny James was.

"Xantippe said that there's a breach between you she's been trying to heal," Danny said. "She sounded upset."

Dee's laugh was hoarse. "She doesn't want to heal anything. And she's not upset."

"Then what is she?"

No, this she couldn't deal with sitting down. Climbing to her feet, she walked to the edge of the circle, where violets dotted the grass and the sky seemed endless. Beyond the cliff, the river reflected a sporadic moon, and the town faded into geometric shadows. It was what she was painting right now.

Dee pulled in a deep breath. How to explain Xan to this seemingly normal, wholesome man? *She's Maleficent and Marilyn Monroe. She's a carnivore masquerading as a flower. She's every man's fantasy and every woman's nightmare. Corrupt, clever, and concupiscent. Xan feeds off people like a vampire, and gets them to smile as she does it.*

But if Danny James was telling the truth, he'd never understand.

"Xan is the person who orchestrated my parents' downfall," Dee finally said, shoving her hands in her pockets. "My father wasn't the one who created that donation program they all skimmed off of. It was Xan. My father wasn't that clever. Xan made a fortune nobody ever traced and conveniently disappeared about a month before the feds arrived with the warrants." *Then reappeared just in time to murder her own sister.*

"You're sure?"

She smiled out into the night. "Oh, yes. I'm sure."

She heard Danny climb to his feet and approach. She didn't turn away from the view. The evening star had just winked on and she made her instinctive wish. *Let us be safe.* Danny came to stand right behind her and laid his hands on her shoulders.

"I'm sorry," he said. "I didn't know."

Dee found herself fighting tears. "Yeah. I'm sorry, too."

She'd grown to love this nondescript little valley, this camouflaged altar. She didn't want to leave. Danny James had left her no choice.

"I'd like to hear your side of the story," he said. "I'm sure I'll get your aunt's."

Dee turned to face him and realized he was too close. So she stepped away from his touch, where she could have enough space to better appraise him. He looked so open. So true. Was he that clever, or was he so honorable he hadn't been able to see what Xan was? Those were the men she specialized in, after all.

"What's in it for you?" she asked.

He watched her for a minute. "It's my job."

"No it's not. At least not only that. I can hear it in your voice. Why are you and Mr. Delaney making such a bizarre left-handed turn into nonfiction?"

"Because too many people have suffered from a belief in what isn't true."

Dee didn't bother facing him. "Many people say the same about religion."

"There are truths in religion. Not in this."

Dee shook her head. "This is personal, isn't it?"

He spent a moment looking out over the valley. The wind ruffled his hair, and the tree whispered above them. "I've seen the damage quacks can do," he finally said.

It was as if a light had flicked off in him. Dee saw the shadows settle and wondered.

"Can you tell me?"

He looked up, his eyes glowing oddly in the dusk. "Oh, I knew someone once. Lost her husband and son in a plane crash."

Dee sighed. "Fell prey to people telling her they could contact her loved ones?"

He didn't even nod. "It wasn't even the money she lost that was the worst. It was the waste of her life."

"Yeah," Dee said. "There are con artists out there. No question about it."

"But were your parents?"

For a long moment, Dee just looked at him. Weighed the ramifications of her words. Of the book that Mark Delaney was going to do, with or without her help. Did she reinforce Danny James's prejudice or discount it? It shouldn't matter. She'd be gone soon.

"Is there really a book?"

He looked affronted. "Of course there's a book."

She nodded. "They truly believed that they helped people."

"Did they? Help?"

"A lot of people said so." People who sent in money for readings. Money that had gone into houses and cars, and all that gaudy jewelry that had kept the Fortune sisters afloat lo these twelve years.

Until those terrible final days when everything had fallen apart. Dee could still see her parents standing there like stunned cattle waiting for the worst, the television cameras that had loved them for so long turning on them, Xan already safely away. She saw them again on that awful morning when she'd stumbled over them, empty husks sprawled on the floor.

"And you?" he asked. "Did they ever help you?"

She almost laughed. It was a question no one else had ever thought to ask. "You can't think I'd discuss that with you, knowing you're going to be talking to my aunt."

"You're right," he said. "That was out of line. I'm sorry."

She could hear him approaching. She didn't move. She had a feeling she knew what he intended. Hell, she hoped she knew. Her heart had picked up speed again. She ached, knowing this man was the last person from whom she should seek comfort. *Why not?* she thought, bracing herself for his first touch. Why not enjoy him, just for this little while? God knew he felt good enough. That curious lightning was sparking between them again, skittering all the way down to Dee's toes and causing them to curl. There were parts of her body that should have glowed in the dark. Surely she could accept this one gift before leaving?

Turning her in his arms, he smiled down at her. "I'm glad I met you, though."

Dee thought his hand might have been shaking a bit as he brushed a loose curl from her forehead. His body radiated warmth, strength. Security. Dee couldn't think of a thing she craved more.

She rested her hands on his chest. "Me, too."

She could do this. She could enjoy this man. She wanted to. She wanted to seduce him. She wanted him to seduce her.

But always Xan lived in her head. *You don't have the control, Deirdre. You never will. Without me, you're a failure. Without my guidance, there will be disaster.*

Danny bent his head to her. Dee fought down the instinctive panic and lifted her face to meet him. She could control herself. She did it every morning when she shifted for her painting. She kept from doing it at the bank when she became so frustrated she could chew glass. She could do it now.

He held her face in his callused hands. Her knees had grown wobbly, until he was all but holding her up, and he hadn't even kissed her yet.

He did. Oh, he did. For a blissful eternity, Dee basked in the unfettered delight of it. He nibbled, he courted, he seduced. He unleashed the kind of fire that shattered cells. He urged her mouth open and slipped inside.

There went her knees again. She was glowing, her breasts pebbled and aching. She wanted him to touch her. She wanted him to lay her down in her stone circle and not let her up until someone else was crowned Oldest Virgin in North America.

She was doing so well. Open-eyed and participating, pulling his shirt free so she could search out those taut muscles with her fingers. So she could explore the delicious terrain she'd seen from the top of a chifforobe. The feel of him was mesmerizing, the smell of him delectable. She could almost hear the racing thoughts in his head as he fumbled with the buttons Mare had tried to loosen no more than an hour earlier.

Yes, Dee thought, arching toward him, never breaking the kiss. *Please. Just this once.*

Her body felt incandescent. Chills chased down her spine and sapped her strength. Her heart battered at her rib cage, and she was pressing against him as if she could climb inside. She felt explosions of light in her very cells.

There will be disaster.

Danny slid his hand inside her blouse and cupped her breast. Dee gasped, lurching against him, struck by a bolt of pure lust from just the brush of his fingers. Dear God, what would happen when the rest of him was involved?

She might have made it. Might truly have thrown caution to the wind and consecrated her hill with a bout of lovemaking that would have gone down in the annals of lost virginity. But just as Danny bent to lay a kiss on her throat, suddenly in her mind Dee saw the face of a woman. Gray-haired and sad, with Danny James's eyes.

Dee shoved so hard Danny almost fell down the cliff.

"What the hell . . ."

"I'm sorry," she gasped, desperately fumbling with

her buttons before her body could betray her. "I . . . oh, I'm just sorry."

Xan had been right. She was about to fail all over again. And she found that no matter what she'd thought, she just couldn't bear what she would see on Danny's face when it happened. So she ran. She ran all the way down the mountain and into the house where men weren't allowed, and she hid beneath the black duvet in her room.

"The cat has to go," Elric said, and Lizzie opened the door to shoo Py out, only to come face-to-face with Mare, home from work. She could feel the color drain from her face, but Mare didn't even blink.

"Hello," Mare said to Elric. "I was looking for Py."

"That's Elric," Lizzie said and stood her ground, daring Mare to say anything about the taboo about men in the house.

Mare looked from Lizzie to Elric to Lizzie and back to Elric again. "How you doin', Elric?"

"Very well, thank you," he said. "And you?"

"I've been better, thank you for caring," she said. "Come on, Py."

She took the cat and retreated upstairs, and Lizzie closed the door.

"Will that be a problem?" Elric said.

"If that had been a problem, there would have been blue sparks," Lizzie said. "So now what?"

"Now we start . . ." The loud thumping on the front

door stopped him, and he said, "Sweet Jesus, is this Grand Central Station? Get rid of her."

"Her? It's probably Charles," she said, resigned.

"I don't think so." He had an oddly smug expression on his face. "Hurry up. I'm getting bored."

"You can always leave," she pointed out, heading for the door.

It was Maxine from the diner, odd enough in itself, odder still because Maxine seemed to be twitching with nerves. "Hi, Lizzie," she said. And then she sneezed. "You'll never guess what I'm here for."

"I can't imagine," Lizzie said faintly. She glanced behind her. She could just manage to see Elric's shimmering outline. A definite advance from earlier in the day, she thought.

"I'm collecting for the Salem's Fork Wetlands Project. We're . . . er . . . planning an auction, and we're looking for donations." She stumbled over the words, as if she'd memorized them.

Lizzie just looked at her. "I didn't know Salem's Fork had any wetlands."

"That's an amethyst, isn't it?" Maxine said, her beady eyes focusing in on the pendant. "It's new, right? You could donate that—I bet it would bring in a lot of money. And think of the poor frogs and salamanders."

Instinctively, Lizzie wrapped her hand over the amethyst, shielding it from Maxine's eyes, and it pulsed in her hand. "I don't think so. I'm sorry, Maxine. Maybe Dee could write you a check—"

"Don't tell Dee!" Maxine said, clearly worried. "I've never seen you wear jewelry before, wouldn't you rather donate it—"

The door slammed in her face, and there was an audible click. Lizzie reached for the doorknob, but it was hot to the touch, and Elric was standing behind her shoulder, looking bored.

"Sorry, Maxine," she shouted through the door. "The wind must have blown it shut. Come back tomorrow and we'll give you a check."

"But I can't . . ." There was sudden silence on the other side of the door.

She whirled around to face Elric. "What did you do to her?"

"Sent her back to work. Which is what we need to do. Come along. I'm not in the mood for any more interruptions."

He motioned her into the workshop. "This is a fairly simple array." He began to draw a circular design on the rough wooden floor there. "Just enough to help focus the energy. When you get better at this you'll probably tweak it a bit, find one that works better for you. There are thousands of variations, carried down through history—you're bound to find one that's just right for you."

She looked at him, doubtful. It was late, and the wind outside was growing stronger. She could hear the creak of the branches overhead, the occasional rattle of the windows as a gust swept through. She'd spent the entire day listening to him, and she should have been tired and bored and restless. And in fact she was restless, though she couldn't figure out why. Even Mare had been an intrusion, somebody to be gotten out of the way. Something was building inside her, in concert with the coming storm, and she kept thinking her life was about to change.

Of course it was. Elric was showing her the secrets of the gift she'd struggled with so long, hated for so long, and she soaked up every word with rapt attention, mesmerized by the sound of his deep voice and his magical words.

They'd been at it for hours, with only a couple of breaks for food and tea. She'd offered him wine, but he'd taken one look at the ordinary chardonnay Dee kept and shook his head. "Working with a gift like ours is tricky enough without throwing alcohol or drugs into the mix. If I were you I wouldn't touch anything for at least five years, until you're a master at transmutation."

"Five years without a drink?" she'd replied. "You're kidding!"

"Is that a problem?"

In fact it wasn't. Beer gave her a headache, wine upset her stomach, and the harder stuff made her shudder. But she wasn't about to tell him that. "Next you'll be telling me I have to be celibate, as well," she shot back. Then strongly regretted it. Mentioning sex in his presence had the most unsettling effect. She glanced around to see whether any untoward shoes had popped up, but for once she was spared.

He pushed his long, dark blond hair away from his beautiful face, and the silver stud glittered. "It all depends. Sleeping with someone like your fiancé will dull your gifts. Eventually they'd disappear altogether."

Her instincts had been right about that. Every time she was around Charles, the shards of magic faded, leaving her safe and quiet and dull. "Isn't that what you'd like?" she said. "Since you say I'm so dangerous?"

He looked at her, considering. "It would be a loss," he said finally. "You have more talent than I've seen in decades, and it would be a shame to waste it. Particularly on an oaf like your fiancé."

"Decades?" she echoed, amused. "I doubt you were that aware when you were a kid."

"In fact I was very aware as a child, but I'm older than you think."

"How old are you?" He couldn't be much over thirty-five, though she would have guessed closer to thirty.

"Older," he said in a voice that allowed no further discussion. "Are we going to do this or are you going to throw everything away on true love?"

He sounded annoyed by the notion. Was it simply that she'd be wasting her talents, or something else? That had to be some bizarre streak of wishful thinking on her part.

"Don't you think true love is worth risking everything for?"

"It depends on how you define it," he said. He'd taken off his jacket and tie, rolled up his sleeves, and his long hair was rumpled. He should have looked more approachable. In fact, the more human he appeared, the more nervous it made her, and she wasn't sure why.

"I bet you don't even believe in true love."

"To quote the Queen of Hearts, I try to believe in six impossible things before breakfast every day. Are we going to do this or are you going to keep talking?"

"We're going to do this," she said, eyeing the chalk circle doubtfully.

"You'll need to take off those shoes." At some point her espadrilles had been replaced by black patent Mary Janes, an odd look beneath her jeans, but then, she was used to having strange things on her feet. She kicked them off and under the workbench.

"Socks, too," he said. "Your body needs to be in contact with the circle."

She peeled off the white socks with the lace trim, grumbling under her breath, and then stepped into the middle of the circle. Immediately the pendant went into hyperdrive, thrumming against her heart.

She met his dark eyes for a moment, startled, and he nodded. "Very good. You're even more receptive than I thought. This would work better if you were naked, but I'm assuming I can't talk you into that. At least, not yet."

"Not in this lifetime," she said, half expecting him to mock her on that blanket statement. His silence was even more challenging.

He picked up one of her shoes and set it on the wooden workbench, in the center of the smaller circle he'd drawn there. "This should be easy enough to start with—it's already been transmuted once, and I can still feel the energy. What do you want to turn it into?"

"Gold," she said promptly.

"Don't be so single-minded," he chided her. "The first time you ski you don't go down a double black diamond run, the first time you sail you don't head across the ocean. Try something small."

"A diamond?" she suggested, ever hopeful.

"Go for something you'd wear," he said patiently. "Just a small transmutation, nothing drastic. You'll learn by small steps."

"I'm going to have to learn fast if you're only going to be here three days."

"You'll learn. Close your eyes."

That was the last thing she wanted to do. Standing barefoot in a circle with her eyes closed made her feel too vulnerable. But the longer she hesitated, the longer it would take, so she dutifully closed her eyes.

"Relax. You're tight as a spring. I'm not going to tickle you."

Her eyes shot open again. "You're not going to touch me," she said, and she wasn't sure whether it was a warning or a question.

He didn't respond. "Close your eyes, take a deep breath, and relax all your muscles."

Easier said than done. She exhaled, letting the pent-up breath out, and tried to release the tension that was knotting her muscles. She rolled her shoulders, shook her hands, and tried to concentrate on the single black patent shoe.

Of course nothing happened. "Maybe you need some wine after all," Elric muttered. "Are you always this tense?"

In fact, she wasn't. She liked life to be peaceful, easy, and she went out of her way to make sure things went smoothly. He jangled her, unnerved her, made her jittery and upset in ways she didn't even begin to understand. Or didn't want to.

"I'm trying," she said. "I just . . ."

"What was that?" Elric froze.

"I didn't hear anything."

"You haven't learned to listen properly. Someone's in your bedroom."

"Don't be ridiculous. Why would someone . . ." Elric had already moved past her, not touching her, shoving the door open.

A blond man in a charcoal suit and a hideous green tie stood there, rummaging through her underwear.

"What the hell are you doing?" she said.

His eyes narrowed as he stared at her neck, and then he dove at her.

Instinctively her hands came up, knocking him away, and then he was gone, vanished in a puff of purple smoke.

"Jesus, Lizzie," Elric muttered, picking up a small, noisy frog from the floor. "You really read too many fairy tales." He opened the window and dropped the frog outside, and in the distance they could hear an anguished screech.

"At least this time I didn't cross elemental boundaries." She peered out into the darkness. "Is he going to be all right?"

"I expect so. He should regain his natural form in a few hours. Unless your sister turns into an owl again and offs him. The question is, what was he after and who put him up to it?"

"He was looking at the amethyst. Like Maxine."

"Very interesting," Elric murmured. "I may have to make a few calls. But in the meantime we have to concentrate on you. Back to the workshop."

She followed him, her hand still cradling the stone. "You've been trying too hard," he said, closing and locking the workshop door behind them. "Hold on a second." He pulled off his shoes and socks, and even though she knew what was coming, her body froze into a block of ice as he stepped inside the very small circle with her.

He circled his arms around her, pulling her back against his body, and ice met fire, melting, against her will. He, however, seemed supremely unaware of the effect he was having on her. Odd, because he'd seemed so intuitive before.

"This is another way of making an array," he said, his voice calm in her ear. "When you get really good you won't need one at all, you can simply visualize it. In the meantime, if you simply put your arms in a circle it can do the trick." He pulled her arms up, wrapping them around his as they formed a circle in front of them. "Now relax, and think about nothing."

"I . . . I can't." He was so hot, vibrating with energy just as her pendant was vibrating. She felt trapped in his arms, assaulted, warmed, aroused, blood coursing through her in response, and she knew, with awful certainty, just where her dreams had been coming from. That same powerful, erotic intensity was flowing through her, from the man who surrounded her.

"Of course you can," he whispered, and his breath

smelled like the peach and raspberry tea she'd given him. She loved peach and raspberry tea, she loved . . .

"There you go," he said, and her eyes flew open. A plume of lavender mist hung over the workbench, and a pile of shimmering gold silk lay on the rough surface in place of the shoe. "You do have a thing for gold, don't you? It's the wrong color for you."

He'd released her, stepping back, and she put out her hand to touch the fabric, watching in fascination as the color deepened, shifted, moved like a living thing until it settled into a deep rich purple.

She looked back at him. "Did I do that?"

He shook his head. "You made it. I fixed the color."

She picked it up, letting the silken fabric slide through her fingers. It still seemed to hold a trace of energy, and she could feel it dancing through her veins, settling in her breasts, between her legs, and she dropped it, horrified. "What is it?"

He reached past her and picked it up. "It's a nightgown, Lizzie. Just an ordinary piece of clothing."

Now that was where he was dead wrong. There was nothing ordinary about the nightgown at all—it was alive with sex and sensuality and magic, and it made her extremely nervous, and if . . .

"Goddammit, Lizzie," he grumbled, picking up the purple rabbit that had taken the place of the nightgown. Another puff of purple mist. "Stop getting rattled." The silk streamed from his hands again, a rich swathe of fabric in his long, elegant fingers.

A squirming purple bunny in his long, elegant fingers. He looked up at her, astonished. "How did you do that?" he demanded.

The room was slowly filling with purple mist, and she wondered whether it could escape through the cracks in the ill-fitting windows. Even if it could she didn't need to worry. It was late—no one would be around to notice puffs of purple mist drifting from their unremarkable little house.

"I don't know," she said, nervous. "I don't think I could do it again if I tried."

"Good," he said, setting the bunny down on the counter as it flowed back into the nightgown. "Did anyone ever tell you that you have hang-ups about sex?"

She could feel the color flood her face, feel the tingling grow stronger in her body. "Charles has no complaints," she said, defiant.

"Charles wouldn't notice." Elric dismissed him. "I think you need . . ." He stopped talking, abruptly, almost as if he'd said too much.

"What do I need?" It came out as not much more than a whisper, but it was one of the bravest things she'd ever said.

He stared down at her for a long, thoughtful moment, and she could get lost in his eyes, she thought. He could kiss her again, and wrap her in purple silk, and those long elegant fingers could touch her, soothe her, teach her . . .

"You need to sleep," he said.

And everything went black.

About the same time that Elric was drawing circles on Lizzie's floor, Crash was climbing the trellis outside Lizzie's workroom. The ancient lattice on the closed-in sun porch at the back of the O'Briens' beat-up little Carpenter Gothic house was as rickety as ever, possibly more rickety than it had been five years earlier, but Mare would be stretched out on the porch roof outside her bedroom window, Crash was sure of it, so he put two Dairy Queen hot fudge sundaes on the low edge of the roof and climbed up the wooden frame, just like old times, holding his breath as he got to the top and the lattice shook harder.

She was there, stretched out on the shingles with her hands behind her head, the cords from her iPod lanyard tangled in her silky hair as her head bobbed to whatever she was listening to, the shadows from the tossing branches making the moonlight dance across her white overalls. Py, her tiger cat, raised his head and fixed him in his yellow gaze as Crash climbed onto the roof. Then Py put his head down on her thigh and watched Crash pick up the sundaes and walk across the roof and sit down beside her. Crash wasn't sure of his welcome since Mare had said, "Tomorrow," but there was only so much a man could do when the woman he loved was this close and susceptible to DQ hot fudge.

She rolled her head on her hands as he eased himself down beside her, her eyes pale in the moonlight, almost as pale as her smooth skin, white against her blue-black hair. She pulled the iPod buds from her ears and he heard Kim Richey faintly singing "Here I Go Again" before she clicked it off and said, "Took you long enough," and he relaxed and held one of the sundae cups out to her. She sat up and he watched the curves of her body, the plumpness of her breasts and the arch of her back, strong and graceful in everything she did. She was Queen of the Universe, and he wanted her so much he ached with it.

Slow, he thought, and Py raised his head and watched him as if he knew what Crash was thinking.

Well, he was a male cat, he probably did.

She cracked the plastic lid off and said, "Spoon?" and he pulled one out of his jacket pocket and handed it to her and then took the lid off his own cup.

"So," he said. "How's things with the universe?"

"It's screwing me over." Mare scooped up some ice cream and fudge, and then closed her eyes as if savoring it for a moment before she swallowed.

Crash looked down the front of her overalls while her eyes were closed, all that blue lace and round flesh, the shadow of her cleavage, probably damp with sweat and—

Mare opened her eyes. "I asked it for a choice in my life, and it sent me two I can't take and didn't offer me the one I need. It's just cruel."

"One of them's me, right?" Crash started on his ice cream.

"Yes."

"Why can't you take me?"

"I can't leave Dee and Lizzie."

Crash almost said, *Bring them along,* until he remembered Dee hated him. "You're going to have to leave them sometime. You're not going to live together forever until you rot and die, right?" What a waste of all that heat and flesh and—

"It's complicated," Mare said. "But basically, I can't come to Italy with you. I'd have liked it a lot, but I can't. Sorry."

Crash nodded, and thought, *Maybe.* If family was the only thing keeping her back—

It couldn't be just that. Nobody refused to get married because she couldn't leave her sisters. It must be something else, the damn secret she could never tell him, the reason he could never stay the night, never climb inside her bedroom. Whatever it was, he didn't care. He still wasn't sure how he'd ended up back in Salem's Fork, but he was growing more and more positive that he wasn't leaving without Mare.

"What kind of cat is Py?" he said, spooning up more ice cream.

"Tiger cat," Mare said.

"Where'd you get him?"

"Lizzie found him at the zoo."

"You had that cat the whole time I knew you, and I never asked you anything about him," Crash said, carefully building his argument, which wasn't easy with so little blood in his brain.

Mare blinked up at him, beautiful and hot in the moonlight. "Well, you know. He's a cat. You weren't a cat person."

"I'm not a cat person now, but now I want to know because he's yours. I'll pay attention this time. Whatever you get from your sisters, whatever you need, I'll give it to you, I swear. I'll give you more. You can trust me. You can leave them. I'll give you what you need." *I'll give it to you right now, swear to God.*

"You can't." Mare leaned against his shoulder as she worked on her ice cream, and he closed his eyes because she was finally touching him. "You're a good guy, Crash, the best, but you can't make this work."

Oh, yeah, I can. "I can make anything work. Wait'll you see this little town I'm living in. You'd love it there. The whole town comes through the shop sooner or later, all of them, grandmas and little kids, too, everybody, because they all love the bikes because the bikes are so beautiful. Ducatis and Moto Guzzis and—"

Below, someone kicked a motorcycle into gear, and he stopped to listen, and she said, "What?"

"Triumph TR6." He listened as the sound faded into the distance. "Who do you know has a classic Triumph TR6?"

"It must have been Danny James," she said. "Dee's guy."

"Dee's dating? Good for her." Maybe Dee would get married. That'd be one down. "My mom heard that Lizzie's engaged to Charles Conway."

"That's off," Mare said around her ice cream. "He went to Alaska. She has a new guy, though, and I think he's a keeper."

"Well, if they're getting married, you can," Crash said, the Voice of Reason.

"They're not getting married." Mare sighed. "So tell me more about the bike business."

They sat in the moonlight and finished off their ice cream while he told her about the business and the bikes and his partner Leo and Leo's wife Amelie and their baby and the little house he owned there—"Does it have a red tile roof?" she asked, and when he said, "Yes," she said, "Oh," and he couldn't tell if that was good or bad—and the sun and the heat and the thousand things he loved about it, and when he was done, they put their cups down for Py to lick and then sat silent in the moonlight. Beneath them, the roof throbbed as if music were playing below, something with a strong bass, but it was quiet down there, just a silent pulsing with a drift of purple smoke around the windows every now and then that Mare said came up from the river, which didn't make sense. Crash didn't care, although the throb under him made it hard to concentrate on Italy and almost impossible not to touch Mare.

"So what are your other choices?" Crash said when she'd been silent for a while.

"Hmmm? Oh. New York. Jude offered me a job in New York City."

"Oh." He shifted on the roof. "Jude's the guy in the suit at the video store."

"Yep."

"You might like New York," he said, trying to be fair.

"I'd love New York," Mare said. "But I can't go there, either."

You're twenty-three, he wanted to say, *you can go anywhere you want,* but he wanted her in Tuscany, not New York, so he didn't say it. "And the third one nobody's offered you?"

"My Aunt Xan," Mare said. "My mother's sister. I'd kind of like to learn some stuff from her. The only problem is I don't know where she is, and Dee hates her so I can't go looking for her."

"Maybe your aunt would like Italy."

Mare turned to him in the dark. "Are you telling me that you're going to support me *and* my aunt?"

Crash sighed. "No. I'm just trying to find a way to make this work."

Mare shook her head. "Crash, you don't know me. At all. You think you do because you knew a little bit about me five years ago but—"

"I know, there are secrets. I got real damn tired of those secrets, of getting shut out, of feeling like the guy you called around when you wanted a good time and then sent home." He stopped because he was getting mad again, and getting mad was what had kept him out of Salem's Fork for five years, that "If I'm not good enough to come in the house, the hell with you" feeling that he was old enough now to know was a lot more about pain than it was about anger, not that that made it any damn better. "What I'm trying to tell you is that you don't need to keep secrets anymore because what I know about you is that it felt right to be with you then, and it's felt wrong to be without you for the past five years, and now that I'm back, it feels right again, and I'm ready to make this permanent, so I don't care what your secrets are, I'm for you."

"Oh," Mare said, a little breathless. "Oh. Well. Well, you don't know my aunt at all. She's a real piece of work."

"I'm good with little old ladies."

Mare snorted. "Xan is not a little old lady. Xan is Vampira and Elvira, Queen of the Night and the Dragon Lady and Morticia Addams with a little bit of Jackie Kennedy thrown in to make things interesting."

"That's everybody you ever dressed up as for Halloween," Crash said, his mind flipping through images of the past, each of them hotter than the last, each of them cooling his anger considerably, along with Mare pressed up against him again.

"She's kind of a role model," Mare said. "But the important thing is, Xan would have you for lunch. She's ruthless and dangerous and Dee's probably right that I should stay away from her, but she knows things that I need to know. And she's always been very good to me."

"Her favorite little niece?" Crash grinned at her in the darkness. "I bet you were a cute kid."

"Not really," Mare said thoughtfully. "Dee was the beauty and Lizzie was the fairy child. I kind of clumped. I was the Amazon kid. I don't know why she paid the most attention to me. Maybe because I'm the youngest. The dumbest."

"You're not dumb," Crash said, surprised.

"I'm dumb compared to Dee and Liz," Mare said, sitting up straighter. "I wonder if that's it. She's the one who told me I was the Queen of the Universe. Maybe she has me marked as the weakest link."

"Weakest link in what?" The roof beneath them began to throb harder, and Crash put his hand on it, distracted. "What is that?"

"Lizzie's working." Mare began to gather up the cups. "Well, I've got another long day tomorrow . . ."

She was leaving. Without thinking, he blurted, "How about if I moved back here?"

Mare jerked back. "Here? To Salem's Fork? You just got finished telling me how much you love Italy. And your business there, everything about it. You're *happy* there."

He was a little stunned himself. "Yeah, but you're not there." Now that he'd said it, it began to seem like a possibility. "Maybe we could open an American branch. Be international."

Mare stared at him, looking hopeless. "You can't give up your life for me. *You don't know me.*"

"Well, come to Italy and we'll get to know each other again," he said, exasperated. "I'll get you a round-trip ticket. You don't like it, you can come home. What's the worst that can happen? You get a vacation in Italy." He leaned closer. "And what's the best that can happen? Us, that's what. Have you missed me at all?"

She looked at him with her heart in her eyes, and he knew that she had missed him, knew she still cared, and the last of his anger evaporated, and then the roof trembled under them, and she looked away and Crash said, "What the hell?"

"You know Lizzie," Mare said. "Something probably exploded."

She was too far away, but he'd seen the look in her eyes, so he put his arm around her, and when she sighed and put her forehead on his arm, he said, "Listen, you can go anywhere you want. I wish it was Italy, but if it's New York, you'll be amazing there, too. You can do anything, Mare. You don't need your sisters or your aunt Xan or anybody else. You really are Queen of the Universe."

She turned her face up to him and said, "I love you," and he kissed her, dizzy with wanting her, loving her, and tasted heat and hot fudge and Mare. He fell into her, felt her yield under him, needing to taste all of her, drink her in, and then she broke the kiss and pulled back, breathing fast, hot and real under his hands, inches away from him, too far away from him. He held on to her, jerking his head toward her bedroom window. "We're going to fall off this roof," he said, breathless, "how about you finally show me your room?" and Mare stiffened.

He tightened his grip on her. "Sorry, too fast—"

"The mountain," Mare said.

He stopped as thunder rolled in the distance.

"Let's go to the mountain. Like we used to." Mare stood up, pulling his hands with her, and Py stretched to his feet beside her.

The mountain again. "Mare, it was always great on the mountain, but it's going to storm—"

"Not until Sunday," she said. "Not until Beltane. And even if it does, I want to make love with you on the mountain again." She held on to him in the dark, tugging gently on his hand. "Just like we used to. I want you so much."

The wind blew her silky black hair across her face, and the moon silhouetted her, tall and round and strong in the darkness, and he wanted her anywhere, any way, always, just because she was Mare and he loved her.

"Let's go to the mountain," Crash said.

C rash's bike was beautiful, even in the dim glow of the streetlights, but then, everything about Crash was beautiful, and Mare was drunk on him.

"It's a Moto Guzzi Le Mans I," he told Mare and handed her a helmet. "A guy in Annapolis bought it from us. Put this on. And roll down your sleeves."

"Yes, sir." Mare put the helmet on and looked at the bike, trying to get her balance back. "This thing is gorgeous. Should we be riding it up the mountain?"

"Sure," Crash said, swinging his leg over it. "Test drive. I'll take it to Maryland before I leave the States." He patted the seat behind him. "Let's go."

"Okay." Mare settled in behind him, scooting so that she was pressed against him, her breasts against his back, her thighs gripping his, and the memories rushed back, the old heat bubbling in her veins, and she sighed. "No hurry. Let's take good care of this classic." She rocked her hips closer so she was pressed tight against him where she fit just right, feeling the good stuff start low.

"You want to make it all the way up the mountain, stop that," Crash said, and she laughed into the back of his jacket and tightened herself around him again, loving the way he felt against her again. Okay, she didn't have choices, but tonight she had Crash. That was a hell of a lot.

He kicked the bike into motion, and she drew a deep breath as they rode down the street, closing her eyes and smiling as the vibration made her breathe harder still. "Take Cobblestone Street," she said, and he laughed and said, "Why?" and she thought, *Cobblestones, of course,* knowing he knew why, rubbing her cheek against his back because of everything he did know about her, concentrating on the hum inside her as they rode and he turned down the streets, taking the long way, feeling it build until they hit bumpy Cobblestone Street, and she felt the heat rise and twist and thought, *yesyesyes* and began to shudder and bounce. *Don't stop*, she thought, clenching against him, *God, yes,* drawing in her breath, *yes,* sucking in energy from everywhere, drawing everything to her, and then Crash cursed and swerved and she cried out as a trash can went hurtling by them.

He slowed the bike. "*Damn* it," he said, and Mare straightened away from him, shaken, watching the trash can roll away now that she'd let go, cold with knowledge she didn't want. "You okay?"

"No," she said faintly.

"I'm going to personally go around nailing down every damn trash can in this town," he said as they turned down the road that led up to the mountain.

That's the street we were on after prom, Mare thought, trying to catch her breath. *I told him to take the cobblestones then, too. I wanted the ride.*

I pulled that trash can to us when I came. I sucked in my breath, I sucked in everything, and I pulled it to us, and we wrecked because of me and he left because of me.

Everything was my fault, it was all my fault.

She held herself away from him, trembling, all the way up the mountain, trying to tell herself that she hadn't known, that she'd always been careful when she'd had sex, always had it outside, up on the mountain under the big oak, where there was nothing but rocks too big to move so that nobody got hurt, that she'd thought the little bubbles she got on the back of the bike hadn't counted, the real thing was Crash inside her, not just her hugging him, giggling and popping on the back of the bike, she hadn't known—

My fault.

Crash turned the bike into the violet-filled meadow at the top of the hill and cut the motor, then took off his helmet and turned to her. "Are you okay?"

"Yes," she said, and took off her helmet and got off the bike, hating not touching him, hating herself for touching him. *My fault.* "No."

"I know, it was just like prom night," Crash said, getting off the bike. "Listen, if you don't want to, we don't have to—"

"It was my fault," Mare said miserably. "The accident prom night. It was my fault."

"It was an accident," Crash said, sounding confused. He put his hand on her arm. "If it was anybody's fault, it was mine. If I'd slowed better, you wouldn't have fallen off—"

"My fault." Mare put her arms around his neck, keeping her mind in check so that nothing moved anywhere. "It's my fault you left town. It's my fault—"

"*Hey.*" Crash put both arms around her and she drew in her breath as he pulled her close, the bulk of his body a comfort. "It wasn't—"

"I'm magic," Mare said, holding on to him. "I make magic. That's my secret, I'm psychokinetic, I can move things with my mind, that's why I always brought you up here, because everything up here's too heavy too move. I came on the back of the bike and when I came,

I threw that trash can, and that's why we wrecked. It was my fault."

"Uh, Mare . . ."

"No, I really can move things." Mare looked around the clearing. There was the Great Big Rock and the circle of the other Big Rocks, but they were all too big, that was the whole point of being up here, that she couldn't throw things while she was thrashing around. The wind had picked up, and the tree branches were waving, and there wasn't anything light enough for her to move that the wind wasn't already moving, everything was beyond her power. Maybe one of the helmets . . .

Crash was looking at her with sympathy in his eyes. "Look, Mare, if this is that Queen of the Universe stuff, it's okay, I believe you."

"No you don't." Mare stared at his helmet, trying to get the weight of it in her mind. She lifted it up off the seat of his bike, but then the wind scooped in under it and it toppled to the ground where Crash caught it and tied it to the seat.

"I really can," she said desperately, looking for something light enough, anything, maybe she could put a violet in his buttonhole or something, and then he put his arms around her and drew her close again.

"Look, I don't care," he said. "Because you know what? Even if you could do that stuff, even if the wreck was your fault, it would be good that it happened. I grew up. I got out of town, I learned things, I made a great life, a life I want you to be part of, I'm ready to settle down now, so it turned out all right, didn't it?"

Mare bit her lip and leaned against him. "No. No, I missed you *too much*."

"I know," he said, holding her tighter. "I missed

you, too. But now it's our time, Mare. We've earned each other."

"You don't understand," she said, but his arms were warm around her, safe, and she sighed into him, grateful to have him at least for tonight, even though she couldn't keep him, even though there'd be no tomorrow for them and she'd be lost without him again. "You've definitely earned me tonight," she whispered, and then she reached up and kissed him, hard, desperate for him, felt his arms tighten around her, remembered the way he'd felt rolling hot against her, and didn't care about anything but now. If all she had was now, that would be something. "Come on," she whispered, and pulled him with her under the massive oak.

She popped the snaps on her overalls and let them fall to her feet and Crash said, "You shouldn't do that all at once, I get dizzy," and she laughed, taking off the rest of her clothes, watching him strip, too, trying to keep the tears from starting, and then she pulled him down to the ground with her, shivering because the air was cool with the approaching storm. He was hot against her, his hands gentle on her again, and she closed her eyes, remembering him, trying to remember him forever, the taste of him and the scent, the way his skin scraped on hers, the way his mouth covered hers, the way his hips fit into her. They were made for each other, both strong and tall, and she said, "Do it hard," the way she had the first time she'd brought him up to the mountain, and he laughed the way he had then, and he said, "We'll do it every way we can," just like he had then, and she closed her eyes tight and thought, *Don't cry, he'll think it's because he's doing something wrong,* and he was doing everything so right.

"I love you," she whispered into his skin, and he whispered, "I love you, too, and God, I've missed you,

Mare," and he moved his hands over her, remembering her, touching her everywhere. She shifted against him, thinking, *Yes, you fit there,* and *Yes, that was right there,* and *Yes, I loved feeling you there,* rolling against him and shuddering as he discovered her all over again. Then she bit his earlobe and he bent to her breast, and she sucked in her breath as he worked his way down her body, and she arched under him, her eyes wide open as the oak tree moved above her, the leaves pulsing as he gently bit her stomach and moved lower, then lower still, licking into her, and she breathed with his rhythm and the oak leaves did, too, and the branches heaved as her blood pounded harder and she twisted her fingers into his thick hair. *Oh, God,* she thought, and began to rock, and the earth did, too, and so did the branches as he held her hips trapped and she felt the pressure everywhere, in her fingertips and behind her eyes and most of all *there,* until she writhed and reached up and saw the branches above her writhing, wildly, almost *snapping,* and she stopped herself just in time before they broke. *"No,"* she said, and pulled on his hair, and he looked up at her, confused.

"Make love to me," she said, breathless, and he said, "I was," and she said, "No, condom, inside me," and he reached for his pants, and she thought, *I hate having power,* and let her head fall back and looked up at the tree that at least had all its branches still in place. Heavy suckers, too. *You never did that before,* she told the tree, and realized that to keep all those branches up there and not plummeting down on them, she was going to have to fake an orgasm. With the man she loved. Who was perfectly capable of blowing her mind. Literally. And who was going to leave her on Monday.

Life sucks and so do you, she told the tree, and then he was beside her again.

"Something you want to tell me about?" he said.

"I tried," Mare said and kissed him, pulling him down to her as she licked inside his mouth. "You taste good."

"I know," he said. "That's you."

"I know. I just taste better on you." She rolled against him, and said, "Let's try the old-fashioned stuff. You know, you inside me, moving in and out."

"Old-fashioned is good," he said, and tried to roll so she was on top.

"No, real old-fashioned," she said, pulling at him so she'd be on the bottom. Missionary position. Harder to come that way. Plus, she could keep an eye on that damn oak tree.

He let her pull him over her, balancing above her on his hands, and she wriggled underneath him, wrapping her legs around him, feeling him hard between her thighs.

"You sure you're okay?" he said, and she moved her hand down his stomach and let her palm slide against him, taking him gently while he sucked in his breath.

"I'm thinking yes," she whispered, tilting her hips and guiding him to her, and then he eased himself inside, and she drew in her breath and thought, *Oh, God, I forgot how much I love him on top of me.*

He moved into her slowly, the way that always made her shudder, with his mouth on her neck, on that nerve that always made her shiver, and she looked up at the oak, checking on those branches as her eyes unfocused and thought, *Oh, Christ, there was a reason I cried for him for a year,* and lost herself in him, stroking her hands over his back as he moved inside her, tracing the lines of his muscles the way he loved as his fingers traced hers, biting the place on his shoulder that made him crazy as he whispered in her ear, tilting her hips at the angle that made him moan as he moved deeper inside her and made her gasp, loving the scent and the taste and the sight of him, drowning in the rhythm they made together, and five years fell away as if they'd been nothing, as if he'd never been away at all, except this time the throb and the heat and lust he built in her, the incredible grinding need she had for him had an ache behind it—*he's going to leave me*—and even while the flutter in her blood began to itch and then to sear, even while she clenched herself around him, arched up into him and rocked hard against him—*yesyesyesyes*—even as the oak tree waved above them like a storm, all that time she was hanging on—*don'tcrydon'tcrydon'tcry*—because it was too much to bear, he was going to leave again, *he's going to leave,* all that glory, she was never going to have it again, never again, never again, never again, she rocked with rhythm of it, and so did the ground and the tree and her blood, and her breath came quicker, little gasps as he moved in her, hard in her, never again, neveragain, neveragain, *again, again, again*—tighter and tighter and then it all broke and she cried out in his arms, and held him to her, felt him shudder against her, too, and something soft as tears rained down on her, covered her as she sobbed but didn't cry, great gulping breaths as she fought back real tears and rocked in his arms, breathing, "I love you, I love you, I love you," over and over again, trying to get her breath back, holding on to him for dear life, afraid to let him go.

"I love you, too," he said finally, when his breathing had slowed again, and then he picked something off her shoulder. "What is this?" he said and held it up.

Mare focused on it. Something blue. "A flower?" She looked up at the oak. It had bloomed, little blue flowers everywhere. *Violets.* She looked over to the meadow and saw a bare patch in the wildflowers there. *That's where my tears went. I didn't cry, I pulled the violets into the oak.*

Crash started to sit up, and she held him tighter. *"Don't leave me."*

He pulled her closer, their damp bodies sliding together, and brushed the blue petals from her hair. "I thought that was an oak tree."

"Oh, yeah, now you're a botanist," she said. *"Kiss me."*

He did, and she kissed him back and thought, *My heart is breaking,* and for once, drama queen of the universe though she was, it was true.

Xan stood in the middle of the room, silent in liquid silver silk, gripping the see glass that hung around her neck like a pendant as she tried to slow her breathing. Deep slow breaths, from the diaphragm, cleansing breaths, because if she didn't, she was going to turn Vincent into something unfortunate, and that would be too good for him.

"You've really completely lost your sense of humor, darling," Vincent said, flicking an invisible speck of dust from his satin lapel. "Jennifer meant nothing by that remark."

"I'm sure she didn't." Jennifer was such an airhead, she didn't have the concentration to mean anything by any remark. Xan opened the cupboard hidden in the silver paneling and took out a plain glass decanter of deep red wine, burgundy, like blood. *I'm in the mood for blood.*

"When she said her grandmother had known you, she didn't mean you were the same age as her grandmother," Vincent went on, his smile sly.

"Of course I'm near her grandmother's age," Xan said, taking down two goblets. "But Vincent, you're *older* than her grandmother. Her grandmother slapped you for taking liberties when she was a teenager."

Vincent's smile vanished, and Xan filled the goblets.

"Jennifer is a silly girl, but she'll get older and wiser." Xan handed him a glass. "Everybody does." She looked at Vincent's stupid, smiling face. "Well, they get older anyway."

"I don't think you quite understand," Vincent said, taking his wine.

"I understand." Xan picked up hers and leaned back against the paneling, knowing the silver background was kind to her, along with the goddamn candlelight. "You're turning into an old goat chasing much too young women who probably laugh behind your back."

Vincent sipped his wine and then checked his reflection in the silver mirror on the wall. "No, you really don't understand." He smoothed back his already smooth white hair. "Jennifer has agreed to become my wife."

Xan's hand tightened on her glass. "You proposed to that bubblehead?"

"Two days ago. I think you and I had about run our course anyway, don't you?"

There was a rushing in her ears and the room shimmered a little. *That would be the blood rush,* Xan thought. *And, of course, the rage. I'm being discarded by a moronic bastard before I could dump him. I really have to stop letting my work get in the way of my social obligations.*

"I know this comes as a shock."

"Only because I didn't get there first," Xan said and drank more wine.

"Oh, please." Vincent drained his glass and put it down on the table in front of her. "Everyone knows you're mad for me. That's why I waited until after tonight to tell you. I knew tonight was important—"

"Wait a minute." Xan straightened. "Are you telling me that everyone at the gala knew about this *except me*?"

"Well, Jennifer wanted to show people her ring."

Xan looked at his slack, arrogant face and thought, *You were this close to getting out of here alive.*

He shook his head at her, smugly with faux sympathy. "I'm afraid there's nothing else I can do for you. My future awaits."

"Sit."

"Really, Xan," he began, straightening his white tie, and then he sat down, surprised.

"I've been seeing you for exactly three weeks, Vincent," Xan said, not bothering to hide her contempt anymore, which was not only a great relief, but also a great pleasure. "During that time you were arrogant, boring, stupid, and only mildly interesting in bed."

"Well, I guess we're not taking rejection very well, are we?" Vincent said, still trying to get up.

"Vincent, nobody takes rejection well except the bottoms in S and M pacts, and even they want it their way. Even so, I would be delighted to let you go on disappointing dim-witted, barely legal Jennifer in every way it is possible for a man to disappoint a woman except for one thing: you have just humiliated me in public." She leaned forward. "That was dumb, Vincent."

"Oh, and now you're going to punish me." Vincent

waggled his fingers at her. "Big scary witch. Well, I have powers, too. So take *this*!"

He flung out his arms and nothing happened.

"You had powers, Vincent," Xan said. "Now I have them. It was the only reason I was seeing you at all. You didn't think I was sleeping with you for your wit and charm, did you?" He gaped at her and she went on. "I took your powers, Vincent. I *earned* them. Three weeks with you was like three years with anybody else."

"My powers?" Vincent looked around. "What did you do with them?"

"I put them under my pillow," Xan said, exasperated.

"You can't *do this*!" Vincent said, not smug for the first time in his life. "Do you know who I am?"

There was a rattling behind the paneling, and Xan said, "Oh, hell," and looked at Vincent. "You're a cockroach," she said to him.

"Name-calling is so middle-class," Vincent said.

"No, Vincent," Xan said. "You are a cockroach." She waved her hand and he turned into a cockroach on the table in front of her, and while he sat there stunned, she leisurely upended his empty wineglass over him. He scrabbled at the sides of it then, trapped there, the only thing human about him, his weak, pale gray eyes.

Xan sat back with her own wine as Maxine stumbled through the paneled doorway holding a frog.

"It's Jude," she screamed. "Turn him back."

"Jude," Xan said, looking at the frog. "Why am I not surprised."

"We were stealing the purple necklace just like you told us—"

"A moment, please," Xan said. "That was not 'us' I told to steal the necklace, that was you."

"I couldn't get them to give it to me, so I went and

got Jude," Maxine said, almost sobbing. "And he was *wonderful*. But then that blond guy—"

"Elric," Xan said, thinking, *Elric wouldn't have looked twice at that bubblehead Jennifer*.

"—threw him out into the yard and he was a *frog*—"

"Well, it happens," Xan said, and waved her hand.

"—and I caught him and brought him—"

Jude rose up from the silver rug, as naked and beautiful as the sunrise, and Maxine stopped talking and gaped.

"Ciao," Jude said, looking panic-stricken.

"What happened?" Xan said, unmoved.

"The middle sister," Jude said. "She hit me and I turned." He cast a nervous glance at Maxine.

"She can do that," Xan said, trying to be kind. "She doesn't have control of her powers." She waved her hand and he was dressed again. "As long as you're here, aside from *failing completely at taking the necklace*, what's happening?"

"Dee and Danny were very cozy at dinner," Maxine said, talking fast, still not taking her eyes off Jude. "Dee had two martinis, so she was very receptive."

"Martinis?"

"I did it for you, Xantippe," Maxine said, talking faster. "I knew martinis would loosen Dee up so I served them for you. They were going up the mountain the last I saw of them. And Lizzie and Eric—"

"Elric."

"—Elric were in her bedroom, so that's good, right?"

Wonderful, Xan thought bitterly, ignoring the scrabbling inside the wineglass.

"But I don't know what happened to Mare after work." Maxine looked at Jude who shrugged.

"She went home," he said. "I tried to get her to come out for a drink, but she said no."

"She must be *nuts*," Maxine said explosively.

Xan picked up the see glass and polished it with her sleeve.

"Dee," she said, and saw Dee weeping in her bedroom, and sighed. Dee was always going to be the most difficult.

"Lizzie," she said, and saw Lizzie sleeping with Elric beside her. Lizzie didn't deserve what she was getting. It wasn't fair. Just a slight miscalculation and it would no longer be a problem.

"Mare," she said, and saw Mare rise up under a dark-haired man on the mountain, flushed with passion while blue flowers rained down on her—

"*Bloody hell!*" Xan said, and rose up to glare at Jude. "What the hell have you been *doing*?"

"I don't think she likes me," he said, licking his lips.

Maxine licked hers, too.

"You listen to me," Xan said, grabbing Jude's tie and pulling him close. "You're her true love and you're letting her get seduced and confused by some blast from her past. You get down there and you give her everything she's ever wanted so she realizes that you're what fate intended for her, do you understand? *Everything she's ever wanted. Whatever she wants, she gets.*"

Xan gripped the tie tighter, trying not to panic. Everything was very finely balanced—if Mare went off with the wrong man, one Xan couldn't influence, then everything might collapse, all her careful plans, the youth and energy she so desperately needed might be denied her. She couldn't let that happen. It *could not happen*—

"I think Mare wants *him*," Maxine said, craning her neck to see into the glass where Mare was thrashing in the arms of the dark-haired lout.

"You do realize that if I have to come down there, I won't need the two of you," Xan said quietly as she let go of Jude's tie.

"We'll make it happen," Jude said, taking Maxine's arm.

"You bet," Maxine said, turning for the door and knocking over the wineglass on the table as she did.

Vincent made a break for it and hit the floor; Maxine saw him and screamed, "Cockroach!" and stepped on him; and silence filled the room.

"Ew," Maxine said, looking at the bottom of her shoe.

"Scrape that off on the Dumpster, will you?" Xan said.

"You bet, Xantippe," Maxine said.

"I'll get right on Mare," Jude promised.

"Lovely thought," Xan said and waved her hand.

A moment later she watched Maxine scrape Vincent off onto the Dumpster in Salem's Fork.

"Jennifer owes me," she told the see glass and went to bed.

CHAPTER FIVE

Lizzie moaned. She was asleep, but she could hear the sound she made—a soft sound of pleasure and protest. She didn't want to wake up—the dreams were too delicious. Sexual dreams, so powerful that she felt her body spasm in her sleep, this time so real she could have sworn she was actually being touched. And this time the phantom lover had a face, a body, the mouth of a fallen angel and the eyes of a sinner. It wasn't real, but it was wonderful, and she didn't want her sister dragging her away from such a deliciously sinful fantasy. Some distant part of her brain could hear Dee in the front room, and the noise filtering into her subconscious.

But she pushed the noise away, snuggling deeper into the bed, into the silky sheets, into the arms of the man who touched her . . .

Her eyes flew open. He was asleep beside her, and her head had been resting on his shoulder, his arm draped loosely around her. The covers were pulled up to his waist, but from what she could see he was naked.

They weren't her sheets. Instead of the percale with the tiny flowers, her bed was now covered with sheets that were either silk or a cotton of such an astronomical thread count that it might as well be, and the color was deep, rich purple. The color she never wore, the color that she secretly loved. She moved slowly away from him, so as not to awaken him, and sat up in the bed, looking down at him in shock and awe.

Asleep, he couldn't cloud her perceptions, and she could see him quite clearly. He was beautiful—there was no other word for it, a beauty so classic that it shocked her. He looked younger than she'd thought— her age or even younger still, and yet curiously ageless, and his body was strong, lean, with smooth, golden skin. His dark blond hair lay rumpled against the deep purple sheets, and she reached out a hand to touch him, then pulled it back.

She looked down at her own body, and just barely managed to stifle a gasp. She was wearing the purple silk nightgown she'd conjured up the night before. It made her pale skin glow, and it draped her body, clinging to her slight curves, and she must have made a sound after all, a tiny squeak of distress.

He opened his eyes, and she could see a rim of purple around his irises, something she hadn't noticed before. He didn't move, but his voice was low and just slightly amused. "Don't panic," he said. "I didn't touch you."

Then why did her body still vibrate with remembered pleasure? Why did her skin feel hot and shivery at the same time?

The tapping on her door made her jump, and for once Dee didn't wait for a reply. She opened the door, and said, "Lizzie, did you—" and then stopped, her mouth open, and Lizzie waited for the shit to hit the fan.

"Good Lord, Lizzie, where did you get that night-gown?" Dee said, a fairly minor question considering there was a naked man in her bed.

Lizzie glanced down at Elric, who'd rolled on his side to look at her, a faint smile on his mouth as he tugged at the hem of the silk nightgown. "I know this is upsetting for you but . . ." she said lamely.

"Why would your choice of nightgown upset me?" Dee said.

Lizzie gave Elric another confused look, but he simply smiled and shrugged, saying nothing, although his hand was touching her foot beneath the silk, and she could feel the tremor of response dance across her skin. And then she felt a flash of relief. Dee couldn't see Elric lying in her sister's bed. As far as she could tell, Lizzie was simply sitting alone in an inappropriate nightgown.

"It's time to talk about Xan," Dee said.

"Xan?" Lizzie echoed absently. Why was he touching her when he knew there was nothing she could do about it? She couldn't respond as some dark, secret part of her wanted to, she couldn't slap him away without Dee noticing. All she could do was sit there and shiver in delicious anticipation.

"Did you see her? You shivered. You saw her."

"No, no," Lizzie said.

"Well, come out for breakfast," Dee said. "It's time for the vote."

"We voted yesterday," she protested.

"Somebody told Xan we're here, and we need to get the heck out of Dodge."

Instinctively Lizzie glanced down at the man in her bed. His hand froze, his beautiful face an unreadable mask, and she knew who had betrayed them.

She scrambled out of bed, jerking the quilt with her to wrap around her. Elric lay back under the sheet.

"It's okay, Lizzie," Dee said. "Just get dressed, and we can decide what we're going to do. Not that there's much to decide, apart from which piece of jewelry . . ." Dee's eyes widened. "What are you wearing? What's that around your neck?"

Lizzie had forgotten all about the Borgia pendant that Elric had placed around her neck just before he'd kissed her. It lay between her breasts, a comforting weight against her heart, and she knew it belonged there.

Just as a beautiful, treacherous creature like Elric belonged in her bed. She was going out of her mind— she must be. She started to pull off the pendant, but he sat up, reaching out and covering her hand, stopping her.

"Liz, what's going on?" Dee said.

Lizzie shook her head. "I'll be out in a minute—we can talk about it then."

Dee looked surprised and not pleased, but she shut the door, and Lizzie flinched automatically before realizing that she wasn't feeling her usual emotions of dread and disaster. She was going to leave the room, and Dee and Mare were going to fight, and then there'd be shoes and bunnies and wildlife everywhere.

But right now the only wildlife in the room was in her bed, watching her warily.

"Xan sent you," she said.

He seemed totally unmoved by her accusation. "I was planning on coming here anyway—she just pointed me in the right direction. Someone needed to stop you from making such a mess of things."

She had no words for him, none that she was comfortable using. Mare could have told him off—Lizzie just wanted to cry.

She wasn't going to let that happen, not in front of him. Nor was she going to strip off her clothes so he could watch. She grabbed her discarded clothes without another word and disappeared into the workroom, tripping over a new pair of shoes. High-heeled sandals with gold coins dripping off the ankle band—both tacky and charming. She didn't bother to look too closely—if the coins were real gold and she'd somehow managed to transmute something into the precious stuff, she didn't want to know. She was too overwhelmed.

When she came back through the bedroom he was nowhere in sight. It was only a small relief—he wasn't gone forever. The bed was made, the deep purple sheets smooth and inviting. He should have changed them back, but then, Dee had probably seen them, even if she hadn't seen the naked man lying beneath them. She could feel the pendant against her skin, even through the layers of clothing, and its slow pulse calmed her. Calmed her enough to face the calamity her life had become overnight.

When Lizzie walked into the dining room, Mare was sitting at the end of the table with Pywackt in her lap and a cup of coffee cradled in her hands, looking like her last friend had just died. She looked up when Lizzie sat down. "So who's this Elric? I'm all for him, I'm just curious. The roof over your workroom was practically bouncing last night."

"I don't want to talk about it," Lizzie said. There was just the hint of defiance in her voice, and she hoped neither of her sisters would notice that the sweet little peacekeeper was developing a backbone.

It was a vain hope. "You sure you're okay, Lizzie?" Dee said, coming in from the kitchen, coffee mug in hand. "It's not like you to sleep late. And why did you take the Borgia pendant from the jewelry case?"

Lizzie took a deep breath to steady herself, answering the easy part. "The jewelry belongs to the three of us, and this particular piece belongs to me."

Dee looked as if one of Lizzie's bunnies had turned around and bitten her. "I'm pretty sure that needs to be the next piece to go—"

"It's not going anywhere," Lizzie said. "It's mine."

"Lizzie, do you know how much that piece is worth?" Dee said.

"I don't care. You can do what you want with the rest of the stuff—I don't need any of it. I can take care of myself. I should have had this years ago—it was supposed to be mine." There was something about Dee's distracted behavior that alerted her. "It was, wasn't it?"

Dee sighed. "Honey, it was in mother's jewelry box—"

"But it was supposed to go to me."

Dee rubbed her forehead. "Xan said you should have it, but as far as I knew, it was a trick, maybe some way to track us."

"That's fair," Mare said, watching both of them with melancholy interest. "But you should have told us what Xan said."

Lizzie nodded. "Or if it's dangerous, you should have gotten rid of it years ago."

Dee sat back, clearly upset. "I tried. I even threw it in the Pacific Ocean one year. It just kept ending up back in the jewelry box."

"Well, if that's where it's supposed to be, then it

will be there." Lizzie sat at the opposite end of the table. "Somebody tried to steal it yesterday, too, and that didn't work, either. Maxine even tried to take it for some fund, but it's still with me. It belongs with me."

"Maxine was collecting for charity?" Mare said. "What is the world coming to? But the signs are clear. The amethyst belongs to Liz."

Lizzie looked at Dee. "Are you going to call the meeting to order?"

Dee looked uncertain. It wasn't an expression Lizzie was used to seeing on her practical older sister's face, as if Dee's entire universe had shifted unexpectedly. Just as Lizzie's had.

"Let me just get the jewelry box . . ." Dee said.

"Dee, don't bother," Mare said tiredly. "It's a waste of time. Just call the vote and get it over with."

Dee sat down. "Well, Xan has found us. I'm afraid it's time to leave. I'm sorry but I vote yes, we go."

Mare nodded, all fight gone. "As long as I'm in Salem's Fork, I'll never get over Crash. I vote yes, we go."

Dee looked over at her. "No Italy?" she asked gently.

"Nope."

Dee patted her hand. "Lizzie?"

They both turned to look at her, only a formality, since sweet, spacey Lizzie avoided conflict like the plague.

But sweet, spacey Lizzie had changed. She felt the amethyst throb against her heart, and she lifted her head to look at them squarely.

"I vote no."

Lizzie could feel her sisters' amazement, but she wasn't about to back down. "I'm tired of running," she said.

"I'm not a frightened child anymore. I like it here, and I'm not going to let anyone drive me away."

Mare blinked at her. "Lizzie?"

Lizzie stared back at her, implacable.

Mare looked at Dee. "We're not leaving Lizzie."

"Listen to me," Dee said to Lizzie. "We cannot stay here. We don't even have a plan!"

"Then we'll come up with one," Lizzie said, and her voice didn't waver.

Mare tilted her head at Lizzie. "Something's new."

Dee put her hands on the table. "You're damn right something's new. We're in danger. There's something about this time that's different. Worse."

Lizzie folded her arms, unmoving.

Dee took a deep breath. "Okay, we're not leaving. Let's think this through. Xan sent Danny James, and we know she deals in men and sex so he's probably not the only one. Who else is new in town besides Danny?"

Mare put her chin in her hand. "Jude the VP from Value Video!! I already have my suspicions about him, but he's dumb as pond scum, so I don't see him as a major threat. And Crash, but I can't see Crash and Xan plotting together. She'd hate the motorcycle."

Lizzie felt Dee's bright green eyes turn in her direction. "Lizzie?"

She couldn't lie about Elric. Not now, not to her sisters. But she had no intention of sitting there and having them pepper her with a thousand questions about him, particularly when she had no answers, particularly after she'd just called the shots in her family for the first time in twenty-six years, something that would have made her giddy with power if the responsibility hadn't been so terrifying.

"What about Charles?" Dee said.

"It can't be Charles," Mare said. "He's gone."

"Gone?" Lizzie echoed, astonished.

"Pauline said he decided to move to Alaska. Quit his job yesterday afternoon and took off. And nobody has missed him."

"Well, hallelujah," Dee muttered into her coffee cup.

Lizzie knew who she could thank for Charles's unexpected disappearance. One more thing her mysterious visitor would have to answer for. Who the hell did he think he was, sending the man she loved . . . no, she didn't really love him, but the man she was going to marry . . . no, she wasn't going to marry him, either. And this way she didn't have to tell Charles anything, which was a blessing. He'd dumped her for a magic spell and Alaska.

"Maybe we need to talk about Elric," Mare said, with her usual tact.

"Who the heck is Elric?" Dee said.

Lizzie stood up. "Someone I need to have a little talk with. And that's all I'm saying. You two should probably talk to your . . . whatever they are. And don't overlook Crash—there's more to him than you might expect. We could come back, pool our information, and see what we can come up with. Find a way to fight back."

"Fight back?" Mare said, interested. "You're going to fight back? Go, Lizzie!"

"But—" Dee said, for the first time outmaneuvered by her younger sisters.

"It's a plan, Dee," Lizzie said firmly. "We'll meet for lunch and compare notes."

"I'll ask Crash why he picked now to come to Salem's Fork," Mare said as she stood up. "And I will beat some answers out of that little toad Jude, but then

I'm taking an early lunch break at Mother's Tattoos.
I'll meet you there."

She headed for the stairs and Dee called after her,
"You get any more tattoos, you're gonna look like a
biker!"

"What's wrong with bikers?" Lizzie said.

Dee didn't look happy. "I guess I'm going to find
out. Where are you going?"

"I'm staying put."

"But you haven't told me about this Elric person . . ."

"He'll come to me," Lizzie said in a dangerous
voice. "And he's going to wish he hadn't."

*No shoes. No bunnies, ferrets, or wisps of purple
fog,* she thought, heading back to her supposedly deserted bedroom. Just one extremely pissed-off Miss
Fortune, about to find out what the hell was going on.
And maybe see whether she'd gotten good enough to
turn a wizard into a frog.

They were staying. Dee should have been terrified.
She should have been grabbing her sisters by
whatever body part she could reach and dragging
their asses out the front door so fast they left a dust
cloud. And oh, yeah. She was terrified. She knew better than anyone just what they were up against. The
truth? Xan could crunch them like cockroaches. And
she didn't even have to show up to do it.

But, God. Dee'd been wanting to face off with that
pernicious bitch as long as she could remember. She'd

had the girls to think of, though. She'd had her mother looking at her with those big Lizzie eyes of hers, begging Dee to protect them.

Seemed she didn't have to anymore. At least not alone. So no matter what, it was time to put on her big-girl panties and get on with it. For a second, Dee actually managed a smile. She damn near giggled. Until she remembered just what she had to do to get to that face-off.

She'd thought she'd never have to see him again. That as bad as last night had been, she could be safely away long before he came to demand explanations. She should have known better. Ever since Danny James had knocked on their door, nothing had gone the way it should.

Yanking on her gray cardigan and grabbing her purse off the table, she turned for the door. "All right, then," she said with forced bravado, "let's get this over with."

She should have known. She threw the door open, ready to march out like Carrie Nation in search of a saloon, only to be stopped dead in her tracks.

"Oh, good," he said, standing on her porch in his white T-shirt and bomber jacket and jeans. "I hoped you'd be home."

Dee knew she was probably goggling at him. But what did you say to the most handsome man in the world, whom you'd run from the night before? *Sorry. I wasn't sure how well you liked your mother*? No. Too much to explain. *It was better this way*? Not that, either. Dee decided she wasn't the *Casablanca* type.

"Yes," was all she could come up with. "Here I am."

She couldn't take her eyes off him. Those wonderful, water-clear eyes, that chiseled chin and the glint of silver above his T-shirt. The easy, comfortable-with-myself, happy-to-see-you stance that made people smile and set her palms to sweating. She couldn't breathe again. She could never seem to breathe around him.

She'd run from him last night. She'd have to do it again soon or lose her mind altogether. But not right now. Now she had a mission. Yeah. That's all it was. A mission for her sisters.

He was smiling. Of course he was. "May I come in?"

Dee blanked. "Uh, no."

He looked over her shoulder, as if expecting a parent with a shotgun. "Well, can you come out?"

She fortified herself with a breath. "Why, yes," she said, closing the door behind her. "I can. I need to talk to you."

"Funny. I was just about to say that very thing."

Dee tried to smile, but she knew it looked stupid. She swore her heart could be heard down the block, it was beating so hard. And it was fragile enough right now that she feared serious injury. "Um, there's a garden bench in the back."

"Perfect," he said. "I love sitting in a jungle on a nice day."

They did have to wade through a veritable sea of rhododendrons, wisteria, and lilac to get to a bench, and Dee caught sight of Pywackt prowling in the shadows like the predator he was. But the garden was out of sight of the street. On the other hand, she'd be isolated with Danny James where every sharp memory from the night before would hover between them. What a choice.

Dee was about to sit down on the cedar bench when Danny held her back. Dee jumped at his touch. Hot, sharp, sweet. God, she was going to have to get what she needed from him and run like a coward. She looked over at him, but he just held up a hand. Then, pulling a handkerchief, of all things, from his back pocket, he bent to wipe the fallen petals and pollen from the bench. Dee's breath simply left her body.

He turned, held out his hand, guided her to her seat. Dee couldn't take her eyes from him. It was such a simple thing, a gift of courtesy. But it made her want to cry. Nobody ever thought to do for Dee O'Brien. Dee knew it was because of the face she put on, that she was in charge, in control. But Danny had done this little thing anyway, and that perilously fragile heart that had been in such danger simply failed.

Oh, she thought, gazing up at him like a besotted girl as he settled in next to her. She could so fall in love with him.

Then he sat down himself. "I have a message from your aunt."

Well, so much for fantasies.

"Pardon?"

He pulled out his keys and started playing with them, a sure sign of discomfort. *Oh, no. Oh, no, no.* Her poor, sore heart.

"I talked to her."

Dee pulled herself up, as if posture were protection. "I gathered that."

He nodded, still not facing her. "I know you think she's—"

"The spawn of Satan? The inspiration for every succubus in history?"

That got a grin out of him. "I really wish you had an opinion on anything, Dee."

Oh, don't be charming. That makes it worse.

"What did she say?"

He was at the keys again, so that they jangled. He kept that up, he'd end up with Pywackt in his face.

"Your aunt wants to meet with you."

Worse and worse. "I bet she does. And when does she get in from Santa Fe?"

"Uh . . ." Danny James couldn't seem to keep a secret to save his life.

Dee lurched to her feet. "Oh, my God. You've seen her."

"Well, yeah. She's at the Lighthorse."

Dee didn't say another word. Shoving wisteria aside like an advancing defensive line, she turned and stalked off. She didn't even get past the front gate before Danny caught up with her.

"I really wish you'd stop doing that," he said, trying to hold her back.

She batted his hand away. "I have to see my aunt."

Danny took her arm. "Well, that was the point of the visit. But she wants to see all three of you."

Dee tried to pull away, and found that she couldn't fight hard enough. Suddenly the smell of lilac was cloying, and she hated it. "No," she said. "She sees me or she sees no one."

And if she did, Dee could save them all a lot of time and grief and just rip her eyes out and feed them to her on a plate.

"Let me give you a ride down there," Danny suggested. "It'll be faster."

That took the starch out of her. He was trying to protect her, to help her, and it hurt. Because for the first time in her life, that was what she wanted.

So he could take her to Xan, whom he'd seen.

"Dee? Honey, you okay?"

Dee just nodded, her eyes closed. God, how could she smell him over the overwhelming scent of wisteria and lilac? She did, though, a bracing hint of wind and the sea in this claustrophobic little garden. That awful temptation of freedom and flight. He still had her by the arm, but his hold was gentle. It made Dee want to cry all over again.

"Before we go," he was saying, "I really need to know something." Dee didn't move. Danny hesitated. "Last night . . ."

Oh, no. Not last night. Not when she had to fortify herself for Xan.

"Did I hurt you?"

Dee's eyes snapped open. "What?"

His eyes were soft and uncertain. Vulnerable. As if he'd thought what had happened had been somehow his fault.

"You're the bravest woman I know," he said. "Good God, Dee, you've raised your sisters alone since you were sixteen. I just couldn't imagine you running unless I'd done something terrible. I wanted to follow you, but . . . I stood outside your house for hours. I saw your sister's friend show up and almost knocked then . . ."

Well, this certainly was the end. Dee was as lost as a romance heroine. How could she not love Danny James?

"Oh, Danny," she said, unable to resist the urge to cup that strong face in her hand. "How could you think you could ever hurt anybody?"

"Then you . . ."

The wind caught the flowers and sent some of them spinning, a shower of purple and magenta that rained around them like fireworks. "The problem is mine," she said. "I'm so sorry. I would never want to make you feel responsible."

"You promise."

Tears she allowed for no one pooled in her eyes. "On my honor. And the girls can tell you I'm tough on that kind of stuff."

He took her hand in both of his and raised it for a kiss. "I've never met anybody like you, Deirdre Dolores O'Brien."

He'd met Xan. Dee came so close to asking him if she was more. More beautiful, more compelling, more everything a good man wanted.

"You sure you want to go see her?" he asked, again echoing her thoughts.

"Yeah. But I have a question for you first." She found herself holding tight to those work-roughened hands, really afraid now. "Who was she?"

"Pardon?"

Had the wind died? It sounded so suddenly still, as if breath were being held.

"How would you describe her? Sophia Loren? Susan Sarandon?"

He considered, her hand still captive. "Delilah."

And Dee had thought she'd lost the capacity for surprise. "Delilah?"

He grinned. "I see what you mean about how she gets people to do what she wants. But there's something . . . sad about her. Empty, I guess."

Dee couldn't move. She couldn't look away from him. How do you answer a statement like that? He was wrong, of course. Xan wasn't sad. She was evil. But she *was* empty. Just a shell fabricated from manipulation and cupidity.

"Do you trust me?" she asked.

It was his turn to reach out, running his fingers down her cheek. "Yeah, oddly enough. I seem to have a taste for sharp-tongued shrews."

Dee stiffened, until she saw that sly gleam in his

eyes. "Nobody's called me that and lived to tell the tale, mister."

"But I *like* sharp-tongued shrews. Or weren't you listening?"

She wasn't breathing. The wind must have risen, because she swore she had dust in her eyes. And the dust carried that brief, bright sight of Danny James smiling at her. At *her*. She ached to live that moment, even knowing that by facing off with Xan she was probably tossing out her last chance for it.

There will be disaster.

She hadn't hurt this hard since she'd shoved her sisters onto a bus at three A.M. and made off with them and her mother's jewels.

"Well," she said, as if it were all a game, "this sharp-tongued shrew needs to see her aunt. You wanna come?"

"I wouldn't be anywhere else."

Dee climbed on the bike, much easier in jeans and sweater, and wrapped her arms around Danny. Beyond the trees, the sky had gone sulky again, and the burgeoning foliage hung limp. The air was thick as molasses, with that faint promise of lightning and rain. A storm, huh? She'd sure give Xan a storm.

"I don't understand," Danny said five minutes later as they stood with Verna on the porch of the Lighthorse. "She was in room 2A this morning. I know."

"No, dear," the little woman protested. "We've had that room closed for redecoration. You're sure it wasn't a dream?"

"No. She was wearing a white dress, and . . ."

White. Ah, Xan, such delusions. Dee grabbed Danny by the arm and steered him for the steps. "Jet lag," she said brightly. "Thanks, Verna."

Danny turned on her. "But I saw her."

"I know you did. Now, we're going to find out where she's gone to ground and take her out before she wreaks havoc."

Two feet from his bike, he stopped and turned on her. "Dee, she's only a woman. Just let her go. I mean, what can she really do to you?"

Dee looked up at that dear, honest face and struggled again with the truth. She had no choice, now. She had to at least try to make him understand, no matter that it would send him screaming for the hills by sundown. Oh, well, he would have run screaming eventually anyway. Why not get it over with?

"No, Danny," she said, holding on to his hand. "She's not only a woman. She's far more powerful than that."

"Now, Dee . . ." He was already trying to turn away. She couldn't let him. Not anymore.

"She killed my parents, Danny."

He froze. "You said they died of hypothermia."

"I lied." She shook her head, so frustrated with what she knew, what she realized he wouldn't want to hear. Hell, *Mare* didn't want to hear it. "The official report was hypothermia. It matched the findings. Cold. They were so cold . . ." Like wax dolls tossed aside by an impatient child. She thought she'd never get warm again after holding her mother. "I found Xan bent over them and I screamed and everybody came running, but there was nothing they could do. She convinced the authorities that she'd been trying to save them, but I know better. I don't know how she did it, but she . . ." Dee laughed, knowing perfectly well how outrageous her words sounded. Even so, she straightened and faced Danny. "Somehow I think she sucked the life out of them."

"You can't believe that."

"And now she's come after us."

Danny stiffened like an outraged minister. "Now, Dee . . ."

There was nothing for it. She had to show him. "Come on," she said. "We're going someplace to really talk."

She directed him to a nondescript field at the north edge of town, where Old Church Street crossed a vague path that had once been an Indian track. Weeds littered the vacant lot nobody liked to use, and a straggly cottonwood struggled to leaf. The sky seemed darker of a sudden, the clouds full-bellied and the breeze fetid. Dee hated this place. She walked Danny straight up to it and stood him in the center, right where the paths crossed.

"What?" he asked, looking around. "Is she here?"

"What do you hear?" she asked, standing carefully away.

Danny shoved his hands in his jacket pockets. He opened his mouth. He shook his head as if to clear it.

"Screams."

He tried to walk away, but Dee grabbed him. "What else?"

"This is—"

"What else, Danny?"

"Jeering. Shouts. And those . . . *screams*." He'd lost some of his color, and his eyes looked stark. Dee knew.

"You know those witches who danced on the mountain?" she asked, her voice gentle, her hand holding him still.

"Of course."

"This is where they were burned."

Danny gaped like a landed fish. He threw off her

hand as if it scalded him and stalked over to his bike. "That's ridiculous."

Dee didn't move. "There *is* power out there, Danny. My mother had a great amount of it. My father didn't have so much, but Xan made him believe he did. Xan can make you believe anything. She impressed you so much with her whispers you named your damn bike after her without ever even meeting her. She whispers, and what she whispers is believed. My sisters and I have power, and I think she wants it."

"Don't be—"

"Ridiculous? Xan wasn't there this morning, Danny. Not in the room. But she made you see her. And believe her." Dee smiled, shaking her head. "Although it seems she couldn't do a complete job of it. She'll use you to get to us. And then she'll try and sap our power to strengthen hers. She's a predator. A carnivore. A psychic vampire."

"There are no—"

"Psychics? Yes there are. And you'd better start believing it, because you are one."

For the first time she saw Danny James truly angry. "Oh, yeah, that's what they told my mother. Every goddamn one of them. 'Just believe. There is great power, and I have it. I'm a psychic. I can tell you . . . I can—' "

Dee thought her heart would break. " 'Communicate with your husband.' It was your mother who fell prey to the con artists."

"And they took every dime she had. It's bullshit, Dee, and the sooner you get that through your head the sooner you might join the real world again and stop jumping at phantasms. That woman you're so afraid of is nothing more than a standard-issue drama queen."

She kept her voice so gentle. "And the voices you just heard in your head?"

"My imagination! I told you. It's very good."

"Danny, if you'd just listen . . ."

And then Danny James did the first rude thing Dee had seen. He simply turned away from her and climbed on his bike. "No," he said, kicking it into gear. "I won't."

And then, as she stood alone in a bare field that rustled with an incoming storm, he left.

A re you just going to let him go?" Dee heard from behind her.

She didn't even bother to turn. She knew that voice. It had haunted her nightmares for years.

"Hello, Xan," she said, hoping her voice didn't betray her. She suddenly felt like she was twelve again. "I was wondering when you'd show up."

Right there in the middle of the Burning Field. How appropriate.

"Darling, aren't you even going to look at me?"

Dee couldn't see Danny anymore. The sound of his bike had faded into traffic noise. All that was left was Xan. "I don't look at snakes."

For a moment there was silence, then a sigh. "Oh, Dee."

Dee had to turn around. She had to face her worst nightmare, or she was never going to get past it. She just hoped Xan couldn't see how shaken she was.

Ready or not . . .

Xan didn't look a day different. Elegant and sleek, her thick raven hair caught in an effortless chignon, her maroon suit a Chanel, her ears hung with chunky gold earrings that gleamed in the sullen light. She looked as if she'd just stepped out of a salon on Madison Avenue—or from backstage at the *Fortune Hour of Psychic Power*. Dee wanted to run. She wanted to fight. She wanted, God help her, for her aunt to approve of her.

"A little overdressed for the occasion, aren't you?" she said instead.

Xan held out her perfectly manicured hands with their bloodred nails, and all Dee could think of was talons. "Style is never out of place." She smiled. "You look lovely as ever. Always appropriate."

Tilting her head, Dee motioned to the severe lines of her aunt's attire. "Is that how you think I see myself? Appropriate? Like you?" She shook her head. "I need to toss out some gray suits."

Oddly enough, Xan looked as if she were amused. "I should have looked harder for you. I'm going to enjoy getting to know you again."

"Don't put yourself out," Dee said. "And now, if you don't mind, I have things to do." *People to warn, pitchforks and torches to collect . . .*

Pretending she felt nothing but disinterest no matter how hard her heart was beating, Dee turned and walked away.

"You're not going to make this easy, are you?" Xan asked.

"Any reason I should?" Xan didn't need to know that her palms were sweating.

"You really have nothing to say to me, Deirdre?"

Dee stopped, her focus firmly on the steeple of the

Third Baptist Church that thrust through the trees down the block. "Besides 'you two-faced, venomous murdering bitch,' no. I really don't."

"You don't want to know why I'm here?"

"Nope."

God, she could *hear* Xan smiling behind her. "Believe it or not, I've come to tell you that you won."

Okay, that got Dee to turn around, if only to gauge the look on Xan's face. "It wasn't a game," she said.

Xan took a step toward her. The grass didn't even seem to bend beneath her. "No," she said. "It wasn't. It was a sincere difference of opinion. You never understood that I would never have hurt you, and I couldn't believe you would shatter your family the way you did. But I can't discount the fact that you did keep your sisters safe all these years. You did a good job, Dee. They're exceptional women."

Dee couldn't even find the breath to answer. How did she do it? How, after all these years, did she know just where Dee's weakness was? She was saying everything Dee had yearned to hear all these years, in those moments when she felt small and selfish and put-upon. Just to have one person appreciate what she'd done.

And it had to be Xan. Damn, damn, *damn*.

"They are," Dee said. "And without you."

"And whether you believe it or not, I want to say thank you. I love them, too." Xan considered her a minute, obviously gauging back. "I'm not going to insult your intelligence by trying to convince you there was never any animosity between the two of us, Dee. You do have a legitimate case against my behavior all those years ago."

Dee couldn't move, mesmerized. "You mean the part about your murdering my parents?"

Xan waved an elegant hand, as if discounting bad

grammar. "No, dear. I didn't murder anyone. They simply didn't have the stamina for what they asked. They wanted their powers gone. They had misused them and thought it would be an appropriate penance. I . . . obliged them."

"And they died."

"Well . . ." Xan sighed, actually frowning. "Yes. I'm afraid I wasn't as proficient then. I couldn't pull away in time. They surprised me. I learned a terrible lesson that day."

"Yes. How to cover up a crime."

"The verdict was death by accident, Deirdre." Her voice was so gentle, so understanding. Dee wanted to break something. "And it was just that. I'm sorry. And I hope you'll be able to accept my gift in the spirit it was intended, as a gesture of reconciliation."

"Gift?" Dee demanded. "Like a fruit basket?"

She got Xan to smile again. "If you're getting fruit baskets that are nearly as delicious as Danny James, I need to stop in for the holidays more often." She looked down the street in the direction Danny James had just disappeared. "I looked all over the world for him. I wanted to find someone who would help you free yourself from all your responsibilities, and every search led to Danny James. He's your true love, Dee."

Again, a thrust straight through the heart. "He can't be. He doesn't even believe in what we are."

Xan actually looked a bit regretful. "I know. I didn't realize that until I saw him here with you. I talked to him this morning, but I just don't think that's going to change. He's been too hurt."

"Then how can he be . . . ?"

"Your true love?" Xan shrugged, looking disconcerted. "Truly? I don't know. I just know that this chance comes along once in a lifetime, and that you can't throw him away."

Dee wanted to close her eyes, to stick her fingers in her ears. God, Xan was good. Satan in Chanel.

She shoved her hands in her pockets. "Why should I listen to a word you say?"

"Because you know I'm telling the truth."

"A lovely thought. But what if I feel I can't accept such a generous gift?"

Xan walked right up to her. "Do you really want to find yourself my age and all alone?"

"Like you?"

Xan's eyes sparked red, betraying her frustration. She looked away a second, and then faced Dee head-on. "Yes. Like me. I chose power, Dee. It's too late for me to change that. It's not too late for you." Dee could smell the cinnamon and sulfur that was Xan's power signature. It made Dee want to sneeze. Even so, she couldn't look away from those mesmerizing black eyes.

"Why am I seeing a Trojan horse in my head?" she asked.

Xan laughed and shook her head. "You don't have to trust me. Go to him and you'll know. I'm just hoping you don't throw away the best thing that ever happened to you because I brought him to you. I hope you know just what he's worth."

"Because he's my true love."

"*Yes.*" Xan took Dee's hand before she could stop her, twining their fingers together until Dee could feel the warmth of Xan's skin. "Get out of this town, Dee. Go travel the world and find out who Danny James is. Love him. Have babies with him. And if you have to compromise to get him, you should. I promise you, there isn't anything too great to sacrifice for this chance."

Dee was shaken to her toes. She'd never heard Xan sound so sincere. So passionate about anything. She'd never seen ghosts of any kind in her aunt's eyes. She saw them now. She felt such warmth spread through her, as if Xan had poured it from her fingers.

Xan straightened, retrieved her hand. Dee stumbled, suddenly off balance and shivery.

"It would be nice to reestablish a relationship with my nieces," Xan said. "After you think about this, after you decide what you want to do about Danny, let me know. I'll help any way I can. I've spent the last long years making sure I learned how. Correctly, so I can't hurt anyone else."

And just like that, Dee was alone once again with nothing but a sense of sudden cold and the growing suspicion that for once in her life, Xan had told the truth.

Elric really was gone. Lizzie couldn't believe it—when she went through her deserted bedroom back into the workshop, there was no sign of him. She'd assumed he'd just been masking his presence, and she closed her eyes and tried to sense him, tried to conjure up the flowing colors he seemed to emanate, but the air was flat and still. She looked down, and she was barefoot. How odd—even when she didn't deliberately put shoes on, she always ended up with something interesting on her feet. But ever since she took her shoes off last night, she'd stayed barefoot.

Never in her life had she gone against her sisters' will—she was the peacemaker, the problem solver, the one to figure out something that would make everyone happy, or at least marginally satisfied. She'd automatically stepped into the middle of the array he'd drawn on the floor the night before, and she could practically feel him around her, hear his voice in her ear. The rat bastard. He'd told Xan where they were. For all his "oh, I'll help you," he'd turned around and given them up. He'd lied and betrayed them. Not only that, but he'd sent her fiancé off to the ends of the earth, and probably given him amnesia, as well, at least as far as she was concerned.

Bastard. All that shimmering charm was nothing but a charade, just like her father's facile charisma, and beneath it—

"Stop thinking so hard."

She whirled around. He was standing in the entrance to her workshop, as if he thought he'd be welcome. He'd changed his clothes—whether he'd literally changed what he'd been wearing into something new or had somehow found a new set of clothes, she didn't know and she didn't care.

"You son of a bitch," she said.

He seemed undisturbed by her greeting. "Don't overreact. I'm not the only one who's arrived in this godforsaken little town. If I hadn't told her, somebody else would have."

"Who else has she sent?"

"Didn't you listen to your sisters? Xantippe understands people far too well—she sent exactly the sort of men who'd most distract your sisters. Their soul mates."

"Is that what you're supposed to be? My soul mate?"

For some reason his laugh sounded slightly hollow. "I think Xantippe thought you wouldn't be interested in sex. I was simply going to distract you until she arrived."

"Why you?"

"I offered. I came to her in the first place—Xantippe always knows things, and I thought if anyone knew what was upsetting the flow, then she would. She told me it was you."

"And sent you to stop me."

"I told you, I offered. I have no idea what she wants with you, and I don't really care. I just wanted to stop you from wreaking havoc."

"And how did getting rid of my fiancé serve that purpose?"

He didn't look the slightest bit guilty. "He was the wrong man for you, and you knew it. I just saved you the trouble of dumping him."

"Why, how thoughtful," she said, acidly polite. "So if you were so determined to stop me, why did you teach me things? And don't pretend that you didn't—I already feel different. I'm more focused. More powerful."

"I was afraid of that," he said, not sounding particularly pleased. "You're a fast learner. And you're going to need to know these things sooner or later, I thought I might as well start your education."

"Why bother? Why didn't you just seduce me to shut me up?"

He looked startled. The violet ring around his pupils seemed to have widened, a dark, smoky look that made her think of long nights and purple silk. "Would it have been that easy?"

"Would it have been that hard? You assured me you were very good in bed. Wouldn't it have been simpler to distract me with sex? Unless, of course, you don't want—"

"Don't even go there." His voice was low, dangerous.

"Go where?"

"You know what I'm talking about."

The last twenty-four hours had been a mass of simmering emotions and frustrations, feelings she couldn't even begin to understand, and suddenly she cracked, the last of her nervousness vanishing. She turned on him, coming right up to him as he filled her doorway. "I don't know what you're talking about. I don't know why you stayed once you found us, I don't know why you decided to teach me things, why you sent Charles away, I don't know why you have such a crazy effect on me."

"Sure you do," he said, sliding his hand behind her neck, pulling her face up to his. "You know too damned well."

This time she was prepared. He was going to kiss her, and she steeled herself, determined not to respond. Why should she respond? she thought. She didn't like him, she'd just been engaged to another man, and besides, she didn't really like kissing . . .

"Maybe you just haven't been kissed by the right man," he murmured.

She jerked away. "You can't read minds!" If he'd been reading her mind for the last twenty-four hours she was in deep shit.

"Can't I?" He seemed no more perturbed than if one of her magicked bunnies had hopped out of his reach. "Normally I can't. But every now and then I get a glimpse of what's going on in your tortured little brain, and it terrifies me."

"Nothing terrifies you," she said. "What is it you

want from me? You've done your job, Xan's coming. Why are you still here?"

He shoved his dark blond hair away from his face, the silver earring gleaming against his skin, and his smoky eyes were troubled. Odd, he didn't seem to be the kind of man who troubled easily. "I'm not sure I know."

"Then go away and don't come back."

He stared at her. "That's what you really want?"

"That's what I really want," she said. Because if he stayed he'd kiss her again, and she couldn't afford to let that happen.

It was that simple. One moment he was lounging in her doorway, all golden beauty and shimmering colors, and the next moment he was gone. She put out her hand, knowing she would feel him if he'd simply altered her perceptions, but nothing was there. He'd really, truly gone. Forever, as she'd asked him to.

And she burst into tears.

Lizzie worked on transformations, deliberately messing with the fabric of the universe, until finally she had to admit that he wasn't coming back. When the full realization hit, she ran. She shoved her bare feet into the first shoes she could find, a pair of feathered mules that Mare had drooled over, grabbed her purse and dashed out of the house, slamming the door behind her. The day was dark and overcast, unseasonably warm, and she could feel the storm brewing, the one that had been dancing over their heads since yesterday. The wind had died down, replaced by a sullen torpor that did nothing for Lizzie's state of mind. She needed cool, crisp spring air to clear her mind, and instead she was assaulted with the onset of a storm that was almost tropical in intensity.

She hadn't even planned where she was heading, and the shoes had been a bad choice. High-heeled mules weren't exactly boots made for walking, and she stopped to look down at them in frustration. If she tried to change them they might turn into ferrets, and she couldn't very well walk into town with livestock attached to her feet. But high-heeled, feather-bedecked slides weren't doing her much good, either.

She could feel his arms around her, encircling her, bringing her own arms into a circle as his low voice breathed in her ear, filled her head and her body with shivery hot feelings. She needed an array, he'd said, but she couldn't very well stop and draw one on the sidewalk. It wasn't going to work, but she had to try. She wrapped her arms around her body, envisioning a circle, trying not to think about Elric's body pressed up against hers, his heat melting into her bones. She closed her eyes and thought about sneakers.

They were purple, but at least they were easier to move in. She stared down at them in both triumph and bewilderment. Had it become that easy?

"That's wonderful, Lizzie," a soft voice said, and when Lizzie looked up, Xan was there in all her fanged glory.

Not that she was really fanged, of course. She looked far younger than her years, which had to be somewhere in her fifties, her raven hair tied up with bejeweled chopsticks stuck in it, her beautiful, pale skin glowing, and she wore a bright red kimono jacket and black silk pants that Lizzie immediately craved.

She looked as exotic and out of place as Lizzie had always secretly felt.

"Darling Lizzie," Xan said, holding out her arms.

Lizzie looked at her doubtfully. If Dee had been there, she would have told her to run the other way. If Mare had been there, she would have flung herself into Xan's arms. As it was, Lizzie was stuck in the middle, unsure which way to go, only knowing instinctively that she didn't want to piss this woman off. She could feel the amethyst humming against her heart. It was tucked inside her shirt, out of sight, and yet she had the odd sense that Xan could see it quite clearly through the layers of cloth.

She gave Xan a dutiful hug and a polite peck on her perfect cheek. She smelled of cinnamon and sulfur—an odd combination. "I didn't realize you were in town," Lizzie said in a neutral voice.

"It's not really my kind of place, is it?" Xan said, looking around. "But then, it's not really your kind of place, either." She smiled at Lizzie. "You'd do so much better in Toledo."

Lizzie said nothing.

"And what do you think of Elric?" She ducked her head a little to peer at Lizzie. "I sent him, you know."

"I know."

"He's quite extraordinary, isn't he? And I sent him to you. I'm feeling quite pleased with myself for that." She made a little comic flourish with her hands. "The perfect aunt."

"Why?" Lizzie said, suspicious.

"Because he's your destiny, darling. He's the most powerful sorcerer I've ever known, but he's always been beyond my reach. I thought it was just because he doesn't like powerful women—he doesn't, you know, positively *loathes* them, and I was so besotted with him I was even willing to give up my powers for him—but when I cast a spell to see if I was his true love, I found out . . . you are."

"Yeah, right," Lizzie said, ignoring the sudden surge inside her. Xan wasn't telling her something she didn't already know. She'd taken one look at Elric and known they were mated, bonded, forever.

She just didn't have to like it.

"I'd give anything to be you," Xan said, and the ring of truth in her voice was undeniable. "Give up my powers, anything. He's worth any sacrifice. It's hopeless for me, he'll never love me, but if I were you . . ." She leaned close to Lizzie, cinnamon and sulfur again. "Let passion take you, Lizzie. To be Elric's one true love is a destiny worth any gift."

And all I ever wanted was to get rid of my gift, Lizzie thought, looking at Xan's beautiful, ageless face.

So why was she suddenly feeling manipulated when her long-lost aunt was telling her to reach for everything she ever wanted, true love and no inconvenient powers?

But Dee's decade of warnings still stuck in her brain, and while she might have been spacey, she was never stupid. "What's in it for you?"

"For me, darling?" Xan echoed, pulling back. "What could be in it for me? Except your happiness. Happiness and true love."

Yeah, right, she thought, but this time she didn't say it out loud.

"Go to him, Lizzie. He's everything you ever wanted." There was the faint glint of a tear in Xan's eyes, a real tear, and her voice was true. She took Lizzie's hand in hers, her fingers twining, and the amethyst went wild. Hot and sparking against her skin, a fiery warning that Xan didn't seem to notice. "Don't let your sisters tell you power is more important than love. *Nothing* is more important than love."

She held on for a moment, and then released Lizzie's hand, turning and walking away, graceful in those beautiful silk pants, the red kimono lifting gently in the wind. Lizzie stared after her, dizzy and confused. *That was sincere; she really meant that.* But that was also Xan.

The day had grown suddenly cold, and the amethyst against her skin seemed lifeless, as if, after giving off that major electrical charge, it had burned out. Lizzie pushed her hair out of her face and realized her hand was shaking. On top of everything else, she must be coming down with some kind of flu. It only needed that to make her life complete.

She needed to get to her sisters, to see if she could reclaim some kind of sanity. Mare had said Mother's Tattoo Parlor for lunch, and that was as a good a place as any to figure out exactly what was going on, and whether Aunt Xan really was the she-devil of the western world. The cold began to seep into Lizzie's bones and she hugged herself and turned toward Mother's, feeling sicker with each step. With luck she wouldn't have to think about Elric for a very long time.

Mare got to Value Video!! at ten wearing her work clothes which, since Saturday was *Corpse Bride*, consisted of a wedding dress and veil she'd found at Goodwill, ripped up, and dyed blue. Dreama met her at the front counter.

"That's a *great* dress." Dreama said.

Mare got a box of Junior Mints out of the case and gave it to her.

"Thank you." Dreama opened the box. "The leak in the beanbag chair got worse last night. I think we really gotta just move it outta here."

"I'll do it," Mare said. "Where's Jude?"

"In the office discussing sales with William." Dreama shook her head. "Jude is cute, but he doesn't have much sensitivity."

"You are a keen judge of character," Mare said.

Dreama nodded, serious. "When William took his dinner break last night, I got all the sharp objects out of there."

Mare looked at her, surprised. "*Very* good, Dreama."

Jude came out of the office and smiled when he saw Mare, his green eyes glassy with delight, his tie still vile.

"Ciao, Mare! I'm so glad you're here." Then he looked at her dress. "Oh. That's interesting."

"Well, we all become the remains of the day," Mare said.

"Huh?" Jude said.

"Emily," Dreama said helpfully. "*Corpse Bride*. It's in her song. Mare's wearing her dress."

"Right, right," Jude said. "Great marketing. But in New York, you're going to have to give up anything that's *out of the normal*."

"I'm not going to New York," Mare said, and ignored Dreama's fallen face. That was life. One crushing disappointment after another.

"But it's a tremendous opportunity," Jude said, and then turned when Crash knocked on the plate-glass door.

"We don't open until ten-thirty," Jude said through

the glass, but Mare reached around him and unlocked the latch. "No personal conversations on Value Video!! time!" he told her, his voice rising, and she opened the door.

"I got your message," Crash said as he came in. "Nice dress. *Corpse Bride*, right?"

Mare picked up the broken beanbag chair and jerked her head toward the storeroom.

"Both of you, in there," she said to them. "Take care of the store, Dreama. The boys and I are going to have a little talk."

When they were inside the storeroom, Mare dropped the beanbag chair on the floor, folded her arms, and said, "Okay, which one of you bitches is my mother?"

Jude said, "Huh?" but Crash said, "Phoebe Cates. It's from this bad movie she made me watch once."

"*Lace,*" Mare said.

Jude still looked perplexed. "Who's Phoebe Cates?"

Crash frowned at him. "You never saw *Fast Times at Ridgemont High*? The pool scene? Every guy knows that scene."

"Exactly," Mare said. "He also never saw *Curse of the Were-Rabbit*, *Corpse Bride*, *Young Frankenstein*, the third *Indiana Jones*, or *Ghostbusters*."

"Son," Crash said. "You're in the wrong business."

Mare leveled her eyes at Jude, who was breathing heavily now, his Adam's apple practically palpitating, his fingers rubbing his tie tack so hard, she almost expected a genie to appear. "You don't happen to know a tall, dark-haired woman in a red dress, do you? Very beautiful? Dark eyes with a red ring around the iris? Looks like she could cut you in half with them?"

"I don't know what you're talking about," Jude croaked.

"The hell you don't," Mare said. "My aunt Xan sent you, you little bastard."

Jude shook his head, his chest heaving.

"Back to Aunt Xan, are we?" Crash said.

"I have a few questions for you, too," Mare said to him, suddenly angrier with him than with a lying VP she didn't care about anyway. "Five years you've been gone but all of a sudden you want to marry me. How'd that happen?"

"It was time," Crash said. "You're mad about that?"

"You've been gone for *five years,*" Mare said. "Why now?"

Crash shook his head. "I don't know. The business is on its feet. I bought a house. We're making money. I was tired of chasing girls."

"Oh, *thank you,*" Mare said.

Crash looked confused and more than a little annoyed. "This guy in Annapolis ordered a bike and it was ready to ship, and I thought, *I could deliver it and see Mare again.* The bike I've been restoring for you is finished. I looked out the door one day and thought about you standing in the sun, and I missed you so much I couldn't breathe. It was just *time.*"

"Just like that," Mare said, trying to ignore the "couldn't breathe" part. "I find your timing suspicious."

Crash shrugged. "You're the Queen of the Universe. Maybe you made it happen."

"I'm not the queen of anything," Mare said grimly. "So what did my aunt Xan tell you?"

"Nothing," Crash said, definitely annoyed now. "I don't know your aunt. What's this about?"

"I think you're both Xan's evil minions." Mare swallowed hard, appalled to realize that she was upset, almost crying upset. "She was always trying to get control of us, and I think she sent men after us this time, and I got a doubleheader. At least I only fell for one of you."

"I don't know what you're talking about," Jude said, trying for the high ground and just sounding slimy. "I'm offering you a promotion and the chance for great earthly power. All you have to do is stop doing anything"—he gestured to her dress—"strange. It's corporate America. We don't do strange."

"And I told you, I don't know your aunt." Crash straightened, his face dark now. "But you know me. You knew me for three years before I left Salem's Fork, so if I was going to be an evil minion—and who the fuck talks like that anyway?—you'd have known back then. You really think I'd hurt you, do *anything* that would hurt you? Jesus, Mare, if you can really think that, you don't deserve me."

Mare's mouth dropped open. "What? You're mad at *me*?"

"Hell, yes, I'm mad at you. You drag me up on that damn mountain last night, you give me some kind of dumb story about magic, we have great sex, but then you tell me there's no spending the night because you live in a damn nunnery with your sisters, and now you're accusing me of being a minion? Yeah, *I'm mad*. What did I do to—"

"Listen, *you*," Mare said, stabbing him in the chest with her finger. "*You left me.* I loved you and *you left me,* for five years *you left me,* bleeding and alone and then you came waltzing back in, all charm and marriage proposals like I'm just gonna fall right back into you, and of course *I DID*—" She blinked back tears. "Because I missed you so damn much, *you bastard,* and you did not just show up here by chance out of the blue by a wild coincidence at the exact same time that Xan sent men to Dee and Lizzie, so yes, I think you're a minion, you rat bastard, and how *dare you* come back here and make fantastic love to me and *minion* me when I love you and trust you and *love you*, and—" She smacked him on the chest, gulping back tears, and he caught her fist and shoved her away.

"Tell you what," he said. "When you get your head out of your butt, you give me a call." He headed for the door and she moved to block him, sticking her chin out as he loomed over her. "Out of my way, O'Brien."

"Give me one good reason to trust you!"

"Because it's me," he said, and moved her roughly aside, kicking the beanbag chair out of his path and spraying pellets everywhere as he walked out the door.

"Well, he's obviously not a gentleman," Jude said when the door had closed behind him. "Now about New York, I think you can go right to the top if you don't do anything that's not normal and give up—"

"Shut up, Jude," Mare said, fury and pain making her savage. "You are *so* evil minion, it's written *all over you*. You probably even have the goddamn T-shirt. Go back to the lair and push the button, Igor, or do whatever the hell it is that evil minions do when the jig is up. Just get out of my face."

"Huh?" Jude said.

"Jesus," Mare said, "I've lost all respect for Xan." Then she went back out to the counter.

"What happened in there?" Dreama said. "Crash looked really mad."

"He was," Mare said miserably. "So am I."

"Heads are gonna roll, huh?" Dreama said, grinning. "The Queen of the Universe is gonna kick some ass."

"I'm not the Queen of the Universe," Mare said,

close to tears. "I'm not even Queen of Value Video!! and that's about as low as you can go."

Dreama's face went slack. *"Mare!"*

Mare picked up a stack of DVDs. "I'm going to re-stock these. And then I'm taking my lunch break. That okay with you?"

"What's *wrong* with you?" Dreama said, with a catch in her voice.

"Everything," Mare said, and went off to shelve movies. Starting with *Girls Gone Wild Cleveland.*

M are went to the Greasy Fork to pick up lunch on her way to Mother's, threading her way through the crowd of locals and tourists. It was easy to tell them apart; the locals didn't bat an eye when she walked in wearing her ripped blue tulle wed-ding dress, but the tourists all gaped. "Are you in a play?" one of them asked.

"No," Mare said over the tops of her heart-shaped glasses. "Why would you think that?" and then moved on without waiting for an answer, heading for the register.

Pauline went past her, carrying her tray shoulder high like the pro she was. "There's a lady over there in the booth, said you could sit with her."

"A lady?" Mare said, turning to look at the booths. "I don't know any . . ."

In the last booth, a brunette beauty with a fine-boned face and flawless skin sat looking at the menu with barely concealed distaste. Her ruby earrings and cashmere blue hoodie were drawing more glances than

Mare's blue tulle, but she didn't seem to notice. Then she looked up and saw Mare and smiled, her red lips curving an invitation, and Mare began to walk toward her without realizing she was moving.

"It can't be you," she said, taking off her sunglasses as she reached the booth. "You haven't changed. It's been thirteen years and you haven't changed."

"Diet," Xan said. "Exercise. Plastic surgery." She waved a languid hand. "Magic. Have a seat, Mare. You look beautiful."

"Well, blue is my color," Mare said, trying to get her snark back as she slid into the booth, the scent of cinnamon and sulfur taking her back to childhood. "I should have known you were here. They're serving martinis here now. That had to be a sign of the apocalypse."

Xan closed her eyes for a moment.

"So you sent guys after us and now you're here in person," Mare said. "What's going on?"

"Guys?" Xan said innocently, but the red flash in her heavy-lidded eyes was just like old times, and the red ring around the black iris said Xan was cooking, magic at work.

"Danny," Mare said. "Jude. Eldred."

"Elric."

"Exactly," Mare said. "You sent them."

Xan laughed, the lovely, liquid musical laugh that Mare had tried to emulate as a child, only to have Dee yell at her for sucking the helium out of her balloons. "Just trying to get back in touch, darling. Bring the family together again."

"How sweet," Mare said. "But you know how the holidays are with families who eat their young. So that would be no." She looked closer at what Xan was wearing. "Is that cashmere?"

"Yes," Xan said, and peeled it off, shaking out her

hair so that it fell over the white silk tank top she wore underneath.

The man in the next booth almost fell into his chili.

Xan held out the hoodie to Mare.

"Really?" Mare said, looking at it like it was a snake.

"You can't think I'd really wear a hoodie," Xan said.

"Okay, what'll it be?" Pauline said, appearing beside them and pulling her pencil out from behind her ear.

"I've never seen a waitress actually do that," Xan told her.

"Pauline has studied waitressing on all the major TV shows." Mare held out the hoodie to see it better. "Wait'll she cracks her gum and calls you honey."

"Funny," Pauline said. "So that'll be crackers and water for you."

"With a side order of medium rare hamburger and chocolate shake," Mare said. "Hold the crackers. And make the water a Diet Coke. And add some fries. To go." With a great deal of self-control, she put the hoodie on the table and pushed it across to Xan. "I'm not staying."

"I'll have the chicken Caesar salad," Xan said, closing the menu. "Dressing on the side. And Perrier with lemon."

Pauline raised her eyebrows at Mare.

"She's my aunt. She's not from around here," Mare said. "She's not staying, either."

"Looks more like one of your sisters," Pauline said, surveying Xan with a critical eye.

"That would be the plastic surgery," Mare said. "And the magic. I'm starving, Pauline, and I have to be somewhere in, like, five minutes."

"Coming right up," Pauline said. "Plastic surgery, huh?" She picked up the menus. "Did it hurt?"

"They give you drugs," Xan said.

"Huh," Pauline said and left.

"Don't be so quick to reject me, Mare," Xan said. "I have things to give you. Besides the hoodie."

"Well," Mare said. "Jewelry is good. And money is always in fashion."

"Or your One True Love?" Xan sat back. "That took some heavy-duty magic, finding three soul mates for you all. And then convincing them to come to this backwater." She looked around the diner. "I did manage to find them, though. Yours took the longest. Jude. He was in Italy and I—"

"Oh, please." Mare put her chin on her hand. "If Jude is my soul mate, I'm putting in for a new soul."

Xan leaned forward, her beautiful face smooth but her dark eyes intent. "I sent the men as a goodwill gesture. I don't want you to be lonely, Mare, I want to help you. Jude can give you love, but more than that, he can give you real power, earthly power, not the parlor trick your magic gives you. He can take you straight to the top of the business you've chosen."

"Renting videos?" Mare said, incredulous. "You think that's my future? God, I'm going to kill myself, I really am. I think William has some rope left—"

"Not renting videos," Xan said. "Have you even listened to Jude? He thinks you're brilliant. He wants to take you to New York. Mare, you could run the entire company. You could . . ." She stopped as Mare squinted at her. "What?"

Mare tilted her head. "You know what's freaking me out? There's no expression on your face. It's in your eyes, but your face is like this mask. Is that the surgery?"

"Botox," Xan said. "Grace Kelly didn't have expressions, either."

"Grace Kelly was serene, not embalmed."

"If you're trying to drive me off with insults, it's not going to work." Xan reached out and put her hand over Mare's, twining their fingers together. "I'm here to help you, but you have to grow up. Life isn't a game, Mare. It isn't about who's got the best comeback or"— she gestured to Mare's wedding dress—"who gets the strangest looks in the local diner."

"Says the woman who's nine parts snake venom," Mare said, taking her hand back. "Or whatever the hell Botox is."

Pauline appeared and slid their drinks in front of them. "Anything else?"

"Got any antitoxin?" Mare said. "My aunt may want to show fury shortly."

"Fresh out," Pauline said. "We got steak sauce."

"That will be all," Xan said, and Pauline evaporated, probably in fear for her tip. "Look, darling, you can be as flip as you like, but I know you. I know you've been living with Dee for too long, I know how she treats you, like a child, patting you on the head, trying to run your life—"

"That's not going to work," Mare said. "You know I'm fed up with Dee, but I know I can't trust you. Yes, Dee's a pain in the ass sometimes, but she's smart, and she's strong, and she's right most of the time, and more than that, she's part of me, she's a third of who I am, and that means that while I fight her tooth and nail when it's just us, when somebody comes at us from the outside—that would be you—I am her girl. So if you think you're going to do an end run around her by hitting at the soft underbelly of the group—"

"That would be Lizzie," Xan said, and sipped her ice water.

"You haven't seen Lizzie lately," Mare said. "What

I'm saying is, this isn't going to work. You can't divide and conquer. We don't divide."

Xan shrugged. "Well, at least you have Jude."

"Oh, Jesus, kick a girl when she's down." Mare looked at her watch. "Damn it. Pauli—"

"Gotcha," Pauline said, appearing with a Styrofoam container with her burger and fries and a lid for her Coke. "You got time to make it yet."

"What's wrong with Jude?" Xan said.

Mare capped her Coke cup. "Jude is not my type, and that's being charitable."

"Who's not your type?" Pauline said.

"The Value Video!! VP who's in town," Mare said.

"The one who looks like Jude Law." Pauline nodded.

"How could he not be your type?" Xan said. "Your entire generation is mad for Jude Law."

"Well, some of us felt he lost some luster over the nanny thing," Mare said.

"And besides, there's Crash," Pauline said as Mare put her sunglasses on and slid out of the booth.

"Crash," Xan said dangerously.

"Christopher Duncan, Mare's old flame, he's back in town," Pauline said, in her best news-at-eleven voice. "He proposed. She's thinking about it. He wants her to go to Italy but she doesn't know if she's going. We're still waiting for the update." She looked at Mare over the tops of her glasses. "The pool stands at even money."

"There is no update." Mare looked at Xan. "I'm going to get a tattoo now. You should go back to wherever you came from. We're not interested."

"You lie," Xan said without rancor. "And you can't speak for the others. Lizzie might be interested. Even Dee might be tempted by the chance to have a normal life."

"Maybe, but not if it means dealing with you," Mare said. "Enjoy your salad. Tip Pauline good. She's the sole support of twelve orphan children."

"And a dog," Pauline said solemnly.

"And a dog," Mare said. "Thanks for the speed with the Styrofoam, Pauline. Have a safe trip home, Xan."

"Wait," Xan said, and Mare paused. "This Crash. You think he's the one you really love?"

"I don't know," Mare said.

"Yes you do," Xan said and took a deep breath. "It's in your voice. I don't know how I missed him, but he's the one. Isn't he?"

"Probably," Mare said. "It's definitely not Jude."

"And you say he lives in Italy?" Xan said, and she sounded sincerely interested. Sincerely puzzled but sincerely interested.

"Tuscany." Mare settled into the booth again. "He came back because he was ready to settle down, not because of your spell, he didn't have anything to do with you—"

"That's where the spell found Jude," Xan said, half to herself. "I *thought* it was odd."

"Jude's not my type at all," Mare said. "Maybe the spell was slow and Crash had just ridden by. He rides those bikes at suicide speeds."

Xan nodded. "That could be. Long distances like that are tricky for finding things. I must have cast that spell a dozen times because the result was so strange."

"Well, Jude's a good-looking guy," Mare said charitably. "You couldn't have known he was that much of a loser."

Xan shook her head. "You know, magic. After a while, you start to think it can't go wrong."

"I wouldn't know," Mare said, taking her sunglasses off. "Mine goes wrong fairly often."

"You did get the short end of the stick, didn't you, darling?" Xan said sympathetically, reaching out again and twining her fingers with Mare's. "But from the sound of things, you're making up for it with your Crash. And if you're sure he's the one . . ."

She let her voice trail off, as if asking, and Mare nodded, feeling warm in the moment, connected to Xan somehow.

Xan nodded back. "Well, then, don't screw it up. Follow your passion, Mare. Sacrifice anything for it. Your sisters, your power . . . real love is worth anything."

Mare blinked. "Boy, for a minute there, you sounded like a real aunt."

Xan smiled at her, holding on tightly, the warmth from her fingers spreading. "So you're going to Italy. Tuscany?"

Mare nodded. "That's where he lives. But I can't go. I—"

"Of course you can go." Xan sounded indignant. "My God, Mare, the man you love lives in one of the most beautiful places on earth, and you have nothing holding you here. Why can't you go?"

"Well, Dee and Lizzie . . ." Mare stopped. She couldn't go because they had to stay together because they were running from Xan who had just given her a cashmere hoodie and hadn't taken her soul in return, who instead had taken her hand and made her feel warm and safe. "We need to stick together."

"Why?" Xan said. "Dee has Danny and Lizzie has Elric. It's not really *normal* for sisters to stay together forever."

"Well . . ." Mare looked around the diner and then leaned forward. "In case you've forgotten, we're not normal sisters."

"You could be." Xan smiled. "You have choices, Mare. You're not trapped."

Mare blinked at her.

"I know your powers haven't made it easy for you, and it's especially irritating since they're not particularly good for anything, but you don't have to keep them, you know. Any time you don't want them, you can get rid of them. I'll help you get rid of them. You can be as normal as the next person, all of you, go off with your true loves completely safe, have normal lives, normal children, truly live happily ever after. It's possible, Mare."

Mare sucked in her breath. *Give up my power?*

But there was Crash and the sunlight in Tuscany and even that laughing baby, if she gave up her power . . .

Xan patted their clasped hands and then let her go, and Mare felt a chill. "Just think about it, darling. Take your time. And take this, too. You look cold."

She tossed the hoodie across the table, and Mare caught it, and said, "Thanks," fairly sure she shouldn't keep it, but it was a cashmere hoodie and she was cold.

She got up and headed for the door, her thoughts racing, dizzy with them, and a woman at a table she passed said, "That looks like my old wedding dress. Did you get it at Goodwill?" Mare said, "No, this was my sainted mother's, God rest her soul," and slammed out the door, not looking back, shivering with cold now, wondering what Xan had up her sleeve, wondering if Xan was being tricky and pretending that she hadn't sent Crash or if he really had come back just because he loved her, wondering what it would be like to be free of her power . . .

She was shuddering with cold now, feeling dizzy and sick in the heat of the day, chilled in the sun, not sure what had just happened.

Something's wrong, she thought and put the hoodie on and headed for the tattoo parlor.

A butterfly," Mare said to Mother ten minutes later as she handed her the drawing, still shivering, and now really annoyed about everything. "And I don't want to hear any crap about how it's the most common tat for a girl. My name's Mariposa and I want another butterfly." She felt like pouting, life was so unfair. Pouting and shivering and throwing up. "It's *cold* in here."

"Feeling testy, are we?" Mother said, straightening her white lab coat. She looked at Mare strangely, her cool gray eyes level under her neatly razor-cut gray hair, and Mare took a deep breath and relaxed a little. "That's better."

"Well, it was either a butterfly or the Statue of Liberty." Mare dropped her bag in the middle of the floor and stepped over it. "I think of her as a kindred spirit."

"She stands in one place holding a light for everybody else," Mother said, picking up Mare's bag and moving it to one side. "How is she like you?"

"She's tall, everybody knows who she is, she's a classy dresser, and nobody kicks her around." Mare hiked up her skirt and sat down with her back to Mother. "And in moments of stress, I could beat somebody senseless with that big torch."

"Of course," Mother said, looking at Mare's *Corpse Bride* dress. "Where do you want this tattoo?"

"Right there at the base of my spine. Only tilt it.

Like the world's tilting." The world felt like it was tilting. She really was going to throw up if Mother didn't get a move on.

"Trailer trash license plate." Mother tucked the skirt of Mare's dress into the neck of the hoodie and then held the drawing up. "Very buff butterfly." She put it on the copier and punched the button.

"Yeah," Mare said, trying to sound chipper as the copier hummed and her stomach churned. "I'm surrounded by jerks. I need a butterfly that can kick a little ass on my ass. Jesus, it's cold in here." Her skin felt damp, clammy, and she shivered again.

"Color?" Mother said.

"Just black," Mare said. "If I wanted color, I'd have said color, okay?"

Mother put her hands on her hips and looked at her, as if something was wrong or something.

"I'm broke, okay?" Mare said, looking away. "Plus, I like tribal. More butch."

"Yes, the world needs more butch butterflies." Mother snapped on latex gloves and picked up a razor. "Anything happen today I should know about?"

"There'd be a hell of a lot fewer victims if butterflies went armed," Mare said, and then Lizzie came into the back of the shop hugging herself and shivering and said, "Mare?" in this tiny little voice, and Mother looked up from shaving Mare's tailbone.

"Mother, this is my sister Lizzie," Mare said. "Lizzie, this is Mother. What's wrong with you?"

"Hello, Lizzie," Mother said. "Lovely to meet you."

"You, too," Lizzie said, shivering hard, her voice breaking, and Mare realized she was close to tears.

What a wimp, Mare thought and sighed. "What happened now?"

"He's *gone.*"

"Charles?" Mare said. "Well, yeah, I told you, he's in Alaska. And good riddance—"

"*Elric,*" Lizzie said, and sat down on the floor in a heap, her arms crossed over her chest. "My heart hurts."

"Oh, okay," Mare said. *Drama queen. We're gonna be ass deep in rabbits here in a minute.* "Deep breaths." She shivered as Mother spread cream on her lower back and then smoothed the drawing over it. She was really *cold,* dammit. And her stomach hurt, probably got ptomaine at the Fork. "So what did Elric say when you asked him if he knew Xan?"

"He said yes." Lizzie made a little aching sound in her throat. *"He said yes."*

"Well," Mare said. "Points for honesty. Did he say what he was supposed to do? Like wrap us up and deliver us or something? Because I just met her—"

"No. He came because I was screwing up . . . things." Lizzie began to rock back and forth. "My heart really hurts."

"Yeah, I know, I got a stomachache." Mare looked over her shoulder to see Mother studying the transfer on her tailbone. "How we doing?"

"I'm doing fine," Mother said and handed her a mirror. "Your sister is sick. Doesn't that bother you?"

"She gets like this." Mare gave the mirror a perfunctory glance. "Great." She handed the mirror back to Mother. "He said you're screwing up things," she prompted Lizzie.

"I was doing things against the rules."

"The rules."

Lizzie leaned forward. "Of the universe," she whispered, her face pale and damp.

"Oh." Mare thought about telling her that rules were for the little people, but given the scope of Lizzie's powers, that could lead to mushroom clouds and planet-sized charcoal briquettes, so she said, "So did he help you?"

"Yes," Lizzie said, almost sobbing, "but then I told him to go and *he did*." She curled up and lay down on Mother's floor in the fetal position, still rocking.

"Quitter." Mare sucked in her breath as she heard the hum and felt the bite of Mother's needle. She shivered and her stomach turned over again. "Oh, sit up, Lizzie, he'll be back. He's your true love. Xan sent him."

"I know," Lizzie, still in the fetal position, said, her voice breaking. "She told me."

"She talked to you, too?" Mare felt disappointed. That was no good, Xan wasn't supposed to talk to anybody else, only to her, because she was *special*. "She told me we could be normal if we wanted to. *Ouch*." She looked over her shoulder. "Hey."

"You want painless tattoos, get a rub-on," Mother said serenely.

"She told me to sacrifice anything for true love," Lizzie said, tears leaking from her eyes, the big baby. "She said Elric's love was worth anything, even my power. I thought I didn't want my power, but ever since Elric's been here I've been changing my mind, and now I can't even think straight . . ."

Mare frowned at her and jerked her head toward Mother, who appeared to be oblivious. "Shhhh," she said to Lizzie, but Lizzie just kept rocking and shivering.

Well, Mother was keeping it damn near freezing in there, so no wonder.

"Is there a *reason* you have the air-conditioning on 'frigid'?" she snapped at Mother.

Mother turned the needle off. "I think I'll make some tea."

"Or you could just turn the goddamned air-conditioning down," Mare said and went over to do it herself.

It was off.

"What the fuck?" Mare said, and then her stomach roiled again and she pressed her arms against it.

The door opened.

"Xan's here," Dee said, sounding like Eeyore as she closed the door behind her. "I'm really confused. But I think we have to go. No, I know we have to go. God, my head hurts."

"I don't want to go." Mare crossed her arms over her stomach tighter, both for warmth and to block Dee.

Dee started pacing. "You don't understand," she said, rubbing her forehead. "She killed Mom and Dad. It was an accident, she said, she was just trying to take their powers to help them, but she killed them. She says she knows how to do it right this time, but I'm afraid."

"I don't care, I'm not going, don't care what you say, not going," Mare singsonged, shivering.

"All right, that's *it*," Dee said, walking faster, her voice rising to a thin whine. "I have a headache, I'm freezing, and I'm tired of saving your ungrateful ass. Do I *always* have to make the decisions in this family? A little help would be *nice* for a change. But that's fine. I'll save you—*again*—and damn well drag you along."

Mare leaned forward. "Make me. I dare you. *Make me.*"

Lizzie started to cry.

"You know, it's not enough that I have given up *my* life for you," Dee said, "and now I've lost Danny—"

"How could you lose Danny?" Mare pulled back, determined not to feel sorry for her. "You just *found* Danny."

Dee ignored Mother, who was bringing in a tray of tea things, and dropped into the chair next to where Lizzie was curled up on the floor. "Danny's going to hate me when he finds out. He hates people with powers and he's going to hate *me*." She scrubbed at her face with both hands. "Maybe I *should* just give Xan my powers. So what if she *kills me*."

"Well, that's the first thing we've agreed on," Mare said. "Not the killing part, but the powers part. I talked to her and thought the same thing. Sure would make life easier."

"I think my heart is breaking," Lizzie said from the floor, and Dee looked down and saw her and got to her feet.

"How long has she been like that?" she said to Mare, suddenly sounding frightened.

"Couple minutes," Mare said. "You know Lizzie. There should be bunnies any time now." She looked around and felt a chill that had nothing to do with her lowered body temperature. "Wait a minute. *Why aren't there bunnies?*"

Dee was on her knees beside Lizzie, gathering her up into her arms. "It's all right, baby, it's all right, I'm here, it's all right. I'll take care of you."

"I'm so cold," Lizzie said to her. "And my heart is breaking."

"What's *wrong* with her?" Mare said, dropping to the floor beside Dee, really frightened now. *"What's wrong with her?"*

"Xan," Dee said, holding Lizzie tightly against her, as if to wrap her in warmth. "That's what Mama said right before she died, when Xan took her power." She met Mare's eyes over Lizzie's bright curls. "She was cold and shivering and rocking like this and that's what she said *and then she died*."

"You're cold, too," Mare said, putting her arms around them both. "And so am I. I was cold after I left Xan. *What did she do to us?*"

Mother put the tea tray down on the floor beside them: a teapot, three cups, and a plateful of cookies covered in sugar. "Eat. You need sugar."

"Sugar's going to take care of this?" Dee said, incredulous, as Mare tightened her arms around all of them for warmth.

"Cookies, just like the ones they give you after you give blood," Mother said cheerfully. "Instant energy."

"We didn't give blood," Mare said.

"Oh," Mother said and left them alone.

Dee looked stricken. "What did Xan do? Did she touch you? She took my hand. She twisted my fingers with hers. And she was holding Mama's hand the same way right before . . ." She turned to Lizzie. "Did she *touch* you?" She looked at Mare.

Mare nodded. "Yeah. She did. Just like that. That twisting thing."

"She took our power," Dee said, still rocking Lizzie. "I know you think Xan's my nightmare in the closet, but she took our power."

"No, I believe you, I'm with you now." Mare picked up a cup and held it to Lizzie's lips. "Drink, Lizzie."

Lizzie sipped and made a face. "Too sweet."

"Drink it anyway, baby," Dee said, and Lizzie did, sipping at first and then gulping, and when Lizzie was done, Mare gave Dee a cup, too, and then picked up the third cup and drained it.

"Did Xan take all our power?" Mare said, and then answered her question by lifting the needle off Mother's tray from across the room. "Still got that." She tried for her bag, much heavier, and couldn't budge it. "She took part of it. A pint. Like at the blood bank, she took some off the top. What was she doing?" She picked up a cookie as if it were a life source and chomped her way through it.

"Maybe she didn't have time," Dee said, sipping and rocking. "We'd have noticed if she'd taken more. We'd have fought. But if she finds a way to take it all . . ."

"I become a spoiled brat forever," Mare said, and called out, "I'm sorry I was rude, Mother." She picked up the teapot and filled everybody's cup again. "Tea. Cookies. Eat. Drink."

"And I become the most annoying victim on the planet," Dee said, her voice already stronger. "And Lizzie . . ."

They both looked at Lizzie, gulping her second cup of tea as if it were a lifeline.

Lizzie curls up and dies just like Mama, Mare thought. *We'd all die.*

"You three feeling better?" Mother said, coming back in. "I've turned up the heat."

"Thank you," Mare said.

"You shouldn't give blood when you're not feeling well," Mother said. "I'll fill in the black on your tattoo now."

Mare thought about saying, "You know damn well we didn't give blood," but if Mother was rewinding to normal, that worked for her. She got up and sat down on the chair again, feeling the chill abate. It really was like giving blood, she thought. Probably in a couple of hours, she'd have built her power back up again. As long as nobody came along and sucked more off. Or took too much. Like her mother. Xan had taken too much from her mother. Dee had been right all along.

Any fascination Mare had for Xan died on the instant.

Lizzie pulled away and reached for another cookie, and Dee took a deep breath. "We need to think. We need to work this out. Xan wants our powers, and she has a plan and the guys have something to do with it. But I think she's telling the truth about them being our true loves."

"She thinks she made a mistake with Jude," Mare said. "And I have to agree there."

"I think we have to go back to the guys and ask them about it," Dee said. "Tell them what just happened and ask them. If they really do love us, they'll tell us the truth."

"Elric loves me," Lizzie said, sounding stronger. "He left me, but he loves me. When he finds out what she did . . ."

Mare frowned. "Jude doesn't love me, but I bet he knows something."

"Can you seduce it out of him?" Dee said.

"No, but I can beat it out of him," Mare said, looking over her shoulder as Mother filled in her tattoo.

Lizzie watched her finish.

"What's it look like, Liz?" Mare said when she was done.

"Like you," Lizzie said. "Like a warrior." Her color was back, her hands were no longer shaking, and for the first time in her life she looked strong and determined. "I want a butterfly," she said to Mother. "But not a warrior. I want a sorcerer butterfly. I want the magic."

Mother handed Lizzie a book of flash and then smeared cream on Mare's back and covered it with plastic wrap, while Lizzie began to look for her sorcerer tat.

"That one, the sorcerer butterfly," Lizzie said a few moments later, handing Mother the book as she took

Mare's place on the chair. "But small on my ankle. Something that'll look great with my shoes. Whatever they turn into."

Dee put down her cup and got to her feet. "I think that's my cue to leave. We all know about Xan now, we're all protected because we know, we'll talk to the guys—"

Mother turned those gray eyes on Dee. "Three sisters. Three tattoos. Different but the same."

"I am *not* getting a tattoo," Dee said.

Mother nodded, still serene, and handed her a second book of flash.

"Save yourself a little time," Mare said to Mother, "don't bother with Dee and the flash. It's not going to happen."

Mother sighed. "You'll be fine, Mare. Stop trying to control the universe. It's not trying to control you." She put a gentle hand on her arm and Mare almost burst into tears. "And give my love to Crash when you see him."

Mare sniffed. "Okay," she said, and headed for the door.

The last thing she heard was Dee saying, "Really, I am *not* getting a tattoo."

Xan was lighting the candle under her chafing dish when she saw Maxine in the see glass, huddled next to the Dumpster, looking tense. She frowned and then waved her hand and opened the portal, and Maxine stumbled into the room.

"What's wrong?" Xan said, not unkindly.

Maxine looked around, trying to hide her nervousness. "Hey, it's nice in here. I never been in this room before."

"It's my kitchen."

"Yeah," Maxine said, reaching out to stroke the black granite countertops. "Are those cherrywood cabinets? They're really red. This is something."

"Thank you." Xan watched her for a moment and then went back to the silver chafing dish.

The cream there was warming beautifully, thick and rich, and Maxine inhaled and sneezed.

Xan sighed.

Maxine moved closer to the bowl. "What is that?"

"Cream," Xan said. "A few spices. A little coffee. Some dark chocolate."

Maxine leaned closer and sniffed. "What are you making?"

"A spell." Xan picked up three cinnamon sticks from an intricately painted box that held dozens and, for the moment, her see glass. "Lean back, Maxine, I do not want you sneezing into this."

Maxine stepped back. "Is it dangerous?"

"Very." Xan broke the three cinnamon sticks into the cream.

The rich spice filled the room, the cloud spiraling up in three curling strands, rust-colored arabesques with tiny red sparks that made Maxine's mouth drop open. "Whoa," she said, leaning closer again as the spirals turned and twisted, and Xan watched, smiling, her eyes half shut.

"What kind of spell is that?"

"It's a libido spell, Maxine," Xan said, watching the cinnamon curl. "I went to Salem's Fork today to nudge the plan back into place, and this spell is going to make sure it stays there. Tonight the sisters and their lovers are going to find each other irresistible. Tonight seals the deal."

"I'm sorry we couldn't get the necklace, Xantippe," Maxine said, watching the cinnamon, too.

"It's all right, Maxine," Xan said. "You can try again tomorrow."

"Jude will help," Maxine said eagerly.

"Jude will not help," Xan said. "Jude is finished. Mare has chosen Crash. It's going to make things difficult, but I'll simply have to adapt."

"No." Maxine drew closer. "That's what I wanted to tell you, Jude will try harder. Don't fire him or turn him into something, he'll do better, really . . ."

The cream was ready, so Xan tuned Maxine out and picked up three glass beads strung on a silver thread, beads she'd separated temporarily from the see glass. "Deirdre, Elizabeth, and Moira," she said over the cream and the beads, as Maxine leaned still closer, pleading with her. "May your deepest passions be unleashed—"

"Please, Xantippe," Maxine said.

"—may your wildest fantasies come true—"

"—he'll try *really* hard—"

"—may this night make you one with your true love—"

"—Xantippe!"

"—so I say, *so be—"*

Maxine moved to grab her arm and knocked the cinnamon box and the see glass into the cream.

"—it," Xan said, and watched as the cream began to turn dark as the entire box of cinnamon sticks and the see glass sank to the bottom of the pan. She sighed and dropped in the Fortune sisters' beads, too.

Maxine stood frozen as Xan turned to her.

"That was bad, Maxine."

"I'm sorry, Xantippe."

Xan looked down at the rapidly darkening cream, sighed again, and then took a glass rod from the table and fished out the see glass, letting the cream drip from it before she wiped it clean.

Maxine swallowed. "What's going to happen now?"

"Now?" Xan poured herself a drink. "Now there's going to be a hot time in the old town tonight."

Maxine's eyes got huge. "It's going to burn down?"

"Only figuratively. Go home, Maxine."

"What did I do?"

"The spell was meant for the sisters only," Xan said. "That's why there were only three beads. But you blundered. You knocked the whole see glass in, so now the entire town—"

"What about Jude?"

"Forget Jude. He's finished."

"What do you mean, finished?"

"Go home, Maxine."

"No, please!"

"Home, Maxine."

Maxine backed toward the paneled door, sniffing, her breath coming in mewing sounds. She stopped when she had it open. "Xantippe?"

Xan was still watching the dark cream bubble. It had been such an elegant spell, so beautifully subtle, so carefully aimed.

Now it was going to be a fuckfest.

She put her forehead in her hand.

"Xantippe?"

Xan raised her head, looked into Maxine's terrified little eyes, and raised her hand.

"No!" Maxine screamed and dove through the door, letting the panel slam behind her.

Xan watched in the see glass as Maxine landed in a sobbing heap behind the Dumpster.

She was going to have to do something about Maxine. She turned back to the glass, decided that Salem's Fork was not something she wanted to see tonight, and covered it with a velvet cloth before leaving the room.

CHAPTER SIX

Dee was still a block away from the inn when she spotted Danny's Triumph at the curb. Absently rubbing at her right shoulder blade, she stopped dead in the street.

Should she go on up? More important, would he talk to her? Would he understand?

Dee didn't even want to think about the scars Danny could inflict before he left. Or that she could inflict on him. What choice did she have, though? What choice had she ever really had?

Her pulse had speeded up again, and she had to lay a hand on her chest to help her breathe.

"Danny?"

He was sitting on the white wicker swing on Velma's front porch. Dee realized he was bent over, his head in his hands. She strode up the sidewalk.

He jumped to his feet. "Dee?"

His face looked drawn, his hair spiked from where he'd been tangling it in his hands. His smile, when it came, was lopsided and sweet. Dee ignored the flare of panic in her chest and kept walking. She met Danny at the bottom of the porch steps.

"I went to your house," he said, giving her a quick, hard hug, "but you weren't there. I'm sorry." Another hug, then he pulled back, running a hand down her face, as if apologies had to be tactile. "I really am. I wish I had a good excuse for taking off on you like that. My mother would have called me everything but a Republican for what I did."

She fingered his hair back into a semblance of order. "It's all right. I'm sorry I upset you."

He dipped his head. "I guess I'm a little touchier than I thought. After what happened to my family, I'm afraid all New Age psychicbabble just sets me off."

Well, good. Dee wouldn't have wanted to feel too good before she had her come-to-Jesus meeting with him. Over his shoulder, the curtains shifted in the front window, and Dee caught a flash of Velma's face. She was amazed the little woman had the restraint to stay in the house.

"Would you like to take a walk?" she asked Danny.

He took a wry look at the sky. "It looks like it's going to rain."

True. Dingy gray clouds scudded fast, and the air was thick with the smell of unsettled dust. Dee wished like hell it would just rain and get it over with.

"Not yet," she said.

"Are you a prognosticator, now?"

The clouds reflected in the cerulean of his eyes, like a portent of things to come. Dee tried not to shiver. "Nah. I just know the weather here. Come on."

"Will you go to France with me when we get back?"

He was smiling. She did her best to smile back. "Only if we can bring Lizzie, Mare, and Pywackt."

"All of them?"

"Well, it wouldn't be fair if I saw Montmartre and they didn't. Besides, Py's always had a hankering to see France. He collects Edith Piaf records."

Danny shook his head. "Cool cat. Come on."

Somehow they ended up hand in hand. Dee didn't mind. She relished the feel of his callused fingers as they wound around hers. The sense of belonging. It was nice for a moment to just pretend she was doing nothing more than taking a walk with her honey.

It was Saturday. A chorus of lawnmowers serenaded the street. A couple of kids were skateboarding beneath the overgrown elm trees that lined the sidewalk. Pete Semple had his garage open and was hammering on something. Mrs. Ledbetter hurried past with an armful of groceries. Nobody paid attention to Dee and Danny.

Dee rubbed at her shoulder again, wondering what she'd been thinking to believe she was brave.

"Has Xan called you again?" she asked.

"You want her to?"

"It doesn't matter what I want her to do. It just matters that she doesn't hurt you."

Danny looked over at her, every instinctive suspicion plain in his bright blue eyes. "We've had this discussion, Dee."

"No we haven't," she said. "Not really. It's why it's important we have it now. Has she called?"

"No. Should she?"

"I imagine she will, and when she does I need you to tell me right away. I'm not exactly sure what her strategy is this time. I just know she has to be stopped. Which is why I'm talking to you now."

"I guess I still don't understand."

"Well, I hope I'm going to clear it up for you."

Because above and beyond the obvious dilemma, if

Dee couldn't prove what she was, he would never understand what a threat Xan was. Not just to her and her sisters. To him. Xan would delight in breaking Danny James.

"What do you need to tell me?" he asked.

"I'm a shapeshifter."

Good God, where had that come from? *Hi, my name is Dee and I'm a shapeshifter. I'll be taking questions now.*

She wouldn't have been surprised if Danny just picked up and ran off. Instead he pulled her to a halt, still holding hands right in the middle of the sidewalk. One of the skateboarders missed them by inches and yelled invectives.

"My sister Lizzie changes silverware into shoes," Dee said before she could chicken out. "My sister Mare can rearrange furniture without using her hands. My mother could tell the future, and Xan can . . . well, you saw what she could do this morning. We've had these gifts since we were young. Well, actually, since puberty. For the women they arrive then and then wane . . . change at menopause. I think that's why Aunt Xan is on the warpath again. She's just about that age, and I think it terrifies her."

Danny gave her a bemused smile. "All she did this morning was convince me to see you."

"She wasn't there, Danny," Dee said. "No matter what it looked like. She was a suggestion. Xan deals in suggestion."

"And you, uh, shift into . . ."

She rubbed a finger between her eyes, where a headache was blooming. "It depends. I'm still working on control. When you came yesterday morning, you remember the owl sitting on the table?"

His smile had long gone. Now he was looking nervous. "Yeah?"

She did her best to smile. "Twee. Twee."

Brandon Upshot rode by on his paper route and almost clipped Danny in the head with a copy of the *Salem Tines*. A car came the other way. Danny didn't notice.

Suddenly he grinned as if it were the greatest joke in history. "Of course you were. And I . . ."

Dee pulled her hand away. He could have at least tried. She'd already turned for home when he caught hold of her—unfortunately by her right shoulder, which made her yelp.

"What's wrong?" he asked.

"Nothing. I think it's just time for me to go home." Especially since her shoulder had started to burn the minute he'd touched it. Maybe she should have somebody look at it.

"No, really," he said, frowning over her back. "Did you hurt yourself?"

And before she could protest, he'd pulled her cardigan and T-shirt down far enough to make her blush.

"Dee?"

"Yes," she snapped. "It's a butterfly. It's a symbol of, oh, I don't know. Having the courage to fly. Well, I fly all the time. I didn't need an insect on my back to help me. I'll probably be the only hawk with a butterfly on its back. All the other hawks will laugh at me."

He was smiling. "It's beautiful. And so small. I really like the color."

Dee turned, trying to see. "Color? It's black."

"It's green."

Which made Dee shake her head. "Of course."

She tugged her clothes back up. "We've gotten off

topic, Danny. You either need to take me seriously, or I go home alone."

He flailed a bit, shoving his hand through his hair. "You're asking a lot, Dee."

"I know." She was asking everything. "Believe me. Will you come to the house?"

"Of course."

She nodded. He took her hand again and they walked on. The trees were beginning to writhe as they passed, and Dee could smell cut grass and a hint of rain. The very air was in turmoil, as if Mare had been weaving her fingers through it. It gave Dee a chill.

They reached the house to find it dark and empty. Lizzie had obviously cleaned, because there wasn't anything out of place. The only thing Dee heard was the throb of complete silence.

Something was wrong, though. Off. Dee stopped in the middle of the living room floor, but she heard nothing but her own steps echo off the hardwood. She thought to call out, but Lizzie's door was closed. She looked hard into the shadowy corners without seeing anything. She took a sniff.

Ah, that was it. It was the power signature in the air. She caught Mare's licorice and a whiff of Lizzie, gardenia and roses. And there, underlying it, a new scent. A tang of spices that made her think of something ancient and powerful and beautiful. She looked toward the bedrooms. Even though she couldn't hear anything, she felt it. Power. Hell, there should have been waves of purple wafting out from beneath the door.

Was Lizzie here? Was she okay? Was it this Elric she was sensing?

"She's fine," Danny said.

Dee turned on him. "Could you at least wait for me to say it out loud?"

"You did."

"No, Danny. I didn't. And how do you know Lizzie's okay? She just lost her guy this morning. This guy I've never met . . ."

"I hear it. Like I heard the witches. This gives me a good feeling. A . . . hmmm, wow. Whatever she's been up to, she's enjoying it."

"Well, thanks for putting *that* image in my head."

His grin was impish. "You wanted me to believe I can hear things."

"I just don't want to hear what you're hearing. Not about my little sister."

"From what I saw of her, she's not so little."

Dee physically turned him for the stairs. "Come on. I brought you here to see my studio. Not eavesdrop on my sister."

Dee's studio shared the second floor with Mare's bedroom. Fourteen steps up and a slide of the hand along the banister from the outside world to hers. She had no control over the outside world. The downstairs rooms were kept fairly anonymous. Even her own bedroom was nondescript. Pale gray walls, black duvet, and thrift store dresser. Zen, Lizzie called it. Disinterested was the truth. What was the point of decorating a room that would see such uninspiring use? Dee saved all her whimsy for her studio.

She climbed the fourteenth step and led the way into her room. She flipped the light and held her breath.

"Good God," Danny breathed, frozen to the spot.

Dee stayed where she was by the white hutch she used as a storage cabinet. This room was her sanctuary, her soul. It was what kept her sane when the responsibilities and the isolation wore her away. It was the only place on earth she didn't feel like somebody's mother.

The studio faced south, a stark wood-floored, slant-ceilinged, well-windowed space furnished in secondhand rockers, her grandmother's trunk and a pair of cluttered worktables she'd painted cobalt teal, the very color, she realized, of Danny's eyes. Multicolored bottles filled the sills to catch the sun, and every flat surface held a vase or bowl or pot stuffed with flowers from the garden. The air was thick with their scent. Her easel stood by the north wall, and jewel-toned saris draped the windows in purples and reds and oranges. Travel posters took up the stark white walls. Vienna, Rome, Bali. Peru. And, of course, Montmartre.

"You've really never been to those places?" Danny asked, bemused.

Dee looked at the Byzantine dome of Sacré Coeur. She knew how many steps it took to get to that door, too. "Some day."

He turned to look down at her. "I'll take you."

God, she wanted to just say yes. "Thanks for the offer. But there's stuff you need to know first."

"About your painting, obviously." He walked over to where canvases sat stacked against the bare white walls. He bent, hands clasped behind his back as he studied each one carefully. Dee rubbed her hands along her jeans and prayed for strength.

"Do you know what that is?" she asked Danny as he stood considering a painting that looked like a patchwork quilt of greens and golds. "Salem Valley. See the river snaking through? And the cliffs at the edge? See the design?"

It was what she painted. The designs of her life. All experience reduced to geometrics and color, as primary as it got.

"I shifted into a hawk to get that perspective. I also

ate two mice and chased a pigeon for three miles. And that one, the violet and green? It's the flowers on Salem's Mountain."

He tilted his head, trying to pull a flower from the simple lines.

"I was a hummingbird to see that. Exhausting. Those little bastards never stop fighting. And a cat to see the white one. It's a garage door." Titanium white on Payne's gray on burnt sienna with just a stroke or two of alizarin crimson, the composition of genteel decay. "I trotted all over town for two weeks before I found that one. A subject has to strike me, and it usually doesn't until I'm shifted. The one by your arm is the sun reflecting off the rim of Linda Rose's trash can. I was a rat that day. Rats see a lot. And they have a passion for trash cans."

And, of course, if I even tried to have sex with you, I'd turn into your mother faster than you can say Oedipus.

He stopped in front of each painting. He fingered through the stacks as if checking CDs in a record store. He was silent. Dee waited where she was, her hands twisted together, her chest suddenly constricted with dread. *Say something.*

"These are beautiful," he breathed, turning on her, his hands up as if trying to take it all in.

"I use acrylics. They're cheaper, have purer color, and they work faster. I get up before the sun comes up so I can be shifted and anonymous by the time I'm seen. I've only been caught once. Fortunately it was a frat jock on the way home from a kegger. Much better than the time in Ames, Iowa, when I got mad at Lizzie's high school principal and turned into a rottweiler in his office chair. That was the second time we moved. The third was when Mare started her period in the middle of chemistry lab. Everything in the room started flying. She almost burned down the school. Well, we didn't move because of that, really. It was that Xan smelled Mare's power coming on and—"

"Dee," he said softly as he came up to her. "Shut up."

He laid his hands on her shoulders, stilling her. He looked down at her as if discovering something amazing. His eyes, like pools at sunset, seemed to glow in the dim light. "You don't show these, do you?" Not a question at all.

"Of course not."

"Why?"

"They're personal."

"They're unique and amazing. You could be famous."

Dee scrunched up her face. "Oh, yes. I enjoyed being famous so much I changed my name and moved across the country. I'm happy as I am."

Her heart had gone on alert again. She was trembling. He stroked her shoulders as if it were the most natural thing to do, and it took her breath, because it was so alien to her. It made her shoulder flare, as if his fingers had lit that butterfly into sunlight. It made her ache. This was so important. Didn't he know how important this was?

"You're not happy," he said. "You're in prison here. You're dying and you don't even know it. God," he said, shaking his head in amazement. "I knew you were special, but I had no idea. I don't think even you have any idea."

"I didn't bring you up here for that," she protested, suddenly afraid of things she hadn't even anticipated. Beautiful? They were beautiful? "Weren't you listening? Didn't you hear how I painted them?"

"I don't care if you rode a monkey in a wet suit to paint these. They're magnificent."

Dee was rubbing her forehead again. "I. Shape. Shift. I'm not delusional. I'm not lost in Dungeons and Dragons. When I was thirteen I shifted into a wolverine and treed Mare for two hours when she broke my bike. I do this, Danny. You have to believe it."

For a long moment, he just looked at her. Just held her, his big hands gentle on her sore shoulder. Dee couldn't look away. He was mesmerizing, a phantom in the shadows who dangled terrible possibilities before her.

"Dee," he said. "You don't belong here. You belong out in the world, where your work can have a chance to be seen."

"Much tougher to turn into a ferret if you're famous, Danny."

"You can be anything you want. Don't you get that? This can get you out of the bank and off wherever you want. The rest doesn't matter."

She looked at him a long time. "Does it matter to you?"

He shook his head. "Dee . . ."

She closed her eyes and made a last-ditch grab for courage. "I'm going to have to show you, aren't I? Oh, this would be so much easier if Mare were here. She'd just hit you in the head with a muffin and be done with it."

"You don't have to do this. I don't care."

"What's your favorite animal? And don't make it too big. Or a golden retriever. I have too many breakables in here."

"You don't need to prove anything. I love you."

That brought her eyes wide open. Even Danny

looked stunned. "I mean it," he said, and suddenly grinned, hands up in the air. "Good God. In twenty-four hours I've fallen madly in love with a four-star, grade-A—"

"You say 'shrew' and I'll have Lizzie turn you into a wart." How could he make her want to laugh when she was inches away from losing him?

His grin softened, and he bent to cup her face in his hands. "Genius. I'm in love with a goddamn genius, and I want to show her to the world. She doesn't have to prove anything to me."

It was almost enough to make her melt. She wanted to close her eyes and lean into him and be comforted. She wanted to meet him skin to skin, clothes tossed in a heap, mouths bruised with the force of their kissing. She wanted to be safe and she wanted to be free, and there was only one way that was possible. She lifted her own hands and laid them over his.

"I do have to prove it, or I can't trust that you love me."

"Why not? It sure feels like it." He touched noses, his eyes whimsical. "I thought it was gas, but that would have gone away."

"Because you don't know me. Not the real me. You have to meet her before you can decide. Now pick your favorite animal."

"Why?"

She struggled against the tears that crowded her throat. "Because it's who I am, Danny. It's inseparable from the rest of me. If you can't live with it, then you can't love me."

"Hedgehog."

She pulled away. "Your favorite animal is not a hedgehog."

"Of course it is. It reminds me so much of you."

She glared. "Fine." Pulling out the rubber band, she let her hair loose, shucked her sweater and kicked off her basic boring white tennis shoes. "I'll be a freakin' hedgehog."

She did a couple of stretching exercises. *Hedgehog. Hedgehog.* She tried to concentrate, but Danny was standing there with his hands on his hips, a silly grin on his face as if he were waiting for a card trick. She closed her eyes. *Hedgehog.* The image appeared, a quivering, sharp-nosed little thing. Great. Well, at least it wasn't a shrew.

She eased herself down and curled her legs up under her, which saved time when she had to minimize. Four legs, round body, a quiver of bristles. He couldn't have likened her to a fawn. Maybe a kestrel. The air around her seemed to congeal. Sound sharpened, light intensified, and she could smell the charge of her power as it gathered. Lime. Lizzie got flowers. Mare got candy. She got a garnish.

Another charge shot along her nerves. Something alien that glittered a dozen colors behind her eyes. Was Lizzie setting something off downstairs? It was distracting her.

She'd find out later. Right now . . .

Hedgehog.

The tingling began in her chest, a disruption that spread and congealed like the air, so that her blood slowed, settled. Her lungs contracted. Her skin shrank.

Hedgehog.

One last push and she should have it. The power coalesced. Her body fizzed and itched, trembling so hard she was sure her cells convulsed. She squeezed her eyes shut, wrapped her arms tightly around her legs, gathered that odd little animal deep until . . .

Poof!

She coughed. She opened her eyes. She found herself waving away the cloud of green fog that filled the room. With hands.

"Damn."

She stared at her fingers as if they'd betrayed her. She hadn't changed. Something had thrown her off.

"Dee?"

"I'm going to try again."

She tried three more times. All she got was a lot of fog and a couple of lame snapping sounds.

"The green fog is a nice touch," Danny offered, sounding bemused somewhere inside the cloud. "It kinda matches the butterfly."

Dee didn't move from where she was curled up on the floor, her face in her arms. "Green is my color."

Silence. She'd exhausted herself with the trying. She wanted to lie down. She wanted to eat chocolate and cry. She didn't have the luxury. She'd wasted too much time already on this party trick.

"I do love you," Danny whispered, and Dee realized he'd crouched down on his haunches right in front of her.

She lifted her head, miserable tears sliding down her cheeks. "I love you, too."

He looked startled. "Really?"

She nodded, trying to keep from openly sobbing. "I'm so sorry."

He wiped at her tears. "Why?"

She wailed like a little girl. "Because now we're going to have to have sex!"

"God, no. Not that." He was grinning, the bastard.

"It's not a laughing matter."

Gently, he reached over and pulled her to her feet. "If we have to have sex, then we'll just have to take one for the team."

"Oh, Danny. You don't understand. I shift when I have sex."

"Well, unless it's into Jude Law, I don't see a problem."

Dee sighed. "I think you should. And don't joke about Jude Law. The way Xan's been screwing with things, he's suddenly a candidate."

He took a second to lift her hair behind her shoulders. "God, I love your hair. I'm dying to see you wearing nothing but that."

Dee fiddled with his silver chain. "It can be arranged." There was a medal on the end that somehow came free of his shirt. "Saint Michael?" It was still warm from his skin.

"My mother gave me that," he said. "She said it would keep me safe."

Carefully Dee tucked it back inside his shirt and gave it a pat. "Well, for your sake I hope Saint Michael stays on alert."

"Does that mean we're having sex now?"

Dee shook her head. "I need to eat something," she said and sat back down to put on her shoes. "Misfires always make me hungry. Since Mare exploded all of Lizzie's muffins, it'll have to be something else. Nutritional value is strictly optional."

Danny grabbed her shoes before she could and crouched before her. "I know a place we can get all the Nutter Butter bars you can swallow," he said. Lifting her foot, he fitted her shoe.

Dee blinked away new tears. He was putting on her shoes. "If you can also score me a giant order of onion rings, you have a deal. Don't forget to double-knot. I'm tough on my shoes."

He double-knotted. Then he brought her to her feet and dropped a kiss on her nose.

"Thank you." Her smile was a bit watery.

He helped her slide her sweater back on. "We also need to call your aunt."

She'd been all set to turn off the light. His words stopped her. "You really know how to bring a party to a crashing halt."

"You said you wanted to talk to her."

"I don't want to talk to her." Hitting the wall switch, she stalked out the door and down the stairs. "I want to find her before she finds me."

Danny guided her down the stairs. "*Then* can we have sex?"

It was overcast and threatening by the time Lizzie made it home, and darker than it should be at two in the afternoon, and she moved fast, avoiding the neighbors. She didn't have it in her to make cheery small talk. The tattoo was burning against the inside of her ankle. It wasn't a painful burn, more of a needful throbbing. She didn't want her mind to go in that direction, but then, life wasn't going the way she wanted it to.

The purple satin sheets were still on her bed, and the wallpaper with its splash of flowers had disappeared, leaving the walls a rich, creamy shade, even in the darkness. She reached for the light switch and then stopped, the tattoo burning brighter, the amethyst resting against her heart pulsing with life. She looked down at the plain black Asian-style butterfly on her ankle, and it had turned a rich shade of purple, strong and beautiful, like her amethyst. It was as if the tattoo had claimed her, turning from stark black to the rich violet shade that made her think of endless nights and sex and impossible true love. How could a color mean all that?

It was dark in the workshop, the only light coming from the candle that sat in the middle of the circle he'd drawn on the workbench. The array was a new one, more complex than the one he'd used originally, and in the light of the candle his eyes glowed with a deep, lavender light.

He was wearing white, an open shirt and loose white pants, barefoot, watching her, and his dark blond hair was loose around his beautiful face.

"I thought you weren't coming back," she said. And then could have kicked herself. She wanted him back, no matter what she'd said, no matter what she'd told herself.

The teapot was sitting on the workbench, the porcelain Imari cups beside it. He filled hers without a word and held it out to her. And she knew if she took it there'd be no coming back.

She took the cup, careful not to touch his hand, and drank. The perfume filled her senses, spreading through her body, and the frantic pulse of the amethyst slowed, calmed, soothed.

"I put a guard on the door. Your aunt can't touch any of you."

"It'll keep her out?"

He shrugged. "Xantippe shouldn't be underestimated. But as long as the three of you are in this house she can't touch you."

"Why?"

"It's a simple enough protection charm but surprisingly effective . . ."

"Not why does it work. Why did you come back and set it?"

"It's not something that can be done from a distance."

She set her teacup down. "You aren't answering my question. Why did you come back and set a spell to protect us when you're the one who betrayed us in the first place? And why are you still here?"

He didn't answer her question. Instead he pulled up his loose pants leg. "I wondered if you could explain this? It suddenly appeared on my ankle, and I'm thinking it has something to do with you."

She stared down at his feet. They were narrow, beautiful—she never thought she'd be thinking about a man's feet. And then she saw the tattoo glowing on the inside of his ankle, a match to her Asian butterfly, deep purple and glowing.

"What's that doing there?"

"I thought you might know. You didn't have a tattoo when I was here earlier."

She didn't ask him how he knew that. She still wasn't sure how she'd ended up in the purple nightgown, and she preferred to think it was through magic, not his hands on her. "I just got it an hour ago. But I don't understand why it showed up on you, as well."

"I do." He put his teacup down, moved the candle to one side, and before she realized what he was doing he'd picked her up and set her down on the workbench, her butt directly on top of the array.

It was like sitting on a hot burner, the power spiking through her body, turning her insides to molten lava.

"Oh, hell," Elric muttered. He was standing in front of her, and he put his hand on her face, pushing her tangled hair back. "Your eyes are purple," he said, sounding impossibly gloomy.

"My eyes are blue," she protested in a strangled voice. She didn't want his hand to leave her skin—the feel of his long fingers gently stroking the side of her face was a sensation so astonishing that she wanted to cry. "*Your* eyes are purple."

"What?" He sounded appalled, starting to pull away, but she reached up and covered his hand with hers, holding it against her face.

As if he couldn't fight it anymore he leaned forward and rested his forehead against hers. "Doomed," he said bleakly.

Horrible things ran through her mind—had his protection spell backfired, infecting them both with some deadly disease? Had Xan done something unspeakably terrible, poisoning them both?

"Are we going to die?" she whispered, not sure she minded as long as he was with her.

His breathless laugh was only a slight reassurance. "Eventually," he said. "Most people do. We'll just be a lot older when it happens. A lot older than everybody."

"Then what's wrong with our eyes?"

"Disaster. A fate worse than death. I thought I'd done everything to keep this from happening, but my best efforts weren't good enough. The universe *will* have its way."

He lifted his head and looked down at her, and even in the murky candlelight the lavender glow of his eyes was unmistakable.

"What are you talking about?"

"This," he said. And kissed her.

Had he only kissed her once before? Why did it feel so hot, so powerful, so right? There was nothing tentative about the kiss—his mouth covered hers as his hand cupped her face, and he kissed her fully, holding nothing back, and she felt a tremor dancing through her body, something she'd never felt before. Except in dreams.

He moved closer, between her legs, coming up against the workbench, and she slid her arms around his neck, opening her mouth for him, kissing him back, and between their bodies the amethyst hummed and pulsed.

He wrapped her legs around his hips and pulled her off the workbench, and she could feel him, hard and hot against her, and another quiver of reaction danced across her skin.

He left the candle burning, moving through the shadows back into her bedroom, setting her down on the rich, purple sheets.

"Take off your clothes," he said, and the door to her room closed and locked, the clicking sound reverberating in her stomach.

But he was no longer touching her, and some unwanted but unavoidable doubt had reared its ugly head.

"What do you think you're doing?"

He was stripping off his loose white shirt, and even in the darkness she could see the perfect glow of his chest, the smooth golden skin, the taut musculature. A man shouldn't be that beautiful—it was unfair.

"Making a very big mistake. Take off your clothes or I'll do it for you."

She slid backward on the bed, out of reach, suddenly wary. "Don't make any dire mistakes on my account." She couldn't keep the stiffness from her voice, from her body. "I didn't ask you to come back, I didn't ask you to kiss me."

That wasn't exactly true. She'd held on to his hand as he'd tried to pull away, and then it had been too late.

The storm was picking up outside, and the sky was as dark as night, but even in the shadows she could see him quite clearly, the look of annoyance and resignation on his beautiful face. "Yes you did," he said. "Every time you look at me you're asking me to kiss you, whether you know it or not. I should have gotten the hell out of here the first time I touched you. God knows I've been trying to avoid such a disaster for most of my life, and after all these years I thought I was safe."

He was making no sense at all. "Safe from what? From me? I'm no threat to you."

He moved so fast she doubted it was by human means. One moment he was across the room from her, the next his hands were gripping her shoulders as he shook her.

"Are you that blind, Lizzie? Do you really have no idea what's going on here? I know you're not a virgin, even though you might as well be, considering how clueless you are."

She wrenched herself away, moving farther back, to the very edge of the bed, against the wall. "Okay, I get it. I'm clueless and blind, life as we know it will cease to exist. Exactly what has caused this Armageddon?"

"We fell in love."

She couldn't help it—she had to laugh. First, because he seemed so angry and resentful at the thought, and second because it was patently absurd. "Don't be ridiculous," she said. "You're incapable of it."

"That's what I was counting on," he said, almost sounding sullen. "I happen to like my life very well, indeed. I have a castle in Spain, a house in Provence, a flat in London. I have friends, I have lovers, I have a rich full life and there's no room for you in it."

"I don't want to be in it."

"Liar."

She'd been feeling hot, angry, ready to explode, but

suddenly she felt cooler, as if a breeze had washed over her skin. She looked down and jumped. He'd somehow managed to change her sensible jeans and T-shirt into the clinging silk nightgown from the night before.

"Hell, no," she said, furious, and a moment later she was wearing a nun's habit, a puff of purple mist shimmering around her. She only had a moment to be pleased with herself, before he moved.

"Don't bother," he said, and the voluminous folds of cloth disappeared, leaving her in skimpy underwear that might have come from some cosmic Victoria's Secret. Her slightly small breasts spilled out of the lace bra, and the thong was riding up, both arousing and uncomfortable.

She growled, and a moment later she was frozen, immovable, and something was pinching her butt a lot harder than the strip of lace. She tried to move, only to be rewarded with the sound of clanking metal.

"Armor, Lizzie?"

She was totally immobilized. She threw her weight to one side and fell over, pinned to the bed by the weight of the metal.

It didn't help that he was laughing. "Let me help you with that," he said in a kindly tone, and a moment later she was lying on the bed without any clothes at all.

She shrieked as she dove for the covers, wrapping the silk sheet around her.

He knelt on the bed, moving toward her as she huddled in the corner with the covers wrapped around her like a shroud, and he was lean, feral, and the hottest thing she'd ever seen. He was also clearly out of his mind, and even for the sake of great sex she wasn't going to sleep with a crazy man.

And it would be great sex—she had little doubt of

that. Bone-melting, soul-shattering sex, hot and wicked and everything she never thought existed.

She pulled her knees up to her chest, one more layer of defense. "Go away, Elric. You'll get over this if you try. You think I'm a scatterbrained idiot, and I'd drive you crazy if you had to spend much time with me."

"You already drive me crazy," he said. "The fact of the matter is, we don't have any choice."

"You may not have a choice, but I do. Go away or I'll start screaming, and one of the neighbors will call the police."

She had no place to retreat to, and he knelt in front of her, grabbing her hands as she clutched at the sheet. "Look at me, Lizzie," he said in a gentler voice. She closed her eyes tightly, shutting him out.

He was holding her prisoner and she didn't like it. Except that the hands encircling her wrists were oddly gentle, and she knew she could break free any time she wanted to. And she knew she should want to.

"Look at me, Lizzie," he said again, and she couldn't resist the wry note in his voice. She opened one eye, cautiously, then the other.

"What do you want from me?" If she sounded sullen and childish she didn't care. He'd already said that she was a disaster of epic proportions—she had no intention of encouraging his delusions. Even if she had the almost overwhelming urge to put her mouth on his flat, golden stomach.

"Sex. Companionship. True love. Take your pick."

"You're crazy," she said, appalled.

"I know," he said. "Let's start with sex."

She should have said no. Her entire life had turned upside down, all thanks to the man kneeling in front of her, and he seemed to regret it even more than she did. And it wasn't helping that every time he touched her she could feel light and color flooding through her body, and she was tired of being gray and ordinary.

But she wasn't going down without a fight. "Okay, let's look at this logically. You've got some delusion that we're trapped in the curse of true love, though I'm not sure I understand why it's a curse. So if I sleep with you, it'll either free you from that delusion, which would be a relief, or convince you that it's true, which would be revenge. If I sent you away right now, I know that you'd go, and sooner or later you'd realize it was only temporary insanity and you'd forget all about me, and I'd marry Charles if he ever gets back from Alaska and remembers who I am, and I'll have a safe, ordinary life, which is everything I always wanted. The trouble is, I don't want to marry Charles after all."

"Oh, God," he said weakly. "Do I have to marry you, too?"

"Revenge is sounding good to me," she said, half to herself. She scooted down on the bed, the purple sheets pulled up to her armpits, and closed her eyes. "Have at it."

If Elric had any doubts as to the scope of this catastrophe, looking down at Lizzie as she lay on the bed, swaddled like a mummy in purple satin, her blond curls tangled around her pale face, her eyes tightly shut, convinced him it was all too terribly, horribly true. He was in love with her. He didn't need the purple rim around his eyes to prove it—all he had to do was look at her and he was lost.

She was fighting it even harder than he was, but then, she didn't know it was hopeless.

He leaned over her, taking the edge of the sheet and tugging gently. She quivered for a moment, keeping her hands at her sides, effectively keeping the sheet over her, but he was a lot more experienced than she was, and he simply pulled it down, away from her body, tossing it on the floor beside the bed.

She was the most luscious thing he'd ever seen in his entire life. Smooth, creamy skin, smallish breasts, soft and small and sleek. A far cry from the experienced, sophisticated women he tended to sleep with, and she was absolutely, shyly irresistible.

He put his hand on her ankle and she jerked, her eyes opening for a minute and then shutting again. This was probably the way Charles did it—with Lizzie lying passively, missionary style, while he groaned and sweated over her. He might have to kill Charles.

Or at least turn him into a moose. Moose did well in Alaska, didn't they? Maybe a polar bear would eat him.

But he wasn't interested in thinking about Charles at the moment. He kissed her ankle by the side of her brand-new tattoo, tasting the rose-scented soap she'd bathed in. He kissed her behind her knee, and he could feel the tremors run through her body. Fear or arousal? Or a heady combination of both? He kissed the inside of her thigh, the soft skin at her hip, and she was trembling in earnest now, her eyes tightly shut. Poor baby, she had no idea what was in store for her.

He kissed her other ankle, moving up her legs with slow, lingering kisses, and his hands cupped the full sweetness of her hips.

"Open your legs for me, Lizzie," he whispered.

She opened her eyes instead. "What?" she demanded, shocked.

"This doesn't work with your legs together, sweetness. Hadn't you figured that out yet?"

"But . . ."

"Open your legs for me," he said again, helping her, pushing them apart and moving between them, and she braced herself, expecting God knows what. He hadn't even taken his pants off yet.

She really was the most adorable, pathetic creature right now. So frightened, so needy. So why was he shaking, too?

He pulled her toward him and put his mouth between her legs, because he needed to, and she let out a shriek loud enough to rouse the neighbors. Her hands left the bed to clutch his shoulders, pushing at him. "Don't do that," she said, a thread of desperation in her voice.

He looked up at her. "Why? Is it sinful?"

"You shouldn't . . . I can't . . . you wouldn't . . ."

"I like it," he said, touching her. She was slick and wet, even before he'd gone down on her, and she was wound up so tightly she might burst. He wanted her to burst. To split apart, into a thousand pieces, and then he could pull her back together again.

All it took was the touch of his tongue, and she began to spasm, her body contracting in helpless pleasure. He held her there, for long, endless moments, letting the waves of her release fall around him, and as each one began to subside he would bring it on again, with his fingers deep inside her, with his tongue, his lips, his teeth, until she was sobbing, rigid, gasping for breath, and then he took her further still, into a dark, hot place that even he seldom reached.

When he sat back on his heels, kneeling between her legs, she tried to curl up, in on herself, hiding her face, hiding her body, sobbing, and he knew if he let her she'd keep hiding. He pushed her back against the sheets, gently, covering her body with his and kissing her mouth. And another orgasm caught her body with weary pleasure.

He hadn't even realized how fucking hard he was—he'd been concentrating so intently on her response that he hadn't even realized he was about to explode. He'd barely started with her, hadn't gotten to the sweet perfection of her small breasts, the smooth curve of her back, the softness of her butt. He wanted to touch everything, inside and out, he wanted to take her places he barely knew himself, and he shoved the loose white pants off, leaving him naked and so painfully aroused he didn't know if he'd ever manage to get off.

"No." The voice was no more than a plaintive whisper, and yet it was like a death knell. He could change her mind, all he had to do was touch her and she'd forget that she ever said no. But her hands came up to push at his chest, and he fell back, away, onto the bed beside her, barely able to catch his breath. If she really wanted revenge she couldn't have picked a crueler one. He closed his eyes, trying to control the tension that drummed through his body. He didn't know where he'd get the strength to move, to leave her, he only knew he had to, because she'd said no after all, and maybe he'd been wrong about the purple in her baby blue eyes, and maybe . . .

Her mouth touched his, her lips feathering across his with sweet, soft kisses, and he stared up into the lavender shadows of her eyes, confused and so damned needy he thought he might never walk again. She'd gotten to her knees, leaning over him, her scattered curls falling in her face as she kissed him, his mouth, his eyelids, the pulse in his throat, moving down his chest with slow, delicious, torturous bites and licks and kisses, and he needed her to just touch him, just lightly, please, so he could die a happy man, as her tongue touched his navel, working downward, and he knew he was going to die and he was happy to do so.

Her hands were cool, soft, as she touched him, encircling him, holding him, and he wanted to teach her, tell her what to do, but her very helplessness made it even more powerful, and when she leaned down and put her unpracticed mouth on his cock he felt the power of it through every cell in his body.

And he knew he certainly wasn't going to last long at that rate. He let himself absorb the sweetness of her mouth for a moment, then gently lifted her away, ignoring her sound of protest.

"Later," he said, sliding her onto her back. "We have time for everything." And he pushed inside her, filling her tight, clamping sweetness with his cock, pushing in so deeply that she gasped, her breath catching as he filled her.

They both froze, staring into each other's eyes. Lavender into violet, wizard into wizard, and it was so right he would have cried, if he was a man who cried.

She reached up and smoothed the moisture away from his eyes, her fingers shaking, and then she pulled him down to kiss him, and he lost the last tiny bit of control he'd been clinging to. He pulled her legs up, tight around his hips. He tried to move slowly, deliberately, but her fingernails were digging into his back, she was shivering and shattering in his arms, and he could feel her body clamp around his, and there was no holding back. He followed her down the dark slide into eternity, feeling it burst around them in a flame of colors. And there was nothing left at all.

Dee told herself she was on a mission from God. She couldn't just sit in Salem's Fork waiting for Xan to bring disaster down on them. She had to try and prevent it, and the only way she knew was to find her aunt before she had a chance to act. Xan was close, metaphysically. Dee could feel it. So she searched for her like Tommy Lee Jones tracking a fleeing felon. She refused to admit that she was using her search as a means of avoiding Danny.

He'd bought her Nutter Butter bars. He'd fed her onion rings. She hadn't even been able to dredge up the courage to so much as kiss him thank-you. After all, how gracious would it be to respond to such kindness by sending the man into therapy for the rest of his adult life? Especially a man who'd just said that he loved her.

What if Xan was right? What if Dee actually had found her true love, only to have to give him away again? She'd never had to survive that kind of alone before.

So, she ran. The problem was, Danny James refused to be left behind.

"Butterflies make me hot," he whispered as they stalked the halls of the General Lee Motel. Dee was trying to be surreptitious, but she knew she looked like a German shepherd sniffing out bombs. Come to think of it, if she weren't so distracted, it might have been easier to shift into one. Nobody stared at a dog that sniffed the air.

"From what you've told me today," Dee said, "breathing makes you hot."

"If you're the one breathing."

Dee flushed, unaccustomed to the flirting. Terrified to anticipate anything beyond his escort through motel halls.

There was no Xan here. Not that she should have been surprised. It was one of those brown-and-gold-paisley kinds of places with a pool smack in the middle so the chlorine clogged up your nose. But even chlorine couldn't mask cinnamon and sulfur. At least not Xan's mix. And there wasn't a trace of it.

Dee had only caught her scent once, at the Peaceful Garden B and B down the road in Martinsville. The owner swore the only guest she'd had was a shy librarian sort who'd checked out that morning. Dee had nodded and moved on to the next place. She wasn't going to give up until she'd checked out every hotel, motel, and rented room in a ten-mile radius.

Danny held open the General Lee's front door. "Why don't you just meet with her?"

"I did."

Danny frowned at her. "Then why are we chasing her around town?" Dee struck the General Lee off the list she'd scrawled on the back of deposit slips and stepped out onto the cracked parking lot. "Because I can't let her get another jump on me. Next time, she could really hurt us."

"She *hurt* you?"

"Not enough to matter. Not like my parents. I was right. She killed them. So I'm not going to let her kill my sisters."

"She told you that?"

"She did, actually. I shouldn't have been surprised, I guess. She said it was their fault, of course."

"Can you tell me anything else?"

Dee considered him a moment, with his clear honest eyes and his untested power. "Not yet. I'm sorry."

Danny nodded. "Okay."

He steered her to the bike.

Dee stopped. "That's it? Okay?"

He shot her a bright smile that could make a girl forget her name. "Sure. Witch hunts make me hot."

He bent far enough that his lips fluttered over the shell of her ear. "Especially when the hunter is a gorgeous redhead with a butterfly tattoo on her shoulder."

Dee damn near melted into a puddle on the spot. God, she wished he'd stop doing that. He was driving her insane. Already she felt as if she needed to borrow one of Mare's bras. Hers suddenly seemed so tight. He handed her in and out of doors, on and off the bike, and always managed to find a bit of exposed skin to brush against. Wrist, throat, the gap between her jeans and T-shirt above her hip. She felt as if he'd stroked a live wire over her. And he kept riding her back and forth across those godforsaken cobblestones. How did he know?

"I'd say I should dye my hair," she challenged, "but you'd tell me that brunettes make you hot."

"Do they have tattoos?"

She giggled. She couldn't help it. He was keeping her in an agony of ambivalence. He tempted her so much, with his mad blue eyes and sly smiles. But he terrified her even more. She'd seen the horror in men's eyes. She couldn't bear to see it in his. For all the brave talk in her studio, all she wanted was to put off the inevitable as long as possible.

They stopped by a Dollar Dayz and got Dee a

small spiral notebook to replace her deposit slips, a package of rubber bands for her hair, which Danny immediately snatched, and ten more Nutter Butter bars. Witch-hunter supplies. They also discovered that Xan had been in. Of course everybody in the place remembered the stunning visitor from the day before. Staying over to Bicksburg, they thought. Two of the men even pulled out phone numbers. Dee would have told them how hopeless a return call was, but Fred Norton had tried to bully Mare in high school. Mare had knocked two of his teeth out, of course. Dee figured Xan would make him grovel like a serf. She tucked her new notebook in her purse and headed for the door.

"Can we have sex now?" Danny asked, following.

Dee patted him like a toddler. "After Bicksburg."

"You promise?"

"Don't you ever think of anything else?" she demanded as they walked across the parking lot.

He never slowed. "No man ever thinks of anything else. Well, except rare moments when they're trying to remember football statistics."

She was smiling again. Damn him. He made her want him.

"You don't have to kill yourself, Dee," he said, touching her arm again. Always touching her. "You know she'll find you."

"The best defense is a good offense."

He grinned. "Football coaches—"

Dee laughed, pushed him again. "We can't have sex."

She should just get it over with. She should haul him into one of those cheesy pressboard-furniture-and-industrial-carpet rooms they'd been scouring, toss him on the bed, and break most of the cardinal rules of nature. He sure wouldn't be whispering in her ear after that.

"You're not going to have sex with me until you find her, are you?" he asked.

Dee stood by his bike, running her hand over the butter-soft leather. "I have responsibilities. Since you showed up, I've forgotten most of them. But that's not going to keep Xan from coming after us. If we don't stop her first, we'll never be safe."

"Coward."

She straightened to find that he wasn't smiling anymore. The storm shadows collected in the hollows of his cheeks and made him look fierce.

"I am not a coward."

"You're hiding behind your sisters, behind the threat of your aunt. Behind the door of that little house of yours. You're braver than that, Dee."

"I'm not hiding. I'm trying to live a normal life, just as I dreamed when I was a little girl. Hell, I even have a white picket fence."

She knew she was trembling again. Her stomach was suddenly in turmoil. Right there in the middle of the Dollar Dayz parking lot, for God's sake. Couldn't he challenge her in private? Couldn't he not challenge her at all?

"You have a prison surrounded by a big garden."

"You don't understand," she whispered, her voice suddenly hoarse. "You don't know what Xan really is."

"I'm not talking about Xan."

"Then what?"

He bent over so he could face her eye to eye and took her face in his hands. "Not everyone hides her passion in the attic, Dee. Come out into the sunlight."

"As what?" she asked, pulling away. "I can be a

bulldog. Or maybe a seagull, except nobody really wants them around, no matter how cute they are."

He ran a finger down her cheek, setting off sparks all the way down her arm.

"As the woman who painted those paintings."

He brought her to a stop. *They'll see me.*

Danny frowned. "Who'll see you?"

Dee started. "You're doing it again."

"Then maybe I am psychic. Tell me, Dee. Who'll see you?"

She drew in a deep breath, struggling to quell the hot rush of tears that crowded the back of her throat. She couldn't bear to look at him. She watched the street.

The Dollar Dayz took up a corner of Main near the highway, a graceless stretch of fast food and strip malls. She'd painted it in shades of umber and gray. "Do you know what a nightmare it was to be Delightful Dee-Dee? To never have privacy? To have strangers think they had the right to you? Those paintings are . . ." She picked at a loose button on her cardigan. "They're me." She knew her voice was small. "I should have the right to say who I share them with."

Gently Danny lifted her face. "You showed them to me."

The button came off in her hand. "You don't understand them, either."

"I understand that they're the product of an amazing, beautiful, talented woman who should be able to share her vision with the world. I understand that I want her to smile more and worry less. That I've been thinking about wandering the world with her just so I can watch her paint my favorite places, because I can't even imagine how they'll look through her eyes."

How could something that sweet hurt so much?

Danny took her by the arms. "The rest doesn't matter, Dee. I promise."

Damn. The tears were swelling, searing her throat and forcing her to swallow. She nodded. "I promise you. It does."

"Then make love with me. As the woman who paints those paintings."

For a minute Dee couldn't manage a single syllable. She could barely see him through the tears she kept sniffing back. "You don't believe in her. And I don't think you'd like her."

"I have the courage to try. And I don't think I'm going to be disappointed. Do you?"

There was no air to breathe. Her heart hammered like an off-balance washing machine. Dee opened her mouth twice before she could answer. "Will you promise me something?"

"My life, my wealth, my body."

"If you suddenly see somebody you recognize, just close your eyes?"

His laugh was sharp. "You do make life interesting, Dee."

"Promise."

"I promise. But I'm not inviting anybody to this party but you."

His eyes were so sweet. So very dear and bright and clear. Dee sighed. "You may be surprised by who shows up."

"And you'll make love to me without consideration of whether Xan is confronted or not. Or whether your sisters are having man troubles or Xan troubles or tattoo troubles. I assume they got them, too."

Dee gaped. "How did you know?"

He grinned. "Because I know you'd never do that on your own. But you'd do anything for your sisters. Now, are you agreed?"

"Where? When?"

"Dee," he said with a chuckle. "We're not scheduling a root canal. These things are better done spontaneously."

"Not in my house they aren't. Lately, you just don't know what's going to happen there. Besides, I really, really don't want any surprises. Well, more than are inevitable."

Her heart picked up even more speed. She was damp all the way down her back. She shook like a terrier, and a fire burned in her chest that threatened to melt her.

Oh, God. She was going to try.

With Danny James. Her lover.

Well, there was no better way to spit in Xan's face. If both of them survived, anyway.

"The mountain," she blurted out.

Danny took a second to consider. "I like it. Dancing up with the witches. It's just about Beltane, isn't it? I know the moon's almost full. Doesn't sex play a big part in the celebration?"

"How did you know?"

"Researcher, remember? We're all frustrated *Jeopardy* champs. I say we go right now. After all, my policy is to never put off something you want to do. Only the things you have to do."

She giggled like a nervous virgin. "It's only five. A bit of discretion from the local personal banker is always a good idea."

"On the other hand, if you shatter your reputation like cheap ceramic, it'll give you the excuse to take up painting full-time."

"I don't want to traumatize the girls."

"Are you kidding? The girls are going to throw a parade in my honor."

"I beg your pardon."

Reaching over, he pulled off her current rubber band and sent her hair flying. "You," he said, dangling the limp oval before her, "need to let your hair down more."

She wanted to giggle again, but she was too breathless. He was smiling, but his eyes gleamed hot. His eyes took the stuffing out of her knees.

"Also, when we're traveling the world, being sybaritic and feckless, I absolutely forbid you to wear cardigans. Math teachers wear cardigans. You will wear silk and linen and the odd feather in your hair."

"On a researcher's salary?"

He kissed her nose. "I'm going to live on your art. Clever, don't you think?"

She nodded again. She was beyond fear. Somewhere between anticipation and terror, she thought. And before she'd even so much as shed her shirt.

He pulled her against him. "Kiss me to seal the deal?"

Dee took another anxious look around. "Right here?"

"It's part of proving how brave you are." He blew gently in her ear. "And how feckless."

Dee was glad he had a hold on her. Her knees failed again. Her nipples snapped to attention and showers of sparks washed down her neck. He was smiling down at her as if she were the last drink on a desert. She couldn't have looked away if Xan had tapped her on the shoulder.

She managed to lift her face and smile back. It was all the invitation Danny needed. Dee thought she heard a sigh of relief from him as he bent to her.

Dee had been kissed before. Good kisses, bad kisses, kisses that curled her toes. In all the history of kisses, though, none was more perfect. His lips were so soft she wanted to lick them. His whiskers chafed her skin. His eyes, open so she couldn't mistake him, darkened to midnight.

He didn't just kiss her. He claimed her, his mouth ravenous, his hand curled behind her head, his other arm wrapped so tightly around her she had no room for escape. He branded her with his lips and his tongue and his breath, and Dee couldn't bear the idea of stopping. She raised her arms and wrapped her hands around his neck, and oh, yes, his hair was just as silky as she'd hoped. And fun to winnow her fingers through. Just another color of sensuality; damson maybe, rich and deep and delicious.

For the kiss she'd use vermilion. Hot and sweet and impossible to turn from. Dee dined on that kiss. She let Danny plunder her lips and then returned the favor. She traced the tiny scar she hadn't noticed at the edge of his mouth, and nibbled at his lower lip like a forbidden sweet. And his tongue. Oh, she couldn't think of a thing that could give proper homage to his clever tongue. He sought out every part of her mouth, tracing ridge and hollow and the sweeping slope of her tongue. And then he returned to engage it in an unbearably erotic dance.

Dee lost track of time and place and propriety in that kiss. She felt him harden against her and envisioned them skin to skin. She didn't ever want to stop. She wanted to wallow in the sudden glow of her own body. She was nothing but liquid and light, and only one thing could have brought her up short.

Her body warned her. It wasn't insistent yet, but it was obvious. A hot ember that lodged right behind her breastbone and flared to life. It kept expanding until she thought it would consume her, a pulsing, living lucency that seemed to coalesce in her belly. Her very cells began to hum.

She jerked back, pushing at his chest. "No . . ."

Danny was panting like a long distance runner. "Oh, yes." He was smiling, the rat.

"I'm sorry," she said instinctively, giving him another little push.

He let her go without hesitation. "You're not allowed to apologize. Official Feckless rules."

She shook her head, trying to get her breathing and heart rate back under control. She wanted nothing more than to grab him by the ears and pull him back into that kiss. She wanted to go down on him like a hooker. She *wanted*. She sucked in a series of calming breaths, and inevitably the glow faded to safety. It made her want to cry again. She wanted to go up the mountain so badly.

Danny tucked a couple of curls behind her ear. "You want to go to Bicksburg now?"

She blinked, still trying to pull her senses together. "Just like that?"

"Are you kidding? I'm going to spend every second we're there fantasizing about what crimes we're going to commit on that mountain tonight."

He didn't just fantasize. He aided and abetted. In Bicksburg he bought her a red feather boa. In Martinsville it was scented warm body oil. Citrus. An odd choice, Dee thought until Danny told her he liked his pleasures tangy and tart. Like her.

While Dee was checking out the Burns Bridge B and B, Danny was at the Sweet Tooth confectioner getting liqueur truffles. And next door to the Motor 8, he found a string of pop beads.

"Okay, I wanted pearls," he told her as they sat in

Miss Mamie's Tea Parlor for dinner. "But we'll have to settle for these."

Dee pulled the beads apart and then reattached them with a lovely, well, popping noise. "You want me to wear a necklace of hot-pink pop beads when we make love?"

Danny's grin was purely salacious. "Honey, they're not going to be anywhere near your neck."

Dee was sure she was a fluorescent shade of crimson. "Oh."

But oddly enough, it was Xan who furnished the best accessory. After a long day of not even coming close to finding her, Dee gave up and asked Danny to run by the house. It was sundown, and the storm still threatened. The temperatures ahead of it had risen unnaturally, so that she'd even ditched her cardigan by about four. But it was almost dark now, and Dee had plans.

She was so hungry. So anxious. So damned ready. No matter what, she was going to walk up that mountain and see this through. She might have a spectacular flameout, but she might actually succeed. The only way she'd know for sure was by taking the chance.

So, Danny's saddlebags loaded with everything from whiskey to a lovely suede French tickler, just in case one of them got spunky, he pulled up to the gate and shut off the motor. Dee swung off the bike and almost stumbled. Something hit her from behind. Something soft, like a wash of air from an open oven. She spun around, wondering what Danny had done now, but he was checking something on his front wheel.

Suddenly there was a rustle in the bushes, and Py let out the most incredibly soulful yowl Dee had ever heard. His call set up a veritable glee club from hell all up and down the block.

"Pywackt?" Dee called, shoving open the gate.

"Seems to have quite a following," Danny said, looking up the street. "Must be all that Edith Piaf."

It wasn't just the cats, though. Dogs howled. Birds chattered and trilled. A veritable squadron of rabbits was suddenly doing maneuvers on the Ortballs' yard, and the Coxes' Chihuahua could be seen nuzzling the Nelsons' Saint Bernard. Dee kept turning in circles, wondering at the sudden heat that was crawling down her spine, at the softening of the stormy air so that it seemed the sun shone anyway. Damn, her flowers were multiplying again, and it was almost dark out.

Her first thought was that Lizzie had had another experiment go wrong. She checked the chimney, but there wasn't any new smoke. She couldn't blame Mare. She certainly couldn't blame herself. She didn't do that kind of stuff.

"Is that Frank Sinatra?" Danny asked.

Dee cocked an ear to hear the vague tunes above the caterwauling. "And Michael Bolton and Andrea Bocelli and Liza Minnelli. And, wait for it . . . yes. Barry White. Every neighbor on the block must be getting in the mood."

And the Foleys next door were well into their eighties. But that was definitely their silhouette in their front window.

"I'm impressed," Danny marveled.

"Me, too. Mr. Foley's been in a wheelchair for a month."

Her own senses were heightened. She could hear Danny breathing as if he were whispering in her ear again. She could smell that wonderful soap and man musk on him, and his power signature had strengthened. Not just an approaching storm, but one about to break. She could see the pale glow of his eyes, and couldn't bear to turn away.

She was suddenly aching and hot and hungry. She took a look at the oak tree next door and thought how delicious it would be to scrape her back against that bark as Danny took her against it, driving hard into her until her skin was raw and everybody on the block heard her screaming.

"Dee," Danny said from right behind her. "Are you thinking what I'm thinking?"

He wrapped those wonderful long-fingered hands around her breasts. Dee sucked in a desperate breath. "Probably not," she had to admit. Then she closed her eyes and savored every stroke of his fingers.

"I'm thinking I might not make the mountain. What are you thinking?"

She sighed. "That Aunt Xan's sent out a libido spell."

Well, there went his hands. "Now, Dee. Everything isn't from your Aunt Xan."

"No, but I can guarantee this is. The Foleys haven't spoken to each other since he had an affair with her sister fifteen years ago. Besides, they both loathe Sinatra. They listen to polka music."

Danny looked over to where the silhouette was gyrating to "Luck Be a Lady Tonight." "And you really believe it's a . . . libido spell."

Py set up another grating racket, making Dee wince. "Yeah. When we were younger, we tried a libido spell for me. We hoped it would improve my results. It didn't. But I know the feeling. Only Aunt Xan's is much stronger. Either that or it's just exacerbating the fact that I'm already horny enough to howl."

"Uh-huh. Well, what do you plan to do about it?"

Dee laughed so hard three of the rabbits stopped and turned to look. "Are you kidding? Say thank you and head up the mountain."

M are had walked back to Value Video!! in time
to see William moping in the storeroom. "Go
eat something," she said and sent him to the
diner, in no mood for any more depression. Then she'd
taken her Styrofoam out to the counter and found Jude
talking sternly to Dreama, who looked rebellious.

"Ciao, Mare!" Jude said.

"Now what?" Mare said to Dreama.

"I caught Dreama making a personal phone call,"
Jude said stiffly.

"I called Algy," Dreama said.

"That wasn't a personal phone call," Mare said to
Jude. "Stop being such a damn bean counter." She
looked at Dreama. "Is Algy coming back tonight?"

"No," Dreama said miserably. "He wouldn't even
talk to me."

"Well, you did your best."

"You could have gotten Algy back," Dreama said
even more miserably.

"The hell I could have," Mare said. "I'm a complete
failure." And Dreama scowled at her.

"Now about New York," Jude said, trying for busi-
nesslike and just sounding fussy. "I can guarantee you
a vice presidency in public relations, but you'll have to
promise to give up anything *out of the ordinary*—"

"No. Also, I sent William on a lunch break. He
needed hot protein." Mare put her Coke down on the
counter.

"No food at the front of the store," Jude said automatically.

"Don't make me hurt you," Mare said. "I want to talk to you. *In private*."

Jude blinked and said, "I really don't have the time right now, perhaps later," and made tracks for the back of the store, and when Mare followed him, he was gone.

"Little weasel," Mare said when she came back to the front.

"I don't like him," Dreama said.

"Hold that thought," Mare said.

Jude stayed MIA, but William came back very late in a slightly better mood after Pauline fed him, the afternoon went by without incident, and then the six-thirty showing of *Corpse Bride* went off without a hitch except for Mare's almost uncontrollable urge to weep when Emily turned into moths at the end. *That's me*, she thought, *I'll end up a bunch of blue moths, unloved in this creepy little town.* She was so bummed by the thought, that she almost missed the weirdness that started around eight o'clock, just as the sun was going down.

First William didn't come back from his dinner break, although the fact that he'd taken not only a lunch break but a dinner break, too, was noteworthy in itself. Jude came back and called the Greasy Fork to track him down, incensed that Value Video!! was missing fifteen minutes of quality morose manager time, and they told him that not only was William not there, but Pauline had gone AWOL, too. "He didn't kidnap her and take her hostage, did he?" Dreama asked, and Mare said, "For what? Extra ketchup on his fries?" Then Algy called and asked to talk to Dreama, and when she hung up, she was pink-cheeked.

Mare said, "So?"

"He's coming to the nine-thirty show," Dreama said, blushing brighter.

"That's good," Mare said, starting to smile in spite of herself because Dreama looked so flustered. "And why is that?"

"He said he'd come if I'd sit with him," Dreama said. "And I'm, like, off work then, so I can. He was really cute about it. Forceful, even."

"This is excellent," Mare said. "I think— *Hey, you!*"

Across the store, the boy who'd put his hand down his girlfriend's blouse straightened up.

"What were you *thinking*?" Mare said. "The sun isn't even down yet," and he sank back into his chair.

That was when she noticed everybody was sitting closer than usual.

"You know, Algy is *really cute*," Dreama said, fluffing up her hair a little. "I told him to come early so we could like, talk."

"You did," Mare said, looking around.

Over on the love seat, Katie stuck her tongue in Brandon's ear. Brandon almost passed out.

Jude caught her eye from the back of the store and motioned to her.

"Stay here," she told Dreama. "Watch everybody. There's something weird going on."

"Well, fix it," Dreama said.

Mare sighed. "I told you, I'm not—"

"Yeah, but that's crap," Dreama said. "I've been working with you for two years. I know what you do. I watch you talk to the people who come in here. I watch you walk down the street. People stare at you, but it's not because of the weird stuff you wear, it's because you know stuff, because you're not afraid to say things, because you make a difference, you make things happen." She stepped closer. "You can catch DVDs, no hands. Pencils don't fall on the floor when you're around. I was right behind you when you found William, and we were clear across the storeroom, but you lifted him off that rope before we were even close. You *saved* him before we were close. You really are the Queen of the Universe. So I know you're having a bad day, but snap out of it. Because we need you. Queens of the Universe do not get days off, so just suck it up and get back to work."

Mare blinked at her, and Dreama stuck her chin in the air and went back to the counter.

Mare thought, *Well, hot damn, Dreama,* and then Jude called, "Mare, I'm ready to have that talk now," and she went to the back of the store and followed him into the storeroom, still stunned by Dreama and the backbone she'd grown while nobody was watching.

"So, Mare," he said, when he'd closed the door.

"So, Jude," Mare said. "I know Xan's up to something because she damn near killed me this afternoon, and I know you're part of it, so tell me everything right now and you'll get to keep all your working parts."

"You were right, I do know your aunt," Jude said. "She told me all about you, she showed me your picture, she told me you worked in one of our stores, and Mare, I fell in love right there."

Mare rolled her eyes. "No you didn't. You're the wrong guy. She probably put a spell on you or something. Now what's her plan? We know the whole taking-the-powers bit, but exactly *how* is she—"

"No, Mare," Jude said fervently. "*You* put a spell on me, I loved you from the moment I saw your picture, and *I wanted you*—"

He lunged for her, grabbing her arms, and she said, "*Hey,* watch my veil!" and tripped backward into the shelf behind her, knocking over the plastic bottles of orange popcorn oil, bouncing them onto the concrete floor and breaking one as Jude tried to slide his arms around her, aiming for her lips and kissing her cheek instead, his tongue flicking out at her ear.

"God, *no, stop it.*" Mare pushed him away, trying to keep her veil from ripping, but he grabbed again and got her breast this time, squeezing it as if he'd never felt one before, and she smacked at him with the flat of her hand, catching him on the nose so that he jerked back. Then she kneed him in the stomach and he slipped in the oil, and she lifted the broken oil bottle with her mind, and dumped the rest of the oil over him so that he slipped again and again on the floor. She looked around for something else and levitated the ripped beanbag chair, letting the pellets fall out to hover in the air in a blanket above him and then dropped them on him all at once so that he was covered in them while she smoothed out her blue tulle skirt.

She didn't mind kicking a guy around, but she drew the line at screwing up her Corpse Bride dress.

"For the last time," she said, shoving her veil back into place so she could see him better. "You're an *evil minion.* You do not get the girl, you do not get laid, you do not get anything but humiliated." She shook her head at him, splayed on the concrete floor, covered in orange goo and white pellets. "Why anybody ever applies for the evil minion job is beyond me. Didn't you see this coming?"

"I'm a *vice president,*" he said from the floor, outraged.

"You're a *minion,*" she snapped. "You might as well have a target painted on your forehead. Now what the hell is my aunt doing? And while we're at it, what the hell is going on out there?"

"Out where?" he said, looking legitimately confused as he kept a wary eye on the empty vinyl beanbag still hovering above him.

"Out there in the store? All the PDA?"

"PDA?"

"Public Display of Affection," Mare said, exasperated. "Don't tell me that's not a spell. What's Xan doing? Or is that your idea of foreplay?"

"I don't know," Jude said, still watching the vinyl bag overhead.

"Oh, great," Mare said, "a *clueless* evil minion," and dropped the bag on him.

She detoured around the popcorn oil slick and locked him in the storeroom and then went back to Dreama. "How's it going?"

Dreama looked perplexed. "I never thought *Corpse Bride* was a very *hot* movie, did you?"

"No."

"Well, a lot of people are necking to it."

Mare cast an eye over the escalating PDA in her audience. "Wait here." She walked around the counter and out the door into the street. People were walking hand in hand, stopping to kiss in the twilight. In darkened doorways, they were doing more. In bouncing parked cars, a lot more. Dogs howled. Cats yowled. The birds in the trees twittered with more enthusiasm than usual.

A passerby said, "Hey baby," and tried to kiss her, grabbing her butt in the process, and she gave him a bloody nose.

He staggered on down the street and she got out her cell phone and called Dee.

"Hello?" Dee said breathlessly.

"Dee, it's Mare. I think Xan's doing something. Jude just attacked me in the Value Video!! storeroom, and now everywhere I look, there's sex."

"It's a libido spell," Dee said.

Mare looked at the phone, stunned. "A libido spell?"

"She's made the whole town hot to get us into bed with the guys she sent."

"Oh." Mare thought about it. "What's that going to get her?"

"I don't know," Dee said. "Make us fall in love faster? She really wants us with these guys. Are you okay?"

A guy stopped and opened his mouth to say something, and Mare looked him straight in the eye. He moved on.

"Yep."

"Good. I have to go."

Mare frowned at the phone. "Go where?"

"Up on the mountain with the guy she wants me with. This is a good libido spell. No point in wasting it."

"Danny's back? That's gr— No, wait. This is Xan's plan. You tell that man good-bye and get your butt back home. What are you thinking?"

"I'm thinking it's about time I had sex on a mountain."

Mare started to yell and then reconsidered. "Oh. Good point. Be careful."

"Not this time," Dee said and hung up.

"I'll be damned," Mare said, and went back inside. Algy was behind the counter with Dreama.

"Good to see you, Algy," Mare said. "Take any liberties with Dreama, and I'll rip your heart out and feed it to my cat."

"Mare," Dreama said.

"I'm Queen of the Universe. I can do that." Mare dialed her cell phone again and waited until Crash picked up. "I was wrong. I apologize."

"I accept," Crash said. "What took you so long?"

"I've been mostly dead all day."

"Princess Bride," Crash said. "Your roof at eleven?"

"Yes," Mare said. "Do *not* talk to another woman until then."

"Why would I?" Crash said and hung up.

Dreama was smiling at her. "Feeling better?"

"Jude's locked in the storeroom covered in popcorn oil and beanbag peanuts." Mare straightened her veil and put her sunglasses back on. "Take Algy with you when you let him out, just in case he has Ideas."

"Oh, my," Dreama said, impressed.

"Yep." Mare swished her blue tulle skirt which looked *fabulous*. "I'm back. And I owe you, baby. Have another box of Junior Mints. Take two. Knock yourself out on the Jujubes, too. In fact, take anything you want."

"Cool," Algy said.

"Respect this woman," Mare said to Algy as she headed out to the floor to break up the worst of the PDA. "She's gonna be Queen of the Universe someday."

"I'm *glorious*," Dreama said and handed Algy his Junior Mints.

Lizzie lay on the bed, purple smoke floating in the air above her, the purple silk sheets smooth and sensual beneath her body. She could smell roses—she hadn't realized the ones in the dining room were so strong. And then she realized the scent was coming from the bed. She opened her eyes, to see her body covered with lavender rose petals. Elric lay on his stomach beside her, a few stray petals in his tangled blond hair. He looked exhausted, and she couldn't blame him. All she wanted to do was curl up next to him and sleep in his arms—the emotions swamping her body were too new, too strange. It was as if a protective covering had been washed away, and the new Lizzie, the one lying naked and exhausted and replete beside her wizard lover, was a stranger.

And yet she wasn't. This Lizzie had always been inside her, hiding from the arguments, trying to keep her magic from getting noticed, doing her best to fix things. Right now she didn't have to fix a thing, didn't have to listen to anybody. All she had to do was slide up against Elric's strong, beautiful body and try to ignore the sudden resurgence of desire that was sweeping through her. For heaven's sake, they'd done it three times in a row, and each time had been more powerful. There was no way she could want more.

But she did. She rolled onto the scattered rose petals, and the fragrance drifted up as she snuggled against him, trying to quiet the sudden stirrings. He opened his eyes to look at her, and the deep iris hue was glowing. He plucked a rose petal from her shoulder.

"I should have known," he said, resigned. He picked up a handful of the feather-soft petals and let them drift down over her body. "It only needed flowers to seal the deal. There's no escape now." He shook his head, and a loose petal landed on his elegant nose. "We may as well accept our fate."

"Oh, I've accepted it," she said. "I'm just . . ." Words failed her.

"You ready for more?" he asked lazily.

She should have been embarrassed. Except that he rolled onto his back and he was clearly as interested as she was. "This is crazy," she whispered, sliding up beside him.

"No it's not. It's Xantippe."

"What?" Lizzie jumped back from him in horror, almost falling off the bed.

He sat up. "Not that I want to keep my hands from you, my love, but normally even I would like a rest at about this point. Your aunt must have cast some kind of libido spell."

Lizzie grabbed the sheet from the foot of the bed, wrapping it around her as she climbed off the bed, and the flower petals scattered everywhere. "You mean the only reason I had sex with you was because Aunt Xan made me do it?" There was no way she could hide her horror.

His expression was so tender that she wanted to cry. "Haven't you been paying attention? Up until about fifteen minutes ago it was just us. The rose petals prove it—if Xantippe's spell had been working they never would have appeared, trust me. This spell is brand-new. Your aunt's been trying to disturb things, and she'd use just about every trick in the book. You don't need to worry about it—the spell doesn't work unless the partners are more than willing. God knows she's tried it on me for decades and I have yet to succumb."

She stared at him, unmoving. "Decades? You and Xan? Ew."

"*Not* me and Xan. I've never been interested. She likes men—surely you know that much. She likes men with power even more. The problem is, I see her a lot more clearly than she likes. I wouldn't touch her with a ten-foot pole."

She glanced down at him. "That might be a bit of an exaggeration," she murmured, and then clapped a hand over her mouth, horrified, and the satin sheet began to slip.

"That's the spell, you saucy creature. It relaxes

inhibitions, and puts one's libido into overdrive. But don't worry—we can ignore it."

"We can?"

"Of course. Singly we're more than a match for Xantippe's waning power. Together she doesn't stand a chance. Though I think I like the idea of you being just the slightest bit raunchy."

"Let me build up to it," she said faintly. "So what do we do?"

"Talk?" he said, and laughed when he saw the expression on her face. "We can talk about how powerful you've become."

"I *know*," she said, curling closer to him. "Isn't it amazing?" She smiled to herself. "Maybe it's because you're such a good teacher."

He shook his head. "It was you, Lizzie. You had that power all the time. I don't know why you weren't using it."

"We had to be so careful," she said, relaxing into the sheet as it slipped farther down. "Always looking over our shoulders, making sure that nobody thought there was anything wrong with us, never calling attention to ourselves." She pushed her hair out of her face as she looked at him. "No smoldering purple smoke coming out the windows, no green fog seeping out the doorway, no blue sparks shooting out the chimney. We just *sat* on ourselves all the time. I practically buried myself in that workroom."

"*Buried yourself?*" Elric said, grinning. "How *tragic*."

"We were good little girls," Lizzie said primly, letting the sheet slip a little more. "And I was the best. And then you showed up."

"The big bad wolf."

"The big bad sorcerer," Lizzie said. "And now I

feel . . . *unleashed*!" She threw her arms open and the sheet dropped to her waist and Elric laughed and reached for her and she grabbed for the sheet again as he pulled her to him.

"Xan's spell must have made me do that," she whispered, and he kissed her.

"I don't think so."

"I'm hungry," she said.

And he let her go and said, "Then eat something." He saw the expression on her face, and laughed. "Not that, Lizzie! We'll find something for dinner, and I'll tell you about Spain, and just to prove how weak Xantippe is, I won't even touch you."

"Okay," she said, not necessarily pleased at the notion. "I'll just take a shower. Alone," she added, catching his eye. "If we're going to circumvent Xan we need to avoid temptation. How long do these things usually last?"

"It should be gone by dawn."

"We have to wait that long?" Lizzie wailed.

"We don't have to do anything . . ."

"Never mind. I'll take a shower and then cook us dinner."

"So will I," Elric said. "A cold one. And I'm going to cook for you. Oysters. And strawberries, and champagne . . ."

"Saltpeter," she said firmly, clutching the sheet more tightly around her. If she jumped his bones, as she wanted to so desperately, then Xan would win. And she couldn't let that happen.

Her own shower didn't do much good. The feel of the hot water beating down against her skin was an erotic stimulus, and she couldn't wipe lascivious thoughts from her brain. She hadn't had a chance to really use her mouth on him, and she was getting obsessed with the idea, fantasizing about it, her hands soaping between her legs—

"No!" she said out loud, turning the water to icy cold. But even that was arousing, and she turned off the water with a curse, wrapping herself in a towel, rubbing her skin briskly, then more slowly, languorously . . .

"Goddammit," she muttered. She was standing stark naked in the middle of the bathroom, wearing nothing but red patent hooker stiletto heels, and she yanked on her clothes with shaking hands. The fresh tattoo on her ankle glowed with an almost malevolent sensuality, and she shoved open the door with a little moan.

She headed down the stairs, careful in her hooker shoes, to find Elric in the kitchen, shirtless, a helpless expression on his face. "I can cook," he said. "I promise you, I could cook you an absolute feast out of nothing. But right now . . ."

"Right now we've got better things to do," she said. "You have any problems giving in to Xan's spell?"

"I thought you'd never ask." And he picked her up, tossed her over his bare shoulder, and headed back into the bedroom.

The moon shone after all. It wasn't perfectly full. Beltane wouldn't officially start for a few more hours. If anybody felt compelled to light bonfires, they'd have to do it the next night. Which was just fine. Dee had an idea she was going to create enough of a conflagration as it was.

They approached the stone circle at dusk. Danny

brought the whiskey and truffles. Dee brought the feather boa and pop beads. She even wore what she considered to be her ritual garments. She'd ridden up the hill covered in her long raincoat, her hair caught in a ponytail to keep it out of the way. She carried two blankets and a couple of green pillows she'd pulled from her studio.

When they reached the stone circle, though, she revealed her true colors. Laying her burdens across the grass at the foot of the Great Big Rock, she set her boa and beads alongside. Danny pulled whiskey glasses from his jacket pockets and set them up alongside the bottle of Midleton he'd managed to unearth in town. He was just turning when Dee slid out of her coat.

"Holy Mother of God," he breathed in awe.

For the first time in her life, Dee O'Brien appeared outside her house wearing nothing but the long white silk slip dress she wore to paint. She pulled the band from her hair and shook it out so that it caught the breeze and whispered into lazy motion, her Irish witch's banner flowing well past her shoulders. She slid off her sandals and stood on the sacred ground in bare feet.

"I decided not to hide in the attic," she said, and hated the fact that her voice sounded uncertain.

For the first time since she'd known him, Danny James was struck dumb. He just stared, hands out, breathing hard, face frozen in a stunned kind of yearning.

"What?" she asked, his amazement bolstering her. "You don't think the virgin-on-the-way-to-a-sacrifice look is good for me?"

"I think it's about to make my eyes melt." He unfroze,

walking up to her and lifting a trembling hand to her hair. "My sweet God, Dee. You're an earth goddess."

She smiled. "That's actually what I was hoping for. Something in the Persephone line. Innocent but brazen."

"I couldn't have said it better." He kept fingering her curls. "Great dress, by the way. Do you wear it for any other guys?"

"I wear it to paint."

He nodded, still looking stunned. "I bet you do. It goes great with your butterfly."

Dee felt the fizz of his arousal along every nerve ending. "An added bonus, just for you."

He nodded. Swallowed. "Um, would you like a drink? I sure think I'm gonna need one."

Dee wanted to laugh. She'd never felt so strong before, for once in her relationship life not the supplicant. He needed a drink. And not because he was disgusted. Okay, that might come later, but for now she was damn well going to enjoy the feverish light in his eyes.

"I'm not used to drinking," she said. "It makes me a little nuts."

Danny held out a hand, as if calling her to dance. "Oh, but this night demands a little nuts, don't you think? And I promise. You're going to like this."

"As much as the pop beads?"

Good heavens. His eyes simply went black. "Oh, no. But it's a close second to the feather boa."

Dee grinned and laid her hand in his. As tenderly as if he were escorting her to a cotillion, he guided her over to where the blankets were spread and helped her down to sit with her back against the Great Big Rock. She faced the edge of the cliff, which gave her a lovely view of the sleeping fields and the deepening twilight sky overhead. Peacock and carmine and a slash of gold where the lowered sun licked the top of low clouds.

And there, the evening star. *Let us be safe. And let me not disappoint this good man.*

Sliding out of his jacket, Danny laid it on the slab of granite and took the glasses in hand. With those in one hand and the bottle in the other, he slid down to nestle right next to Dee on the thick plaid blanket. "Now, this is some of the finest whiskey the Irish make. And the Irish make great whiskey." He poured two fingers each and handed Dee her glass.

"Have you been to Ireland?" she asked, measuring the light that glinted off the amber liquid.

"Often." He carefully set the bottle over his head on the rock. "You think the fields are green here in the spring. In Ireland they're so intense they make your eyes ache."

"And Paris. You said you've been to Paris. Have you walked Montmartre?"

Danny laced the fingers of his free hand with hers. "It's a flea market of a place with narrow, steep streets and quaint cafés and one of the most beautiful churches on earth. Would you let me take you there?"

Dee held on tightly to him, both with her hand and her eyes. "I can't think of anything I'd love more."

"But we'll see?"

She opened her mouth. Shut it. Shook her head. "This isn't a test, Danny," she said. "It's not pass\fail. I want to make love to you because I love you. But it could well prove that we're not able to go any farther."

"You mean me."

"I know who I am. You don't."

"I told you. I know enough. Did I tell you I love you?"

Her smile was wistful. "You did."

"And you'll let me show you?"

"As long as I get to show you back."

He leaned down, so that he blocked the last light of afternoon and the breeze, so that he brought the stillness of night with him, and he kissed her. Hot and wet and openmouthed, but with unspeakable gentleness. Heat swept through Dee. Longing such as she'd never known. Terror.

She denied the terror its root, and leaned into the kiss with every ounce of passion she'd stored up for twenty-six years.

This time it was Danny who pulled back, panting. "You haven't had your drink yet."

Dee ran her tongue over her lips to capture the rest of his taste. "You want to take the time?"

He scowled at her, flicking the end of her nose with his finger. "This is a seduction," he informed her archly. "Not a blitzkrieg. Proprieties will be observed at all times."

"Oh, good God," she said with a scowl. "Another movie quote. Are you sure you shouldn't be dating Mare?"

He laughed. "Another reason to love you. You recognize *The Quiet Man*. A classic in film."

"You aren't a John Wayne fan, are you?"

"John Wayne is God. It's tattooed on my left buttock. Wanna see?"

"It is not. I already have."

He looked astonished. "You've been peeking?"

Dee lifted her glass and grinned at him over its rim. "Twee. Twee."

Danny spun around on her. "Good God. It wasn't stuffed."

"Not the owl. And yes," she said. "She did like you.

Especially that star birthmark on the inside of your right thigh."

"Wanna see it again?"

She grinned, giddy. "Birthmarks make me hot."

He drew a finger down the hollow of her throat. "That can be arranged."

Dee took another sip of the whiskey. Danny was right. It was smoky and smooth and the perfect accompaniment for a tryst in the middle of a stone circle. It settled into her stomach and sent tendrils of warmth spreading through her. Good. A few more of these and she might relax enough to avoid disaster.

Danny finished his drink in a gulp and set both glasses aside. Dee damn near gulped herself.

"There is one thing you should probably know," she said.

"You shift. I heard."

He reached both hands out to her. Dee shied back. "Uh, no. This is something else. A direct result, if you will, of the shifting."

Danny lowered his arms. "I'm doing the best I can here, Dee. But my patience is not what it usually is tonight."

"The libido spell," she said with a nod. "I know. It's affecting me, too. Do you know you smell like the sea and the air right before a storm?"

"I hope you like those things."

"Hugely. I'm a virgin."

She'd done it again. What had happened to her tact? She squeezed her eyes closed in humiliation, knowing damn well Danny would be appalled.

"It hasn't just been a long time," she babbled. "It's been never. Not because I didn't try. I did. But . . . so far there isn't a guy who's lasted past the point where

I shift. At least one wasn't heard to speak again for four solid months."

"Never?" he asked, his voice oddly small. "Not even in college?"

"By then I'd given up. Besides, I was too busy. Mare was going through puberty, and it was spectacular." She shrugged and rested her head against his chest. "I hope you're not allergic to dust bunnies. I really want to do this."

She surprised a laugh out of him, which got her eyes open fast. "I'm sure it amuses you. It's not quite so fun from here."

He wouldn't let her pull away this time. Reaching out, he slid his hands into her hair and pulled her toward him. "I promise," he said, his face no more than inches from hers so she couldn't miss his sincerity. "You will not leave this mountain a virgin. I think you can trust me to make it past the dust bunnies and lost socks. And I further promise you're going to enjoy it."

Dee couldn't help smiling. "Did I tell you I love you?"

Danny smiled back, and it was incandescent. "You did."

And then he kissed her. His hands still tangled in her hair, his body warm and strong, his breath a whisper of enticement.

"Did I tell you I've been to Peru?" he said against her mouth.

She did her own kissing. She could survive on nothing but his mouth. She explored, savoring every curve, every secret recess that carried the taste of him. She nibbled and licked and teased her tongue against the nascent whiskers that lined the edge of his lip. She dipped her tongue into a dimple and traced his lips with her own. Then she closed her eyes and traced them all with her fingers.

"I'd love to go to Peru," she said, stroking her thumb over his upper lip, sliding it up to measure the slight crook in the bridge of his nose.

Danny took her hand in his own and kissed it. Then he took his turn, kissing her forehead, her cheeks, her chin. He kissed her eyes closed and then paid tribute to the shells of her ears.

Dee gasped, shuddering with the startling pleasure of having someone lave her ear with his tongue. Who knew? No one else had ever taken the time. Then he sipped lower, along her pulse point, which she knew was erratic and bounding. She felt as if she had a hummingbird trapped in her chest, her heart beat so fast. She was sure that was why she couldn't catch her breath. Not the fact that when she finally got the chance to give in to temptation and explore the lovely contours of his chest with her hands, she met rock-hard muscles and the surprise spring of hair. Oh, and she knew the line that lovely mahogany hair followed. She wanted to trace it down. She wanted to yank his shirt off and discover the texture of his skin with her hands and lips and tongue.

"Would you like to go to Giverny?" he asked, sliding her straps off her shoulders. "I could take you to Giverny."

Dee arched a bit to give him better access. It seemed as if her breasts anticipated him, already tingling and taut and heavy. Please, she thought in desperation. Take them in your hands. Take them in your mouth and suckle so hard I feel it in my toes.

He must have heard her again. He set his mouth to her and feasted.

"I'd love to . . . oh . . . ah, go to Giverny. What about . . . oh, yes . . . Tahiti? If I'm following great painters I should . . . go . . ."

Her gown was at her waist, and his mouth was on her breast. She couldn't keep her eyes open or her hands still. She measured his back, his strong, lean back, and traced those lovely biceps. She fought that ember when it sparked. But then Danny nipped at her breasts with his teeth, and she forgot control.

"Tahiti," he said, taking her breast into his hand, "would be lovely. As long as you dress like a native. I want to be able to see these magnificent breasts every day."

He licked her throat, inciting fierce chills.

"My breasts are too small."

"Shut up. Your breasts are perfect."

And to prove it, he devoured them all over again. Dee didn't mind losing that argument. She was melting, the wicked witch in water. Sliding down to lie on the blanket with Danny following her as he traced her arms, her hips, her legs with his wonderfully callused hands. As he slid the dress completely off.

"Not fair," she gasped, arching with the pressure of his palm against her belly. "You're the only one in clothes here."

"Easily remedied."

Immediately remedied. She'd thought he'd looked impressive before. It was nothing to Danny James rampant.

"Dear Mother of God," Dee breathed, unconsciously mimicking his earlier words. "Do you think you're appropriate for a virgin? I mean, shouldn't I start out on something smaller and work my way up?"

Danny burst out laughing. "You do know how to make a man happy." He lay down next to her, nestling skin to skin, just as she'd dreamed. "Now, relax. It's a man's work I have before me this day."

She groaned. *Another John Wayne . . . oooooohhh-hhh . . .*

He kissed her, slowly and sweetly and absolutely sinfully. He fitted himself against her, shoulders to toes, so she couldn't be confused about how happy he was to be there. He let his hand drift from breast to belly to mons.

"Open for me, Dee. Let me give you as much pleasure as you give me."

Dee wasn't sure her legs worked properly, but she did her best to oblige. And gasped again when she felt his hand on her inner thigh. When he slipped his fingers into her.

"God," he moaned. "You're so beautiful. You're so wet for me. Feel it?"

Feel it? She was writhing with it, stunned with the sudden shaft of pure, sweet pleasure his fingers unleashed. It consumed her, sweeping away every other thought or action. She couldn't speak, couldn't breathe, and he was still tormenting her with the most cunning fingers ever attached to a hand. He slid a finger inside, then two. Pleasure speared through her, igniting unquenchable holocausts, freezing and burning her at once, confusing her body, her power, so she didn't know how to gauge her danger. So she couldn't care.

But oh, his hands. His mouth. His sweet, hot breath fanning across breasts dampened by his tongue. His words, raw words of need and want, promising, pleading, propelling her to new agonies.

"Danny . . . *please . . .*"

She was scrabbling at him, sobbing and cursing, fighting the inevitable explosion. It was coming, and he wouldn't allow her to rest, to hide from it. She was going to change. God, her body had to be glowing with the building power. She had to be too close to stop it.

"Close your eyes . . ." she begged. "Oh, close your . . . ooooooh . . . my . . . . *God* . . . !"

Cataclysms, catastrophes, colors that simply didn't exist in the universe spun within her, gathering, intensifying until she couldn't stop moving, until she couldn't stop begging, until, suddenly, she disintegrated into shards of light and color and sound, gasping and weeping and bucking hard against Danny's touch, convulsing into the night sky like fireworks on the Fourth of July.

She was panting like a long distance runner, and she knew tears ran down her cheeks. "Never," she admitted, "this has never . . ."

"Well, it will again," he promised, still stroking her. "And there's even better."

"There can't be. I'd never survive it." She opened her eyes and almost came right off the blanket. "Oh, no! I told you to close your eyes."

Danny easily held her to him. "Why should I, and miss the most beautiful sight ever?" His smile was so bright, so wicked. "You in the throes of orgasm."

He was acting as if nothing had happened that wasn't natural.

Dee frowned, still struggling with the aftershocks that shuddered along her limbs. "But I've shifted."

"Shifted? Into what?"

Dee caught her breath. The idea was inconceivable. "Who do I look like?"

Danny brushed her hair away from her damp forehead. "Persephone."

Suddenly she was sobbing, and she couldn't stop. "I'm me?" she demanded. "I'm really me?"

He looked so confused, so concerned. He kept stroking her, soothing her sobs. "There's nobody else I'd be making love to."

"Oh, Danny." She laughed and cried at once. "Make love to me." She took his face in her hands. "Banish the dust bunnies. Please."

"With pleasure."

He kissed her, mouth and breast and the tender, sleek skin he'd just been torturing with his fingers. He stoked those terrible fires all over again until Dee couldn't breathe well enough to beg. And then he lifted himself over her and nudged her legs open and kissed her hard, plunging his tongue deep in her mouth, stroking her to incandescence, and then he slid into her, tight into her, impossibly large for her, and he gentled her and incited her and brought her right back to a shattering, gasping climax at the very moment he plunged home, past the slight resistance that didn't matter after all, so deep into her that she thought she'd die, that she thought she had died, and he pumped into her, slowly at first, but gathering speed, murmuring delight to her, murmuring encouragement and gratitude and love as she felt the pleasure spiral yet again to impossible heights, matching him move for move, murmur for murmur until she convulsed, screaming, and he emptied himself into her, emptied the last of him into her, and fell into her arms, spent and struggling for breath.

"I really look like me?" she asked a few minutes later as she stroked his hair where he'd rested his head between her breasts.

"Like no one else."

She chuckled. "Oh, hell. Now I'll never be able to convince you that I'm a shapeshifter."

And then she slept, with Danny James in her arms, up on the mountain where the witches danced.

At eleven o'clock, Crash climbed the rickety trellis again and found Mare waiting for him on the roof, dressed in her Corpse Bride dress and holding two DQ hot fudge sundaes. Py was stretched out at her feet, eyeing the cups.

"You look great," he said, sitting down beside her, using every ounce of self-control he had not to touch her.

"Thank you for coming," she said, primly. "That was very forgiving of you."

He looked at her, round in the moonlight, smiling at him. "Not that much to forgive."

The moonlight was bright enough that he could see straight through that blue tulle to her spectacular legs, long strong legs, and the urge to run his hand up under that skirt was damn near overpowering. He reached for his sundae instead, but she cocked her head at him, holding it out of his reach. "So that's all it takes? I call up and say, 'I'm sorry,' and you come back?"

"What am I, stupid?" Crash said. "Of course that's all it takes. This is True Love. You think this happens every day?' "

"Princess Bride," she said. "I don't know why anybody ever quotes any other movie."

"Well, there are other really good ones." Crash closed his eyes to keep from lunging for her since he was sure he was in a good place right now. Mare smiling at him was always a good place. "Can I have my sundae now?"

She stuck her chin out. "You remember what I tried to tell you last night? That I was magic?"

"Mare, I have *always* believed you were magic," Crash said.

"Uh-huh. Here's your sundae."

Crash reached out, but the sundae floated over to him of its own accord, bobbing along on the cool night air, ignoring the stiff breeze that was still promising the storm to come.

He froze for a moment, watching it hover in front of him, while Mare took the lid off her sundae and spooned up the first bite as if nothing unusual were happening. His stayed just out of reach, moving up and down, side to side, back and forth, as if sliding on invisible strings. It had to be a trick, he told himself, but when it slid closer to him, he ran his hands around it, trying to find the supports and couldn't.

"You're good," he said finally. "How do you do that?"

"Magic." Mare spooned up more sundae.

He took his and still couldn't find the wires that had held it up. "You're really good. Got a spoon?"

The spoon floated over to him, too, spinning in lazy circles until it arrived at his cup and stuck itself into the ice cream.

Okay, that was beyond good. Granted, he never did think clearly when he was with Mare, but this . . . He looked over at her.

She looked back at him calmly, heat in her eyes.

"My uncle used to do magic tricks," he said, staring at the sundae and the spoon and then at her again. "Nothing like this."

"I didn't say 'trick,'" Mare said carefully. "I said 'magic.' I'm magic. My family is magic. I'm psychokinetic. Dee's a shapeshifter. And Lizzie transmutes things. She's trying to turn straw into gold right now. That's why the shed roof hums."

Crash looked at the sundae again, took a deep breath, and dug the spoon into the ice cream. Mare was not crazy. She was odd, she did and said odd things, that was one of the reasons he loved her. But this . . . "Shapeshifter?"

"Usually some kind of bird. She's into flying. I think it's a metaphor for her need to escape, but that's just me." Mare licked her spoon, sounding very matter-of-fact, but his mind latched on to the "licking the spoon" part as something pleasurable and understandable and much preferable to "My sister is a shapeshifter," and it was with real regret that he dragged his mind back to the part he was going to have to deal with.

"Straw into gold."

Mare nodded. "That's Lizzie's big project. She does smaller things. Like when she gets nervous, she turns things into rabbits. On bad days, we're up to our asses in bunnies. If she's turned on, it's shoes. Usually, whatever she transmutes turns back on its own. Sometimes it doesn't."

Py lifted his big head and stared at Crash, his golden eyes solemn in the darkness, and Crash began to believe against his will because those were not house cat eyes.

"Where did you say Lizzie found Py?"

"The zoo."

"Right." He rubbed his forehead with his hand. "Let's try this again."

"We come from a long line of witches," Mare said, as if they were having a completely normal conversation.

"No real trouble aside from the odd pond ducking and one burning at the stake." Her voice darkened. "We ever get time travel, somebody's gonna pay for that one."

Crash took a deep breath. "Uh-huh."

Mare scooped up more ice cream. "Our aunt Xan convinced Dad and Mom to go on TV and we ended up the Little Miss Fortunes, and you'd have thought somebody would have seen the play on words there, wouldn't you? But no, and the show was a success, but then something went wrong, and there was a fraud conviction, and Mom and Dad asked Xan to take their powers for some reason, and she took too much and they died."

Crash straightened at the bleakness in her voice there. That wasn't magic, that was real, he knew that part, and suddenly her whole preoccupation with Xan began to make sense, magic or not. "Dee took us and ran from her, and it's been thirteen years on the run since then, what with all kinds of people wanting to get hold of us."

"Hold of you," Crash said, losing all appetite for his ice cream. He put the cup down for Py, having a feeling that anything he could do to make Py like him might pay off big in the future.

"We were the Miss Fortunes," Mare said. "Very big deal. Especially for Aunt Xan. All those powers, you know?"

"I'm starting to. That's the secret you could never tell me?" Okay, she thought she was magic. Except there was that spoon spinning around and sticking in the cup. So maybe she was magic.

"It's a lot to wrap your head around," Mare said. "I've never told anybody before. I don't know what the time frame on the learning curve is. Maybe never."

Crash took a deep breath. *Keep an open mind. This*

*is the woman you love. No matter what happens, this is
the woman you're with for the rest of your life, so . . .*
"So what else can you do?"

Mare put her cup down on the roof for Py. "Nothing. I have the suckiest power in the family."

"Hey," Crash said. "It's a great power. I just got
here, so I'm not fully clued in yet, but it's amazing."

Mare looked at him oddly.

"Well, it amazes me," Crash said, with absolute
truth.

Mare nodded. "So you believe me. Just like that."

"I saw it," Crash said, pretty sure he had.

"It could be just a great trick." Mare stuck her chin
out. "I'm pretty smart, you know."

"Smarter than I am," Crash said. "But you wouldn't
lie." She wouldn't, he realized. And she wasn't crazy;
Mare was a little off the wall, but at base, she was the
sanest person he knew. "You wouldn't lie about something like that. You'd lie about getting a tattoo while
I was gone—"

Mare groaned and put her head on her knees.

"—but not about something like this. You're serious
about this. And I have to tell you, there are weirder
things in the world. So why not? I saw it. Do it again."

Mare looked away from him, biting her lip.

"Hey." He put his arm around her, and when she
looked back at him her eyes were bright. "Don't cry.
We're good."

"We're great," she whispered. "If you can hear all
that in five minutes and believe it and still say, 'We're
good,' we are fucking great."

"Well, we knew that," he said, and kissed her, and
any doubts he had went away in the heat and the rightness of that kiss, the way she fell into his arms and became part of him, the way he went dizzy, wanting her.

When she broke the kiss, she sniffed, and he thumbed away the tear on her cheek. "Hey, I love you," he said. "You were always magic to me," and she sniffed louder.

"Okay, then." She rolled to her knees and wiped her eyes. "Look in here." She took the front of his jacket in her hand and pulled him toward her bedroom window, and he peered inside and got the first good look at it he'd ever seen.

The room looked like Mare. The walls were draped with mismatched blue velvet and satin curtains with glittery gold butterflies embroidered on them and dark blue flowers painted on them. There was a long backless couch covered in blue zebra skin and a vase full of the black satin roses he'd given her for prom—she'd kept his roses, that was something—but the biggest thing in the room was a broken iron bedstead, huge and black with spirals and circles, spinning and turning in on each other, making Crash dizzy when he looked at it, mostly because it was Mare's bed and he wanted her on it. A big black witch's hat was stuck on one of the high posts, and the mattress was piled high with blue and lavender and green pillows, and even as he saw them, they began to stir and flip and tumble to the floor on their own—*she's doing that,* he thought, *she's magic*—and when the watery blue satin comforter rolled slowly back, no hands, he drew in his breath and looked at Mare, and she smiled at him in the moonlight. Then the blue-striped top sheet rose up and floated toward the curlicued iron foot of the bedstead until the bed lay open and inviting in the full moon, and all the blood left his brain, and he pulled her closer to him, feeling her soft flesh yield to him under that slippery, torn blue tulle dress.

Mare whispered in his ear, her voice full and rich,

making him shiver. "This is my room. No man has ever been in here before. We don't bring men into our bedrooms. We're magic in there and we can't trust them."

Oh, Christ, he thought, and nodded and began to turn away, and then she whispered, "Come to bed, Crash," and he shuddered as a wave of lust hit him and damn near knocked him off the roof, but she caught him and climbed through the window, pulling at his arm, and he fell into the magic that was Mare's bedroom.

Her room seemed smaller with Crash in it, a little kid's room with a witch's hat on the bedpost and the cheesy crystal ball and black fake flowers on the vanity, and she swished her Corpse Bride dress a little from nervousness because it was one thing to boink with her boyfriend on a mountaintop and another thing entirely to bring her One True Love and future husband home to meet her bedroom.

"So this is my place," she said, fighting back the heat that washed over her every time she looked up at him because that was the libido spell and she had to keep a clear head for this next part. He looked around, taking his time, and she did, too, biting her lip, seeing through his eyes the moth-eaten secondhand draperies she'd tacked to the walls every place she'd ever lived, covered with the sloppy blue flowers she'd painted on them when she was ten and the crooked gold butterflies she'd embroidered on them at twelve; and under them the beat-up iron bedstead she'd found in a junk-yard at fourteen, its spirals broken and bent and some of them missing; and the silky blue comforter she'd gotten on sale when she was sixteen, the day she'd decided to have sex with him someday, whenever his dad stopped calling her "jail bait." She remembered that first time, how careful he'd been, and she put her hand out to steady herself on the bedstead as the libido spell got her again, or maybe it was just that memory. She jerked her mind back to the room and all its failings: the tacky zebra-covered fainting couch was missing one leg that she'd replaced with her copy of the OED, the cheval mirror that was so speckled with age that it looked like it had mildewed, the threadbare rugs and the cracked lamps, the whole place just so . . .

"Great room," he said, his voice a little unsteady.

It's a mess, she thought, *it's junk. Why would any man want to marry a woman who lives like this?* "It's not much," she said. "But you know, it's—"

"No, it really is great," he said, looking at her. "It's hot and it's magic like you," and she looked around again and saw the splashy flowers and the jaunty butterflies and his wicked black silk prom roses that Lizzie had gathered up off the road for her after they'd wrecked, and Py stretched out yawning on the windowsill—

"I like it here," he said. "Do I get to stay all night?"

"Yes," she said happily, and took off her veil and tossed it toward the bed. It floated through the air—she gave it a little help—and landed on the bedpost opposite the witch's hat, the ends curling down to fold themselves like arms over the post.

"That's *amazing,*" he said.

"I can do better," she said, and pulled her dress off over her head and tossed it into the middle of the room where it pirouetted, its skirt spinning out around it, and then curtsied to him. "How about that?" she said, and turned to look at him, but he was looking at her. "Hey, you missed it."

"I didn't miss anything," he said, looking at her blue lace bra.

She sighed happily, and he didn't miss that, either, so she kicked off her shoes and went over to crawl onto the bed and sit cross-legged with her back against the headboard, rosy with heat for him, smiling all over but determined to make sure he understood everything before they ripped into Xan's libido gift.

When he tried to join her, she pointed to the footboard. "Sit."

He sighed, but he took off his boots and sat down there.

"Is there anything you want to know?" she said, gathering her hair up off her neck where the heat was making it stick.

"Yeah," he said. "How long am I going be stuck down here?"

She let her hair drop. "I mean about me. About this." She gestured to her dress, and it pirouetted again.

"What's to know?"

"Well, it's *hereditary*," she said, a little annoyed.

"All right."

"So if you're serious about getting married and having kids—"

"I am."

"—there could be some surprises down the road," Mare finished.

"Okay."

Mare leaned forward, her elbows on her knees. "That's it? *Okay?*"

Crash leaned forward, too. "You sit like that, anything you say, I'm going to say 'okay.' But yes, okay. Our kids will be all right. They'll be ours. Now can we practice making one?"

"You sure you want to have them?"

"Yes," Crash said. "We can start tonight if you want. I'm ready. I want to get married to you, and I want to have kids with you. But mostly right now, I want to have sex with you. Lots of it. As much as we both can stand. All night."

"Libido spell," Mare said. "My aunt cast it."

"No," Crash said. "I always feel like this about you. I always have. But you always had to come home and shut your window, keep your secret, shut me out. Now I'm inside. I'm staying. Anything else?"

"Just like that," Mare said. "You want to marry me and have kids, my aunt does libido spells, my magic's no problem."

Crash sighed. "Okay. Tell me the part I'm missing that makes it complicated." He leaned back against the footboard, patient. "Put a little speed on it if you can. I want you."

"Well," Mare began, and thought about it.

She wanted to marry him and spend the rest of her life with him. She wanted kids. She wanted them while she was young. If she thought about it, she was ready now. There wasn't anything she wanted to do that she couldn't do while backpacking a baby. Crash's baby. Maybe two. Two would be good.

"Two?" she said.

"Two would be good," Crash said. "Maybe three. Four."

"Two," Mare said. "They shouldn't outnumber us. We don't know what they can do yet."

Maybe it wasn't complicated.

Crash stood up and stripped off his T-shirt. "Is this

something we could discuss later?" He sat down on the edge of the bed and shoved off his jeans.

"Why, yes, I think we could," Mare said, looking at the muscles in his back. In his thighs. Well, everywhere.

She cautiously let go of the edge of her control and let the libido spell in just as Crash rolled onto the bed and reached for her.

He touched her and she shuddered, sliding against him as the memory of him came back.

"Huh," she said, as the heat washed over her, the bubble in her blood and the prickle under her skin.

"What?"

"You're right. It always feels like this." She arched up and kissed him, loving the feel of him against her, the sure pulse he started everywhere. "Just one more thing."

He groaned and put his head down on her thigh, and she patted the top of his head, loving the way her hand bounced on his thick, springy dark hair, loving more the weight of his head there, the heat of his breath, wanting to pull him into her.

She drew in her breath. "You know how we always go up on the mountain?"

"Yes," he said, his voice muffled.

"That's because everything up there is too heavy for me to lift."

He picked up his head and looked at her.

"When I get distracted," she said, smiling down at him, breathing hard now, "things move. So when we're rolling around on this bed, as we're gonna be very shortly, and I start to lose my mind, as I'm gonna very shortly, this place is going to get active. Try to keep your head down."

He sat up on the edge of the bed and looked around. "Anything in here I should know about?"

Come back here. "I don't know." She leaned forward and put her chin on his shoulder, refraining from biting it only by Herculean control, and looked around with him. "I've never had sex in here. I mean, there's loose stuff like hairbrushes and shoes and my jewelry, that stuff, and I collect a lot of things, but I've never done an inventory. I wasn't *expecting* to invite you tonight, so I didn't go through looking for projectiles, you know? I didn't, like, *sex-proof* it."

Crash looked over his shoulder at the dressing table.

"We can go up on the mountain," Mare offered, praying he wouldn't take her up on it. The mountain was *minutes* away.

"Oh, no. It's taken me years to get in here, we're staying." He looked at the pointed witch's hat on the bedpost. "This is the first time in my life I'm wondering if it's a good idea to be naked for sex."

She bit him gently on the shoulder.

"So that's a yes," he said, and kissed her, and she kissed him back as he slid his hand up her thigh, and the kiss lasted longer than they'd meant it to, neither one wanting to stop.

"We could start slow," she whispered against his mouth, when they broke for air, breathing hard against him. "See what happens."

"Uh, Mare?" he said, looking over her shoulder.

She turned her head. Her Corpse Bride veil was floating behind them. "It's all right," she said. "No pins. That crown thing is a headband. *Kiss me again.*"

He kissed her again and she closed her eyes and sighed against his mouth, letting the kiss seep into her brain as his hand moved to her breast, her blood hot now, breathing with him, but when she opened her eyes, he was looking up, his mouth still on hers and his hand still curved around her, but not really paying attention. She pulled away and looked up, too.

The veil was spiraling above them.

"Is that good?" Crash said.

"I'm *happy*," Mare said, but she snapped her fingers and the veil fell down into her hand. "You know, you're going to have to just let go and ignore this stuff or we're never going to get anywhere. You sure you don't want to go to the mount—"

"I'm sure," Crash said, and bent her back onto the bed onto cool blue sheets that were infinitely better than the rocky ground up on the mountaintop.

This could bring a whole new dimension to sex, she thought and dropped the veil and tilted her hips, rolling him over so she could be on top, straddling him and looking down with her hands on each side of him. He looked new, too, with pillows all around him instead of grass and leaves, and then he shifted under her and she felt him hard against her and shuddered as the heat flared, and she smiled and rocked against him until he grabbed her neck and yanked her down, snagging her crystal ball with his other hand as it zinged by her ear.

"Whoa," she said. "Good catch."

"Jesus." He hefted it in his hand. "This thing is heavy."

"Well, it's solid crystal." She took it from him and rolled it under the bed, stuffing the veil after it.

"A crystal ball. Did you look in it for us?"

She sat up and looked at him sternly, which wasn't easy because he was naked and beautiful and hard between her legs. "Crash, I can't see the future, nobody can. Human beings have free will. The crystal ball is just a joke. I got it in New Orleans because I liked the dragonfly stand."

"Right," Crash said. "But you can do magic. How am I supposed to know the difference?"

"Because magic makes sense." Mare slid her hands up his chest. "It's like sex. It's too good to be true, but it works." She bent to kiss him and then started working her way down. "Every. Single. Time."

"I believe in magic," Crash said and closed his eyes.

He was hot under her lips and her hands, hotter as she moved against him, and then he moved, too, and the night grew darker and the stars came out and Mare sighed against him as he took her in his arms and she wrapped herself around him as he slid inside her, hard inside her, and became part of her. She felt the draperies shift on the wall as their bodies slipped together, felt the room begin to throb as her blood began to pulse, but mostly she felt Crash, breathing with her the way he always did except this time it was in the quiet of her room and this time he was holding her tighter, this time when she said, "I love you," he said, "I'll never leave you, I swear, I'll never leave you," and she bit her lip so she wouldn't cry, and he kissed her, and she cried anyway, and it didn't matter, he didn't stop. He held on and rocked her until the heat wiped everything else away and there was just him and his rhythm in her blood, the bubble and the shudder there, the weight of him on top of her and the backbeat of the crystal ball bumping against her butt under the mattress, and she dug her fingernails into him, gasping for breath in the heat, rocking against him harder, and harder, the whole room rocking, the walls moving with them, the black roses rustling in their vase, the zebra couch dancing across the floor, and then something gold glittering in the air like the blue sparks she saw behind her eyelids when she scrunched them closed, and then Crash rocked and hit something good and her eyes flew open and there was gold everywhere, fluttering everywhere, and Py was pulsating on the windowsill—tiger cat, tiger cat, tiger, cat, *tiger, cat*—and the cheval mirror was spinning, and Crash was looking into her eyes, his eyes so blue she fell into them, into him, his eyes spiraling into her, his hips spiraling into her as he moved closer, higher, harder, the heat built and built and built inside her, and then she cried out and grabbed the headboard and it writhed under her hands, and she looked up to see the ceiling spinning around and around, closer and closer as she came and came and came and *came* . . .

When the bed landed with a thump, she held on to Crash, gasping for breath, and realized the ceiling was fine, it hadn't moved, it was the bed.

A few minutes later, when they were both breathing evenly again, when they'd come unstuck from each other and were curled together and Mare was so happy she thought about weeping from sheer exuberance except she was too damn exhausted, Crash said in her ear, "So we bolt the bed down."

"Maybe," she said, rolling onto her back, taking a deep breath just to feel her body ache from all the places he'd touched, all the places he'd been. "That was really good."

"There was a tiger on the windowsill."

She smiled at him and then picked something gold out of his hair, a tiny awkward butterfly that fluttered in her hand briefly and then flew back to the drapery and stuck on. "Huh." She let her head flop back and saw the headboard. It looked different.

She eased herself up on one elbow, feeling fat with satisfaction.

The iron headboard was now the same on both sides, no broken places, no missing pieces, and the pattern was different, more intricate, more beautiful. It took her a minute, and then she realized that she'd straightened out all the pieces of it with her mind, rebent them so they'd matched. Whatever rhythm she and Crash had been moving to, the headboard had gotten caught in it, and her mind had moved and curled the two halves to match.

"What?" Crash said, looking up at her, exhausted, while she tilted her head, looking at the iron twists and curls.

"We just did that," she said, pointing to it.

He squinted at it.

"That's how we make love," she said. "That's what the way we make love looks like. Isn't it *beautiful*?"

"I like it." He let his face drop back into the pillow.

She patted his back and found another butterfly so she peeled it off and set it free to fly back to the curtain.

"It must have been something to see in here," she said, pulling her hair off her sweaty neck and piling it on top of her head, loving the stretch in her back, and he said, "It was," into the pillow.

"I mean for everything else, too," she said, laughing. "I bet there were blue sparks everywhere."

He moved his head so his face wasn't buried. "What blue sparks?"

"My magic," she said, setting free another gold butterfly. "It's blue sparks."

"I didn't see any blue sparks."

She shook her head at him. "You were distracted. Look."

She waved her hand at the cheval mirror, and it rose and minced across the room on its three curved legs. No blue sparks.

She straightened, letting her hair fall back down. "What the hell?"

"That wasn't like that, was it?" Crash said, squinting at the mirror.

Mare looked at the freckled mirror. The freckles were all in spirals along the edges now, the center clear. "No. Never mind that. Where are my sparks?"

He rolled over on his back to watch her, putting an arm behind his head, and she was momentarily distracted by how gorgeous he was, but then she looked around. "Maybe I have to do something . . . more complicated. Like . . . all the butterflies."

"Butterflies?" Crash said, but Mare concentrated on them, visualizing all the little gold filigree wings and then threw them toward the drapery they'd come off of.

Crash yelped as dozens of little gold wings went hurtling across the room to splat on the fabric, some of them peeling off him, but there weren't any sparks.

"I want my sparks back," Mare said, flustered. "When I make magic, there are blue sparks, damn it."

"Weight?" Crash suggested, looking over his shoulder for more butterflies. "Maybe it has to be something heavy."

"Yesterday morning, I got them lifting *muffins*," Mare said.

"Well, things have happened since yesterday," Crash said. "Maybe you've gotten stronger."

Mare nodded. "Okay. Hold on." She took a deep breath, wrapped her mind around the bed, and lifted. It got about a foot off the floor, some blue sparks shot out, and then it thumped down again.

"Ouch," Crash said, holding on. "But I saw blue sparks."

"This sucker was *spinning* when we were coming," Mare said, disgruntled. "I should be able to do that again."

"Hey, anything I can do to help—"

"Shhhh," Mare said, and sat back against her beautiful new headboard to think.

Okay. Time to stop going on instinct and think about how her power actually worked.

With the muffins, she'd seen dust motes in the air turn into blue sparks. That must have something to do with friction, that her power moved things at a really small level. Like the sugar cubes. Like there was something in the air—what? molecules? atoms? germs? tiny little Legos?—that she could latch on to and wrap around things and then—

"Mare?"

Mare bit her lip and went for something easier. *Whatever that is,* she thought, *I'm gonna string it together, wrap it around this bed, and lift.* She put her head down and began to wrap her power around and around the bed in a big spiral, tightening as she went, putting her tongue in the corner of her mouth, her head lowering as she concentrated, her arms spreading out naturally, fingers spreading, too, and then she *lifted* . . .

"Oh, shit," Crash said, and grabbed on to the headboard.

"Sparks?" she said, concentrating on keeping them afloat.

"Ceiling," he said, and she looked up and saw it right above her nose.

"Right," she said and set them down gently. "Huh."

"Well, I can see why you never let me in here before." He swung around and put his feet on the floor.

"Too much?" Mare said, suddenly afraid.

"No," Crash said. "Well, a lot. Not too much." He looked over at her and smiled. "We're bolting the bed down. This one and the one in Italy. You're coming to Italy, right?"

Mare relaxed. "I have to talk to Dee and Lizzie first. If it's okay—"

He shook his head, and she leaned forward and put her hand on his arm.

"Crash, they're like me, they're magic, they can't be alone. I think Elric is okay, but I don't know about Danny, he doesn't like magic, and if my sisters haven't found anybody like you, I can't leave them alone. You know? I just can't. They need me."

He kissed her forehead. "I know. But then they come with us. Honest to God, Mare, they'd love Italy. And I'll help. Dee turns into birds, right? And Lizzie turns stuff into . . ." He frowned, trying to remember.

"Bunnies and shoes, mostly."

He shrugged. "It's Tuscany, it's a country town. Nobody will notice birds and bunnies. And shoes, well, hell, it's Italy. Dee can paint there. I'll build her a studio and Lizzie a workshop. They'll be safe. I'll keep them safe."

"Oh." Mare felt heat behind her eyes and tried to blink it back, but it was too late.

"Hey," he said as she picked up the sheet to wipe the tears away.

"I've loved you forever," she told him, sniffing. "I'm going to love you forever."

"I know," he said. "I'll love you forever, too."

"There's just one thing," she said, blinking back tears.

He closed his eyes and nodded. "Whatever it is, I'll fix it," he said, patience incarnate.

"The footboard."

"What?" He looked around.

"I was holding on to the headboard when I came," Mare said. "That's why it got rearranged and it looks so beautiful now. So I was thinking if I held onto the footboard and you—"

"It's just one damn thing after another with you," Crash said, and reached for her.

CHAPTER SEVEN

Dee woke to see the sky in turmoil. A broad bank of roiling clouds allowed only brief glimpses of the setting moon. The trees on the mountain writhed and whispered, making Dee think of those witches dancing in the dark, and far down in the valley a train whistle blew. Within the stone circle, it was curiously quiet. Dee was absolutely content, tucked close to her lover after their second bout of lovemaking, this one involving the pop beads.

Dee decided that she definitely had a preference for a man with an imagination. Who knew what pleasure pink pop beads could incite when pulled across some of the more sensitive areas of the body. Then again, they were also a great hit wrapped around a rousing erect penis. She couldn't wait to see what Danny had in mind for the boa.

"You'll marry me, of course," Danny murmured, pulling her more snugly into his arms. "After all, I've stolen your virtue."

Busy running her fingers through the curiously soft

hair that traced Danny's sternum, Dee chuckled. "You can't steal something that was offered on a silver platter."

He yawned. "Nevertheless, my honor demands it."

"Consider your honor upheld. Right now I can't think past what we're going to do next. I have to say that I'm sorry it took so long to find out what fun this is."

"I'm not. If you'd found out sooner, it wouldn't have been with me."

"It was meant to be, I think."

"True. After all, the first person you failed to shift with just happens to be your one true love."

"It might also be because he's the first one who tried to make sure I had an orgasm first. Maybe it was a protective mechanism."

"Nah. I prefer the true love idea."

"If you must." She could hear his heart, and it soothed her. She'd never been this close to a human before. Oh, she'd held Lizzie and Mare, but she'd never been given the gift of a lover's comfort.

"I really do want to marry you," he said, lazily stroking her hair. "Did I tell you I love you?"

"Better than that," she said, spreading her hand over his heart. "You showed me. I am honored by your offer."

"You're not allowed to say no."

"I have two sisters to think of, Danny."

"Let 'em get their own husbands."

"Until they do, we need to stick together just to survive."

"I work, too, ya know."

Dee lifted her head so she could face him. "Could you work from Salem's Fork? We could live here to save money. I could stay in the bank. That way I could be here for the girls."

He stroked her cheek with his thumb. "What if I can't? What if you need to come to Chicago with me?"

She frowned. "I don't think we'd have the money to commute. Could you wait? The situation here can't last that much longer. Especially if we can finally take care of Xan."

"You'd give me up for your sisters?"

"Give up is not the idea. Postpone at most. I have a responsibility to them, Danny. I mean, right now Lizzie hasn't even been able to hold down a job."

"Why?"

She shrugged. "She's distracted by trying to change straw into gold. She thinks it would save us all. I think Lizzie's greatest gift is that she loves us enough to try."

"And Mare?"

"Mare will be okay. But if I could stay, I could help out."

"So if I could base my activities out of Salem's Fork, you'd marry me?"

"Before you could get the question out. I know it wouldn't be easy. Neither of us makes a lot of money, and you'd need to travel. But we could make it work." She knew her smile was anxious. She wasn't sure her heart could stand a rejection.

"What about me?" he asked very quietly.

"If you're close," she said, "we'd have more time for impulse activity. I mean, we're not really far from anywhere. And I get three weeks' vacation at the bank."

"And your art?"

She briefly closed her eyes. "I don't want to lose my anonymity."

"If I could guarantee you that you won't?"

She frowned. "There is no artist protection program, Danny."

"I know people."

She considered it. "I've always wanted to share my vision. I just can't bear the idea of intrusion. Do you understand?"

Danny pulled her down to him for a brief, searing kiss. "Better than you know, sweetheart. So if I move here and promise to keep you anonymous, you'd live off my less than stellar salary until you can sell paintings?"

"I'd hope we'd share all the responsibility. But of course. Although I think you're setting too high a store on those paintings."

"And I think I'm not." He kissed her again. "Okay, missy. You have a deal. When do we ask your sisters' permission?"

"When Mare wears a gray suit. Don't worry. They love you already. Mare will offer to have your babies if you take my attention away from her. Hey, I don't suppose you could help me talk her into college."

Danny laughed. "*Mare?* Oh, Dee, don't waste your breath. Mare's going to end up creating something wonderfully bizarre, like, oh, an interactive movie-watching game that everybody's going to want, and she's going to become a cultural phenomenon."

Dee sighed and settled back on Danny's chest. "Fine. Outvoted again."

"I will do one thing for you."

"What's that?"

"Show you why I bought the feather boa."

She was up again and smiling. "Boas make me hot."

Danny James could look very smug when he wanted to. "I thought they would."

Lizzie opened her eyes, slowly letting them adjust to the predawn light. She was lying sprawled across Elric's perfect body, exhausted and deliciously, perfectly happy. She had no idea where, or when, or how she'd gone—at some point the arcs of color had speared through her body, turning it into tiny shards of crimson, blue, and gold, fairy dust spread across the universe until it settled back into lavender and then into flesh once more. It had been endless, glorious, and instinctively she tightened her grip on Elric's shoulder, afraid he'd gone.

He murmured something sleepily, but his arm was locked around her back, and there was no way she could escape. No way she wanted to.

The door to her room was open. Someone must have come in to check on her during the night and she could only guess they'd found nothing. Lizzie and her phantom lover had vanished, at least for the time being, which was probably just as well. She wasn't sure either of her sisters could have withstood the shock of seeing peaceful little Lizzie turning into . . .

What had she turned into? A raging sex addict? If you considered exactly what she'd done, what he'd gotten her to do with nothing more than a gentle tug, then she was the most wanton creature on the face of this earth. Except that she wanted no one but him.

The bastard was right after all. They were in love, bonded, and there was no breaking away. No safe life in the suburbs with a mini-van and two children. There'd be children all right, but the thought of what they might produce was enough to send chills through the heart of any prospective mother. A child with both their gifts would be something to reckon with, indeed.

She turned her face to look at him. He looked so young, so beautiful. And most astonishing of all, he was hers.

The door closed and locked again, and he opened his eyes to meet hers. "Has someone been snooping around?" he murmured.

"Probably my sisters. Are you ready to meet them officially?"

"God, no," he said, sliding his hand up the smooth line of her back. "I can think of much better ways to spend our time. Even if we have more than our fair share I don't want to waste a minute of it."

She slid back down in the bed, back on the purple sheets, and smiled at him. "Don't you think the next fifty years will be enough?"

He made a face. "I think it'll be more than that," he said. "And even then it won't be enough."

"Are you asking me to marry you?"

"No. It's a foregone conclusion." At least this morning he didn't seem nearly as upset over the notion. In fact, he seemed quite smug. "The way I figure it, if an average life span is ninety years, then we're both about one third of the way through it."

"So another sixty years, then."

He shook his head. "You forgot what I taught you about traditional alchemy. There are two main quests. One is to change base metals into gold. The other is to prolong life. You've already crossed that border, though I'm not sure when. I expect we'll die within hours of each other, a very long time from now."

"What border?"

He didn't answer. "You don't mind marrying an older man?" he said instead.

"For all I know you're younger than I am," Lizzie said. "And I'd marry you no matter how old you are." She looked into his deep lavender eyes, wondering if hers had the same translucent glow. "Er . . . exactly how old are you?"

He reached up and pulled her down to his mouth, kissing her. "Older," he said.

"How old?" she persisted.

He put his mouth against her ear, hot and sweet and arousing. "Physically, I'm in my late twenties. Mentally, I'm about thirty-five. In actual years . . ." He hesitated.

"In actual years?" she prompted.

"Ninety-three," he whispered.

And she let out a shriek of laughter that woke the entire house.

Dee had long since lost hope of ever waking to the sight of a man in her room. But when she woke up, there he was. Lying on his side, head propped on his hand, just watching her.

"You really will marry me," he said. "I wasn't just dreaming."

Dee laid her hand against his heart. "And all my worldly goods endow. Unfortunately the sum of that is three business suits, a handful of bird feathers, and a closet of acrylic paint."

She'd thought he'd been beautiful last night. This morning he was glorious, a celebration of sensuality in her sterile bed. His beard shadowed the hard angles of his jaw, adding a rakish air to his smile. His eyes were sleepy and sated. He was naked to his hips where the crisp white sheet pooled just south of his navel to expose her favorite torso on earth. She'd traced every inch of it last night with her tongue. She'd followed the hair that decorated his chest straight down to where his cock rose to meet her and tasted that, too. Then when it had gotten too cold up on the mountain, they'd gathered their blankets and snuck inside the house, giggling like teenagers, and she'd explored all over again.

Danny never looked away from her as he traced a lazy hand along her jaw to dip into the hollow of her throat. "And you really won't mind that we'll have to pinch pennies."

Dee savored the shivers his touch unleashed. "I live to hear Lincoln scream."

"You probably won't be able to go on research trips with me."

She sighed. "So all that talk of Montmartre?"

"To get you to have sex with me."

"It worked. I'll save up my own money and go. But I am going . . . one of these days."

He just kept watching her. At first Dee felt cherished. Slowly, though, she began to suspect that his contemplation wasn't all infatuation. He was just too quiet. Too still. After the night they'd had last night, he should be singing like Domingo. He should at least praise the luster of her eyes, or the fact that she was double-jointed.

"Dee, I have a confession to make."

She fell back against her pillow and shut her eyes. "Oh, hell. I knew it was too good to be true. I looked like your mother after all."

"Like my *who*?"

"If I did and you didn't mind, then I'm afraid you're

just too gothic for me. You'll have to leave. Just don't sell my story to *The Enquirer*."

"Nothing short of the *News of the World,* I promise. What the hell are you talking about?"

She cracked an eye open. "It's my usual party trick. Why else did you think I was so frantic?"

"You turn into . . . whoa, that *is* out there."

"The fact that you seem surprised is a good thing." She rose up on her own elbow to face him. "So if it wasn't that—and I thank all the powers of the universe that it wasn't—what is it?"

Danny stopped making eye contact. Dee felt that loss right in her solar plexus where all her dread lived.

"What?" she demanded. "Your wife needs you? Your gay lover needs you? Your bishop needs you? What?"

"I'm, uh, not who you think I am."

That brought her all the way to a sitting position. "I really think this demands an explanation."

Danny reached for one of her hands. She slapped him away.

"You said it yourself," he defended himself. "You can't bear the notoriety. To have people think they have the right to you. That they know you. I, uh, I guess I'm here under an assumed name."

"You're not Danny James."

"I am. Daniel James Mark—"

He never got the rest out. The figurative light went on in a blinding flash, and Dee shoved him ass first off the bed. They should have heard the thud across town. Dee found she didn't care. She leaned over the side to see him sprawled naked on her hardwood floor, his dignity in serious disarray. It would have been easier if he didn't look as if he were posing for a portrait titled *The Male Animal Recumbent*.

Dee swung her feet off the side of the bed, oblivious

to her nudity. Danny wisely scooted beyond immediate range.

"You are *not* going to tell me that you're really billionaire, world-famous author Mark Delaney," she snarled.

He tried to smile his crime away. "He's not such a bad guy."

She climbed off the bed and stalked over to pick up her clothes. When Danny or Mark or whoever tried to rise and follow her, she planted her foot in his solar plexus to dissuade him. He went down with a faint "oof!"

"I hope you know that this is one of my favorite fantasies."

Dee glared him into submission. She was *not* going to allow him the satisfaction of seeing her cry. "So, what was this?" she demanded, struggling into her sweat suit. "A joke? A bet? Are things so boring in Chicago that you have to go all the way to Salem's Fork for a little fraternity humor?"

"Actually, not Chicago, either."

"Shut up."

With a nervous glance to make sure she wasn't in striking position, Danny climbed to his feet. "I was perfectly serious. I just mostly do my own research. And I call myself Danny James so I can avoid the hoopla. When I still did research as Mark Delaney, the only thing I could accomplish was finding new places on teenage girls where they wanted me to sign my name. I *couldn't* tell you."

"Oh, I imagine you could have. Any time during the four times last night you had my legs spread, for instance. Or sometime around that marriage proposal . . . or is that part of the joke, too? See how the poor chick responds to an honorable but poverty-stricken invitation to marriage. Did I score high? Will you at least spell my name right in the book?"

He yanked his jeans on. "All right, I admit it. I was afraid."

Dee laughed out loud. "Of course you were. After all, I'm so fierce."

"Actually," he said with a wry grin, "you are."

She sucked in a calming breath and squeezed her eyes shut. "Snap your jeans. You look like a cheesy Chippendales poster."

He ducked into his shirt, too. It didn't make Dee feel any better. "Dee, listen to me."

She threw out a hand. "From across the room."

She was backed against her wall, where she could see the only art she'd thought to put up, school paintings from her sisters. A pony with big brown eyes from Liz and Lydia from *Beetle Juice* from Mare, all sharp angles and lots of black. It was good to remind herself sometimes just who she could trust. And here she'd been worried about shapeshifting.

Danny speared his hands through his hair. Dee held her position instead of hurrying over to smooth it back down, like she wanted to.

"This has just been a bit overwhelming, ya know." He wasn't telling her anything. "I came here on a mission. I wanted to blow the whistle on self-serving hucksters who took advantage of people in pain. I wanted you to give up your parents. The only thing I knew about you was from your aunt. And I have to admit—" He shook his head. "She doesn't know you as well as she thinks. To be honest, Dee, I didn't think past getting my proof. I told you. What happened to my mother shouldn't happen to anybody."

"I agree. Get to the part where you think it's a good

idea to help me dispense with my virginity under false pretenses."

"What false pretenses? I love you. I meant it. Thursday I didn't know you. Now I can't imagine spending my life with anyone else. The false identity thing was an oversight."

"Not telling me you knew Aunt Xan could be termed an oversight. Having sex under an assumed name is fraud." She stalked up to him and poked him right in the chest. "And I know fraud. My parents were convicted for it."

Danny grabbed her hands and held them to his heart, which Dee could feel was beating far too fast. It hurt her, because she knew that he was serious. He really was afraid.

"I know," he said quietly, holding too tightly for her to pull away. "And I'm sorry. I really am. It's just that the world is different when you're famous. Everybody thinks they know you. I wanted you to fall in love with the real Danny Delaney. Not the hype on a dust jacket. I thought you'd understand."

She was weakening, and he didn't deserve it. Not yet. "What did I tell you about how I feel about liars? I don't even know where you really live."

"The person you know is the real me," he said, sincerity radiating from every pore. "No pretense."

"Where do you live? Is it really Seattle, like the book jackets say?"

He had a great line in chagrined. "Actually, Detroit."

She flinched. "I hate Detroit. We spent three very bad years there."

"We'll move."

She shook her head. "You really think it's that easy?"

"We really can travel. You can paint whatever or wherever you want. I'll hold your paint box. And think about it. I'm the perfect person to show you how to share your art without paying for it." He leaned so close she could almost taste the perspiration that beaded on his upper lip. "Dee, I can take care of your sisters. You never have to worry about them again."

She just shook her head, beyond words.

"You said you loved me," he said.

Oh, why did he have to sound so uncertain? He didn't deserve to be forgiven yet. But she couldn't bear to hear that vulnerability.

"I love you so much that for the first time in my life I made love to a man as me," she said.

"Then it shouldn't matter."

That brought Dee's eyes open again. "It does." It was all she could do to stay strong. "I can't be in a relationship without honesty. I can't give everything and then get my lover in considered bits and pieces."

"Your husband's."

"You're not paying attention. I think you should leave now, and think about what you want from us. I know what I want. I want it all. I want all of you. I won't settle for less."

"You'll have it!"

"Don't make promises you haven't figured out how to keep." This time when she pulled, he let her go. "I'd rather you weren't here when I try and explain this to my sisters."

She could just hear Mare's reaction. *You threw him out because you found out he's richer than God? Oh, yeah. That's thinking.*

Danny cupped her face in his hands. "Promise you'll be here when I get back."

She couldn't look away from those mesmerizing eyes. For the first time, she saw no humor in them. It was enough. "I'll be here."

It wasn't until she'd let him out the front door that she took in her first real breath. Then, where nobody could see her, she allowed herself a slow smile. Life was very, very good.

Waking up with Crash in the sunlight inspired Betty Crocker fantasies in Mare.

"I could be a wife," she told him, lying on her stomach with her chin in her hand, staring at her new beautiful footboard as the Sunday sunshine poured through the window, warming her naked body and making the butterflies on the drapes glitter. "I could be a barefoot wife and learn to cook."

"A barefoot wife with a blue butterfly on her ass," Crash said, tracing the round wings of the new tat on her tailbone with his fingertip. "This works for me."

"It's black, not blue," Mare said transferring her attention to other renovations. "You know, the flowers I painted never went back to the drapes. They're all over the floor and the sheets now, they never went back. Maybe it's because they couldn't fly like the gold butterflies."

"This butterfly is blue," Crash said, letting his finger drift lower.

"Hey, it's Sunday," Mare said, looking over her shoulder. "Show some respect." She sat up and craned her neck, trying to see her new tattoo. "I saw it when Mother was done with it. It was black."

"It's blue now, like your magic," Crash said, looking at her breasts.

"You are entirely too predictable," Mare said, and got off the bed to try to see the tattoo in the newly cleared cheval mirror.

It was blue. The black outline was still there, but now it was filled with blue. The color of her magic. "Huh. Maybe the magic changed it. Maybe something happened last night—"

"Come here," Crash said.

"I think I should make breakfast," Mare said, her hands on her hips. "A good wife makes breakfast for her man. I could start with toast and work up."

"I think we should make something else," Crash said. "I could start with your toes and work up."

"Okay," Mare said.

An hour and a half later, Mare was down in the kitchen wearing an apron over the long striped skirt she'd made for the movie that night—Victoria from *Corpse Bride*, since Sophie had no good clothes in *Howl's Moving Castle*—and doing her damnedest to fix toast. Setting the toaster on "5" turned out to be a bad idea, since it meant darker not faster—"You're not going to eat that," she told Crash when he looked manfully ready to consume charcoal for her—so she sent him out into the dining room with orange juice while she dialed the toaster back to "2" and tried again. But when she went out to the dining room with a plate of reasonably golden buttered squares of hot bread, she found Jude alone in the dining room with Py hissing at his feet.

"Ciao, Mare," he said, smiling, but she scowled at him.

"What are you doing here?" she said, putting the plate on the table. "Where's Crash?"

"He had to go," Jude said. "I came because I have to talk to you."

"No you don't. You're a minion. Where did he have to go?"

"It's about Xan," Jude said and Mare paid attention. "We belong together, Mare."

Mare frowned. "You and Xan?"

"*No.* You and me." He took a step closer and Py snarled so he took a step back. "Xan cast a True Love Spell, Mare."

Mare nodded. "I know. Where's Crash?"

"She cast a spell to bring the three of you, the Fortune sisters, your True Loves. That's how Danny found Dee and Elric found Lizzie. And that's how I found you, Mare. You can't argue with a True Love Spell."

"I can argue with anything," Mare said. "As for my True Love, you are not it. Now where the hell is Crash?"

Py hissed again, and this time Mare heard a faint but angry croaking.

"What's wrong, baby?" she said to the cat, and then looked under the table.

A frog sat there, panting hard, or maybe it was pulsating, Mare was not up on her Frog Basics. Py was in front of her, but just as Mare moved to scoop him up and save the frog, she realized that Py was standing between Jude and the frog, growling at Jude.

"Nice kitty," Jude said.

"Not even close." Mare got down on her knees and picked up the frog. "We don't usually get frogs—"

The frog's eyes were bright blue, like the Italian sky.

Mare surged to her feet, the frog cupped in her hands. *"What did you do to him?"* she screamed at Jude.

Jude blinked in fake innocence. "What are you talking about?"

Mare wheeled and ran for Lizzie's room, her fingers curled protectively around Crash who croaked his fury.

Lizzie was lying sideways across the tattered bed. She opened one eye very slowly. She could hear the wind outside, and it was so dark she had no idea what time of day it was. Not that she cared.

She started to stretch, then realized one wrist was still tied to the iron bedpost with a purple silk scarf. She sat up, looking for Elric, and she grinned.

He was still on the floor, sound asleep, looking as if he'd been hit by a truck. Not mashed by a truck, fortunately. Very little could tarnish his physical beauty. But something had managed to drain every last vestige of energy from him, and the delightful thing was, it had been her. Them.

And the libido spell had worn off hours before they'd gotten to silk bondage. She looked down at him fondly. They were going to have a really good time in Toledo.

They'd lost his heavy silver earring somewhere in the bed—she needed to find it when she recovered her energy. An overenthusiastic bite on his ear and she'd almost swallowed it. He'd laughed, tried to put it in her ear, and then they'd gotten distracted once more and forgotten all about it.

She could hear her sisters moving around in the living room. Dee would probably think twice about marching in here unannounced—in his current state of happy exhaustion she doubted Elric would have the energy to shield his presence, and she really didn't like the idea of her sisters seeing Elric at his finest. He was hers, and for the first time in her life she wasn't going to share.

She untied her wrist and slid off the bed, kneeling down on the floor beside him. He opened his eyes.

"Not asleep," he murmured. "Dead."

She bent to kiss him, but a pounding on the door made her jerk back, Elric catching her in his arms.

"Lizzie," Mare screamed, and pounded again. *"Lizzie, please, PLEASE!"* And Lizzie grabbed the purple sheet from underneath the bed where it had landed hours earlier, wrapped it around her body, toga-style, and stumbled to the door to face her sister.

Mare heard Jude behind her, but she ignored him to beat on Lizzie's door with her fist. *"Lizzie, I need you RIGHT NOW. Please, please, PLEASE—"*

Lizzie opened the door wrapped in a purple sheet looking flushed and rumpled and annoyed.

Mare stuck the Crash frog out at her. "Turn him back. Please, *please* turn him back. I love him. *Please, please,* God, Lizzie, you *have* to."

"I have no idea what she's talking about," Jude said from behind her.

Lizzie looked closer at the frog. "Put him on the floor," she said, no longer angry.

Mare swallowed and put Crash on the floor. "Oh, God, *Lizzie*."

"Step back," Lizzie said.

Mare stepped back, hating to leave him so exposed.

Lizzie looked down and took a deep breath and raised her encircled arms.

"That's vermin," Jude said, and raised his foot just as Lizzie struck.

There was a flash of purple light, a lot more purple smoke than Mare had ever seen before, and then Crash was back, tall and broad and choking and waving his hands through the violet smog.

"What *the fuck happened to me*?" he said.

Mare threw her arms around him and kissed him and then kissed him again. "*I love you,* I really love you, and I will marry you and go to Tuscany because those five minutes you were a frog were *the worst five minutes of my life*."

"They weren't great for me, either," Crash said, holding her close, still sounding annoyed but not as much as before. "Hello, Lizzie."

"Hello, Crash," Lizzie said, but she was looking at the floor.

Mare looked back at her, clutching Crash. "What? What's wrong? He's okay, isn't he? There wasn't any damage?" She began patting him all over. "He's okay, he feels okay, tell me he's okay. Baby, are you okay?"

"Okay?" Crash said, still holding on to her. "I was a *fucking frog*. Are you going tell me how that happened?"

"I think Jude . . ." Mare's voice trailed off as she looked around. "The little weasel ran for it."

"Not a weasel." Lizzie nodded to the floor.

A frog sat there, looking stunned.

"Jude?" Mare said.

Lizzie shrugged. "He was there and then he wasn't. I'm guessing that's Jude."

"You turned him into a frog?" Mare thought for a second. "Yeah, that's fair."

"No," Lizzie said. "That was a restoration spell. He got into the line of fire when he tried to step on Crash. You know, he was the guy who tried to take my amethyst, and when I hit him the last time and he turned into a frog, I thought it was strange. I mean, why not a bunny? Or a ferret? Generally I don't do frogs, but—"

"What?" Crash said, looking around. "Somebody tried to *step on me*?"

Mare looked at the frog again. "Restoration? He *started out* as a frog? Then how did he get to be a vice president at Value Video!!? Although that's not as far-fetched as you'd think."

"Xan," Lizzie said. "She sent us all our soul mates."

"And she thought mine was a frog?" Mare raged.

"Maybe she misunderstood," Lizzie said. "She did find him in Italy. Maybe Crash moved too fast, and she scooped up Jude instead, and then tried to make him . . . more attractive." She shrugged. "She chose a hot movie star. She tried."

"She thought my true love was a *frog*? If I ever get my hands on that bitch—" Mare stopped, as the rest of what Lizzie was saying hit. "Wait. She cast the spell and scooped up Jude because Crash moved too fast." She shook her head. "I've been stupid. That means she brought Crash, too. She caught him with the spell, too."

"Probably," Lizzie said. "She just didn't realize it because only the edge of the spell caught him." She smiled at Crash. "It's nice seeing you again, Christopher. I've always liked you best of all of Mare's . . . friends."

"Thanks," Crash said, confused. "I've always liked you best of all of Mare's sisters. What's going on?"

Mare let go of him.

"What?" Crash said, holding on to her. "Don't look like that."

Mare smiled at him, miserable. "Remember in the diner when you couldn't tell me why you'd come back. It was because of Xan."

"No," Crash said. "I told you, I never met your aunt."

"I know," Mare said. "She never even knew she got you. That's why she made Jude. But that's why you came here, just the same. You're not a minion. You just got caught in a spell."

"No." Crash looked confused, holding on to her. "I couldn't stop thinking about you—"

"Nobody thinks about a woman for five years without doing something about it," Mare said, trying to pry his fingers off her. "You're back because I love you, because you're my True Love, not because I'm yours."

"I never forgot you," Crash said. "I didn't think about you *every day,* but I didn't—"

"No." Mare swallowed tears, determined not to cry. "And the second soul mate she found for me was a *toad.*"

"Frog," Lizzie said.

"You didn't know him," Mare snapped at her, grateful for the anger.

"This is crap," Crash said. "Could we go back to the part where somebody turned me into a frog?"

"He's got a point," Mare told Lizzie. "You better check Elric. For all you know, he's a llama."

Lizzie blinked, taken aback.

"Elric!" Mare yelled.

After a moment, Elric appeared behind Lizzie, looking unamused. "You bellowed?"

"Do it," Mare snapped to Lizzie, and Lizzie turned, encircled her arms, and hit Elric with the restoration spell.

The air went purple again, there were some interesting violet sparks, and then the fog cleared and Elric was standing there, the same as before.

"Funny," he said.

"Sorry," Mare said. "I made her do it. Jude turned out to be amphibian." She looked at him down on the floor. "I'd like to feed him to Py, but it's not his fault he's a toad."

"Frog." Lizzie picked Jude up. "I've got the old bunny cage in here. I'll keep him in that."

Jude croaked, and Mare said, "You shut up," and turned back to Crash. "The spell will wear off soon, and you'll be okay again, so you should probably go now."

"Oh, dear," Lizzie said, "don't do anything dumb, Mare," and went back into her workroom, taking Jude and Elric with her and sending Mare a look of heartfelt sympathy.

Then the door closed and they were alone.

"You're coming with me," Crash said, determination chasing confusion from his face. "You said—"

"Baby, you don't want me." Mare tried to sound matter-of-fact, as she pulled out of his grasp and levitated him into the hall, ignoring his *"Hey!"* "You think you do, but you're under a spell. If it doesn't wear off on its own, I'll go find Xan tomorrow and make her take it off, and you'll be fine again."

"I'm fine now," Crash said, trying to resist as Mare floated him away from her and toward the door. "Or I will be if nobody else turns me into a toad and you come back to Italy with me. Why are we moving? *Stop it.*"

"Frog," Mare said, steering him through the dining

room. "You were a frog. And I can't come with you. You were gotten here under false pretenses." She swallowed hard, knowing she only had minutes before she was going to burst into tears, the pressure increasing behind her eyes even as she blinked at him. "It was a true love spell, just like Jude said. Hell, just like you said, it was true love and that doesn't happen every day, unless your girlfriend has a crazy-ass witch of an aunt who casts a spell because she's trying to take her power. You should leave town now."

Crash tried to stop the push toward the door by grabbing onto the woodwork around the dining room arch. He missed it by inches. "Wait a minute, damn it, what difference does it make how she found me?"

"I knew I loved you," Mare said, guiding him toward the front door. "I never stopped loving you. But you left and didn't come back for five years. If you'd loved me, you'd have been back. When the spell wears off, you won't love me anymore again."

He shook his head, grabbing at the doorframe as they reached the front door. "That's crazy. *I love you.*"

"Then why didn't you come back for five years?" Mare said.

"*I don't know.* I just *didn't.*"

"Bad answer," Mare said, and opened the front door.

"No," Crash said, holding on to the doorframe. "Mare, I won't—"

"You have to." Mare pried his fingers off the woodwork with her mind. "Go. It'll be okay, you won't care at all tomorrow. And I don't want to be with you when you don't care." She waved good-bye, sadly, staying out of his reach. "Have a great life."

"*Mare,*" he said, and she shoved him out onto the steps with magic, folding her arms across her breaking heart, and closed the door in his face.

"And I even learned to make *toast*," she said and burst into tears.

Lizzie shoved Jude in the bunny cage, put the cover over it, and then let her sheet drop, which improved Elric's mood considerably. Then she kissed him, which improved it even more. "I need to talk to my sisters," she said. "You can sleep some more."

He sat up, leaning against the wall. "Let me clean up, and then I'll face them, too."

"The shower is upstairs."

"You forget—I don't need traditional plumbing," he said. And vanished, leaving Lizzie kneeling on the floor, alone. Apparently he wasn't quite as exhausted as she'd thought.

She got Jude some water, tied the sheet tighter around her body, toga-style, and then headed out into the living room.

Dee was sitting at the table, a big splotch of bright blue paint on her cheek, a cup of tea in her hands, and a bemused, besotted expression on her face that Lizzie knew would be a perfect match to her own.

"You have paint on your face," Lizzie said. "It looks good there."

Dee blushed. "I was painting Danny's portrait."

Lizzie raised her eyebrows. "And where is Danny now?"

"Gone," Dee said happily. "He needed to be taught

a lesson. But he'll be back." She glanced at her watch. "I'd say three hours at the most. He loves me."

"I take it you didn't turn into Danny's mother?" Lizzie asked, closing the door behind her just in case Elric reappeared in the same condition as when he'd vanished.

Dee's smile was both shy and extremely pleased with herself. "Uh . . . yes. Er . . . no. No mothers. No nothing. Just . . ." She let out a happy sigh. "Just lovely."

Lizzie looked at her for a moment, astonished. "Finally having sex really does change everything, doesn't it?" she said. "You look like a different woman."

Mare came in from the kitchen. "You're looking pretty lovestruck yourself."

Mare was looking miserable. "What happened?" Lizzie almost took her younger sister into her arms, then thought better of it. For one thing, Mare wasn't into the huggy thing, for another, Lizzie really needed a shower. She was going to have to get Elric to teach her that trick about cosmic bathing.

"I made Crash go," Mare said, sticking her chin up. "He was gotten here under false pretenses. Unlike the *frog*."

"Frog?" Dee asked. "What frog?"

"No," Lizzie said, very sure of herself. "Crash is your soul mate."

"Lizzie's right, honey," Dee said, patting Mare. "He came all the way from Italy for you. What frog?"

Mare sighed. "Jude stopped by this morning and turned Crash into a frog, only it turned out that Jude was really a frog, so Lizzie has him in her room in a bunny cage."

"Uh-huh." Dee gave up on Mare and turned to Lizzie. "So where's Elric? Don't you think I ought to meet him?"

"He's cleaning up."

"Where?"

"I haven't the faintest idea. In Spain, for all I know. He'll be back momentarily. In the meantime I need to take a shower."

"I can make toast," Mare said in a lousy attempt at cheering up. "You want me to make toast for you?"

Lizzie looked at her miserable younger sister. Mare was no longer the Queen of the Universe—she looked lost, broken. "Toast would be lovely," she said in a gentle voice. "I'm starving."

By the time she got back downstairs again, fully dressed, there were three squares of burned toast on a plate, and a distinct odor of charred bread coming from the kitchen.

"Mare got distracted," Dee said. "Maybe we should take her to the Greasy Fork . . ."

"I don't think we should leave the house." Lizzie sat down and reached for the toast. "Xan can't get in here for a very long time, according to Elric." She looked down at her feet. They were bare—for the first time since she could remember there were no extraneous shoes on her feet. Naked feet, with the glowing purple butterfly tattoo to set them off. How appropriate.

"Don't eat that," Mare said. "It'll kill you. I'm working on a second batch. It'll be good. I dialed the toaster back to two again."

Dee pushed the toast away. "We still haven't decided what we're going to do about Xan. We can't hide out forever. And I'm hungry, too. What do we have besides . . . toast?"

Mare said, "There's nothing in the kitchen. Nobody

made muffins this morning. Maybe I'll go make muffins—" She started to get up.

"Elric!" Lizzie called. She knew the moment he'd reappeared in her tiny, wonderful bedroom. The door opened, and she sucked in her breath. He was wearing dove gray this time, and yet the colors shimmered around him.

"Damn," Dee said. "He's gorgeous."

"Mine," Lizzie said. "This is my older sister, Dee. Deirdre Dolores O'Brien."

Elric crossed the room with his usual elegance, taking Dee's hand in his. "Darling Dee-Dee Fortune," he murmured. "It's an honor."

And Dee was so dazzled she didn't rise to the bait. "Call me Dee."

"And you've met my sister Mare."

He nodded in Mare's direction.

"Hey, Elric," Mare said, still depressed. "I'm going to make muffins."

"Please don't," Elric said.

"And this is Elric," Lizzie said to Dee.

"Elric who?" Dee said, smiling at him, her older sister instincts clearly shot to hell by one night with Danny James. "Let's see, what am I supposed to be asking here? Are your intentions honorable? Who are your people?"

Lizzie blinked, glancing at him. Had she just spent the last twenty-four hours doing really wicked things with a man and she didn't know his last name? "Elric the Magnificent?" she suggested.

Elric laughed, and shards of color split the room. Lizzie glanced at her sisters, but apparently they were immune to it. Only she could see the scattered rainbows.

"Then you'd end up being Mrs. The Magnificent," he said, "and I don't think that suits you."

"You're marrying a man you just met?" Dee asked, sounding far less protective than usual. "What am I talking about? So am I. When he comes back, anyway."

"Of course. We're soul mates," Elric said, moving up behind Lizzie and putting his hands on the back of her chair.

Lizzie looked up at him. She wanted to grab him and drag him back into the bedroom. She wanted to send her sisters away and haul him onto the dining room table, and she could see by the deep purple in his eyes that he was thinking exactly the same thing. And the libido spell had worn off at dawn.

She gave herself a mental shake. "I'm starving. We're all starving. Any chance you could go out and get us a pizza?"

His luscious mouth curved in a faint smile. "I think that would be within my capabilities." He glanced at the pile of burned toast, and she belatedly realized he could simply transmute. But he could read her far too well. "How long do we want me to be gone?"

"Just long enough for me to talk with my sisters. Half an hour? There's a pizza place in town—if you walked slowly it would be perfect."

"You don't want pizza from New York? Or Venice? It's much better, I can promise you."

"Salem's Fork pizza will be perfect." *I don't want to be too far away from you,* she thought. Knowing he could read it. "Oh, and set the frog free while you're out, please."

"Half an hour." He released the chair and headed toward the door.

It closed after him, and Lizzie felt suddenly bereft.

"How does he know what kind of pizza we want?" Dee asked.

"He knows," Lizzie said. "So what are we going to

do next? We're safe for now, but sooner or later we're going to have to confront Xan. We can't spend our lives dealing with her like this."

"We're not going to," Dee said.

"I don't know why you two are so pissed," Mare said. "She sent you your true loves. Look what I ended up with. Ribbit."

"Crash came back to town," Dee pointed out.

"And left again. You know, maybe we should just split up, go our separate ways. You're happy with Danny, or you will be as soon as you let him back in. Lizzie's absolutely glowing . . ." Mare's words trailed off as she stared at Lizzie. "You really are glowing, aren't you? Literally." She bit her lip. "That's lovely. Good for you both."

Lizzie was still shimmering a bit. She smiled. "What can I say? He's a wizard."

"I bet," Mare said. "Sometime you'll have to tell me all about it. I'll come visit you in Toledo."

"Wow," Dee said. "I guess I never thought of the three of us ever being apart. I think I saw us living together, sisters to the end."

"Like that cheesy television show?" Mare said. "Kill me now. Even they got married. I'll be the maiden aunt, the one everybody comes to for advice." The smell of burning bread rolled in from the kitchen. "And toast." She got up to save the toast and then said, "Oh, hell," and waved her hand as the newest batch of charcoal floated up out of the toaster and through the doorway on its own.

"The important thing is, we're not letting Xan get away with it this time," Lizzie said firmly. "We have to face her and tell her to stay out of our lives. Are we agreed?"

"Agreed," Mare said, dropping the toast on the table.

"Agreed," Dee said, and they began to talk, making and discarding plans, closer than they'd ever been before.

an stood over the silver bowl, now rimmed with smooth river rock, the see glass like mist in the center. In it, Danny James walked the streets of Salem's Fork, Crash Duncan strapped his bags onto his motorcycle, and Elric, Elric entered a pizza parlor. *A pizza parlor.*

What the hell had Lizzie done to him?

Maxine stumbled through paneling, clutching her fists to her sweat-stained waitress uniform.

"Did you get the talismans?" Xan said.

"What?" Maxine said, gulping back tears.

"The talismans," Xan said. "One piece of silver from Danny, Elric, and Crash. For my last spell," she said patiently, treating Maxine like the idiot she was. "Did you get them?"

"Yes, but Xantippe, please, Jude—"

"I told you," Xan said with no expression. "Jude is of no use to me. Put the silver in the bowl."

Maxine gulped. "What are you going to do? Are you going to hurt them? Are you going to change them into frogs?"

Xan closed her eyes. "Maxine, I need them. They're the men my nieces love. If I change them into frogs, then my nieces won't recognize them, will they? Give me the talismans."

Maxine opened her shaking fists.

A silver medallion. Xan remembered Danny James wearing that.

"He took it off to shower," Maxine said as Xan took it. "Your spell pulled it through the window to me."

Xan dropped it into the bowl and the mist from the see glass curled around it, obscuring it as she looked at Maxine's shaking hands for the next token.

A silver stud, an earring. Xan saw it with a shock. Elric never took that off.

"He gave it to Lizzie," Maxine said. "It got lost in the sheets. Your spell pulled it—"

Xan grabbed the stud from her and felt it hum against her skin. He gave it to *Lizzie*? It had been in his family for centuries, the contact power in it was enormous, and he gave it to *Lizzie*?

She dropped it into the bowl as if it had bitten her and the mist curled and covered it, and Maxine handed her the last piece, a silver tie tack.

"He was packing—"

"I don't care," Xan said and threw it into the bowl where the mist covered it. Elric had given an heirloom to Lizzie, to Lizzie, she'd known the girl was his true love, but he'd given her *power*, he'd given her—

The mist rose up in arabesques, stone gray this time, and the river rock rose, too, and became the Big Rocks up on Salem's Mountain.

Xan shook her head and waved her hand through the mist, curling her fingers in a summoning gesture until the arabesques coiled about her hand in response. "Like to like, silver draws you," she whispered, "like to like, silver keeps you, there to stay, till I release you, so I say, so be it." She blew on the mist and there below in the see glass she saw Danny James stumble into the circle and look around confused, and then Elric appear and look up at her, enraged, and then . . .

Nothing.

Where the hell was Crash Duncan?

"Oh," Maxine said, looking into the glass. "Oh, *no*."

"Maxine?"

Maxine stepped back, visibly upset. "Well, I'll just be going then."

Xan narrowed her eyes.

"Lunchtime," Maxine said, sidling toward the paneling.

"Maxine, that tie tack you gave me. I don't believe I've ever seen Mr. Duncan wearing a tie."

Maxine froze. "Just give Jude one more chance," she whispered.

Xan looked down at the stone circle more closely. Danny James, Elric, and . . . "Oh, for the love of—" She put her head in her hands. "Now I have to get this Crash lout out of town before I can get this charade over with *since he's not in the circle, is he, Maxine?*"

"No," Maxine cried. "But I love Jude, Xantippe, I had to save him."

Xan turned cold eyes on her. "You love him, do you?"

Maxine lifted her chin. "Yes, I do."

"Then you should be with him," Xan said, and waited for hope to dawn in Maxine's eyes before she waved her hand.

A minute later, a frog croaked its distress behind the Dumpster of the Greasy Fork. And then sneezed.

"I should have done that a long time ago," Xan said and then made her plans. She had the men, or most of them, now all she had to do was get rid of the loose ends—Maxine was gone, Crash Duncan would be soon—invite the girls to the mountain, take their powers, leave them to their tawdry true loves—Mare would need an aquarium—and everybody would be happy.

Unless they resisted and she had to kill them.

"Well, they were the ones who made this difficult," she said to the figures in the see glass and went to change for her last trip to Salem's Fork.

CHAPTER EIGHT

The wind was growing stronger outside the house, and Lizzie could hear the sound of their neighbor's garbage cans being tossed down the street. All the lights were on in the house, but an odd shadow remained, maybe just the manifestation of Mare's unhappiness. The computer in the corner was in sleep mode, and Lizzie was half tempted to give it a knock so that the flying toasters on the screensaver would vanish, but she left it alone. She needed food.

"That computer is taunting me," Mare said, watching the toast on the screen.

Dee glanced at her watch again, and frowned. "I thought Danny would be back by now."

"Danny? What about Elric and the pizza?" Mare said. "I'm starving."

The shadows gnawing away at Lizzie weren't from Mare's grief after all, she realized suddenly. Things weren't right. Elric should have been back, even if he'd allowed them a little extra time for the sake of delicacy. Not that Elric was particularly delicate, though he could be, in the most delicious ways. And he could be quite indelicate, as well . . .

The sudden beep of the computer stopped her cold as the screen came to life. No flying toasters, no welcome screen. It was black, not the usual steel gray of a hibernating monitor, dead black, and then a cream-colored dot spun itself into a square-shaped invitation with a sepia-toned script font:

You are cordially invited to a
Fortune Family Reunion
on the Mountaintop at Twilight
at the Great Big Rock
to meet your lovers or lose them forever . . .

"She's got Danny!" Dee said, furious.

"She's got Elric," Lizzie said, astonished.

"She's got Crash," Mare said, panicked, and then she stopped and scowled. "Oh, hell, no she doesn't, she's probably got the frog. Well, she can have him. Maybe she likes frogs' legs." She realized her sisters were looking at her. "Kidding. I'll save the frog. What are we going to do?"

"Whatever it is, we're doing it together," Lizzie said firmly. "We've got five hours to come up with a plan."

"Xan's very powerful," Dee warned. "We can't underestimate her."

"She's powerful on her own," Lizzie said. "But she's nothing compared to the three of us put together. This time she's gone too far."

"Yeah," Mare said. "Who steals my frog steals trash."

Lizzie turned steely eyes on her and Mare said,

"Hey, I'm *on* it. This bitch screwed up my life forever, and for that alone I'd go after her, but she's taken the two men who made my sisters happy, so this chick is toast." She held up the charcoal square on her plate. "And we all know what happens to toast in this house."

Lizzie nodded solemnly. "So we get the toaster from hell . . ."

Mare started to laugh, and Lizzie did, too, and then Dee got a gleam in her eye, and leaned forward.

"Maybe not toast," she said. "But I like the 'kitchen from hell' part. Let's put that bitch where she belongs."

Crash took the afternoon to finish up the last of his American business, pack, and talk to his partner about the Annapolis delivery for the Moto Guzzi, but when it came time to go, he couldn't leave Salem's Fork, not without Mare. All right, so there were some new wrinkles in the relationship, the magic thing was still giving him headaches, he'd been a frog, for Christ's sake, and there was that love spell mess, but at the end of the day, she was Mare, and he loved her, and he'd sworn to never leave her again, and he wasn't going to. So he'd spend the extra week and she'd see he still loved her . . .

What if he spent the extra week and he didn't love her? It had taken him five years to come back for her. What if she was right?

Clueless about what to do next, he went to the Greasy Fork. It was packed because the service was slow—one of the waitresses had disappeared and the place was buzzing with gossip about it—but then a booth miraculously opened up even though the people had just sat down—"Forgot my wallet," the guy told Crash, bemused—and Crash told Pauline to bring him the usual.

"Could you be more specific?" she said, and he looked up in surprise, but when she glared back, he told her.

Fuck, not even Pauline could remember him.

When his burger and fries were gone, and he was trying to drown his sorrows in his milkshake, Pauline came back with the check.

"So what's with you?" she said, cracking her gum.

"What's with you and the gum?" he said, feeling hostile. "You never did that before."

Pauline stopped cracking. "You look like you lost your best friend."

"I did. Mare dumped me."

Pauline nodded. "Eh, it's for the best. She really wasn't the Italian type. Good-looking guy like you, it's too soon for you to settle down. Go back to Italy. Play the field. I hear they got a lot of fields there."

"No, it's not for the best," Crash said, annoyed. "I'm ready to settle down and I always knew I'd settle down with Mare. And she'd have loved Italy. And Italy would have loved her." *And what the fuck's with you, Pauline?*

"You're telling me you're ready to get married. Ha." Pauline cracked her gum again. "With all the lookers in the world, you're gonna give all that up for one woman you probably haven't even thought about for five years."

"The hell I haven't," Crash said.

"Well, it doesn't matter," Pauline said. "She doesn't want you. You think she hasn't been dating and screwing around? I can tell you, she has."

Crash winced. Then something bumped into the window and he saw a butterfly fluttering there, a big blue one with round wings, staring back at him. *Belligerent, aren't you?* he thought. It looked like the kind of butterfly that probably beat up the other butterflies. In fact, it looked exactly like Mare's butch butterfly, tilted above Mare's beautiful round butt. "Well, why shouldn't she have?" he told Pauline, as the butterfly shoved off and disappeared. "I did, too. We lived our lives. We learned things. Now we're going to learn things with each other. We're ready. No regrets."

Pauline cracked her gum. "Yeah, you look ready."

"She wants me." Crash pushed the milkshake away. "I'm the one she loves, damn it, she said so."

"You just don't love her," Pauline said. "Well, them's the breaks. You should go back to Italy."

"Not without Mare."

"You're just being stubborn." Pauline began to clear the table as Crash got out his wallet to pay the check. "You haven't thought about her in five years, so why—"

The picture of Mare's Florett fluttered out of his wallet, looped a loop, and landed face up on the table.

"The hell I haven't." Crash picked up the picture. "Look at this. I've been looking for the parts for this bike for three years . . ."

He stopped, realizing what he was saying.

"Three years," he told Pauline, jabbing the photo at her. "I've been planning on coming back for her for three years. I've always meant to come back for her. I'm just slow." He looked at the bike. "And stupid," he added to be fair. "But that doesn't mean I don't love—" He looked up at Pauline and for the first time noticed the red glint in her eyes. And the red ring around her iris.

Pauline did not crack gum. Pauline knew exactly what his order was. Pauline was not serving his dinner.

"Of course, there's no reason to rush into anything," he told Xan.

"Yeah," she said, cracking her gum.

"I think I'll go back to Italy now," he said, putting the photo back in his wallet.

"Good plan."

He handed her a twenty. "Keep the change."

She nodded, the red glint in her eye getting brighter. "That's real generous of you."

"Well, I'm leaving the country. Gotta get rid of my American money." Crash stood up and bumped into the woman who'd just gotten up from the booth behind his. "Sorry," he said to the top of her head, her gray razor-cut hair neatly parted.

"My fault," the woman said, keeping her head down.

He followed her out the door, and then got on his bike and headed for the O'Brien house to tell Mare that her aunt was at the Greasy Fork possessing waitresses.

And that he'd loved her since the day he'd met her and would until the end of time.

They'd almost reached the top of the mountain, Pywackt padding beside them, the Great Big Rock in view, Mare with "Remains of the Day" stuck in her head, when she heard the purr of a well-tuned motorcycle.

He's not coming back for you, she told herself sternly, but her heart said, *He's coming back for me.*

"Send him away," Dee said. "This is not the time or the place for civilians," and Mare slowed as Crash rounded the final turn to the top, narrowly missing a frog that was hopping along the roadside. The frog sneezed.

"This is so not the time for us to discuss the relationship," she told him as he parked his bike, but she sighed in spite of herself, he looked so good standing in front of her again.

He took off his helmet. "Your aunt is at the Greasy Fork. I think she's possessed Pauline."

"Really," Mare said, smiling at the thought of Xan slinging hash at the Fork. "Well, she hasn't possessed Pauline. Pauline's in Baltimore with William. They ran off together after William's dinner break in the middle of the libido spell. He quit his job at Value Video!! so they tried to make me manager this afternoon, but I'm busy with the whole Antichrist thing so they offered it to Dreama. She's the youngest manager in the history of the company." Mare knew she was babbling, but he was right there, with her, and it was all she could do not to reach out and pat him because he was *right there.*

I love you, she thought. *I have to go do something horrible to my aunt and I'll probably die, but I love you.*

"Okay," Crash said. "So who's at the Greasy Fork?"

"Probably Xan, shapeshifting. What did she want?"

"Me, back in Italy. But I'm not going without you." Crash got off his bike. "So what are we doing here?"

"Mare!" Lizzie called from the top of the path.

"Just a minute," she called up. "This is new." She looked back at him. "I can't talk now. Xan has grabbed Danny and Elric for some kind of Evil Overlord plan and we have to turn her into a geranium. But if we survive this, her power will be broken, and then if you still love me without her spell—"

"You're kidding," Crash said.

"Which part?"

"The geranium," Crash said.

"Oh, no, we have to turn her into something powerless, and Dee said if Xan likes red that much, she could go be a geranium on the kitchen windowsill in Hell. Dee's really had it with Xan this time, and a geranium's as good as anything else."

Crash nodded, looking lost but prepared to follow anyway. "You really can turn her into a geranium?"

"I can't, but Lizzie can if she has enough power, so if Dee and I channel what we've got into Lizzie, then Lizzie can turn Xan into a potted plant, and that should break whatever spell she has on Danny and Elric up there, and we can all go home for dinner, and then you and I can talk about living happily ever after in Italy, which we might actually have a shot at if we can turn Xan into a geranium. Or something equally nonlethal. And sedentary. And if you still love me when Xan's power is gone." Mare drew in a deep breath.

"Okay," Crash said, and she couldn't stand it any more and leaned in and kissed him, loving the taste of him and the heat of his mouth, so glad to see him that the pebbles on the path rose up and swirled around them, and then he put his hands on her arms and kissed her back and some boulders shifted.

"Mare," Dee said, from the top of the path.

"I have to go," Mare said, dizzy with love. "My aunt the Antichrist is up there. She's probably going to kill us all."

"And your plan is to turn her into a geranium," Crash said, breathless. "Okay, if you're up there, I'm up there." He started up the path.

"Not a good idea," Mare said, and followed him.

"No civilians," Lizzie said when he reached them, but she didn't stop climbing.

"I'm marrying in," Crash said, not stopping, either.

"Not if you get fried by a stray bolt of something," Dee said, as they reached the top. "You have no powers to protect you."

"And they do?" Crash nodded over to the stone circle where Danny and Elric were sitting on the Great Big Rock, Danny looking bemused, Elric looking murderous.

"As a matter of fact, yes," Dee said.

"'Bout time you got here," Danny called to Dee. "Okay, Elric and I slept with you and Lizzie, we know what we're in for. But what did the frog do?" He jerked his thumb at a frog on the edge of the rock.

"Hey, Jude," Crash said.

The other frog they'd seen sneezing on the path had made it to the top of the mountain and now was hopping frantically across the green toward the circle, as Dee said, "Crash, I'm sorry, but you have to go. You're going to get hurt."

"No," Crash said.

"Give it up," Lizzie said to Dee. "Neither one of them can take an order. I say he's part of the family and he stays. Now, has anybody seen Xan? Because if not, this is going to be the biggest anticlimax—"

The setting sun hit the Great Big Rock, and Xan appeared from behind it, clad in a long white dress, looking spectacular with her dark hair flowing across her shoulders.

"Nice entrance," Mare said.

"Overdone," Dee said.

"Well, natural light is tricky," Lizzie said fairly.

"Especially at her age," Elric said from inside the circle.

Xan's face darkened.

"Does not take criticism well," Mare said primly. "Needs to improve."

"And she's wearing white?" Dee said. "Who is she kidding?"

Lightning split the sky behind Xan, lighting up the circle with fluorescent clarity, tinting the rocks with a bloodred glow.

"Did she do that?" Crash whispered to Mare.

"The lightning, no," Mare whispered back. "The red light, probably. That's just high school stuff for her. The real magic is keeping the guys in the circle. If we can distract her, they can get out."

"Like if I went and got my bike and rode it straight at her?"

"I'd get you a very nice wreath and put flowers on your grave every Sunday."

"So, Plan B," Crash said.

Dee stepped forward. "Let the guys go, Xan. They're not part of this. You can keep the frog if you want."

Jude croaked and the other frog croaked, too, and then sneezed.

"Of course they're part of this," Xan said, sounding exasperated. "I brought them into this. It's a trade. I brought you True Love—"

"Thanks for the amphibian," Mare said, scowling.

"Do you know how rare True Love is?" Xan said to Dee. "And I found yours for you. And Lizzie." She lifted her head and looked past Dee to Lizzie. "You think you'd ever have gone to Toledo and found Elric? It would never have happened. Without me, you never—"

"Yo," Mare said. "About the *frog*."

"Oh, for heaven's sake," Xan said to her. "I made a mistake. Sue me. You got your mechanic. Stop complaining."

"I'm not complaining about the mechanic," Mare said. "I'm pissed about the *frog*."

"And what are we supposed to give you in return?" Dee said.

Xan smiled. "Your powers, of course."

Dee looked exasperated. "Our powers. Of course."

"Well, you're not using them," Xan said, her voice full of reason. "You don't even like yours, Dee, you're *inconvenienced* by it, and I can set you free. And Lizzie, well, poor Lizzie can't control hers, Elric was ready to take it from her just because of the damage she was doing to the universe, like a baby with a flamethrower. And Mare . . ." Xan turned and smiled at Mare. "Mare doesn't have enough power to worry about controlling it. She'd rather sell videos and make babies with a mechanic—"

"I don't like her," Crash said.

"—except that she can't do that for fear the villagers will burn her at the stake if she goes to the backwoods of Italy and moves something while she's screaming, 'yesYesYES!' So really, girls, I think I'm making you an excellent offer. I'm giving you the loves of your lives and freedom from powers you don't even want. I'm doing you a *favor*—"

"Well, color us grateful," Dee said flatly. "Sadly, we're just going to have to say no. Let them go."

"That's so like you," Xan said, drifting closer. "Making all the decisions, not even consulting your sisters."

"Oh, we're with her on that," Mare said, moving to stand beside Dee, sandwiching Lizzie in the middle.

"We want our powers. And our lives. We're selfish like that."

"Yep," Lizzie said. "Let 'em go."

Xan sighed, and opened her arms, the long sleeves of her white dress flowing like bat wings. "Fine. Then we'll do it the hard way."

"Like there was ever any other way," Lizzie muttered and took her sisters' hands.

"Maybe we should have been practicing this," Mare whispered, praying this was going to work. "Like for thirteen years. Plan ahead."

"Stop it," Dee said. "Strong thoughts. Positive thinking."

I'm positive we're going to get our asses kicked, Mare thought and looked at her sisters' faces, stern and determined as they faced Xan. Well, hell, she'd be stern if Crash were in that damn stone circle, too. She'd be homicidal. "Right. Strong thoughts, positive thinking. Don't cross the streams." And then she concentrated on giving Lizzie everything she had.

In her peripheral vision, she could see Xan turn and raise her arms as if to smite the men in the circle, and there was something wrong about that, too theatrical, too Disney witch by far, but Mare couldn't do anything about it now. She bowed her head, touched her forehead to Lizzie's shoulder to create a deeper contact, and felt the power start to flow. She heard Lizzie draw in a deep breath and breathed with her, felt blue mist flow into lavender smoke and twine with green, the colors making a watery rope that grew stronger as they twisted together, more powerful because there were three, and a part of her sent a silent apology for all the times she'd sneered at the TV for that power-of-three chant. Around them lightning crackled and then Lizzie raised her head, focused on Xan, and lifted her arms, encircled, and before them Xan wavered, and began to shift, elongating into a green stem, her head blossoming into bright red petals while her face grew slack with shock.

She snarled, *"A geranium?"* and then Mare rocked as talons raked at her mind, red claws cutting through the rope of their powers, smearing the colors into grays, Lizzie screaming as red mist filled the air, and then she realized she was screaming, too, and Crash hit her hard, knocking her to the ground, cutting the connection to Lizzie and to Dee and to Xan, who'd been raping their gifts, leaving her mind savaged and bloody, Lizzie weeping on the ground, and somewhere in that red mist Dee shrieking, and Xan rising up before them . . .

Dee felt the hit of energy like an explosion. The geranium was gone, and Xan had turned. All Dee could see was dark red. Old bloodred. She was shaking hard with the energy she'd expended, holding on by her fingertips to Lizzie, and she knew it had all gone wrong. The flow reversed. The rope of their powers tangled and snapped, a living thing that whipped back at them like a live wire. Lizzie screamed and Dee tried to pull her free, but she couldn't manage it; she couldn't see. All she could feel was that terrible shriek of energy shattering around them, and then she was on her ass, the connection broken.

She scrambled up, thinking it was Xan, but it was

Crash who'd hit them, knocking them around like bowling pins and snapping the connection and saving them. But they were separated now, to be picked off at Xan's leisure. Lizzie was weeping, and the men were shouting from the circle, Danny yelling, "Now Dee! Now!"

Now.

It was an instant, and it was filled with rage, with the weight of the accumulated years, with the liquid crimson viscera of Xan's avarice that collected and solidified and grew. Suddenly out of the bloodred mist a dragon rose, black and skeletal and stinking—Xan, her mouth open in a scream of fury. Her eyes glittered crimson. Her neck arched, snakelike, as she reared up to strike Lizzie where she lay helpless on the ground, and Dee thought, *Yes, Danny, now,* and she let her rage gather, coalesce, compress into form and light and fury, and she rose off the ground herself, there off the dust of defeat where her sisters were still in danger, where Xan wanted to leave them crushed and empty and bloody, and Dee could finally call on every ounce of her power and know that her sisters would help her to finally, *finally* call that bitch to task. She rose right up, her cells swelling, the light so hot it blinded her in the red mist that suddenly sparked green. She opened her mouth and filled her lungs and shrieked, a terrible bone-chilling cry she'd never heard before, greater than a hawk's, more awful than any predator she'd ever been or hoped to be, a magnificent full-throated war cry the kind that she'd wanted to let loose her whole life, and she stretched out her hands, but they weren't hands, and she was the one reaching now, because she was going to impale herself on that fearsome neck, she was going to rip out that snakelike neck that rose above her. The red mist had been swallowed by green fog, but she could see. She could see Xan and she was finally going to have her . . .

L izzie stood frozen, staring up as the huge black dragon reared overhead, bearing down on her, lethal, merciless, and then it was engulfed in a cloud of green fog as Dee attacked.

Oh, God, not an owl, Lizzie thought, horrified. They were all going to die. But then Dee speared upward, out of the thick fog, and even in the darkness of the storm, her green and gold scales glittered brilliantly. She had outdone herself—a magnificent Chinese dragon, soaring through the air, flying straight at the black and red Xan beast with a shriek of rage. For a moment, the older dragon wavered, and little Py leaped beneath them both, aiming for Xan's huge black tail with the same determination he'd shown for Lizzie's bunnies, the ballsiest house cat in Salem's Fork.

With a scream, the black dragon fell back beneath Dee's fierce onslaught, howling into the wind with rage and pain, and red mist flew upward like a tornado. The creature within it began to shift again, narrowing, changing, pulsing, until a huge snake remained, black, malevolent, only Xan's glowing red eyes left with any trace of humanity, all of it bad.

"Lizzie!" Mare cried. *"Do something!"*

She wanted to hide. All her power, her self-assurance seemed to have vanished, and she was terrified, helpless. Her sisters were going to die, Elric was going to die, unless she did something. And then she felt it—the power rumbling against her heart, the amethyst pendant burning, and the strength flowing through her, not just her own, but Mare's, Dee's, Elric's, all the power of the universe was surging through her veins, so strong that if she threw a transformation spell it would hit Dee, as well, turning her into a frail human who'd never survive. She tried to move, to get between the two massive combatants, one so ugly, one so beautiful, but the lightning was flashing all around them, and even as she finally slipped between them the snake focused on her, rearing its huge head to strike.

"Lizzie!" She heard Elric's furious cry of warning, and it pulled the last bit of energy through her, enough so that she looked up, arched her back, and threw the spell upward, directly in the face of the snake, as purple smoke exploded around them.

Mare saw Xan draw back to spit poison at Lizzie and lunged to drag her away, but a huge violet crack of lightning split the sky and purple smoke rolled up, gushing over the landscape. Mare screamed, *"Lizzie!"* and crawled toward where she'd last seen her, hearing Crash yell and then a roaring, and then the rain began to fall, beating down the smoke. As it cleared, Mare saw Lizzie standing like a warrior queen, her arms encircled; and beyond her Dee, human again, sitting naked on her butt in the mud; and beyond her, Crash eyeing a large tiger who looked as confused as he was; and beyond them, Maxine, naked, too, looking startled and guilty as all hell; and in front of all of them, a giant gold snake, frozen in the attack position, glistening in the violet rain.

"Huh." Mare looked up at Lizzie, and then at the giant gold snake, and then back at Lizzie. "Finally got that gold thing down, did you?"

Lizzie took a deep breath and smiled and dropped her arms. "Yes. Yes, I did. Told you I could do it."

Danny and Elric walked out of the stone circle, staring at the giant gold snake, even Elric speechless for once, the frog hopping behind them, while Maxine followed, looking lost.

"She looks like a giant war memorial," Danny said as he picked up Dee's silk dress and helped her slip it on.

"Yes," Elric said. "If the war was really strange, and the victors were really rich."

"Maybe we should make a nice plaque to commemorate the event." Mare shoved her wet hair out of her eyes, trying to wrap her mind around it all. "With something from the Evil Overlord Rules. Like Rule Thirty-four: 'I will not turn into a giant snake; it never helps.'" She looked at Maxine. "Hi, Maxine. So, you were a frog?"

Maxine picked up Jude. "Yes," she said defiantly, cradling him in her hands, trying to pretend she wasn't naked.

"Okay, then," Mare said and turned back to Crash, who'd come up beside her, keeping an eye on the tiger.

"She tried to take your powers," Elric said, his arms around Lizzie, as he stared up at the snake. "That's why she wanted you all up here united to save us. She wanted your powers bound together so she could take them all."

"Bitch." Dee dusted off her hands.

Py gave up staring at Crash and came up and rubbed his huge, wet, furry tiger head against Mare's leg. "Hello, baby," she said, scratching him behind the ears. "Do you feel better back to normal? Kind of normal?"

"So it's over?" Lizzie said, safe in the circle of Elric's arms.

"Yep," Mare said, letting her skirt drop. "You and Dee saved the day, all by yourselves. Unless you want me to turn Xan to face the east, I got nothin' here. And she'd hate facing the east, you know how she stayed out of the sun."

Dee and Lizzie looked at each other.

"Yes, it would be a nice punishment," Mare said, exasperated. "But I lied, I can't turn her to face the east, either. I'm not much good at heavy lifting. I'm not much good at anything." She looked at Crash, and took a deep breath. "So the woman who put the True Love spell on you? She's got no power, that spell is broken, you can leave now."

"I love you," he said.

Mare swallowed. "Still?"

Crash looked patient. "I told you this."

"She has abandonment issues," Dee said.

"Who doesn't?" Crash said.

Mare blinked back tears. *"You came back for me and you weren't under a spell?"*

"Like I'd leave you," Crash said.

"I'd rather have the giant snake spitting venom," Elric said, casting his eyes to the heavens. Then his face changed. "Oh, *hell.*"

"What?" Lizzie said and followed his eyes up.

"This isn't over," Elric said, staring up at the snake's eyes. "She's still alive in there."

"No," Maxine said, holding Jude tighter.

Danny pulled Dee closer. "How can you tell?"

"Her eyes," he said. "Just a slight movement, but she's in there."

"How?" Dee said. "She's *gold.*"

Elric shook his head. "You can only turn like to like. The human body is about eighteen percent carbon, so that's what Lizzie transformed. Xan's just a very unstable shell right now. She's going to change back, and when she does—"

"Oh, *hell,*" Crash said to Mare. "I knew the holidays with your family were going to be a bitch. Well, you'll just have to keep changing her into something else. A piano or something."

"The piano from hell," Mare said, leaning into him again. "All it plays is 'Free Bird.'"

"Dee and Lizzie can't do transformation magic again this soon," Elric said. "And since my powers seem to be on the fritz from the damn containment spell, and Mare thinks she isn't good at anything—"

"Hey!" Crash said.

"—I suggest we leave. Xantippe is not going to be up for an intercontinental chase for a while. We should have time for three honeymoons before . . ." He looked at Mare with distaste. " 'Free Bird.' "

Mare looked up at Crash. "You got any ideas?"

"No, but you can stop that I'm-not-good-at-anything moan. You're Queen of the Universe. If you can't move big things, move something else, but settle that bitch's hash. She tried to send me back to Italy without you. Fix her good."

Mare thought, *Yeah, she tried to ruin my life and my sisters' lives, it's time we did settle her hash.* She stared at Xan, trying to see what Elric the master sorcerer saw, trying to believe what Crash the master mechanic believed, and began to imagine what it was like inside Xan right now, what it had been like when Xan had transformed herself from Xan to dragon. If Xan had done it, she could do it. Xan must have just *seen* her human molecules and maybe rearranged the atoms so they were dragon molecules, and then something had gone wrong and the dragon molecules had become snake molecules. And then Lizzie, Lizzie must have gone in and made snake molecules into gold molecules. And if that was what they'd done, Mare wouldn't even have to change anything, all she'd have to do would be to wrap her mind around Xan's molecules the way she'd wrapped her mind around the bed and the sugar grains and the muffins, and then just bang them together and start a chain reaction . . .

She closed her eyes and concentrated hard. She was Queen of the Universe, and she could see the molecules in her mind—*there they were, gold snake molecules with Xan-red centers, right there in front of her*—and if she could see them they must be real and if they were real . . .

She reached out with her mind, blue sparks flying, and surrounded the gold dots. They were feisty little devils, those Xan molecules, but as she started to make her move, she saw purple smoke and green fog in there, too, in her mind, backing up the blue sparks, and then she laughed out loud.

"Mare?" Dee said, and Lizzie turned to look.

"You know my abandonment issues?" Mare said. "I'm over them."

"We're happy for you," Elric said, taking Lizzie's arm. "And now we're leaving."

High above them, the golden eyes turned red, flickering.

"Go," Mare said. "I'm on it."

"No," Dee said, and Lizzie stepped closer, and said, "We're here," and Mare reached out for them, and then she reached out with her mind again and went inside Xan and found the gold molecules there, her blue sparks zeroing in on the weakest part. *That's it,* she thought, and aimed for two molecules that looked crucial. She tried to pull them apart and they stuck together, so she yanked hard, and then there was cool green fog and warm violet smoke and big-ass blue sparks blowing holes through everything, and Mare used it all and broke through to set free two big fat gold molecules. *One more,* she thought, and kicked out a third and set them rotating, spinning faster and faster, as green and violet and blue, fog and smoke and sparkly mist, began to fill the space between the molecules and the space between her fingertips and the space between the sisters, and the whole top of the mountain began to hum.

High above her, the eyes of the golden snake flickered madly red, and Mare felt her eyes flicker madly back. *I know what you wanted, Xan,* she thought, *and so do Lizzie and Dee, it was this, and we've got it now,* and then she clamped down on the thought, *no gloating,* time to concentrate on the molecules, keep those suckers spinning, and as she did, the blue and green and violet became stronger, brighter, driving back the rain and the clouds, until somebody said, "Oh, *shit,*" and then Mare gave the molecules a flick with her frontal lobe and they smacked into each other and then smacked into other molecules that smacked into other molecules that smacked into other molecules . . .

Crash yanked her to the ground and a second later Xan exploded into chunks of gold that exploded into smaller pieces that exploded into little pieces that exploded into golden dust, and Mare laughed into the mud of the mountain and hugged Crash to her, so grateful she had him, and her sisters, and him, and her power, and him, especially him, as the gold went everywhere, and when it was all over, she sat up and saw the gold dust coating everything. Xan was bronzing powder.

"God, she's gaudy," Dee said, trying to brush off her borrowed sleeve. "I hope she washes off."

"Well, that's Xan for you," Elric said. "She always liked things shiny." He flicked at his sleeve and the gold dust fell away, leaving him immaculate.

"You're going to be annoying me for the rest of my life, aren't you?" Dee said.

"Lizzie?" a very small voice said from the underbrush, and when they turned around, Maxine crawled out, covered in mud and gold, still holding Jude.

"Oh, Maxine," Lizzie said. "We forgot about you. Elric, give her your coat."

Elric looked at Lizzie as if she'd asked him to bathe Maxine by hand.

"I don't want his coat," Maxine said. She held out Jude. "I want him. Turn him back, please."

Lizzie swallowed. "I can't, Maxine. He is what he is. I'm sure he's a lovely frog, but even if I made him a human again, he'd turn back into a frog again in a couple of days. He's supposed to be a frog, honey."

Maxine looked at her, tears in her eyes. "Okay, make me a frog."

"It won't last," Lizzie said. "You'll turn back."

"Maybe," Maxine said. "But maybe I won't."

Mare looked at Lizzie. "Do it."

Lizzie hesitated, then circled her arms. There was a swirl of purple smoke, and two frogs sat on the ground staring happily into each other's eyes.

"That's not the weirdest thing I've seen today," Crash said.

Danny looked around the mountaintop. "I still can't believe Xan's gone. Shouldn't we be playing taps or something? I mean, she *died*." And they stood there in silence, trying to summon up some regret.

Finally, Lizzie said, "I can restore her, you know."

Mare put up her hand. "I vote no."

Dee put up her hand. "I vote *hell* no."

Lizzie put up her hand. "Oh, I vote no."

Elric looked at Danny. "That was a very humane impulse you just had. Next time, *save it for humans*."

Danny put up both hands. "Sorry. My bad."

Mare looked at Dee and Lizzie. "So. That thing that just happened. You were there, too, right? That was all three of us together? Inside Xan. Inside me?"

"Yes," Lizzie said. "And we probably shouldn't do it again until the apocalypse."

"And talk about it first," Dee said. "And then vote on it."

"But it was good," Mare said.

"Very good," Lizzie said.

Dee smiled. "The best."

And they turned and went down the mountain as the gold dust settled like a fine sparkly mist.

Dee didn't think her heart would ease for a week. She couldn't believe it. Xan, the snake, was nothing but cosmic dust. She looked back, just to make sure, and smiled. She loved it when a plan came together.

"You're gonna trip over something if you don't turn around and look where you're going," Danny offered, holding tightly to her hand.

She laughed. "You're right." Then she laughed again, swinging hands as if she were strolling down the street instead of off a mountain where cataclysms had happened. "So what do you think? Will the no-eyebrow look be in this year?"

Danny smiled down at her, his eyes unspeakably proud. "I have a girlfriend who can turn into a dragon," he boasted. "All my writer friends will be jealous. Especially the fantasy writers."

Dee looked closely at him. "It doesn't bother you?"

He shrugged, and picked off a few toasted curls. "I told you. It doesn't matter. It's just one more color in your array."

How did he always know the perfect thing to say to her? "What a painterly way to put that."

"I figure I'd better do some research on the subject. Seems I'm not going to be the star in the family anymore. If either of us ever get to the point where we attend celebrity cocktail parties, I want to sound knowledgeable when I boast about your talent. You are going to marry me, Dee."

"Yes," she said through a tear-constricted throat. "I am."

"And you'll go to Ireland with me? And Greece?"

"And Montmartre?"

His grin was devilish. "Didn't I tell you? I have an apartment on the Left Bank."

Dee pulled him to a dead stop halfway down the hill. "You're lying to me."

He brushed away a few more ashes and plucked at her singed hair. "I also have a horse farm in Ireland and a little getaway in Nevis where I escape to write. Oh, and a brownstone in Greenwich Village for business trips. Do you like New York?"

"I don't know." She couldn't take it all in. "I'd like

to find out, though. What about Italy and Spain? I think that's where Lizzie and Mare will be." Suddenly she grinned, exhilarated. "Pretty rarefied atmosphere for girls who spent the last twelve years hiding in small towns."

"You pick the city." He kissed her, a long sweet kiss of reunion. "I'm sorry, Dee. I should have listened to you. I brought that old snake right to your door."

"No you didn't. She brought you. And it was the only good thing she ever did in her life."

Rain dripped down from the trees, but Dee didn't notice. She had eyes only for Danny, who took a moment to look at their joined hands.

"I can't tell you how sorry I am I lied to you. I never meant to hurt you or make you think I don't love you enough to let you in every corner of my life."

Dee thumbed a tear away from his cheek. "Okay."

He stared at her. "That's it? 'Okay'?"

She beamed. "Sure. Authors make me hot."

Hand in hand, they turned for home.

Elric was walking beside Lizzie, uncharacteristically silent. He had his arm around her waist, a good thing, since she was feeling a bit wobbly, but he still hadn't said anything, and Lizzie was starting to worry.

"Is something wrong?" she asked.

"Remind me never to get you too pissed off at me," he said finally.

"I'm not sure you'll be able to help it. You can be awfully annoying."

He smiled, and even in the night air the colors swirled, dancing in the dark. "You're even better than I thought," he said, not sounding thrilled about it.

"Is that a problem?"

"I'll get used to it. I'm usually the one in control." He glanced down at her. "This is good for me. Maybe we'll use those silk ties on me next time around. We'll have years to work it out." The promise in his voice made her pulse race, her tattoo throb, and her entire body tighten in anticipation.

"Er . . . how long am I going to live? Just curious, mind you."

He leaned down and brushed his mouth against hers. "Two hundred, maybe two hundred and fifty. Give or take a decade or two. Time enough for me to figure out how to keep you on your toes."

"You can try," she said, suddenly feeling very sure of herself. "You know, I'm tired. Do we really have to walk down this mountain? I think I need to go to bed."

"I think you do, too," he said, his voice low and sexy. "Close your eyes and think of England."

And a moment later, they were gone.

As Lizzie and Elric disappeared, Mare and Crash stopped at his bike, Pywackt regal beside them. Crash picked up his helmet and handed it to Mare and then climbed on the bike, and Pywackt sat and stared at him.

"Want a ride, Py?" Mare said.

"Py's kind of large," Crash said, but Mare put her hand on Py's head and he became a house cat again. "Okay. How'd you do that?"

"Remember I told you I felt weird?" Mare put her helmet on. "When Xan reached inside us to take our powers, she scrambled ours a little. I can't turn straw into gold, and I'm betting I can't become a hawk, but I can turn Py back and I might try turning into a redhead for you some night."

"Okay." Crash shook his head. "Or not."

"Or a blonde," Mare said as Py jumped in front of Crash on the bike. "You might like a blonde. As long as she was me."

Then Py looked up the mountain and growled.

"Py?" Mare said.

"About the remains of the day," Crash said, looking up the mountain. "That dust is still moving."

Mare looked back.

The gold dust was swirling. It might have been just a small funnel cloud, just a trick of the light. Then again, it might not be.

Mare walked a little way back up the path to see better. The dust seemed pretty well organized for a cloud. Crash called up, "Mare?" and she closed her eyes and thought about the Great Big Rock up there. All those molecules, sitting up there for centuries. Heavy little suckers, too. Once she had them firmly in mind, she opened her eyes and watched blue sparkly mist swirl around the rock, little bits of green and violet in the mix. *Pretty,* she thought, and picked up the rock and held it over the gold dust. The Great Big Rock didn't feel heavy at all, but when she dropped it on the dust, it made one hell of a thump and the gold poofed out around the rock and then fell down silent into the dirt.

"Better," Mare said, and went back down to Crash and Py.

Crash nodded at her as she climbed on the back of the bike. "How long do you think that's going to hold her?"

Mare wrapped her arms around him and put her cheek on his back. "Long enough for us to get to Italy."

"Works for me," Crash said, and carried them down the mountain.

One fine August evening, as Joey "the Gent" Torcelli sat in his deserted diner on the outskirts of Keyes, South Carolina, and rubbed his gun arm to ease his arthritis; and as beyond Joey's diner, the wildlife in the swamps of Keyes County began to emerge into the deep blue twilight to cogitate upon ways to make the encroaching darkness aid them in their endeavors both nefarious and recreational; and as beyond the swamps, the last of the evening sun disappeared into the commingling waters of the Blood River and the Intracoastal Waterway outside the kitchen windows of the white-columned house known as Two Rivers; Agnes Crandall stirred raspberries and sugar in her heavy non-stick frying pan and defended her fiancé to the only man she'd ever trusted.

It wasn't easy.

"Come on, Joey." Agnes cradled the phone between her chin and her shoulder and frowned over the tops of her fogged-up, black-rimmed glasses at the raspberries, which were being annoying and uncooperative, much like her fiancé lately. "Taylor's a terrific chef." *Which is why I'm still with him.* "And he's very sweet." *When he has the time.* "And we've got a great future in this house together." *Assuming he ever comes out here again.*

Joey snorted his contempt, the sound exploding through the phone. "He shouldn't leave you all alone out there. There's somethin' wrong with a guy who leaves a sweetheart like you all alone like that. You should find somebody better."

"Yeah, like I have the time," Agnes said, and then realized that wasn't the right answer. "Not that I would. Taylor's a great guy."

"He's a mutt, Agnes," Joey said.

Agnes took off her glasses and turned up the heat under the raspberries, which she knew was courting disaster, but it was late and she was tired of playing nice with fruit; the raspberries were about to find out who was boss. "Cut me a break, Joey. I'm behind on my column, I've got the Mothers coming tomorrow, I've got—"

"And there's Rhett," Joey said. "How's Rhett?"

"What?" Agnes said, thrown off stride. She stopped stirring her berries, which began to bubble, and looked down at her dog, draped over her feet like a moth-eaten brown overcoat, slobbering on the floor as he slept. "Rhett's fine. Why? What have you heard?"

"He's a fine healthy-lookin' bloodhound," Joey said hastily. "He looked real good in his picture in the paper today. You did, too." He paused, his voice straining to be casual. "How come old Rhett was wearing that stupid collar in that picture?"

"The collar?" Agnes frowned at the phone. "It was just some junk jewelry—"

The oven timer buzzed, and she said, "Hold on," put down the phone, and took the now madly bubbling berries off the heat with one hand. Rhett picked up his head and barked as she reached for the oven door to get the tray of cupcakes inside, and Agnes turned, raspberry pan in hand, to see what he was upset about.

A guy with a gun stood ten feet away in the doorway to the front hall, the bottom half of his face covered with a red bandana.

"I come for your dog," he said, pointing the gun at Rhett

who was now baying at him, and Agnes said, "*No!*" and slung the raspberry pan at him, the hot syrup arcing out in front of it like napalm and catching him full in the face.

He screamed as the sauce and then the pan hit him, pawing at the scalding fruit and dropping his gun to rip the bandana away as Rhett went for him. Agnes ran around the counter and scooped up the pan as Rhett barreled into him, and the guy went down flailing in the doorway, hitting the back of his head on the marble counter by the wall and knocking off every cupcake she had cooling there.

"God*damn it,*" Agnes said, standing over him with her pan, her heart pounding.

The guy didn't move, and Rhett began to hoover up cupcakes at the speed of light.

"Agnes?" Joey shouted from the phone on the counter. "What the fuck, *Agnes?*"

Agnes kicked the gun into the housekeeper's room and peered at the guy, trying to catch her breath. She was pretty sure that if he were conscious, he'd be twitching from the hot syrup, not to mention the slobber that Rhett was flinging his way.

When he didn't move, she backed up to grab the phone off the counter. "Some guy just showed up here with a gun and tried to take Rhett," she told Joey, breathing hard. "But it's okay, I'm in control, I'm not angry." *Goddammit.*

"*Where is he?*"

"On the floor, in the hall doorway. He hit his head and knocked himself out. Joey, why would anybody want Rhett?"

"*Fuck that,*" Joey said. "Get the hell *out of there.* Take Rhett with you."

"Like I'd leave him," Agnes said, outraged. "I can't get out. I told you, the guy's lying across the hall door. I've seen those horror movies. He'll come to and reach up and grab me."

"Get out the *back door—*"

"I can't, Doyle's got it blocked with screen and boards. I'm going to hang up and call nine-one-one."

"*No*," Joey said. "*No cops.* I'm comin' over."

"What do you mean, *no cops*? I—"

The dognapper stirred.

"Wait a minute." Agnes put the phone on the counter and held the frying pan at the ready, hands shaking, as she craned her neck to look closer at the dognapper.

Young, just a teenager. Short. Skinny. Limp dirty dark hair. Stupid because if he'd had any brains, he'd have grabbed Rhett when he went out for his nightly pee. And now that he was unconscious, pretty harmless-looking. She probably outweighed him by thirty pounds.

As she calmed down, she could hear Dr. Garvin's voice in her head.

How are you feeling right now, Agnes?

Well, Dr. Garvin, I'm feeling a little angry that this punk broke into my house with a gun and threatened my dog.

And how are you handling that anger, Agnes?

I never touched him, I swear.

The boy opened his eyes.

"Don't move." Agnes held up her pan. "I've called the police," she lied. "They're coming for you. My dog is vicious and you don't want to cross me, either, especially with a frying pan; you have no *idea* what I can do with a frying pan." She took a deep breath, and the kid glared at her, and she looked closer at his face, seeing the lurid welts of singed skin where the raspberry had struck. "That's gotta hurt. Not that I care."

He worked his battered jaw, and she held the frying pan higher as a threat.

"So, tell me, you little creep," Agnes said, "*why were you trying to kill my dog?*"

"I weren't tryin' to kill the dog," the boy said, outraged. "I wouldn't kill no *dog*."

"The gun, Creepoid," Agnes said. "You pointed *a gun* at him."

"I was just gonna *take* him," the boy said. "There weren't no call to get mean. I weren't gonna hurt him. I wouldn't hurt *nobody*." He touched the sauce on his face and winced.

The boy closed his eyes, and Agnes was reaching for the phone again when he rolled to his feet and lunged for her. She yelped and smacked him hard on the head with her pan, and he staggered, and then she hit him again, harder this time, just to make sure, and he fell back onto the floor, blood seeping down the side of his face, and lay still. She felt a qualm about that, but not much because it was self-defense, and he'd broken into her *house*, he'd scared *the hell* out of her, he had *no right*—

Violence is not the answer, Agnes.

That depends on the question, *Dr. Garvin.*

—and she was not out of control, she was not angry, she was calm, she was shaking, but she was perfectly fine, and anyway it was a non-stick pan, not cast-iron, so she was fairly certain she hadn't done any permanent damage.

Fingers crossed, anyway.

Beside him, Rhett collapsed, overcome by the number of cupcakes still on the floor.

"I *hate you*," she said to the unconscious boy. Then she picked up her phone, and said, "Joey?"

"*Don't do anything, Agnes!*" Joey yelled, the sounds of traffic in the background. "*I'm on Route 17. I'm almost there.*"

"That's good," Agnes said, realizing her voice was shaking, too. "He's just a kid, Joey. He said he wasn't trying to hurt anybody—"

The kid lunged to his feet, and Agnes screamed again and dropped the phone to swing the pan again, but this time he was ready for her, ducking under her arm and butting her in the stomach so that she said, "Oof!" and fell backward against the counter. She scrambled to her feet as he tried to backhand her, and she ducked and swung the pan again and hit him in the head, really hating him now, and then she hit him again, and then she couldn't stop. She hit him over and over, gritting her teeth, and he yelled, "Stop it, *stop it!*" and grabbed for her while she pounded him, driving him back toward the hall door. She heard herself screaming at him, "*Get out, get out, I hate you, get out of my house, get out of*

MY HOUSE!!!" as he lurched back, his arms across his head, and stepped in Rhett's water dish and fell back into the wall, all of his weight hitting it, and then he fell through it, screaming.

Agnes froze, the frying pan raised over her head, as he disappeared, and then the wall was solid again, and she heard a thud, and the screaming stopped, cut off.

She stood there with the pan over her head for a moment, stunned, and then she lowered it slowly and clutched it to her chest, warm raspberry sauce and all, her heart beating like mad. She stared dumbfounded at the wall, waiting to see if he'd come rushing back through, like a ghost or something. When nothing happened, she went over and pushed cautiously with the pan on the place where the kid had disappeared.

It swung open and shut again, the hideous wallpaper that had covered it now torn along the straight edge of a door frame.

"Oh," Agnes said, caught between amazement that there'd been a swinging door behind the wallpaper and fear that there was also a crazed moron behind there.

"*Agnes!*" Joey yelled on the phone.

Agnes took a deep breath and stepped back to the counter and picked it up. "What?"

"*What the fuck happened?*"

"There's another door in my kitchen, right next to the hall door." Agnes went back and pushed it open again, avoiding the rusted, broken nails that lined the doorway edge, and peered into the black void. "Huh."

"*Where's the kid with the gun?*"

"Good question." Agnes dropped her wimpy non-stick skillet on the counter, yanked open the utility drawer by the door, and got out her heavy-duty flashlight. She turned it on, shoved the door open with her shoulder, and pointed it into the void.

"*What are you doing?*" Joey yelled.

"I'm trying to see what's behind this door. I didn't even know it was *here.*"

"*Agnes, you can explore your goddamn house later,*" Joey
said. "Take Rhett and get the hell *out of there.*"

"I don't think the kid's a problem anymore." Agnes held
the phone with one hand and peered down into the pool of
light the flashlight cast on the floor below as Rhett came to
join her, pressing close to her leg so he could peer, too. "He
fell into a basement. I didn't even know I *had* a basement
back here. Did you know—" She played the light around the
floor and then froze when it hit the moron. "Uh-oh."

"*What do you mean, 'uh-oh'?*"

The boy was splayed out on what looked like a concrete
floor, and he did not look good.

"I think he's hurt. He's definitely not moving."

"*Good,*" Joey said. "He fall down the stairs?"

"There are no stairs." Agnes squinted down into the darkness as the light hit the boy's face.

His eyes stared up at her, dull and fixed.

Agnes screamed, and Rhett scrambled back, stepping in
the raspberry sauce, which he began to lick up.

"*Agnes?*"

"Oh, God," Agnes said, as her throat closed in panic.
"Joey, his neck's at a funny angle, and his eyes are staring up
at me. I think I *killed him.*"

"No, you didn't, honey," Joey said around the traffic noise
in the background. "He committed suicide when he attacked
an insane woman in the stupid house she bought. I'm almost
there. You stay there and *don't open that door for anybody.*"

"He's dead, Joey. I have to call the police." *This is bad.
This is bad. This is not going to look good.*

"The police can't help you with this one," Joey said. "You
stay put. I'm gonna get you somebody until we figure this
out."

"Some body. Right." Agnes clicked off the phone and
looked back down at the dead body in her basement.

He looked pathetic, lying there all twisted and dead-eyed.
Agnes swallowed, trying to get a grip on the situation.

How are you feeling right now, Agnes?

Shut the fuck up, Dr. Garvin.

Don't say "Fuck," Agnes. Angry language makes us an grier.

Gosh darn, Dr. Garvin, I'm feeling . . .

She put the beam on the boy again.

Still dead.

Oh, God.

Okay, calm down, she told herself. *Think this through.*

She hadn't killed him, the basement floor had.

You hit him many times in the head with the frying pa *try explaining that one.*

Okay, okay, but he'd *attacked* her in her *house.* It wa self-defense. Yes, he was young and pathetic and heartbreaking down there, but he'd been a horrible person.

Why do you always hit them with frying pans, Agnes?

Because that's what I always have in my hand, D *Garvin. If I were a gardener, it'd be hedge clippers. Thir* *how bad that would be.*

She punched in 911 on her phone, trying to concentrate on the good things: Rhett was fine, Maria's wedding wa still on track, her column would be finished eventually, Tw Rivers was starting to look beautiful and it was *hers,* wel hers and Taylor's, pretty soon she was going to be living h dream, and her cupcakes were burning but she could make more cupcakes—

There's a dead body in my basement and I lost my tempe *and I hit him with a frying pan many times, I was not* *control—*

"Keyes County Emergency services," the police di patcher drawled.

"There's a dead body in my basement," Agnes said, an then her knees gave way and she slid down the cabinet to s hard on the floor as she tried to explain that the kid had br ken into her *house* and had been going to hurt *her dog,* whi Rhett drooled on her lap.

"A deputy is on the way, ma'am," the dispatcher said, as dead bodies in basements were an every evening occurrenc

"Thank you." Agnes hung up and looked at Rhett.

"I have to make cupcakes," she said, and he looked e

couraging, so she got up to get the blackened cupcakes out of the oven and clean the floor and get back to work, thinking very hard about her column and Maria's wedding and her beautiful house and everything except the dead body in her basement and the goddamned frying pan.

Shane sat on a bar stool, in a shady nightclub on the wrong side of the tracks in a bad part of Savannah, Georgia, and tried to estimate how many people he was going to have to kill in the next hour. Optimally it would be one, but he had long ago learned that optimism did not apply to his profession. He felt his cell phone vibrate in his pocket and pulled it out with his free hand, expecting to see the GO or NO GO text message from Wilson. There were only three people who had his number, and they never called to chat. One of them was across the dance floor from him, which left two options. He glanced at the screen and was surprised to see JOEY. *Jesus. First time ever and he calls in the middle of a job.*

Shane hesitated for a moment, then thought, *Hell, you gave him the number for emergencies*, and hit the ON button. "Uncle Joe?"

"Shane, you on a job?"

"Yes."

"Where you at?"

"Savannah."

"Good," Joey said. "Close. I need you home."

Shane frowned. *Home? You send me away at twelve and now you want me home?* "What's the problem?" he said, keeping his voice cold.

"I got a little friend needs some help. She lives just outside Keyes in the old Two Rivers mansion. Remember it?"

Fucking Keyes. Armpit of the South.

"Come home and take care of my little Agnes, Shane."

You adopt another kid, Joe? Gonna take better care of this one? "I'll be there in an hour."

"I appreciate it." Joey hung up.

Shane pushed the OFF button. Joey needing help taking care of something. That was new. Old man must be getting really old. Calling him home. That was—

"I'm a Leo—and you?"

Shane turned to look at her. Long blond hair. Bright smile plastered on her pretty face. Pink T-shirt stretched tight across her ample chest with the word PRINCESS embroidered on it in shiny letters. Effective advertising, bad message.

"What's your sign?" she said, coming closer.

"Taurus with a bad moon rising." The hell with Joey. He had a job to do. He looked at the upstairs landing.

Two men in long black leather coats and wraparound sun glasses appeared on the landing. They took barely visible flanking positions at the top of the metal stairs, just as they had the previous evening at approximately the same time, which meant the target was in-house.

At home, so to speak.

"Do you come here often?" Princess asked, coming still closer, about three inches too close. He scooted back on his stool slightly.

"Never." Except for the reconnaissance the previous evening. He looked up again. Too many people had seen *The Matrix*, he decided as he took in the bodyguards' long jackets and shades.

The Matrix probably hadn't even played in Keyes yet.

Princess came in closer, her breasts definitely inside his personal space. "What do you do for a living?"

"I'm a painter."

That's what Joey used to tell people. *I'm a painter.*
Enough with Joey.

Shane glanced across the room. Carpenter was in place, his tall, solid figure near the emergency exit, the flashing lights reflecting off his shaved ebony skull. *I paint them. Carpenter cleans them.* Shane nodded toward the guard, ever so slightly. Carpenter nodded back.

"That's cool." Princess began to scan past Shane, probably looking for somebody who'd play with her. She must have found him because she smiled at Shane blankly and backed off. "Have a good one," she said and was gone into the crowd.

The phone buzzed once more, and Shane glanced at the screen: GO. Finally. He secured the phone in his pocket, nodding once more at Carpenter, who reached into one of his deep pockets. Princess was over by the bar now, dialing on her phone with a blank look on her face as she tossed her head to get the hair out of her eyes. Then she frowned and pulled the phone away, staring at it. Shane knew no one's cellphone within two hundred feet would work as long as Carpenter kept the transmitter in his pocket working, jamming all frequencies.

He wove his way through the sweaty dancers to the bottom of the staircase and walked up, Carpenter falling in behind him. Both bodyguards stepped out, forming a human wall that he estimated weighed over four hundred and seventy pounds combined with another ten pounds or so of leather coat thrown in. Which meant they trumped him by over two hundred and seventy.

Fortunately, two hundred and ten pounds with brains could usually beat four hundred and eighty pounds of dumb.

"Private office," the one on the right growled.

Shane jabbed his right hand, middle three fingers extended, into the man's voice box, then grabbed the face of the man on the left and applied pressure at just the right places with the fingertips of his left hand, thumb on one side, four fingers on the other. The man froze in the middle of reaching under his jacket, unable to move, while Carpenter caught the man to the right.

"Tell me the truth and live," Shane whispered as he leaned close, ignoring the other guard's desperate wheezing attempts to get air down his damaged throat as Carpenter took him back into the darkness of the landing. "Lie and die. Is Casey Dean here?"

"Uggh." There was the slightest twitch of the head in the affirmative.

"Alone?"

"Uggh." A twitch side to side.

Shit. "Left foot," Shane said. "How many are in there? Tap your foot for the number."

The foot hit the ground twice, then halted.

"Good boy." Shane shifted his fingers slightly and pressed. The man dropped unconscious to the floor. Carpenter already had the other man down, sleeping with the leather. At least they'd be warm.

Shane reached inside their coats and retrieved their pistols. He placed one in his waistband in his back, and kept the other one out, safety off. He stepped over them as Carpenter reached down and grabbed the back of each man's jacket and dragged them to a small janitor's closet and tumbled them in. Then he turned and faced the stairway to make sure no one else came up. He wasn't wearing leather.

Shane walked down the hallway to the bright red doorway with a prominent NO TRESPASSING sign hung on it. He kicked right at the lock, the wood splintered, and he stepped in and to one side, eyes taking in the dimly lit scene, pistol up, sweeping the room, gun in concert with his eyes.

Movement. Two people. A man. Seated behind a desk. A redhead standing on the other side, leaning forward, palms down on the desktop, her skimpy halter top hanging loose, exposing her breasts. *Great*, Shane thought. *I had to hit at playtime.*

He strode across the room as the man jumped up and the woman turned, looking surprised. The man was reaching for a jacket when Shane hit him with a cat paw fist strike to the solar plexus, making him thump back into his chair, gasping in pain and floundering, out of commission for a couple of minutes at least.

The redhead lunged at Shane, who sidestepped her claws, grabbed her from behind, and used her momentum to slam her against the desk, pinning her to it. He got one arm in a half-nelson around her neck and pressed the barrel of the gun against the back of her head. He could feel her tight ass pushing back against his groin, and she began to grind as she struggled against him, putting her arms flat out on the desktop and looking over her shoulder angrily. He shoved her shoulders down on the desk and saw a small tattoo of a compass on the small of her back, just above her jeans. *Like somebody needs directions there*, he thought.

She pressed back harder against him with her ass.

"Stop it," he said.

"Oh, come on," she whispered. "You like it. Come on, we can work this out, you and me. I can—"

Shane pulled the gun back and tapped the barrel against the back of her skull.

The girl rubbed her head. "What the fuck?"

"This is business and you are not part of it. Stay there." Shane backed away, keeping the barrel aimed at her, and when she didn't move, he glanced at the man who was still gasping for air. Not a problem.

Then Shane reached inside his jacket and pulled out an airline ticket. He tossed the plane ticket on the desk in front of the woman. "You've got a problem, here's the solution. A voucher you can use at the airport tonight. Enough for a one-way ticket anywhere in the world."

The redhead stared at him.

"You don't ever want to come back to Savannah again," he told her. "This man hangs with bad men, and they're going to remember you were here and come looking for you."

The girl was nodding, reaching for the ticket at the same time as she tried to put her jacket on.

"You can go, but if you say anything to anyone on the way out, you will die."

The girl was still nodding like a bimbo bobble-head doll, one arm in her jacket, the other with the ticket in hand. Shane kept one eye on her struggles as he focused his attention back on the man. When she was ready and holding the ticket in one hand and her purse in the other, Shane pulled out his phone and hit the speed-dial for Carpenter, knowing he'd have stopped jamming the cellphone frequencies by now. "You got one civilian coming out. Redhead. Let her go."

There was a telling moment of silence. "A witness."

"A *civilian* coming out," Shane repeated.

"Roger," Carpenter said.

Shane nodded to the redhead, and she scuttled to the door and was gone.

Shane turned his attention back to the man. "Same deal for you, my friend." He slapped another ticket voucher on the desk.

"Who—" the man coughed and tried again as he managed to sit up straighter. "Who—are—you?"

"Doesn't matter who I am," Shane said. "I'm gonna ask you some questions. Answer honestly, you take this ticket and go. Lie and die."

The man's face was shiny with pain and exertion, but he wasn't giving up. "What—do—you—want?"

"You were hired by the mob to kill someone the U.S. government would prefer stay alive."

"Listen, we can make a deal—"

"I *am* making you a deal." Christ, this was like talking to some jackass from Keyes.

"Well, I'd like to deal," the man said. "But you got the wrong—"

Shane hit him, an open-handed slap that was more insult than injury. "You're wasting my time, Casey Dean," he said, and the man flinched when he heard the name. "The people I work for do not make mistakes. Unlike you."

"Really—"

Shane reached out and jabbed his thumb into Dean's shoulder, hitting a nerve junction, and the guy jumped as if struck by an electric shock. "Now here's the deal. You tell me what I want to know and forget about the hit, fly away, and never come back, and it's the same to me as if you were dead."

Dean rubbed his shoulder, eyes darting about the room. "That's it?"

"That's it." Shane slid the ticket voucher across the desk.

Dean looked at Shane. "You're really gonna let me go if I tell you what you want and forget about the contract?"

"No. I'm gonna let you go if you forget about the hit *and*

give me the names and contact information of whoever hired you *and* the name of the target."

Dean shook his head. "I can't give the contractor up. He'll kill me."

Shane brought the gun level with the point right between the man's eyes. "Which is worse? The possibility he might kill you in the future or the certainty I *will* kill you in the next ten seconds?"

"Shit." Dean slumped, suddenly looking very old. "Listen, I'm just a business manager. I'm—"

Shane pressed the muzzle of the gun hard against the man's skin just above his nose.

Dean's eyes turned inward, mesmerized by the barrel. "I'm telling you, I don't know the contractor's name. I just got a call that services were needed."

"Who's the target?"

"Didn't get it yet. I swear."

Great. Dean was an idiot, but there was a ring of truth in that.

"Listen, I'm cold. Can I get my jacket?"

Shane looked at him, almost pitying him in his stupidity. *The dumb fuck has a plan.* He pulled the gun back. "Sure." His assignment was to take out Casey Dean, world-class hitman, but if this guy was a world-class hitman, Shane was Princess's date to the prom. Some guys were all PR, no game, and Casey Dean was sure as hell turning out to be one of them.

When Dean had put on his jacket, he looked downright confident, his eyes sly as they went to the desk. "So I really don't know anything, but I'm definitely leaving town, just like you said. Okay if I get my passport from my desk drawer?"

Shane nodded. *You bet. Commit suicide with my gun. That's what I'm here for, pal.*

The man turned his back and opened a desk drawer, and Shane brought his gun up.

Dean swung around, a small gun in his hand, and Shane fired two quick shots, hitting him in the chest. Dean fell back, disappearing behind the desk.

Below, the music pounded, drowning out everything.

Shane walked forward, gun at the ready and rolled the man over, surprised to find there was still a spark of life in his eyes. Not surprised to see his two shots were so tightly grouped they appeared to be one hole, but not happy to see them an inch off target.

Fucking Joey, making him lose focus. Fucking Keyes. Fucking little Agnes, too, whoever she was.

A funny look came over the man's face as Shane aimed the gun at his forehead. His eyes blinked rapidly. "Wait," he gasped. "We can make a deal."

"Oh, come on," Shane said. "You know who and what you are. You lied. You'd have completed the contract because otherwise you'd never get another job."

"No—" Dean said, and Shane fired, the round making a perfect black hole in the center of his forehead.

He pulled out his cell phone and hit number 3 on the speed dial.

It was answered on the first ring: "Carpenter."

"Painting's done. You'll have to help him on to the next world on your own, Reverend. I won't be at debrief."

There was a brief moment of silence. "Wilson won't like that."

"The target had no information on contractor or his target."

"Roger."

Shane put the phone away.

Then he strode across the room toward the window, reached under his shirt, retrieved the heavy-duty snap link attached to the rear of his body armor, clipped it to a bolt holding a drain pipe, turned outward and jumped, the carefully coiled bungee cord snapping out until it jerked him to a halt three feet from the street and bounced him back up half the distance. As he went down the second time, Shane pulled the quick release and landed on all fours. Right next to his Defender SUV.

Keyes again.

Fuck.

A gnes clutched her frying pan tighter as she felt her way through the dim moonlight in the narrow house-keeper's room toward the bedside table and the lamp there, really hating the kid who'd made her feel afraid in her own home, even if he was dead now, hating even more that Joey thought she was in trouble.

"I told you nothing happened in here," she called out, looking around for the cop. "It was all out in the kitchen." *Not that I'm upset with you, sir. Please don't arrest me.*

The wind blew the curtains away from the window by the bed, and she saw that the little bedside table was tipped over, and then somebody clamped a hand over her mouth and said, "Shhhh," and her heart lurched sideways, and she swung the pan up over her head hard and connected with a smack that reverberated into her shoulders.

He wrenched the pan out of her hand. "*Stop it.* Joey sent me."

She yanked away from him, and he let her go so that she stumbled, falling against the bed as she fumbled on the floor for the light and then clicked it on, breathing hard.

He loomed up over her as her heart pounded, a big guy, dressed in black—black pants, black T, black denim jacket—looking like he'd been hacked out of a block of wood: strong weathered face; black flat eyes—*shark eyes*, she thought, *if this guy had come for me, I'd be dead*; cropped dark hair going gray at the temples, now a little bloody on the right; tense, hard, squared-off body, all of it alert and concen-trated on her. But the thing she noticed most as she tried to keep from having a heart attack was that he looked like Joey. Younger than Joey, bigger than Joey, but he looked like Joey.

She swallowed. "Who are you and what the hell are you doing in here?"

"I'm Shane. Joey sent me." He jerked his head toward the kitchen, no wasted movement. "Who's out there?"

Agnes got to her feet, wishing she had her frying pan back. "Shane. Okay, Shane, thank you for scaring the *hell* out of me, but this is my house, so I'll ask the questions." She took a deep breath. "Joey sent you. Why?"

"I'm here to protect some kid. Little Agnes?"

"That's me," Agnes said.

There was a silence long enough to hear crickets in, and Agnes thought, *If he makes some crack about me being not little, I'm gonna hit him again,* and then he spoke.

"I'm here to protect you," he said, sounding resigned. "Unless you hit me again, in which case, whoever I'm supposed to save you from can have your ass."

"Protect me." That wasn't good. She'd been worried about the police finding out about her record, but Joey thought she needed protection from something else, something only somebody like this guy could stave off. Which meant something was seriously wrong. Not that the guy who was now a corpse in her basement hadn't been a tip-off, but if Joey thought something was so bad that she needed this guy, it must be really bad because a guy like this could protect her from . . .

Anything.

Out in the front hall, the ugly black grandfather clock left behind by the house's previous owner began to chime the hour in big gongs that sounded like Death's oven timer, and Agnes looked at Shane again.

Big. Broad. Dark. Strong. Handsome if you liked thugs. Looked like Joey. And he was here to keep her safe.

How are you feeling right now, Agnes?

Could be worse.

"Okay, Shane," Agnes said as the clock gonged twelve. "I got Joey in my kitchen, a cop in my front hall, a dead body in my basement, and you in my bedroom. Where do you want to start?"